S[..]n Nicholls has been a full-time writer since 1981. He is the author of many novels and short stories but is best-known for the internationally acclaimed *Orcs: First Blood* series. His journalism has appeared in the *Guardian*, the *Independent*, the *Daily Mirror*, *Time Out*, *Sight and Sound*, *Rolling Stone*, *SFX* and *Locus* among others. Stan has worked for a number of specialist and general bookshops and was the first manager of the London branch of Forbidden Planet. He currently lives in the West Midlands with his wife, the writer Anne Gay. You can visit his website at: www.stannicholls.com.

Visit www.AuthorTracker.co.uk for exclusive updates on your favourite Voyager authors.

By Stan Nicholls

Quicksilver Rising
Quicksilver Zenith
Quicksilver Twilight

STAN NICHOLLS

Quicksilver Twilight

Book Three of the Quicksilver Trilogy

HARPER
Voyager

Harper*Voyager*
An Imprint of HarperCollins*Publishers*
77–85 Fulham Palace Road,
Hammersmith, London W6 8JB

www.voyager-books.co.uk

Published by Harper*Voyager* 2006
1

A catalogue record for this book
is available from the British Library

ISBN-13: 978 0 00 714153 1
ISBN-10: 0 00 714153 X

Typeset in Postscript Linotype Meridien by
Palimpsest Book Publishing Limited, Polmont, Stirlingshire

Printed and bound in Great Britain by
Clays Limited, St Ives plc

Acknowledgements

With thanks to Stella Gemmell, for the gift of just the
right word at just the right time.
In a spirit of friendship and nostalgia, affectionate waves are
offered to Michael Anft, Dave Baldock-Ling, Ken Brooks,
Jean Dempsey, John Eggeling, Gamma, David & Shirley
Griffiths, Ernest Harris, Ron McGuinness, Alan Moore, Steve
Moore, Cathy Nugent, Michel Parry, Cliff Perriam, Derek
Stokes, Martin Walsh, Di Wathen, and Jenny & Daphne.

Quicksilver Twilight is dedicated to the loving memory
of Eileen Costelloe, John Griffiths, Nick Reynolds,
Barbara Shrestha, and Annie Gleason & Daniel O'Grady.
And it would be great if you could stop doing this
now, please; I'm running out of friends.

The story so far . . .

The known world's magical system was created long ago by extinct race the Founders, though the quality of their sorcery was infinitely more powerful.

Magic serves as technology, an instrument of repression and even legal tender. It defines social status. Its many manifestations, commonly referred to as glamours, include fake lifeforms.

Opposing empires Gath Tampoor and Rintarah are the dominant civilisations, each jealously nurturing their far-flung protectorates. Bhealfa, an island state, has been a colony of both empires at various times, and is currently under Gath Tampoor. Its ruler in name only, Prince Melyobar, believes death to be an animate being, and his sworn enemy. The Prince has created a magic-fuelled floating palace that is literally never still in its attempt to elude the Reaper. It falls to Gath Tampoorian Imperial Envoy Andar Talgorian to struggle with Melyobar's delusions and ensure that the colonialists' wishes are imposed.

But the empires are not unopposed. A resistance movement has grown in response to their brutality and injustice. This insurgency is countered principally by the secretive paladin clans, an immensely powerful militaristic network bound by blood membership. Noted for their cynicism, the clans see no contradiction in contracting their *services to both Gath Tampoor and Rintarah. The clans' High Chief, Ivak Bastorran, is adept at viciousness. Though his efforts pale beside the cruelty of Devlor Bastorran, his nephew and rival for the leadership.*

Reeth Caldason is a thorn in their side. He is a member of the shrinking Qalochian diaspora, his people having suffered bigotry and pogroms. One of the few to survive the massacre of his tribe, Caldason seeks revenge. For decades he has also searched for a cure to a mysterious ailment that pitches him into berserk rages and subjects him to vivid, bizarre visions.

Caldason befriends orphan Kutch Pirathon, a young sorcerer's apprentice shocked by Reeth's antipathy towards the magic his culture sees as perfectly normal. The pair encounter radical politician Dulian Karr, who proves to be one of the leading lights in the Resistance. Karr suggests that Covenant, an outlaw order of unlicensed magicians, might have the knowledge to lift the ills plaguing Caldason. His offer to put him in touch with Covenant leads to Reeth and Kutch ultimately joining with the insurgents.

Serrah Ardacris, employed by the notorious Council for Internal Security, captains what is essentially a government death squad targeting bandit gangs in Gath Tampoor's capital. When the reckless son of an important official dies on her watch, Serrah is blamed and pressured to confess. And her superiors are not above using the pain of the loss of Serrah's daughter, Eithne, to get what they want. Eithne died at just fifteen from an overdose of ramp, a powerful, illegal narcotic. On the point of breaking, Serrah is rescued by a Resistance cell, and manages to escape to Bhealfa.

For all their might, the empires do not rule quite everywhere. The barbarous northern wastes are largely untouched by them. A dominion of savagery and tribal leaders, the wastes have recently thrown up a particularly powerful warlord. Zerreiss, known to his followers as the Man Who Fell From the Sun, possesses a strange power that aids his conquest of increasing tracts of land.

Qalochian Tanalvah Lahn, a state-certified prostitute, has worked

*in the brothels of Rintarah all her life. But when defending herself
against a client who murdered her best friend, Tanalvah unwit-
tingly kills the man. Fearing retribution, she gathers her friend's
two young children and flees to Bhealfa. Once there, they are aided
by pacifist Kinsel Rukanis, a celebrated classical singer who supports
the Resistance. They in turn meet Serrah, who defends them against
government agents, killing several in the process. Kinsel introduces
Tanalvah and Serrah to the Resistance.*

*Reeth Caldason, Kutch Pirathon and Dulian Karr make contact
with Phoenix, the head of Covenant, who uses a fragment of
Founder knowledge to change his appearance at will. They also
meet Quinn Disgleirio, of the Fellowship of the Righteous Blade,
a long-moribund martial order that has been revived to fight for
Bhealfa's independence.*

*The Resistance, Covenant and the Blade Fellowship form the
United Revolutionary Council. Karr reveals that the Council's aim
is the establishment of a free state.*

*Caldason is found to be partially immortal, and his ageing process
has been greatly slowed down. He has no idea why he should be
in this condition. Covenant believes that the Founders left a hoard
of knowledge called the Source. No one knows what form the Source
takes, but it's traditionally associated with the legend of the
Clepsydra, said to be a device for marking off the eons to the Day
of Destruction.*

*The Source could provide the Resistance with a powerful weapon
against the empires, and Caldason with a cure. He determines to
find it, but is constantly frustrated by events.*

*Kutch also has a strange, unsuspected attribute. He possesses the
incredibly rare spotter talent. Spotters can look beyond the falsity of
magic and distinguish illusion from reality. Phoenix offers to coach
the boy in the proper use of the skill. But Kutch soon finds himself
sharing Caldason's terrifying visions.*

*Kinsel and Tanalvah become lovers, and set up house with the
children. But Tanalvah worries that Kinsel runs too many risks*

through his Resistance work. A concern that proves all too real when Devlor Bastorran identifies them as Resistance fellow travellers.

Prince Melyobar plots to massacre the entire population of Bhealfa. His plan is to isolate death, and deprive the entity of the masses to hide in.

Battling her unresolved feelings about the death of her daughter, and taken aback by a temple prophecy, Serrah attempts suicide.

Resistance activity brings down ever greater repression. The paladins are given their head and exploit the leeway with brutal excess.

The location of the planned rebel state is chosen, and at first seems bizarre to many. Batariss, universally known as the Diamond Isle, is a run-down pleasure island. Its owner is one-time pirate Zahgadiah Darrok, who travels on a magically impelled flying dish, having lost his legs to a piratical rival. Darrok agrees to sell the island for a large quantity of government gold, which the Resistance has to steal.

Tanalvah persuades Kinsel to stage a free concert for the poor. But during the event Devlor Bastorran, accompanied by newly recruited aide Lahon Meakin, arrests the singer. Accused of treason, Kinsel will face trial.

As part of his personal campaign against Caldason, Devlor employs assassin Aphri Kordenza to kill him. The female symbiote, also known as a meld, carries her own male twin, a glamour called Aphrim, inside herself. But Aphrim is capable of emerging and having an independent existence.

The waters around the Diamond Isle are infested with pirates, including the infamous Kingdom Vance, the man who deprived Darrok of his legs. It falls to the Resistance to combat this new menace.

As Kinsel goes on trial, Tanalvah discovers she's pregnant. And Serrah is horrified to learn that Commissioner Laffon, head of the Council for Internal Security, and the man who tortured her, has come to Bhealfa to attend the hearing. The trial is a propaganda circus, and Kinsel is inevitably found guilty. He's consigned to the galleys, as a slave rower. In effect, it's a sentence of death.

As the warlord Zerreiss increases his sphere of influence, both empires begin to pay serious attention to him. A concern they share is that he could unite with the Resistance against them, bringing into play his still mysterious power.

Having failed in his plot to have the meld Aphri Kordenza kill Caldason, Devlor Bastorran comes up with another scheme. Under his direction, Kordenza murders his uncle Ivak. Devlor inherits the Clan leadership and Caldason is blamed for the assassination, making him even more of a wanted man. And under Devlor's rule, the paladins are set to become more draconian.

Caldason sets out for the Diamond Isle to deliver the gold Darrok has demanded. En route to the island his visions take on a new character. They now feature Zerreiss. The warlord, in turn, finds himself dreaming of Caldason.

Serrah, her feelings for Reeth growing, decides to travel to the Diamond Isle to join him, along with Kutch. In any event, the secret exodus of Resistance members is due to take place in a matter of weeks.

At the height of his suffering, Kinsel's galley is attacked by pirates and he falls into the hands of Kingdom Vance. Kinsel is only spared because Vance recognises him. The pirate requires Kinsel to entertain him with his singing.

Bastorran has a highly placed spy who feeds him information about the Resistance. On the basis of this, the authorities stage large-scale raids on their hideouts and personnel. Bloodshed and chaos reign in the streets. Serrah and Kutch barely manage to escape on a ship and The Resistance suffers a blow that could prove fatal.

Unknown to all concerned, the traitor is Tanalvah Lahn.

Dulian Karr, Quinn Disgleirio, Phoenix, and Tanalvah and the children are left behind in Bhealfa. Scattered, shell-shocked, demoralised, they go on the run. This takes its toll on Karr. He collapses, seriously ill, perhaps dying.

Caldason, Serrah and Kutch, along with Zahgadiah Darrok, are stranded on the Diamond Isle. Only a few thousand rebels reach its shores. What should have been a populous, self-sustaining state, able to defend itself, has proved a shambles.

Serrah vows revenge on the traitor, whoever they may be. Despite the chaos, Caldason is still intent on finding the Source.

As autumn shades into winter, the dream looks dead . . .

1

The Sun was rising. Icy winds gusted, and a thick mist clinging to the ocean began to disperse. Spectral seagulls wheeled above an island shoreline, its contours emerging from the haze.

The prow of a ship cut through the fog. It was triple-masted and armour-clad, and bore no insignia. Two companion vessels ploughed in its wake, smaller but equally well armed. The decks of all three were crammed with men, pressed to the rails.

A paltry flotilla moved out from the island to engage them; a couple of two-masters accompanied by a handful of smaller craft, flying green ensigns that showed a scorpion. They looked a poor match for the trio of pirate galleons bearing down.

Stealth dissolved with the mist. The three men o' war and the ramshackle convoy put on knots, breasting white foam, heading for each other.

At hailing distance the two groups slowed and came about. Clusters of arrows winged between the ships, hammering timber, canvas, shields, and the flesh of the unlucky or sluggish. The exchange went on until the arrows were spent and

every craft was peppered. Hundreds of wooden bolts floated
in the choppy sea.

So it came to magical munitions.

Rows of hatchways were thrown open along the sides of
the raiders' ships, revealing stout iron cylinders. Spell-driven,
the tubes belched glamoured volleys. Fusillades of shrieker-
needles and concussion beams. Salvos of dazzler bombshells
and ruse-igniters. Befanged and clawed phantasmal beasts,
short-lived but deadly, appeared amongst the defenders and
laid about them. Masses of venomous snakes materialised.
Thunderbolts shattered flagstaffs. Jets of vitriol blistered the
rigging.

The islanders attacked the glamours with nullifying wands
and charmed blades. Using deck-mounted catapults, they
flung back their own ordnance. Sky-bursting hex packets
birthed flocks of carnivorous birds that strafed the enemy
ships. Stun cubes went off with ear-piercing reports. Leathery-
winged gargoyles spat down sheets of flame on enemy heads.

Sorcerers on both sides feverishly conjured protective
energy fields; shimmering, near transparent bubbles shot
through with rippling colours. Enchantments glanced off
them. Incoming spells were dampened.

Shortly, the numinous barrage died down, which came as
no surprise. Everybody knew matters would only be settled
at close-quarters.

Drums pounded. The ships manoeuvred and closed the
space separating them, their scowling crews tensed. Then
hulls collided sidelong, timbers grinding. Seamen roared.
Forests of boarding ladders rose. Scores of tethered grappling
hooks were circled like lassos, and tossed. Waves of fighters,
brandishing pikes, cutlasses, swords and axes, clashed at the
guardrails and the slaughter began in earnest.

Nowhere was the conflict more furious than on the largest
of the raiders' ships. Braver than their opponents, or simply

more desperate, a pack of islanders had fought their way aboard. They were paying for it. The bloody, frantic, trampling melee rapidly thinned their ranks. Outnumbered, forced back, the islanders compressed to a knot. A many-limbed, quilled beast, bristling steel, they stood fast for the final onslaught. Hard-eyed buccaneers started to close in on them.

Men shouted. Not war cries or screams of pain but incredulous yells. Some pointed upwards.

A figure fell from the sky.

He was dressed in black, a billowing cloak giving him the look of a gigantic bat. His hair, long and free, was a raven nimbus. His eyes could have been coals.

As he landed on the deck, sure-footed as a cat, many thought he must be a glamour, or a demon. They were wrong. Only a man could fight with such maniacal fury.

He bore two swords, and employed them instantly. The nearest pair of freebooters went down, gizzards slit, chests ribboned. He was engaging a third before the mob gathered their wits and turned on him. Their quarry didn't flinch. He roared into them. But he seemed careless in telling friend from foe. Only nimble footwork kept allies clear of his lethal blades.

His savagery gave the surrounded group of islanders renewed heart, though many who didn't recognise him weren't entirely convinced he was on their side. Or any side, barring his own. He had the look of someone possessed by furies.

The pirates took to lobbing hatchets at him. He moved lithely, dodging them with an almost contemptuous ease. Twice he deflected hatchets in flight, using the flat of his blades. One embedded itself in the deck, the other ricocheted and struck a pirate's thigh, cleaving bone.

Wrath increased, the black-clad warrior renewed his attack. Bellowing, swinging wildly, he charged into the fray, scattering

raiders. But a bolder trio stood their ground. He met them
headlong. The first to die wore a grubby white bandanna, now
stained with crimson. A thrust to the heart stopped the next.
The third succumbed to a slashed windpipe.

As the fiend looked about for fresh prey the encircled
islanders seized their chance to break out. Accompanied by
the spiky natter of swords, the fight turned more brutal still.

Across a stretch of reddening ocean, another pirate craft
was having a visitation of its own. This, too, came from above.
But its nature, though equally startling, was quite different.

The crew was embroiled in a chaotic two-fold struggle.
Half were trying to board an adjacent island vessel. The rest
were battling to stop the islanders doing the same to them.
Where the sides met, there was carnage.

A thunderous explosion rang out and a plume of indigo
flame erupted against the opposite side of the ship. Splinters
flew. Ropes snapped and whip-lashed, poleaxing crewmen.
A fine shower of briny water pattered the deck. Aloft, where
the fire had licked it, a sail smouldered.

An object soared overhead, describing a tight curve beneath
the pallid clouds. It was disc-shaped, and it glinted in the
rays of frail morning sunlight. Blades quietened, the fighters
below watched as the saucer headed back their way. And
they could see, as they scrambled for cover, that someone
sat astride it.

The dish levelled sharply just above mast height, traversing
the length of the ship. It moved at the speed of a javelin,
bow to stern. As it passed over the stern, where the wheel
stood on a raised deck, with the Captain's cabin behind it,
the disc-rider dropped something. There was another deafening report and an intense flash of light. Debris shot in all
directions. When the dust cleared, the bridge was in ruins.

Banking hard and low, the saucer turned, preparatory
to another attack. By now, some on board had collected

themselves. They loosed arrows and lobbed spears. One or two arrows struck, but were deflected by the disc's metallic hide. A ship's wizard managed to get off an energy burst, an incandescent lance of malevolent particles that hurt the eyes. The beam clipped the saucer's edge, gashing blue sparks, rocking it like a storm-tossed boat, but the rider quickly recovered and completed his turn.

At the galleon's prow was a glamoured figurehead. Twice the height of a man, it comprised a voluptuous woman's body melded with a hydra. Half a dozen writhing, spitting serpent's heads projected from her sinuous neck.

On his next pass, the disc-rider targeted the effigy. Again, there was the glimpse of a dropped object; something that could have been a small hessian sack. The ensuing detonation left the figure a smoking charcoal stump. One dangling head remained, forked tongue wriggling weakly, the magic draining away.

The destruction of the freebooters' beloved icon enraged them even more. But they had no time to dwell on it; the boarders they'd neglected were swarming onto the ship.

The explosions could be heard from the main pirate vessel, though few paid attention. They were too concerned with mayhem. Groups were fighting each other all over the ship. Corpses and wounded men covered the deck.

No one had bettered the warrior in black. His ferocity and stamina were unabated. He'd battled to the nub of the pirate horde and reached their officer corps. This assembly was dandified in their dress, except for the face charms they wore. The glamoured masks were grotesque, fearsome, demonic, and constantly undulating, taking on ever more hideous aspects. They were meant to intimidate. The warrior wasn't deterred, however, and made no exceptions. To him, flesh was flesh.

He gave no let in cracking skulls and hewing ribs. Where

swords were raised against him, he answered with savagery. And even where they weren't. None who stood in his path were spared, whether challenger or capitulator. He scythed through them like a frenzied spirit, mingling a kind of insanity with consummate swordplay.

Then there were no more blades to meet; no more dying screams or pleas for mercy. A true deathly quiet descended. The warrior gazed about him, wild-eyed and bereft, sweat sheening his brow despite the cold.

A tattered cheer went up. Their elite beaten, the remaining pirates were surrendering their weapons. The islanders set to corralling prisoners, and to tending the wounded. But for all that he'd tipped the battle in their favour, they avoided looking at the warrior, except for furtive glances.

He seemed lost, as though dazed at having his purpose taken away.

Of the two smaller raiding ships, one was in limping retreat. The other was on fire. Flames had taken hold of its sails, converting canvas to fluttering ash. Islanders were abandoning ship, shinning down ropes to their waiting boats. The surviving pirates were jumping overboard.

A pall of oily smoke began to shroud the vessel. Moving at a clip, the flying disc sliced out of it and headed for the captured galleon. The rider flew low, letting himself be seen by the victorious islanders beneath, triggering a renewed clamour. Then he spotted his objective, and swooped to the deck.

The disc hovered in front of the fighter in black. Its rider smoothed down his mop of blond hair. There was soot on his cheeks. He was good-looking, his features dominated by shrewd azure eyes, and he sported a neatly barbered goatee. His build was athletic, with broad shoulders and sturdy arms. But his legs hung uselessly from the edge of the floating dish.

He stared at the warrior, who had a glazed expression and seemed unaware of his presence.

'Reeth.' The disc rider's gravel voice belied his looks. 'Reeth.'

There was no answer.

'Reeth!' he repeated. 'Get a grip, man! Reeth!'

The warrior was insensible. A lingering spark of bloodlust still lit his eyes.

A wooden bucket hung from the rail beside them. The disc tilted slightly as the rider reached for a ladle in the pail. He lifted a scoop of water and, turning, flung it hard in the warrior's face.

The icy sting snapped the man in black out of his reverie. He shook his head, shedding droplets, and brought up his blades. His eyes blazed. Passion rekindled, face contorted, he lurched forward menacingly.

'Reeth!' the rider barked, his disc swaying. 'It's over! We won!'

The warrior hesitated.

'Steady,' the rider added, his tone soothing. 'It's me. Zahgadiah.'

Reeth Caldason froze. He blinked, and started to focus. 'Darrok?' he whispered.

'It's over, Reeth. You can stop now.'

Slowly, Caldason came to himself and lowered his swords. He took several shuddering breaths.

'You all right?' Darrok asked.

Caldason nodded, expressionless.

'You look terrible. But I'll take your word for it.' He regarded the Qalochian. 'You certainly know how to ride a fit, I'll give you that.'

Caldason ignored the observation. 'It went well?'

'Look around.'

As though for the first time, he saw the litter of corpses,

many marking his trail. He betrayed no particular emotion.
'Vance?'

'Not here, it seems.'

Caldason spied the burning ship and its sister getting away.
'On that?'

'I doubt it. The bastard's too cautious to expose himself.
He'll be near, though.'

'Pity.' It sounded a strange word to be coming from his lips.

'Let's be grateful for what we've got. Meeting them at sea
was a good plan, Reeth, rather than facing them once they'd
landed.'

The Qalochian let the compliment pass. His attention
seemed to be wandering again.

'We've captured this ship, and destroyed another,' Darrok
went on gruffly, 'and we've killed plenty of the raiders. That's
a good result.' He surveyed the scene and grew sombre. 'But
we can't go on spending our people's lives this freely. We
have to find a way to –'

'Hear that?'

'What?'

'Listen.'

Darrok bellowed for silence. The jubilant islanders
quietened down.

It took a moment for them to realise that what they were
hearing was someone singing.

The sound came from a distance, and drifted with the
wind. But they heard enough to recognise its melancholy
beauty. Though the words couldn't be made out, the song
had the unmistakable air of a lament.

'What the hell . . . ?' Darrok peered around, trying to place
the source.

An exquisite purity of tone added to the melody's eerie,
bitter-sweet quality. Islanders and captives alike stood enrap-
tured, wondering at the strange, haunting refrain.

'What is it?' Darrok said.

Caldason slowly shook his head.

Darrok pointed to a lingering fog bank, well offshore. 'It has to be there.'

'Then Vance is, too.'

'Do we go after him?'

Caldason considered it. 'No. As you say, enough lives have been spent for one day. Why chance an ambush?'

Darrok nodded.

They listened a little longer, then the singing began to fade. The bustle on the ship resumed.

'We've done our bit here,' Darrok decided. 'Get on, I'll take us home.' He extended a hand.

The saucer rose and carried them towards the Diamond Isle.

A series of fortifications defended the island. Heavily armed ships were anchored at the entrances to its bays. Its beaches were scattered with stakes, netting, mantraps and spike pits, along with more subtle magical obstructions. Beyond the beaches, patrols roamed the scrublands, and watchtowers dotted the cliffs.

There were a handful of strongholds spread around the island, some purpose-built, most adapted from existing structures. The largest was also the newest: a fortress raised by the rebels during the several months of their occupancy, and still unfinished, its construction was traditional. It comprised a succession of concentric earth mounds, one upon the other, each three times the height of a man. Where one mound plateaued, giving way to the next, there were deep, encircling ditches, filled with combustible material. After the ditches came high walls made from mature tree trunks, dressed with barbs.

The fort proper, at the top of the mounds, consisted of

several acres of flat terrain. It hosted a collection of buildings for storing supplies and weapons. Barracks and dormi-
tories were being erected, though the distinction between
soldiery and civilians was fine, as everyone was expected to
fight. Stone had been carted up and used for battlements
that surrounded the perimeter, forming the last line of
defence. On a dozen flagstaffs, the scorpion standard fluttered in the blustery air.

A thousand or more islanders crowded the ramparts,
watching the course of the battle out at sea. They'd been
cheering, but now fell silent.

Two observers stood apart. One was a handsome woman
in her prime. She was agile and strapping, though not to the
extent that it threatened her femininity. Her long golden hair
was tied back, and she dressed in the practical, loose-fitting
garb of a fighter. She wore a sword and matching long-bladed
knife. Given the prospect of another raid from the sea, she
had a longbow slung over her shoulder, with the quiver at
her hip.

Her companion wasn't much more than half her age. His
pallid look of youth hadn't completely shaded into the ruddier
complexion of manhood. Nor would it for a while. His hair
was ashen blond, making it harder for his attempt at a beard
to make much impression. But he had a frame that was
toughening under unaccustomed physical exertion, though
it hadn't fully hardened yet. He held a glamoured spy tube
to his eye.

'Come on,' she complained, 'you must be able to see something.'

'It's obviously gone well for our side.'

'We knew that. What about that . . . sound?'

Shrugging, Kutch Pirathon handed her the spy tube. 'It's
too confused down there. Could have been anything.'

'No.' She looked through the tube, scanning the scene

below. 'It was too strange. Too distinctive. And there was something . . . I don't know; something familiar about it.'

'Maybe it was just the wind.'

'You don't believe that, Kutch.' She nodded towards the hushed crowd sharing the battlements. 'And neither do they.'

'Some magical pirate trick, then?'

'Hard to see the point of it.'

'We had the better of them this time. Perhaps they got desperate and –'

'And what? Decided to sing at us?'

Kutch looked suitably chastened. Hesitantly, he asked, 'Is this really about something else?'

'What do you mean?'

The words tumbled out. 'He'll be all right, you know. Reeth can look after himself. He's got a way with trouble.' He shot her a sidelong glance, uncertain of her reaction.

Serrah Ardacris gave in to a smile. 'You are starting to grow up, aren't you? Of course I'm concerned about Reeth. But it isn't just that. It's being stuck here, and everything going wrong, and the raids and the uncertainty.'

The youth nodded sagely.

'But I still think that whatever we heard was important,' she repeated.

'Well, we can't hear it now.' Something caught his eye. He turned seaward again, and pointed. 'Look.'

Darrok's flying disc was heading for them. From a distance it looked like a huge, black bird, gliding the updraughts. Serrah lifted the spy tube and brought the image closer. She glimpsed fire, wreckage and emerald waves. Then she locked onto the dish, reflecting metallically in the bland sunlight. She made out its two riders, one with flowing hair and cape, and didn't hide her pleasure.

The people on the ramparts saw the saucer too, and resumed cheering.

'Let me,' Kutch said.

She slapped the glamoured tube into his outstretched palm.

He focused on the battle scene. 'It looks like we did a lot of damage to them. Using that dragon's blood was a great idea, Serrah. Should make them think twice before they come at us again. Serrah?'

She had a finger to her lips. 'Sssshh!'

'What is it?'

'Use your ears.'

Everybody else was. A chorus of shushing ran through the crowd, and once more they were quietening.

The wind had shifted. It brought the sound they'd heard earlier, but clearer this time. There was no doubt it was a human voice; flawless, lucid, and heartbreakingly poignant. No one spoke or moved, such was the hold it exerted.

At length, Serrah whispered, 'I'm a fool. Why didn't I spot it right away?'

Kutch gave her a blank look. 'What?'

'Don't you recognise it?'

'No.'

'Concentrate. Doesn't it sound like something you know?'

'It's somebody singing.'

'*Obviously*. Think back, Kutch. Remember when we were at the concert in Bhealfa?'

Realisation dawned. 'You don't mean –'

'Yes. It's him. Kinsel.'

'Oh, come on.'

'You've heard him sing. How can you doubt it?'

'It can't be.'

'But what if it is?'

'You must have keener ears than me, Serrah. I couldn't be so sure from this far.'

'Trust me, I'm right.'

'But what's Kinsel doing out here? If it is him.'

'I don't know. Does it matter? He's alive; that's all that counts.'

They listened in silence, lost in their thoughts. The flying disc drew nearer, travelling so low it almost skimmed the waves.

'We have to do something,' she said.

'Like what?'

'Like finding him, of course. And just as important . . .'

'Yes?'

'We have to let Tanalvah know.'

'Tanalvah?'

'She has a right. It won't be easy, I know. But we'll find a way.'

'You're forgetting something.'

She turned to look at him.

'Tanalvah's almost certainly dead, Serrah.'

2

The streets of Valdarr had grown meaner.

Before the Great Betrayal imperial enforcers had shown brutality towards dissenters, while touching only lightly on the lives of most citizens who conformed. Now the gloves were off for everyone. Or practically everyone.

In affluent quarters, where the powerful and well-connected lived, the security forces tended to see their role as protective. In poorer neighbourhoods they were more likely to harass. Emergency laws, curfews, raids and summary arrests beset the powerless but usually left the high-ranking unaffected.

The culling of the Resistance, and the authorities' continuing search for surviving rebels, had left the city edgy. But it was a curious aspect of the atmosphere in Valdarr, or perhaps of human nature, that straitened times made little difference to the games people played.

Many of the rich persisted in flaunting their status. Their clothes, carriages, fine residences and other trappings were part of it, but principally they advertised their rank through costly magic. Mythical beasts waited on their banquet tables; ghostly mummers performed epic dramas on their immaculate lawns;

dry waterfalls cascaded down, and up, the glorious facades of
their mansions.

The poor persisted in their wretchedness. Where they had
magic at all it was mean. There might be a rudimentary jester
glamour, stolen or counterfeit, to divert a hungry child.
Perhaps an image charm to remind a destitute wife of a
husband taken by the watch.

Or, in the case of this bitterly cold evening, a spell in the
likeness of a fire.

It illuminated a filthy alley that snaked between windowless, dilapidated buildings. Its flames looked real enough.
There were artificial sparks, and the crackling of burning logs. It faked smoke and the pungent aroma of
blazing wood. But the heat it gave out was miserable. The
glamour was meant only for ornamental purposes, nor
would it last long. Still, it drew a small crowd of ragged
drifters, glad of what little cheer there was. They huddled
around the deception, trembling hands extended, gazing
into the flames.

One seemed out of place. Recently arrived, she stood in
partial shadow, and was better dressed than the others. Her
hair was inky black, and her smooth skin had a light olive
complexion. Despite her loose clothing there was no hiding
the fact that she was heavily pregnant.

She was breathing hard and looking about nervously, in
the manner of a terrified animal as it tests the air for the
scent of a predator.

A movement caught her eye. Beyond the fire, further down
the drab alley, a number of figures were approaching. They
didn't shuffle, bent-backed, the way the itinerants did. There
was order in their advance, and they moved with purpose.
She retreated into deeper shadows.

When the figures reached the flames' glow they became
recognisable, and her fears were confirmed. Their distinctive

scarlet tunics left no room for doubt. She cursed herself for a fool for daring to think she'd escaped the paladins.

Uproar broke out. Tattered vagrants were elbowed aside. Heedless of the fire, several of the red-jacketed men waded through it. The flames spluttered, flashed through a kaleidoscope of colours, and died. A patrol, four or five strong, was clearly visible now. Everyone scattered from their path.

The woman touched the string of consecrated beads at her throat and mumbled a swift prayer to her goddess. Then she turned and fled again. The commotion behind her went up a notch. She heard shouting and the rasp of swords being drawn.

The alley she hurried along came to a junction. To left and right the lanes were narrow and twisting. The way ahead broadened out into a street. There were more people in that direction, but not enough of a crowd to lose herself in. She chose the right-hand turn. Twenty paces on she came to a passageway, no wider than her outstretched arms. She entered it. The buildings on either side were so tall, and the sky so leaden, she found it hard to see where she was going. And she was splashing through a sluggish stream of icy water, and from the smell, sewage.

In spite of the cold she was sweating. Her bones ached and every step was an effort. But the noises at her back, which might have been the sound of pursuit, kept her moving.

Another alley crossed hers. This led to a tiny deserted square. She went through that, staying close to the walls, and emerged in a street. It was lined with shabby houses, and to one side a stable, abandoned and boarded-up. There was nobody about.

She stopped to listen. It was quiet, bar the distant, expected sounds of a city. Lost, exhausted, she looked for somewhere to rest, daring to hope that no one was following her. All the doors she could see were closed, and most of the windows were shuttered. The only prospect was the maw of yet another alley, almost opposite. A house forming one of the corners had its wall shored up with a low stone prop. It was flat-topped and of a height to sit on, and the alley was dark. She limped to it, hands pressed to the small of her back.

Sighing, she perched on the crude seat. She felt the chill of the stone through her clothes and shivered. Weary beyond reckoning, she took what ease she could. But whenever she allowed herself pause for thought, no matter how fleetingly, the demons were there to torment her. Her mind turned, as always, to the children; and to her man, lost to her now, and what would become of them. She dwelt on the life she carried. The things she had done in the name of those she loved lay on her like a great weight. Her conscience made certain she never walked alone. Guilt and fear were always with her.

Drained, she closed her eyes.

A rough hand clamped over her mouth. A strong arm encircled her. She tried to scream, but couldn't.

'It's all right,' her captor said, speaking in an undertone. 'Don't struggle, I'm not going to hurt you.'

The voice seemed familiar to her, but it was too indistinct for her to place it.

'It's all right,' he said again, trying to calm her. 'I'm going to take my hand away. Don't scream. All right, Tan?'

Hearing her name made the blood run to ice in her veins. She nodded stiffly.

The hand was removed. Its owner faced her.

She almost gasped aloud. 'Think of my child,' she whispered. 'Don't kill me.'

He looked as shocked as she felt. 'Tan, it's me. Quinn. I wouldn't harm you.'

He didn't know. She stared at him. At about thirty summers,

he was roughly her age, and ruggedly built. Except for a moustache, he was clean-shaven. His eyes were quick and dark.

'Tan?'

She blinked and stated baldly, 'Quinn.'

'Are you all right?'

'Yes. Just . . . surprised to see you.'

'We've been looking for you for months, woman. We thought you were dead.'

'No. I . . . I'm not.'

'Evidently.' Quinn Disgleirio smiled. 'And fortunately. Where have you been?'

Tanalvah Lahn wondered if this was some elaborate game. That perhaps he really did know and was playing with her, like a cat with a sparrow. 'Here and there,' she answered. 'Wherever . . . wherever I could find –'

'I understand. It's been a bad time for all of us. What about Teg and Lirrin? Where –'

'The children are safe. With someone I trust.' This was the man who once argued for assassinating her lover. How could she trust him?

'Good.' He scanned the streets. There was still nobody about. 'How do you come to be in these parts?'

'I had some trouble.' She found it difficult keeping a tremor out of her voice. 'A patrol.'

'Right.'

'Paladins.'

Disgleirio's expression froze for a second. 'You know how to pick your enemies, Tan.' He was looking around again, alert. 'Lose them?'

'I think so.' Tanalvah wished he'd stop asking questions. She tried one of her own. 'Are you alone?'

'I started out with a couple of other Righteous Blade members. We had some trouble of our own and got parted.

Look, it'll be curfew soon. I'll take you somewhere safe. I assume you've nowhere to go?'

'No.' She couldn't say anything else.

'Let's move then.' He stopped, and met her eyes. 'One thing.'

'What's that?'

'Whatever made you think I might kill you?'

She had no idea what she would have said, if she'd had the chance.

Disgleirio grabbed her arm and pulled her roughly to one side. Tanalvah nearly cried out. Then she saw what he saw.

On the other side of the street the paladin patrol was spilling from the alley Tanalvah had come out of. Disgleirio tugged her into the gloom, but it was too late. The patrol spotted them, fanned out and headed their way.

'Go,' she said. 'Leave me.'

'You must be joking. I'm getting you out of here.' He drew his sword, and placed himself between her and the advancing paladins. 'Move. Get yourself clear of this.'

Tanalvah backed away from him, as though obeying, but after a few steps lingered at his rear. She couldn't say why she defied her instinct to flee.

The patrol's officer came on at the head of his men, blade in hand. 'Identify yourself!' he barked. 'And throw down your weapon!'

'It's not for taking,' Disgleirio replied evenly, 'and neither am I.'

'You're shielding a suspect. Stand aside!'

'I can't do that.'

'We want the Qalochian whore,' the man spelt out, 'and we're going to have her.'

'You'll have to pass me first.'

The officer's bearded features twisted in fury. 'There are severe penalties for obstructing law-servers. Are you prepared to pay them?'

Disgleirio shrugged. 'We'll have to see, won't we?'

The officer abandoned words. In the time it took Disgleirio to raise his sword the paladin had rushed in to attack. Their blades collided, then fell into the steely clatter of blow and counterblow. The exchange was breakneck fast, each man making a potentially deadly pass a dozen times in the first half minute.

The paladin was a skilled fighter, as were all his persuasion, and his swordplay was near faultless. But he lacked Disgleirio's energy and desperate drive. Blocking a swipe, Disgleirio parried, his blade biting deep into the man's upper arm. Blood flowing freely, the officer staggered and dropped his sword. Pain and outrage inhabited his face. He backed off.

Too confident in their officer's ability, his men hadn't moved. Now they did, as one.

Disgleirio withdrew, and nearly bowled Tanalvah over. None too gently, he shoved her further into the alley. Almost immediately another paladin arrived, enraged and swinging his sword viciously. A swift exchange ensued, made all the more frantic as the rest of the patrol was nearing. Disgleirio cast off subtlety and took to battering his foe.

The stalemate held for a heartbeat. Then one of his blows got through, cleaving the side of the paladin's neck. It was a lethal strike. The man fell senseless, blocking his fellows' path. There was confusion. The injured officer bellowed curses.

Disgleirio seized his chance and Tanalvah's wrist. 'Come on!'

They broke away and fled along the alley. Twenty or thirty paces took them to a corner. They looked back. All four members of the patrol were coming after them, including the wounded officer. And now they were fuelled by vengeance.

Disgleirio glanced at Tanalvah. It was plain she could never outrun their pursuers. They turned the corner and kept moving.

'What are we going to do?' She was already short of breath.

He didn't answer.

'Save yourself. I mean it, Quinn.'

'No.'

They came to the end of the passageway. A tall iron gate barred the way to the street beyond. Disgleirio rattled the bars. It was locked.

'I couldn't climb that,' she whispered.

'I know.'

He snatched her hand again, and dragged her back the way they'd come, to a recessed door he'd noticed. He pushed at it, and found that it too was locked.

The patrol had rounded the corner and was running towards them.

He gave the door a hefty kick. It groaned and released puffs of dust. But it didn't budge. He glanced over his shoulder at the sprinting red-coats. Grasping the frame on either side, he pummelled the door with his boot heel. Wood splintered and it flew open. He bundled her inside.

There was just enough light to see that the place was derelict. They scrunched into muck and decay. The smell of rot was in the air.

One room opened off the passageway. Inside, the floor had given way. The only other option was a rickety staircase.

Disgleirio tried to shut the door. But he'd made too good a job of breaking it. A single hinge held it up, crazy-angled.

A paladin ran headlong into the entrance, sword thrust out. Disgleirio slammed the door into him. The man's sword arm was trapped against the casing. He yelled in pain. Disgleirio commenced battering door against arm until the weapon and its owner went down.

'The stairs!'

Tanalvah began climbing, hands clutching her swollen stomach. She moved slowly and clumsily.

Outside, there was uproar. The remnants of the door shook. Disgleirio threw himself against it and strained to keep the paladins out. The contest was short-lived. To the sound of snapping timber, the hunters simply tore the door off.

Disgleirio leapt to the first stair and spun to face them. Shoulder to shoulder, two paladins barged in. He caught a glimpse of their comrade in the alley behind them, on his knees, nursing his broken arm; and their leader, dripping blood, still roaring.

Tanalvah was near the top of the staircase, her white-knuckled hand on the rough banister. A few more steps would bring her to a small landing, then a turning to the next flight. If she got that far.

Disgleirio stood guard.

The space in the hallway was too confined for both paladins to attack him at once.

They jockeyed before one took the lead, while his partner attempted to vault the handrail. Disgleirio slashed at the man, denying his route, as he backed further up the stairs. The first paladin stalked him at swords-length; the other, deserting the banisters, followed. By the ruined door, the officer urged them on.

More violence was fated and it came quickly. The first red-coat sprinted, charging upstairs with sword outstretched. Disgleirio batted it aside, warding off an impaling. They swiftly traded a dozen fierce blows, with Disgleirio's greater height giving him the advantage. The tip of his blade raked the paladin's face. His follow-through was a massive downward rap that shattered the man's skull.

The paladin fell back into his companion. Both of them

tumbled, landing in a tangled heap at the foot of the steps. Their officer renewed his shrill tirade.

Disgleirio took the stairs two at a time, catching up with Tanalvah. 'Keep moving!'

She gave him a pained look. He took her arm and propelled her forward.

There were two rooms on this floor, their doors ajar. They were as derelict as the one below, and their windows were boarded. Disgleirio hurried her to the second flight. The officer and the last mobile paladin were at their heels.

A bolt of scorching blue light ripped the air. Disgleirio thrust Tanalvah to one side, and ducked. Just above their heads a section of wall flamed intensely. A smouldering fissure the size of a fist had appeared in the plaster. The odour of singeing prickled their nostrils.

As the officer raised his glamour wand again, Disgleirio and Tanalvah rushed for the next staircase. Another cobalt streak flashed their way. It gouged a smoking groove along half the length of the wall, and seared a chunk of handrail. Tanalvah screamed.

Disgleirio hustled her round the next corner. She started to climb. After a few steps she turned, and saw he was still at the bottom of the stairs, flat to the wall. He held a finger to his lips and motioned her on. She hesitated, then kept going while he lay in wait.

Nothing happened for a moment. Then a sword-tip cautiously probed the air. Disgleirio tensed.

But it wasn't the officer who appeared. It was the remaining private, sent ahead.

The space was too confined for swordplay. Both men lunged, grabbed each others' wrists and commenced struggling. With the officer lurking nearby and liable to join in, Disgleirio had to finish the tussle quickly. He delivered a vicious head butt. It broke his opponent's hold and impelled him backwards into the wall. Disgleirio snatched a dagger from his belt and plunged it into the dazed paladin's chest.

He didn't wait for the fatally wounded man to fall. Relieved to see that Tanalvah had already reached the top floor and was out of sight, he began bounding up the stairs after her.

He nearly made it.

A jolt like a kick from a mule almost knocked him off his feet. The officer had unleashed a further energy bolt. Disgleirio was lucky; it struck the blade of his sword, which took most of the impact. But the weapon was unbearably hot and he had to drop it. His palm was blistered. He felt as though a mass of burning needles peppered his arm. Clutching the knife, he raced up the last few steps.

He found Tanalvah cowering. She stared at his burnt hand. 'Gods, you're injured. What –'

'It's nothing,' he lied. 'I'm fine. But now we've only got this.' He showed her the knife.

'What do we do?'

He left that unanswered and took in their surroundings. This floor was very much like the one below; a couple of rooms, one doorless, with blocked windows. There were a few pieces of cheap, broken furniture.

'Quinn.' She pointed at the ceiling. There was a trapdoor, secured by a simple latch. 'But I don't think I could –'

'Wait.'

He glanced at the stairs. As yet there was no sign of the last paladin. Then he went into a room and came out with a shabby wooden chair. 'Could you manage with this?'

'Maybe.'

'Well, now's the time to find out.'

He stood on the chair. Stretching, he slid the latch and pushed open the trap, revealing the evening sky. The stars were just beginning to come out.

'Can you . . . ?'

She nodded. 'I'll try.'

She accepted his steadying hand and laboriously mounted the wobbly chair. Once more, he looked to the stairwell. Nothing stirred there.

'Put your foot here,' he said, 'on the chair back. Don't worry, I've got you. Good. Now the other.'

It took an eternity of straining effort to get the pregnant woman through the trap and onto the flat roof. Panting, he scrambled up after her, slamming the door behind him. There was nothing to secure it with.

The night was growing colder, and their breath expelled in huffing clouds. Ice was starting to form on the pitch.

The roof was edged by a low wall; and as the building was taller than those on either side, getting to them meant a substantial drop. At the back, there was a space too wide to jump separating them from the next jumble of houses. The only thing breaking the flatness of the roof was a brick chimney stack standing not far from the trapdoor. Tanalvah leaned against it as Disgleirio looked for an escape route.

He was checking the roof's opposite end when she cried out. The trapdoor had risen, and the officer was halfway out. He was already aiming his wand.

Disgleirio dived clear, landing painfully, full-length on the gritty asphalt. With a loud report, a power beam smacked into the wall where he'd been standing. The dazzling blast scattered masonry fragments.

He was on his feet again instantly and running, desperate for cover. The officer was out of the trap and moving forward, levelling the wand. Disgleirio zigzagged, trying to work his way to the chimney stack. He saw that Tanalvah had slipped round to its blind side and was all but hugging it.

A sapphire flash hosed the roof just short of his racing figure. Fiery streaks erupted and the surface bubbled. The tar stank. Perhaps thirty paces from the officer, Disgleirio saw only one choice. Aiming as best he could on the move, he lobbed his knife. The officer dodged, avoiding a body hit. But not fast enough to escape entirely. The knife skimmed the back of his hand, gashing flesh and sending the wand flying. It flipped, bounced and rolled out of sight. He dismissed it. Instead he dragged out his sword and, bellowing, sprinted in Disgleirio's direction.

Having no weapons except fists and feet, Disgleirio's sole option was to keep clear. As a strategy it had limited potential. The paladin officer had only to herd him.

Disgleirio retreated in the face of the charging man, who'd now drawn a knife too. But there was little room to move, and soon Disgleirio had his back to the low wall. He was rapidly driven into a corner. The paladin strode forward confidently, a smirk on his face despite the wounds he'd suffered.

'Ready to pay now?' he taunted. He came closer, until he was standing over Disgleirio, his blades raised. 'Die knowing that after you I'll deal with the whore,' he promised, swinging back his sword.

The blow didn't come. Lightning struck instead. Or so it seemed.

An obtuse expression on his face, the paladin froze, sword poised over his right shoulder. He looked down at his chest. His red tunic was smouldering. The outline of a tankard-sized hole began to appear. Orange flames blossomed from his chest.

Dropping his blades, he screamed and lurched forward. Disgleirio stumbled clear, narrowly avoiding the paladin's outstretched arms. As he did, he caught sight of the man's back and a large, vivid wound. There was the unmistakable smell of roasting flesh.

The officer teetered at the wall, flames spreading across his upper body. Then he toppled and fell shrieking to the alley below. Broken against the cobbles, his limbs at crazy angles, he continued to burn.

Tanalvah stood nearby, her arm extended, the wand in her hand. She seemed to be in some kind of daze. He called her name. She came out of the reverie, and as though only now realising she held the wand, let it slip from her fingers.

'How . . . how were you able to use that thing?' he asked, still shaken.

'You know magic,' she said. 'Desire triggers it.' Her words had a faraway quality. 'That's all it takes.'

Disgleirio was inhaling deeply, pulling himself together. He looked down to the alley. The paladin whose arm he'd broken was nowhere to be seen.

'The alarm's going to be raised,' he said. 'We've got to get out of here.'

'Yes.' Her voice was small.

'And, Tan . . . thanks.'

She only nodded.

The way Tanalvah saw it, she had added no more than a feather to the scales of redemption.

3

'How much further?' Tanalvah asked.

'Not long now,' Disgleirio told her.

'We're going out of the city?'

'Not quite. To the outskirts.' He seemed reluctant to say more, presumably on the principle that what she didn't know she couldn't be made to tell, should things go wrong.

They sat side by side in a small gig. As Tanalvah could hardly be expected to walk far, or ride a horse with any ease, Disgleirio had stolen the vehicle shortly after they escaped the paladins. With shadows lengthening and the curfew drawing near, he drove as fast as he dared.

Central Valdarr was behind them and they were entering the city's outer reaches. Even here there was evidence of Bhealfa's successive occupation by both empires. Rintarah and Gath Tampoor had subjugated the island by turn for generations, and their most visible legacy was the muddle of architecture. As conquerors will, each erected monuments that commemorated their victory and acted as a reminder of who was in charge. Many of these structures were extravagant statements of imperial might that dwarfed the humble native dwellings surrounding them.

When one empire cast out the other, the loser's buildings were often demolished to make way for new constructs, or adapted to serve the incomers in a cycle that had repeated itself beyond living memory. The aftermath of recent civil strife also left its mark. Arson had proved popular of late, and the effects of glamour weaponry added another layer of visual discord. In places where they suspected nests of rebels, which is to say in poorer quarters, whole neighbourhoods had been razed by the authorities. All this made for a complicated cityscape.

Wealthy or impoverished, every section of the city had one thing in common: magic was used in profusion. And now that night was falling its expression was more obvious, and spectacular. Far more intense than conventional lamps and candles, a myriad pinpoints of light flickered on and off in every direction. There were dazzling flashes, multicoloured flares, twinklings, sparklings and occasional outbursts that looked like earthbound lightning.

But while the quantity of magical discharges was roughly even, its quality was noticeably variable. The nature of a district could be assessed by the strength or weakness of its emissions, and Disgleirio and Tanalvah witnessed a particularly stark example as they crested a rise. Stretched before them for a moment were two abutting sectors, one well-heeled, the other deprived. The former's magic shimmered with a bright purity; the latter gave off the feeble glow of cheap and counterfeit sorcery. Disgleirio chose the road that ran through the less fortunate area.

They had travelled more or less in silence. That suited Tanalvah. There were subjects she'd rather not dwell upon, and traps she hoped to avoid. Now Disgleirio decided he wanted to talk, though he began innocuously enough.

'How are you feeling?' he said.

'I'm all right.'

'Not finding the ride too bumpy?'

'No.'

'Because if you are –'

'Quinn, I'm expecting a baby; I'm not ill.'

He grinned. 'Of course.'

Nothing more was said for a moment, then he asked, 'What have you been doing with yourself these last few months, Tan?'

It wasn't a question she relished. 'Moving from place to place. Trying to keep the children safe.'

'How did you support yourself?'

'Any way I could. I worked selling unlicensed glamours for a while. Served in a tavern; pounded herbs for a healer one time; scrubbed floors. Of course that's become a bit difficult lately.' She laid a hand on her distended belly. 'But people helped me now and again.' Some of it was true.

'You didn't try to find us?'

'How could I? I didn't dare go to any Resistance places for fear of spies. And you must have cleared out of them anyway.'

'No, I can see that. But as I said; we've been looking for you.'

'Valdarr's a big place.'

'I meant . . . I just wanted you to know we hadn't given up on you.'

It was hard getting her words out after that. 'I . . . I've tried to keep out of sight.'

'Until tonight.'

'My luck ran out.' Perhaps it really has, she thought.

'Why were they after you? The paladins.'

'I sometimes wonder if they need a reason.'

'True.' His features took on a troubled cast. 'Tan. About . . . Kinsel.'

Her insides did a flip. Her knuckles were white from squeezing the seat rail.

'It's just . . .' he stumbled on, '. . . just that . . . I don't know if you heard, but –'

'I heard.'

He didn't think to ask her how. 'I'm so very sorry, Tan.'

'You don't have to be. We don't know that he's . . . gone. Not for sure. Officially he's just missing.' A cold thought touched her. 'Unless you know any different?'

'No. We've heard nothing beyond that ourselves. And you're right; while there's a chance we have to keep hoping.'

Tanalvah came close to telling him she knew he'd argued for Kinsel's death, but she was hardly in a position to do so.

The houses they passed were less densely packed together, and the roads were rougher and pot-holed. There were glimpses of vegetation between buildings. The city's gravitational hold was weaker out here on its farthest edge.

They were heading east. The low mountain range that hugged this side of Valdarr was beginning to loom. In the crisp, moonless night it looked as black as a paladin's soul.

It was cold, fit to snow. She gathered her cloak more tightly.

Disgleirio glanced her way. 'We've never really recovered, you know. From the betrayal.' He made it sound like a confidence. 'It tore the guts out of us, Tan.'

She'd dreaded him bringing up the catastrophe, though she knew it was inevitable he would. A nod was all she could manage.

'We lost . . . well, who knows how many,' he went on. 'Including quite a few you would have known.'

She was afraid he'd wonder why she hadn't asked about that herself. 'I . . . try not to think about it,' she replied truthfully.

'Can't say I blame you.'

'What about Serrah and Caldason? And Kutch? Any word on them?'

'On the Diamond Isle, last we heard. Don't know how they're faring, but at least they got away.'

'That's good. Oh, and what about Phoenix?'

'He got away to the Diamond Isle too. Or at least we think he did. The rest of Covenant linked up with us again within a few weeks of the betrayal.'

Tanalvah shouldn't have asked her next question, but couldn't help herself. She had to know. 'Does anybody have an idea who . . .'

'Sold us out? There are plenty of theories, but no real evidence. Might not have been just one person, of course. Could have been a disaffected faction in our ranks. Perhaps we'll never know. But one or a hundred, I could never understand the mentality of a traitor.'

'Perhaps whoever it was felt . . . compelled to talk.'

'Torture, you mean?'

'Yes.' It was a kind of torture, she reflected.

'I don't want to bring back unpleasant memories, Tan, but Kinsel suffered that and he didn't break.' He shot her a sympathetic look. 'To his great credit. But as I said, I doubt we'll ever know what happened.'

'Is that how everybody sees it? That we'll never know, I mean. Are they getting over it?' As soon as she said it she realised how idiotic a question it was, born of desperation.

'It's not something you get over, Tan.'

'I know. I'm being stupid. Sorry.'

'Don't apologise. We'd all like to forget it if we could. But the prospect of maybe never knowing who betrayed us hasn't dampened our passion for finding out. There isn't a member of the Resistance who wouldn't cheerfully slit the bastard's throat, given half a chance.'

It was getting too uncomfortable for her. She tried changing the subject. 'I didn't ask about Karr. How is he?'

'Damn near died when this thing first broke out. His heart.

He pulled through, but his health suffered badly. Being Karr, of course, he's made little concession to taking it easier. For once I think he's right. We're all working like demons just to stay alive.'

She looked away, her eyes stinging. Guilt's hot knife twisted in her gut.

'We're nearly there,' he said. 'You'll be able to rest soon.'

If only that were true. She made an effort to collect herself, and dabbed at her eyes with a cloth. He was staring at her. 'The cold air makes them water,' she explained lamely.

'Sure,' he said, not seeing.

At length she started taking an interest in their surroundings. The scenery was becoming semi-rural, with buildings standing more in isolation, and now she saw barns and small-holdings. Much further and they'd be in farmland proper.

'Quinn,' she asked, 'where exactly are we going? The only thing I know of in these parts . . .'

'Is the Pastures of Sleep. You guessed, Tan.'

She couldn't suppress a shudder. Had this all been an elaborate scheme after all? A ruse to lure her into a terrible retribution of some kind?

He read her expression. 'No need to look so grim. I know it isn't everybody's favoured location, but it'll be fine, believe me.'

A couple of minutes later they had first sight of their destination.

The Pastures of Sleep was Valdarr's oldest and most extensive necropolis. It had already existed in a modest form when the city was founded, and over the centuries it had grown in size, and in the elaborateness of its monuments and tombs. For generations it served as the last resting place for high and low alike. Bhealfa's leading dynasties maintained grand family mausoleums within its grounds, but less regarded, or easily seen, were the acres given over to paupers' mass graves. Now the cemetery was full, unfashionable and largely unused.

A high stone wall surrounded the burial ground, though many of its more ostentatious memorials stood taller, displaying the tips of decorated spires. Mature trees towered higher still, their skeletal branches swaying in the brittle wind.

'It wouldn't be safe going all the way in this carriage,' Disgleirio announced. 'We'll have to lose it and walk the last part. Can you manage that?'

'I'll be fine.'

He pulled into a small piece of open land with only a single darkened house overlooking it. After helping Tanalvah down he went to the gig's horse and gave it a reassuring pat. 'Don't worry,' he said, assuming her interest in the animal's well-being, 'I'll see he's taken care of.'

They set off.

Curfew was in force and the streets were deserted, though that didn't make Disgleirio any less alert. However, their short walk, hugging shadows, was uneventful, and soon they approached the cemetery's imposing iron gates. An impressive entrance demanded an impressive lock, and the necropolis' gateway was no exception. It bore a mortise larger than a man's hand.

'It's got an alarm spell,' Disgleirio explained as he dug into his pocket. He produced a key the length of a small dagger. The gate creaked shrilly as he opened it just wide enough for them to pass through, then he ignited a glamoured orb to light their way.

It was, literally, deathly quiet. They took the central avenue, a broad boulevard edged with ghostly sepulchres. At the avenue's far end, dark and brooding, stood an imposing temple, now falling into decay. Well before they reached that, Disgleirio led them round a corner and along a much narrower path, which was less well maintained, with crooked gravestones on either side, amid a tangle of untended vegetation. There was barely enough room for them to walk abreast.

A voice growled, *'Remember me!'*

Tanalvah squealed and grabbed Disgleirio's arm.

'Steady, Tan.' He took her hand. 'There's nothing to be scared of; they're only living memorials. Look.'

Several nearby headstones had activated, projecting spectral likenesses of the graves' occupants. The one that had spoken was an ancient man, bald of pate and with skin like yellowed parchment.

'Passing sets them off,' Disgleirio continued. 'Sorry, I should have warned you.'

She disentangled herself from him, feeling foolish. 'Silly of me,' she said.

They carried on.

Every few paces they triggered a glamoured memorial, conjuring animated images of the dead. Men, women, old, young; ailing in appearance or hearty; smiling or scowling. Tanalvah noticed that not all the graves were set off though.

'They only work if relatives keep recharging the magic, of course,' Disgleirio offered, almost conversationally. 'It'll all run down eventually.'

Many of the deceased's glamours were vocal. They presented greetings, pearls of wisdom and dire warnings. Some recounted their life stories or recited poetry. Others mumbled prayers or mouthed prophecies. The voices were beseeching, cheerful, hectoring, doleful, jaunty. A few sang or played musical instruments.

Tanalvah loathed the place. She couldn't help thinking what kind of messages would have been left by the people she'd consigned to their graves. When they rounded another corner and entered a quieter spot her relief was intense.

They trudged on, encountering only the occasional garrulous crypt. An area of dense trees lay ahead and they made for it.

'There's something coming up I need to warn you about,' Disgleirio told her. 'We have sentinels.'

'Are they dangerous?'

'They look dangerous. But they're not top-grade magic. Essentially they're for deterrence. If our enemies knew how feeble our defences really were –'

A long, drawn-out howl sounded. It raised the hairs on the nape of Tanalvah's neck.

'Ah,' he said, 'here they come.'

A creature loped from the treeline, looking grey from this distance. It was joined by three more, sleek and fast. As they got nearer their features became distinct. They had powerful jaws and razor-keen talons. Their silky fur was pure white, and their eyes were pink.

Tanalvah wondered why albino wolves were thought appropriate, before deciding they were probably all the Resistance could get.

The wolves slinked closer, fanning out into a semi-circle, apparently positioning themselves to strike. They growled and snuffled convincingly.

Disgleirio snapped his fingers at each beast in turn, one-two-three-four. The wolves turned into clouds of faintly phosphorescent green mist, then nothing. Tanalvah caught a distinctive whiff of sulphur.

'The next line of defence is human,' he promised, 'and it's just about the last one. Come on, it's not far now.'

He strode towards the trees. She had to hurry to keep up with him.

They entered what proved to be a small wood. It was thick, with trees growing close together, and there was no path. In places, dead leaves had drifted into sizeable mounds, but Disgleirio knew exactly where he was going.

'This copse runs to the foothills,' he said.

'That's where we're going?'

'Yes. We're nearly there. Are you all right with this? No problem with the walk?'

'I'll let you know if I need help.'

Two armed men, black clad and sober faced, slipped from the foliage ahead of them, barring the way. When Disgleirio was recognised they lowered their weapons, but they continued to eye Tanalvah. She didn't know either of them. Disgleirio told them about the abandoned gig and ordered it taken care of. The guards returned wordless nods and stood aside for them. It all happened so quickly and smoothly that it felt like a dream to Tanalvah, but her mind was on other things, and her trepidation was growing ever stronger.

Shortly they reached a wall of rock, smothered in creepers and vines. Another pair of guards appeared, identified Disgleirio and hailed him. A moment later they were at the rock face, dragging aside a mass of netting cunningly woven with scrub. They revealed a cave entrance.

Disgleirio took out another orb and handed it to her. It snapped into life. As they entered, he said, 'This is actually the oldest part of the cemetery, the catacombs. No one comes here any more. Nature formed it, but there was a lot of tunnelling in the past, too. This is where our primitive ancestors first started depositing their dead, Tan.' He stopped and looked at her. 'I should have asked. You're not jumpy about going underground, are you?'

'I'll cope with it, Quinn.' She was much more worried about facing the people she'd wronged. But it was too late now.

'Good. But I think Serrah might have had a problem with it.'

'What?' She focused on him.

'Serrah. She didn't like –'

'Oh, yes. Of course. I don't suppose she would.'

They resumed their journey.

'There are several other entrances.' Disglierio jabbed his thumb over his shoulder. 'Makes getting out in an emergency much easier. The tunnels themselves are a good defence, too. Easy to get lost if you don't know them; and there are chambers that flood.'

They twisted and turned more times than she could count. The sloping tunnel they followed was above head height and unlit. Its floor and walls were smooth from the eternity of flowing water that had carved them. There was a musky, earthy smell she found faintly unpleasant.

Eventually the going got lighter. The tunnels now had glamour orbs and flaming brands fastened to their walls, and as Tanalvah and Disgleirio moved deeper into the tunnel system the nature of their surroundings changed. The drabness began to give way to unexpected colour. Veins of yellow, red, purple and green patterned the rock.

They passed through passages wide and narrow, and in and out of caverns, some vast, housing eerie rock formations. They negotiated forests of stalagmites and stalactites. Tanalvah saw no evidence of the bodies supposedly deposited in ancient times, although Disgleirio assured her that there were plenty.

Soon they heard the distant clatter of habitation and the echoing sound of voices.

Where tunnels crossed they glimpsed people at the end of passageways; men and women engaged in chores, running messages, carrying barrels and crates. There was a distinct sense of buzzing activity.

At last they came to the entrance of a massive underground chamber, its roof so high it was hidden in shadows. A number of passages ran off from the cavern, and scores of people bustled in and out. They scaled mountains of provisions or polished the blades in well-stocked racks. At dozens of benches they fashioned weapons and stitched clothing, while children circulated with water pails, and there were dogs and pigs running loose. Braziers and torches were scattered everywhere. In the centre of the chamber, in a large natural pit, a generous fire was burning, making the atmosphere smoky and pungent with the smell of sweet woods. The aroma of roasting meat mingled with it.

'You look anything but happy, Tan,' Disgleirio told her as they entered. 'What's up?'

'Do I? I suppose it's all been a bit of a shock. Meeting you like that, being brought here.'

'You're safe now. You'll be taken care of. And if it's Teg and Lirrin you're worried about, don't be. We'll look after them, too. You're among friends again, Tan.'

'Friends,' she repeated quietly.

'Yes. Friends who'll be very happy to see you.'

She made no reply.

'I'll be just a minute,' he said, smiling.

He moved off, leaving her standing at the edge of the milling crowd.

Tanalvah was aware of everyone staring; some tactfully, others with open curiosity. One or two faces looked familiar, but most were strangers to her. She wondered how many had lost loved ones.

It was hard to shake off the feeling that they knew what she'd done. That they could somehow gaze into the depths of her soul and see her foul secret. She began to breathe hard. Her head was swimming and she didn't know where to look to avoid their probing eyes.

'Tanalvah!'

Disgleirio was heading back, but it wasn't him who greeted her. An older man walked beside him, and it took a moment for her to realise who it was. Bringing up the rear was a mature woman Tanalvah had no trouble recognising.

'Tanalvah,' the old man repeated, approaching with arms outspread.

'Patrician,' she whispered.

'It's plain Karr these days,' he responded, enfolding her in a hug. 'I can't tell you how glad I am Quinn found you, my dear. We were beginning to think we'd never see you again.'

'So was I.' She tried not to go completely rigid in his arms.

She was shocked. He was thinner and drawn, and what hair he had left was even whiter, if that were possible. His back was bent and his skin looked unnaturally ashen. A distinguished, sprightly politician the last time she saw him, Dulian Karr had mutated into a pallid shadow of his former self. The illness had taken a heavy toll.

Tanalvah corrected herself. *She* had taken the toll.

'Make room for me.' The woman accompanying him came forward, and likewise embraced Tanalvah, planting a smiling kiss on her cheek. It was an unusual show of affection from Karr's closest aide.

'Goyter,' Tanalvah said. 'It's good to see you.'

'And it's wonderful to see you, Tan.'

The woman's appearance was little changed. Goyter remained strapping for her age, and her face had kept its no-nonsense set even while she smiled. She wore her hair in a bun. It was greyer than Tanalvah remembered, and perhaps there were a few more stress lines on her brow, but otherwise she hadn't altered.

'We have so much to tell you,' Goyter went on. 'And you must have a hell of a story for us.'

'You wouldn't believe it.'

'Look at you,' Goyter exclaimed, taking a step back and surveying Tanalvah's ripe figure. 'You must be due soon.'

'Not too long.'

'You're well, are you, Tan?' Karr wanted to know. 'No problems with the baby? And the children? Are they fit, and safe?'

'Everything's fine.'

He swept an arm to indicate the cavern. 'Well, what do you think? The United Revolutionary Council, what's left of it, wound up in a graveyard. A fitting symbol for the state of the Resistance, some might say.'

'It's so . . . unusual.'

'True it's not much, but it's home. And a graveyard seems like a good place to stage a resurrection.'

'A resurrection?'

'The girl doesn't want to hear all that,' Goyter interrupted. 'Can't you see she needs rest?'

Karr seemed stricken. 'Forgive me, Tan. We have a lot of catching up to do, but it can wait until later.' He smiled and took her arm. 'Come on, we have a bed for you.'

Disgleirio had stood apart while the exchange took place. Now Goyter looked to him. 'Quinn, what happened to your hand?'

'Oh, it's nothing.' The grubby makeshift bandage was bunched, revealing angry blisters. 'I wouldn't be here at all if it wasn't for Tanalvah.'

'Really?' Karr said.

'She was very brave, Dulian. I owe her my life.'

'That's our Tan,' Goyter announced admiringly.

They all turned their smiles on her.

Tears rolled down Tanalvah's cheeks. Her shoulders heaved. She covered her face and gave way to sobbing.

'It's only natural,' Goyter cooed, moving forward to comfort her. 'You've been through so much you're bound to feel low. But it's over now. You're back with your family.'

Tanalvah continued to weep uncontrollably.

Up above, the first flakes of snow were dusting the frozen ground.

4

It was starting to snow.

'We should have brought horses,' Caldason grumbled.

'We're nearly there now. Besides, you want to stay fit, don't you?'

'I can think of more pleasant ways of doing that.'

Serrah Ardacris smiled. 'Keep your mind on the job at hand, Reeth. And stop changing the subject. We were discussing Kinsel. What are we going to do about him?'

'*You* were discussing Kinsel. I'm not convinced.'

'He's out there, Reeth.'

'How can you be so sure?'

'I've heard Kinsel sing; you haven't. It's not something you forget. Believe me, it was him.'

'You've got to admit it's a bit unlikely.'

'What's so unlikely about it? Kinsel's galley was lost. Why shouldn't pirates have been responsible?'

'It was a fair way from here.'

'So? That's what ships are for, isn't it? Getting people from one place to another.'

'But why would he be singing?'

'Are you having a particularly dimwitted day? I don't know

why. Perhaps somebody forced him. Maybe it was his way of identifying himself. It doesn't matter; but what we do about it does.'

Caldason grinned. 'You really do think it was him, don't you?'

'*Yes!* That's what I keep saying, for pity's sake. Look, Reeth, if there's even a slim chance I'm right we have to do something, don't we? We owe him that much.'

'Yes, of course we do. I'll talk to Darrok about it, and the council.'

'We need a plan.'

'We'll have one.'

She reached for his hand. 'Thanks, my love.'

It was twilight and the chill winds were biting. The sky was leaden, and just beginning to shed its burden of snow.

They were in the Diamond Isle's interior. The path they trod was ill-maintained, like most of the rundown pleasure resort's walkways. Some of the buildings they passed had fallen into ruin after years of neglect. Others were intact and functional, but as many of them had been designed for purely recreational purposes they were little use as island defences. Serrah and Caldason had seen them so many times they hardly noticed anymore.

'We should try to get word to Tan about Kinsel,' Serrah suggested, negotiating a ridge of frozen mud.

'That could be hard. This place is practically blockaded. The pirates, the empires or all three seem to be stopping most of the glamoured messages we send. Not to mention how low our store of magic is. It wouldn't be easy convincing the council to use any on our behalf.'

'I know the problems, Reeth. We should still try.'

'Wouldn't it be better to wait until we're sure? Give it until we have more than just your certainty about it?'

'Let's not go there again.'

'I'm serious, Serrah. We could be building up Tanalvah's hopes without cause.'

'If I were in her position, waiting to hear about you, I think I'd want to know. Would it hurt so much to give her a straw to clutch at?'

'It could, if the hope's groundless. We should think on this. Besides, we don't even know if she's alive.'

'She's alive, Reeth. Tan's a survivor.'

'I'll talk to some people about it. Anyway, we're nearly there.' He nodded to indicate the towers marking their destination, which were starting to show above the hill they climbed.

Minutes later they had a clear view of the structure the rebels grandly referred to, not without irony, as their central redoubt.

Built as a guesthouse for rich visitors, it was the tallest building on the island, very large, and fashioned sturdily enough. There were half a dozen towers, winding battlements and an extensive flat, walled roof. There was even a portcullis, and a moat, now dry and clogged with leaves. However, its appearance didn't reflect its substance; it had been made to look like a castle rather than be one. Its stone cladding was for show and unlikely to withstand a concerted battering. The doors and windows were equally deceptive in terms of their strength.

Caldason would never have chosen such a place as a fortress of last resort, or approved its location, but it was all they had. The coastal hill fort had been constructed from scratch. It took so much in the way of time and resources that the same couldn't be done for a central redoubt. The rebels had no choice but to beef up this mock bastion.

Hordes of people were swarming over and around the scaffolded building. They created a din with hammering, sawing, and felling trees for timber. Wagons queued with loads of stone to toughen the ramparts, while mortar was being mixed in giant vats.

Serrah and Caldason made their way down the side of the hill, exchanging greetings with the workers.

'There's Zahgadiah and Pallidea,' Serrah said, pointing.

The one-time owner of the island was hard to miss as he floated on his glamoured dish, inspecting a score of black-smiths pounding iron on a row of anvils. His leather-clad female companion walked beside him, almost as conspicuous with her waist-length flaming red hair.

Darrok hailed them in typically gravel-voiced fashion. Pallidea merely nodded.

'Let's get away from this racket,' Darrok mouthed.

They followed his hovering saucer along the side of the wall until the noise faded to a tolerable level. The sky was notice-ably darker and snowflakes were growing more abundant.

'How's it going?' Caldason asked.

'Not bad,' Darrok replied, surveying the scene. 'But there's a hell of a lot more to do yet.'

'Just like everywhere else on the island. How long before it's finished do you think?'

'Couple of weeks. Maybe longer.' He turned his attention to Serrah. 'We haven't had a chance to talk since we beat off the raid, have we?'

'When do we ever?'

'I just wanted to say it was a great plan of yours to use dragon's blood against Vance's men. It really turned the fight in our favour.'

'I can't take the credit; I got the idea from the Resistance back in Bhealfa.'

'You're too modest, Serrah.'

'Dragon's blood?' Pallidea said. It was a rare utterance from Darrok's normally taciturn bodyguard-cum-lover.

'The stuff that caused the blasts,' Darrok explained. 'It's a

powder that explodes on contact with water. Serrah brought
some in with her, and came up with a way of making it
work; an ingenious little water-filled pouch with a breakable
container inside for the powder. And before you ask; it's just
called dragon's blood.'

'Very funny,' his mistress responded dryly.

'Is there any left?' Caldason asked.

Darrok shook his head. 'Not much. I've got our wizards
trying to make more.'

'Zahgadiah,' Serrah said, 'you heard that singing during
the raid, didn't you?' Caldason sighed. She shot him a
glare.

'Yes,' Darrok said, 'I heard it. Reeth mentioned you thought
it was Kinsel Rukanis.'

'Right.'

'I went to a concert he gave once, somewhere. Gath
Tampoor, I think.'

She leapt on the possibility of confirmation. 'So do you
think it was him we heard?'

'Damned if I know. Tin legs, tin ear, that's me.' He rapped
his thigh, raising a muffled clang. 'Never did have much of
an appreciation of music.'

'Why did you go to one of his concerts then?' Her tone
was mildly exasperated.

'It was a place to be seen. That's important for a man in
my position. Or it was until I got stuck out here with you
ragtag insurgents.'

'I notice you haven't left,' Caldason observed wryly. 'It's
not too late to get out even now, you know.'

'So you keep saying. Want to get rid of me?'

'No, but it's not your fight. You shouldn't feel compelled
to stay.'

'Forcing me to do anything I don't want to do isn't easy,
Reeth. And as I understand it, it wasn't your fight either at

the outset. No, I think I'll stay. For now, at least. I've a certain curiosity about how things will turn out. Anyway, I always did favour the underdog and hopeless situations.'

Caldason smiled. His initial opinion of the man had been turned on its head these past few months.

'This is all beside the point,' Darrok continued, 'and I've got something to tell you. As you know, we decided to undertake the island's first census. Well, not much more than a headcount really, but we just got the tally and I thought you'd find it interesting.'

'I certainly would,' Serrah confirmed.

'The survivors of the Great Betrayal who managed to get here, including you, Reeth and Kutch, along with the Resistance pathfinders already installed and my people, amounted to just under two and a half thousand. We've lost a little short of a hundred since to pirate raids and natural causes. But we've gained, too. In the weeks after you arrived we had quite an influx of stragglers. Near as we can tell, the total now stands at a bit over three thousand seven hundred.'

'That's more than I expected,' Caldason admitted.

'Me too. And we're still seeing the odd boatload coming in, though it's a trickle now as getting here's so dangerous.'

'How does that figure break down?' Serrah asked.

'Unbalanced. Which could be a problem for the future. Assuming this place has a future. Approximately two thousand six hundred are men. Women amount to just about an even thousand. The remaining hundred are children, including babes in arms. Good news on the men is that all but around sixty of them are in their prime and capable of fighting.'

'Do you have any idea how many people it'd take to defend this place?'

'From a full-scale invasion of the island by either empire? Oh, about twenty to thirty thousand. Minimum.'

'Damn their eyes!' Serrah spat.

'Who?'

'Whoever it was who betrayed the Resistance and put us in this position.'

'I think we'd all go along with that.'

'If we live through this, and if I ever find out who did it, I'll enjoy cutting their fucking throat,' she vowed. 'Slowly.'

'You might have to stand in line,' Darrok advised.

Caldason steered them back to the question of defence. 'But the force we have can hold off the pirates, can't it? Assuming they don't attack in greater numbers than they have been?'

'Probably.'

'And we've had no word of Rintarah or Gath Tampoor mustering invasion fleets?'

'As far as we know they're not. Though we're basing that on reports from latecomers drifting in, of course. We can't be sure.' He regarded Caldason quizzically. 'What's your point?'

'If I don't act soon I'll never finish what I started.'

'The Clepsydra,' Serrah stated flatly.

He nodded.

'Is this the right time, Reeth?'

'It may be the only time.' He saw the anxiety in her eyes. 'This is really important to me, Serrah.'

'You don't have to tell me that. I'm just wondering how practical it is. A lot's changed since you learned about the Source.'

'Not for me.'

'How can you be sure this Clepsydra thing isn't a myth?' Darrok chipped in.

'I can't. But it's the only chance I have of a cure.'

'Do you know how to find it? Or how it'll lead to the grimoire or whatever it is you're looking for? As I understand it, the Clepsydra's on an islet, not much more than a speck in the ocean, along with a hundred others.'

'Phoenix showed me maps. I think I can find it. As to the Source, whatever it may be . . . I'll just have to take my chances with that, too.'

'Nobody could stop you, of course, and I certainly wouldn't want to. But you're going to have to persuade the council to spare a ship and a crew. That's unlikely in present circumstances, I'd say.'

'I can be very persuasive.'

'I'm so afraid you'll be disappointed,' Serrah said.

'More than I have been?' He softened, smiled. 'Until just lately.'

She brightened, and smiled back.

'You'll be going together?' Pallidea wondered.

Serrah looked to her man. 'Reeth knows better than to try it without me.'

Darrok gave a gritty laugh. 'Never thought I'd see you blush, Serrah.'

She made a suggestion concerning where he could put his hovering saucer, bringing a grin to Pallidea's lips, a rare sight.

The snow was getting heavier. Somebody had planted a scorpion insignia on top of a nearby hillock, and the green pennant fluttered noisily in the bitter wind.

'Whatever you decide, Reeth,' Serrah declared, wrapping her cloak tighter, 'you know I'll back you. But I hope we can do something about Kinsel first.'

'I won't go until we do.'

'Good. You know, Tanalvah told me something about Kinsel from when he was a boy that I've never mentioned to you. His father was arrested by the authorities. Some trumped-up charge, apparently. They forced him into slave labour, and then the army. It killed him. And it really struck me, and Tan too, I think, how that's so similar to what's happened to

Kinsel himself. Like father, like son. Only we can't let him end up the same way, can we?'

'He deserves our help,' Darrok decided. 'You and I should talk this over, Reeth.'

'That was my thought. Tell me, assuming it is Kinsel out there, and Vance has him, what do you make of the singing?'

'Oh, you'd be surprised. For a man who acts like a savage, Vance has some unexpectedly cultured tastes.'

'You think he'd be indulging them during a raid?'

'You don't know him, Reeth. He's perfectly capable of something like that. To add a note of drama to the proceedings perhaps, though the gods know they seemed dramatic enough to me at the time. Or to cosset himself against our victory. He's unpredictable. He could simply have been taunting us.'

'You mean he might know about the connection between us and Kinsel?'

'Who can say? After time on a galley, and left to Vance's tender mercies, your friend might be made to reveal anything.'

'The CIS's torturers couldn't break him. Or the paladins.'

Darrok raised an eyebrow. 'I'm impressed. A brave man.'

'I've often wondered,' Serrah said, 'why they sentenced Kinsel to the galleys rather than just executing him.'

'You need to understand the nature of our rulers,' Darrok offered. 'It could have been a sop to the masses. A way of showing that insurgence won't be tolerated, but without the stigma of actually being seen to put a popular man to death. Politics plays a big part in these decisions. Given the character of our self-appointed leaders, it was as likely to have been pure sadism. They had to know his end would be lingering and painful.'

'That sounds like the bastards,' Serrah remarked.

Darrok absently brushed snowflakes from his tunic and looked to the sky, blinking. 'This is getting too rough. We'll have to call off the exterior work, damn it. Let's get inside.'

Serrah and Caldason slipped arms around each other's waists. With Pallidea walking beside his floating dish, Darrok led them towards the mock fortress's grand entrance. He signalled as he moved, a silent order for the grateful workers to down tools and seek shelter. The swirling snow had the look of countless locusts descending. Fires were doused, horses draped with blankets. A young girl collecting discarded nails in a bucket laid down her burden and ran for cover.

'We shouldn't leave things too long as far as Rukanis is concerned,' Darrok said. 'What he suffered in the galleys wouldn't compare to what Vance can put him through. I feel sorry for your friend if he really is in that devil's hands.'

5

'Go on, have a grape.'

'Thank you, no,' Kinsel Rukanis repeated stiffly, keeping his eyes downcast. He'd found it safer that way.

Kingdom Vance replaced the crystal fruit bowl on a polished oak table. He plucked a grape for himself, popped it into his mouth and assumed an exaggerated expression of pleasure. 'Hmmm. You don't know what you're missing.'

'What I'm missing,' Kinsel said, daring to lift his gaze, 'is my freedom.'

The pirate feigned concern. 'Is my generosity lacking in some way? Is the quality of the wine not to your liking? Are the silk sheets on your bed –'

'I hate to spoil the delight you take in mocking me, Vance, but please don't abuse my intelligence.'

'You think it intelligent to insult my generosity? When someone talks to me like that it's usually a prelude to their death.'

'Then have done with it. Even dying's preferable to your brand of hospitality.'

'You can have your freedom whenever you want. Or at

least a chance to win it. You've only to meet me in combat. We can do it now, up on deck.'

'I've told you before that I won't do that.'

'Should you win, I give you my word that my crew would release you, if that's what you're worried about. Or if it's a question of your skills being less than mine, I'm sure we could find a way of evening the odds. I could fight with one hand tied, perhaps.'

'I'll not lift a sword against you or any other man.'

Vance laughed. 'You fascinate me, Rukanis. You're not a coward, yet you don't believe in violence. Whereas I've always found it an invaluable tool in my line, not to mention a continuous source of entertainment.'

It was no idle boast. Kinsel had seen Vance's fickle brutality toward his enemies and crew alike.

Both men were big, in their different ways. Vance was taller than average and large-framed. A mass of black curly hair framed his craggy, blemished face, and he was full-bearded. He favoured showy clothing; blue ankle-length frockcoat with gold trimming, breeches stuffed into thigh-high leather boots. And he swathed himself in jewellery: bracelets and ear studs, chains and pendants, rings on every finger.

Where Vance was flamboyant, Rukanis was modest by nature; in his life before slavery he could hardly have been called ostentatious. He was a little below the norm in height, and thickset, with a slightly barrelled chest that denoted the extra lung capacity of a singer; though the tattered convict's uniform he currently wore hung looser now. His hair and beard were dark and had started out trimmed short, but now both were growing unruly.

Vance crunched into a red apple. 'If you're not willing to fight for your freedom,' he said, chewing, 'I'm not inclined to grant it.' He discarded the apple after a further bite, tossing

it casually over his shoulder. It joined a clutter of half eaten
fruit littering the floor of his grandly appointed cabin. 'Besides,
you're more use to me alive.'

'Why?'

'The gift of your voice, for one thing. Despite what you
may think, I'm no savage.' He belched and wiped the juice
from his beard with the back of his sleeve.

'What's the other thing?'

'You were sentenced for Resistance activities. Who better
to call for those on the island to give up?'

'I'd be appealing to strangers. Why should they listen to
me?'

'You underestimate your influence. The Diamond Isle's
been taken over by rebels. Chances are you know some of
them.'

'That's quite an assumption. And even if I did, why should
they give up because of me? Their vision's bigger than one
man.'

'Vision,' the pirate mouthed contemptuously. 'They have
as much vision as a eunuch looking for a good time in a
whorehouse.' He fixed Rukanis with a steely gaze. 'Do you
know Zahgadiah Darrok?'

'I've heard the name,' Kinsel replied cagily.

'Darrok's behind this defiance. He's formed a union with
these damned revolutionaries to keep me from what's right-
fully mine.'

'You mean the island? I thought he owned it.'

Vance flashed sudden anger. He brought his fist down hard
on the table, jangling the dishes. 'Own be damned! He as
good as stole it from me!'

Kinsel thought that unlikely, but judged it best to stay
silent.

'Darrok and I share a history,' Vance continued, calming
somewhat. 'We worked in harness to forge a dominion in

these waters, and further afield.' He adopted a theatrically hurt look. 'I thought we were friends. Then he stabbed me in the back. It was a grievous betrayal.'

'I don't see what it has to do with me.'

'Then you lack imagination, singer. That island rightly belongs to me, and to the alliance I've built with my fellow merchant adventurers. We need it as a base, and I'll do whatever it takes to get it. If that means using you any way I see fit, I will.'

'They won't trade, if that's what you're thinking. And I wouldn't want them to.'

'How noble of you,' Vance sneered.

'Look at it from their point of view. My well-being or all their futures. It's no contest.'

'We'll see.'

'This whole thing is insane, Vance. You're wasting lives in pursuit of . . . what? A rock in the middle of the ocean. There are other islands. Why not settle for one of them?'

'Lives are just another overhead in my business. The men who threw in their lot with the alliance did it willingly, and they knew the risks. Lives are nothing. It's my honour that counts.'

'So your honour demands such carnage? Surely it's better to come to some accommodation with the rebels. They might even –'

'Enough! Your . . . reasonableness vexes me.'

Kinsel braced himself for a blow. Or worse. It didn't come. Instead Vance leaned back in his chair and thumped his feet on the table. He supported his head with laced fingers at the back of his neck.

'Sing for me,' he said. 'The way you did the other day, after the raid. Soothe me.'

'And if I refuse?'

'You're so concerned about lives. The fate of the next . . . oh, let's say ten prisoners who fall into my hands will hang on what you decide now. And so will the prisoners.' He laughed at his little joke.

'Very well,' Rukanis replied quietly. He stood, doing his best to prepare himself for what would be an ordeal.

'Make it something restful,' Vance ordered. 'All this talk sets my nerves jangling.'

Given that his captor displayed the volatile emotions of a child, Kinsel decided on a lullaby.

He began to sing. The air he chose wasn't particularly doleful, but his interpretation lent it a certain melancholy, and inevitably it brought Tanalvah to mind, and the children. The thought of them was all that kept him going. Now he was performing a lament for their loss, and found a kind of solace in it.

His thoughts turned to the world of normality he'd been forced to leave behind. Its familiarity, its certainties, seemed so distant and unreal to him now.

Kinsel Rukanis longed for his old life. He craved the sanity of Bhealfa.

Somewhere in the backwoods of western Bhealfa, Prince Melyobar was attempting to eat a raw chicken.

He sat at a small dining table in the spacious wheelhouse of his palace, wearing a look of distaste as he chewed unyielding, rubbery flesh.

'Urgh!' He spat out the meat, grimacing. 'This is disgusting! Whose idea was it to serve me such muck?'

An alarmed manservant hurried forward, bowing low. 'Begging your pardon, Your Highness, but . . . you ordered it that way.'

'What?' He blinked at the man, perplexed.

'You said . . . that is, Your Royal Highness commanded that your food be served uncooked in future. In order to foil poisoners.'

'When?'

'You were gracious enough to issue the order to your chef yesterday, Highness.'

'Nonsense!'

'But, Your Eminence –'

'Claptrap, I say! The fool misheard me. Or somebody's being deliberately wayward.' His plate and cutlery went flying. 'Take it away!'

The servant bent to retrieve the debris, then scurried off, trying to bolt and fawn simultaneously.

'Flog the cook!' Melyobar shouted after him. 'And have yourself flogged for insolence!' Contemplating the empty table, a suspicion dawned. 'Gods,' the Prince muttered. 'Guards! Guards!'

A pair of sentinels rushed to him, drawing their swords.

'Sire?' the sergeant enquired.

'I've reason to believe he could be on board.' They had no need to ask who their monarch referred to. 'I think he's using his shape-changing powers. Sound the alert. Comb the palace for someone impersonating me.' The guards seemed confused, then stared quizzically at him. 'Well it's not me, obviously! Dolts. Now get on with it!'

The duo retreated. Further instructions were unnecessary. They were called on to search for Death at least once a day.

Tense at the best of times, the incident did nothing to steady Melyobar's nerves. Although barely into middle-age, he looked much older, and his thinning hair had greyed early. His shaved face was bulbous, with a sallow complexion; his body was flabby, running to stout.

'Your Highness!' the steersman hailed from the wheel. 'We're approaching the valley!'

Melyobar rose and went to join him, the episode of just seconds before forgotten. The brevity of the Prince's attention span was legendary.

The upper half of the wheelhouse consisted of an expanse of precious clear glass. Melyobar took in the scene. Ahead lay the mouth of a deep valley, though it was hard to see in the driving snow. A trail could just be made out snaking through the valley's floor, edged with snow-laden trees.

Had an observer been stationed on top of either cliff-like wall, enduring the blizzard, they would have witnessed an awesome sight.

The Prince's floating palace was enormous, beyond ostentatious in its embellishments, and now the whole prickly confection bore a coat of sparkling white. Moved by magic whose cost took a sizeable bite out of Bhealfa's gross national product, the palace glided under the direction of a team of top-grade wizards.

Equally impressive was the court's entourage. Several dozen lesser castles and mansions, owned by leading courtiers, and similarly powered, followed in its wake. 'Lesser' in comparison to Melyobar's gigantic folly, that is. They would still appear remarkable if seen without the contrast.

As it drifted regally, the whole procession was bathed in a crackling discharge of magical energy. Dazzling tendrils leapt from one structure to another, like blue lightning, connecting them in a glittery, ever changing web.

Down below, on mere ground, an army kept pace. In fact, two armies; one a military force deserving the name, the other a ragbag of civilian camp followers, tens of thousands strong. They travelled in a multitude of every conceivable wheeled transport, or rode herds of horses. The lowliest plodded on foot. All were stung by driven snow and cut by icy winds.

'Why are we moving so slowly?' Melyobar demanded, slumping into his throne.

'The weather, sire,' the steersman explained nervously. 'This is about as fast as we can go in these conditions.' He pointed to the glass. 'And that valley is very narrow, Highness. Getting us through will be like threading a needle.'

Melyobar snorted.

The steersman, along with his superiors and all their subordinates, would much rather have gone another way, but the Prince insisted on this route; and to fly above the gorge would have taken a ruinous amount of magic.

They entered the valley's entrance carefully, well above the treetops. On both sides the sheer cliffs seemed to press in. Beads of sweat appeared on the burly steersman's brow as he gently manoeuvred his titanic charge. The navigation took every ounce of his skill, not least because his commands had to anticipate the great bulk he was trying to control. It was like steering a mighty ship at sea; there was a lag of some seconds before its phenomenal weight sluggishly responded.

They lost a little height and the base of the palace brushed across the tops of some particularly tall trees. The dislodged snow plummeted onto the camp followers travelling beneath, adding to their discomfort and vexation. They sent up an anguished roar of protest. The steersman gingerly began to regain altitude.

'Oh, do get a move on!' Melyobar grumbled. 'We've no time to waste!'

The startled handler's concentration was fractured. His hand jerked on the wheel, just enough to move the leviathan a degree off course. He struggled to right it.

Inexorably, the palace slowly glided towards the right-hand cliff wall. There was a series of loud crashes, followed by an intense grinding noise as it scraped along the cliff face. Everyone in the wheelhouse, a score at least of functionaries and guards, had their teeth set on edge. The room shuddered. Glassware and china crashed to the floor.

The Prince seemed supremely unaffected, or curiously unaware of what was happening.

Gradually the palace corrected itself and resumed its stately trajectory, but no more than half a minute of relative calm ensued. A sharp bend in the valley loomed ahead, and in order to negotiate it safely the palace's speed had to be further reduced. It was a delicate operation. If the speed dropped too low it could cut off the magical supply, and their means of support.

Taking what felt like an age, with Melyobar's obvious impatience a constant background presence, the steersman took them round the serpentine curve. He was aided by two assistants now, working a bank of levers that operated a complicated system of rudders.

When at last they were back on the straight, to many suppressed sighs of relief, Melyobar again urged more haste. As the valley opened out at that point, the palace could increase its pace.

At the rear, the entourage followed, a line of drones trailing their mammoth queen. They swarmed at the bend in a hovering queue, each slowing as much as they dared to traverse the turn. But one of the last, a multi-turreted affair faced with alabaster, approached a grandiose castle that lay in its path too fast. The speeding structure resorted to braking and swerving at the same time. It clipped the castle, sending it wobbling aside, and careered towards a cliff wall. The speeds involved were relative, so to onlookers it was like watching a clumsy underwater ballet.

The ricocheting palace struck the cliff and literally compressed, a good third of its mass compacting in on itself. Chunks of masonry dislodged and fell. For a drawn out moment the building hung in the air, cerulean lightning playing all over its surface. Then the light went out and its compact with gravity was cancelled.

It plunged like a rock.

That part of the horde unlucky enough to be directly below

stood no chance. The palace, disintegrating as it fell, shedding screaming occupants, came down as an avalanche. Its impact was thunderous, and released huge billows of dust that even the heavy snowfall was hard put to dampen.

Melyobar stood to get a better view of the chaos visited on the gorge. 'I believe that was Count Barazell's residence,' he observed, addressing no one in particular. 'Damned bad luck.' He sank back into his throne, sighing. 'Still, should keep Death diverted for a while. Every cloud and all that.' He waved a languid hand at the crew. 'Full speed ahead.'

The palace gathered momentum. The end of the valley could be seen, and soon the procession would be in the open snow-covered fields beyond.

Melyobar beckoned an aide. The man was ashen, like everyone else in the room; but they differed from the Prince insofar as his features were permanently wan.

'As soon as we're clear,' he said in an undertone, 'have search parties sent back.'

The aide stooped. 'Of course, my lord. I'll have the rescue teams prepare.'

'Rescue? Oh. Very well, if they find any surviving aristocrats they can bring them out. But tell them to give corpses priority.'

'Corpses, Highness?' The aide's rigid, tight-lipped response made him look like one himself.

'Just a selection. I could use a couple of dozen.'

'Does your Highness require any particular kinds of . . . cadaver?'

'I'm not fussy. But come to think of it, bodies of the lower orders serve us best, I think.'

'Very good, sir. Will that be all, Your Highness?'

'Yes, yes. Get on with it.'

When the official had gone, Melyobar rose, passed a gamut of bowing flunkies and left the wheelhouse. Outside, he was joined by an escort of his personal guard, four strong, who fell in behind him. He led them to a corridor terminating in an oak door. The sorcerer lounging in a chair beside it leapt up, and in a flurry of obsequiousness opened the door and ushered in the Prince and his guard, then squeezed in after them.

They were in a perfectly square, wood-panelled room not much bigger than a large cupboard. The only things in it were a glamoured lighting orb on the ceiling and a book-sized slab of brown porcelain, etched with runes, set into the wall by the door. At Melyobar's curt order, the sorcerer laid his palm against it.

The room began to descend. Slow at first, it quickly picked up speed, causing the Prince's stomach to take a little tick-ling flip. It was a sensation he quite enjoyed.

His private elevation chamber was essentially a box. It sat inside a shaft that ran from this high point to one of the palace's lowest, with access to various levels in between. Magically generated pressure, drawing from the same energy propelling the castle, moved the chamber up or down at the direction of its wizard operator. Melyobar prided himself on embracing all the latest conveniences.

The limit of the chamber's capacity was six people. Consequently they were all crushed together, with Melyobar at the centre of the scrum, allowing his bodyguards a unique opportunity to experience his eccentric attitude to personal hygiene. The descent passed in an awkward silence.

When they finally arrived at their destination, to a chorus of expelled breaths, they tumbled into a subterranean corridor. Leaving the sorcerer behind, the group entered a labyrinth of tunnels which led to a lengthy journey through a series of checkpoints and locked gates. At last they came to a pair of heavily reinforced doors guarded by armed men. Melyobar ordered his escort to wait and went in alone.

He was in a large, windowless room with rough stone walls that made it resemble a cavern, though scores of glamoured globes kept it well lit. Perhaps twenty people were working there, most of them sorcerers.

A wizard greeted him. 'You'll require this, Highness,' he added, offering a bulky white mask identical to the one he and all the others were wearing.

Melyobar needed the sorcerer's help to position it correctly over his nose and mouth. The mask had been soaked in some kind of sanitising agent, mixed with a mild perfume, which made the Prince cough.

'How goes the work?' he asked when he stopped spluttering.

'Well, sire. Would you care to see?'

'Why else would I be here?'

The sorcerer guided him to the far end of the room. Four huge metal tanks stood there, each with a glass window. Melyobar went to the nearest and peered in, but all he could see was milky liquid. He was about to complain when a spherical, deathly white object bumped against the glass. The Prince jerked back in shock, emitting a startled squeak.

'No need for alarm, Highness,' the sorcerer assured him. 'Nothing here can harm us providing we're careful.'

Melyobar stared in morbid fascination at the floating corpse's head. It looked as though it had been a man, but as putrefaction had set in, it was hard to tell. One eye was missing, the other bulged. The flesh was bloated and turning green.

'Begging your indulgence, Highness,' the sorcerer went on, 'but we really do need some more subjects.'

'I have it in hand. You've made use of all the others?'

'Oh, yes, sire. But the process is experimental, as you know, and wastage has been high.'

The travelling court yielded dead people on a regular basis.

Melyobar had supposed enemies hung from the battlements in cages until they starved. Others he tortured at random on the chance they might be his shape-changing arch-foe in disguise. Some he merely had stabbed while having dinner with him. But these obviously weren't enough for the sorcerers' needs.

'What else have you to show me?' the Prince said.

'We have our first distillation, sire,' the wizard informed him with a note of glee.

'You've produced the essence?'

'Not quite, Highness. But we're very close. Come, sire. See.'

He took his liege to a secure cabinet and inserted a glamoured key. Reaching inside, he brought out a tiny glass phial. Praying Melyobar wouldn't demand to handle it, he held the container up to be examined.

The Prince blinked myopically. 'It's completely clear,' he complained, 'like water.'

'Don't be deceived, my lord. There is much here that cannot be seen.'

'But will it do the job?'

'In sufficient strength and quantity, sire, yes. Indeed, we've begun testing.'

'Show me.'

An adjoining chamber, one of many, housed a pigsty. It wasn't possible to enter as the door had been replaced with a thick sheet of glass, but Melyobar could see well enough. The sty was filthy. Two mature pigs lay on the straw, shivering convulsively, their legs in spasm. Their skin had a mottled, greasy appearance, and their eyes were glazed.

'How do you get in there?' the Prince wanted to know.

'We don't, sire. Once the subjects are exposed to the solution we seal the chamber. We leave them enough food and drink so that we know it isn't starvation that's making them ill. Then we observe. We could never dare open this room again, Highness.'

'Hmm. What of higher forms?'

'We've had some success there too, sire.'

He showed him to another glass-fronted antechamber, this one having bars in addition.

There were three crude bunks inside. Two men and a woman occupied them. All were covered in sweat, and looked as if they were in a twitching coma. The woman's eyes were open and she was staring glassily, like the pigs.

'Excellent,' Melyobar said.

6

No one would have begrudged the warlord riding in a splendid battle sledge, or on the back of a magnificent charger. But that wasn't Zerreiss's way. He chose to walk, and his followers loved him for it.

He marched at the head of an army unlike any the so called barbarous lands had ever seen before. Its numbers could only be guessed at. The great multitude covered the vast plain it crossed, so much so that the layers of snow they trampled underfoot couldn't be seen. They resembled a plague of ravenous insects carpeting the earth.

As remarkable as its size was the constituency of the horde. Many of its members were drawn from the lands Zerreiss had conquered, yet no element of coercion had been involved. Nor were there mercenaries in its ranks, as was often the practice when armies were mustered. Far from being driven by the lash, or marching for the hope of coin, the prevalent mood was that of a crusade.

The one they followed bore many epithets – the Scythe, the Silk Claw, the Man Who Fell From the Sun – though all had been bestowed, not claimed by him. Yet few men belied his titles as much as Zerreiss. There was nothing outstanding or even particularly notable about his appearance. He was ordinary in face and form, and if he stood in line with a dozen others, he would be the last to be remembered. However, the way he looked had nothing to do with the extraordinary charisma he possessed. No words could describe his allure. His empathy with the troops, and infectious passion for his cause, inspired a loyalty that was genuine and bottomless.

Though still in the region loosely designated the northern wastes, they had made considerable headway in their journey southward. Thus far, no force had successfully stood against them, or even appreciably slowed their progress. But for all that Zerreiss had led them a great distance from his place of birth, in the inhospitable core of the barbarous heartlands, the weather wasn't noticeably kinder. The temperature rarely lifted above freezing. For weeks the snow had been continual. Now they were enjoying a rare day without it, and the sun had appeared to lift their numbed spirits.

The warlord was flanked by his two principal aides. Sephor was the younger of the pair, and might have been thought too tender in years to hold a position of such responsibility were it not for his proven skills. Wellem was an old campaigner, a veteran of many conflicts, whose experience and good sense proved an ideal counterweight to the younger man's comparative rawness. Both had licence to speak freely in the presence of their leader; indeed, Zerreiss insisted upon it.

As they reached the top of a hill covered in ankle-deep snow, they paused to catch their breath and look to the host tramping in their wake. The tundra was black with an uncountable mass of warriors. Hundreds of siege towers bobbed amongst the crowd, and as many massive catapults were being hauled, while thousands of drums kept up an incessant rhythm.

'You must find it very pleasing, sir,' Wellem said, 'to have so many flocking to your banner.'

'When you show them the truth,' Zerreiss replied, 'the people rally.'

'Could it not be, my lord, that they're drawn to power?' Sephor wondered.

'You have a very cynical view of human nature, Sephor, for one so young.'

'I hope that isn't true, sir,' the younger man returned earnestly.

Zerreiss smiled. 'Of course it isn't. But sometimes you're so serious I can't resist tugging at those chains of sobriety you bind yourself with.'

'Our *aim* is serious.'

'Indeed. But you must learn to trust me, and know that through me we will prevail.'

'I have faith in you, sir. It's those we'll be up against that I don't trust.'

'Then you're saying you doubt my power over them, Sephor. Haven't you seen enough of my victories to put such fears behind you?'

'More than enough, sir. But this is different. We've never been so bold as this before.'

'People are people, whether they be citizens of the empires or thought of as savages. The gift I have for them will be equally prized.'

'We've certainly found that to be true up to now,' Wellem chimed in. 'But Sephor does have a point, if I may say so, my lord. We're not going against some chieftain's clan or a city state this time. It's imperial forces we'll be facing, and not just one empire but the pair of them.'

'In attacking protectorates of Rintarah and Gath Tampoor simultaneously we stand a chance of breaking their fragile truce in these parts,' Zerreiss reminded him. 'If their rulers back in their capitals blame each other they'll do our work for us. More animosity between the empires can only serve our long term aims.'

'I can see the possible benefit in tweaking both their tails, sir, but I'm worried about splitting our forces to do it.'

Zerreiss indicated the army with a sweep of his hand. 'You think we lack sufficient numbers?'

'It wasn't our armed strength I had in mind. I'm concerned that you can't be in two places at once.'

The warlord laughed. 'Even my abilities fall short of that, Wellem.'

'Make light of it if you will, my lord, but you can't dismiss the problem.'

'Problem?'

'While you're here for the storming of Gath Tampoor's outpost, the rest of your army approaches Rintarah's without you. How are they going to fare?'

'You overlook the fact that my reputation moves ahead of us. The defenders there, and here, will know about the others who've fallen to us. Don't underestimate that advantage.'

'What about the *morale* of the army marching against Rintarah's settlement?' Sephor wondered. 'If you're not with them –'

'They're perfectly capable of achieving their mission without me. In fact, that's part of my intention.'

'Sir?'

'Wellem here was only stating the obvious by saying I can't be in more than one place at a time. Yet as our campaign proceeds we'll be increasingly fighting on several fronts at once. The army needs to know it can win victory without my presence. To some extent they have to be weaned off their reliance on me. We'll never achieve our goals other-wise.'

'I can see the sense in that, sir.'

'I mean to plan for future eventualities, too.'

'How do you mean, my lord?'

'I'm just as vulnerable as the next man. If I take an arrow in this battle, or get cut down in a cavalry charge, I'll be no less dead. I want to be sure my work doesn't die with me.'

From the looks on their faces, neither aide had considered the possibility of Zerreiss's mortality.

'How could we carry on without you?' Wellem said. 'If you weren't here, the gods forbid, what would inspire us?'

'I'm touched that you should feel that way,' the warlord replied with genuine warmth. 'But that's exactly the attitude that has to change. I'd want the momentum of what I've begun to carry you through. The worst way you could repay me would be to abandon our cause simply because I couldn't finish it with you. My wish is to kindle a movement, not self-aggrandisement.'

They knew this to be true.

'Be assured,' he added in a lighter tone, 'that if our forces attacking Rintarah's outpost run into fierce opposition, I'll travel east to join them. Does that make you feel better?'

His aides chorused that it did, though they found it hard to conceal a note of unease about what he'd told them.

Sephor wanted something clarifying. 'You said that our actions today could set the empires at each other's throats, sir, even more than they already are, that is. But surely when word reaches their capitals they'll know the truth?'

'If we bring about more discord between the empires it'll be a bonus; it isn't our main target. As to word getting back; they'll hear what we want them to. The more conquests we make, the more we control the channels of communication.'

'That will soon be like trying to bail out the ocean, my lord,' Wellem offered.

'The empires used to neglect these lands. Now they

encroach by the day, mostly because of your victories. The expeditions Gath Tampoor and Rintarah sent into our waters are an example.'

'At the moment we need to move with caution. But soon we'll reach a level of dominance where it won't matter what they do. And you've no need to worry about those two little armadas. I've taken steps against them.'

He said nothing more, and they didn't press him. Now rested, they moved on. The sky was starting to darken again, promising the return of snow. The army burrowed deeper into their furs.

The scenery, too, had started to alter. Trees had been felled, and through the expanse of white there were traces of low stone walls slicing the land into growing fields. Clear signs that they were nearing their objective.

'I hope you'll forgive me if I raise a sensitive matter, my lord,' Sephor ventured.

'You've been with me long enough to know there are few sensitive matters in my company. What is it?'

'These dreams you've been having, sir . . .'

'Ah. Sensitive in a way, because they've challenged my view of the world. Though I still think they're a part of nature rather than outside it, for all their incredible vivacity. Not like dreams at all.'

'Do you have any understanding of them?'

'Understanding, no. But there's a . . . compulsion in them. I've no doubt there's a reason why I'm having them. And I'm quite aware of the irony that I, of all people, should pay attention to something like ethereal dreams. But the man I saw in them, though it was more like an encounter than seeing, that man felt like part of what's supposed to happen. I can't put it plainer than that.'

'It's strange to hear you talking that way, sir,' Wellem observed.

'I've never denied the possibility of a spiritual domain, only the malign part it can play in people's lives. Perhaps we *are* directed by gods for their own fickle reasons. Who knows?'

'And you intend seeking this man,' Sephor asked, 'assuming he's real?'

'I'm sure he's real, and somehow I have the feeling that in moving south I'm drawing nearer to him.' He smiled. 'Don't ask me how.'

They were climbing another hill, much steeper than the previous one. The vanguard of the army was close on their heels.

'Have you managed to identify the power lines in this area?' Zerreiss said.

'As best we could, sir,' Sephor replied, 'but there's an abnormality nearby. In fact, we should be able to see it any minute now.'

They trudged to the peak and took in a panoramic view. Straight ahead, perhaps a mile distant, stood a substantial walled township. An impressive fortress rose at its heart, pulsating with magical defences, whilst outside the settlement's gates an army was massed, waiting for the onslaught. It was an arresting sight, but not the most dramatic to be seen; that was to the west, and all eyes were drawn to it.

On the horizon, a geyser of magical energy spurted high into the sky. It might have been said to resemble an anchored tornado, except that it displayed qualities no normal storm ever possessed. Every colour of the spectrum vied for dominance within its swirling interior, and the whole swaying column glowed with a silvery radiance. Its base generated thick clouds of vibrant, sparkling dust which also constantly altered colour. Within those clouds, things moved, shapes that melted, mutated and defied clarity.

The column's tip reached a giddy height. Above it, the snow-heavy clouds acted as a vast canvas for a pageant of images painted by the escaping magic. They were ever changing, and never quite settled on a definite likeness. Yet to any looking on they suggested a myriad possibilities. Beasts real and imagined seemed to dwell there, along with giant insects, birds, blooming flowers, phantom armies, blazing comets, faces beautiful and grotesque, and oceans breaking against imaginary shorelines. The effect was hypnotic.

'A rupture,' Zerreiss stated. 'How long has this been going on?'

'Several months, apparently,' Sephor explained. 'We're not sure what set it off. Possibly a landside.'

'Look on it,' the warlord commanded, 'and see the very essence of what we oppose. You'll have no better portrait of that which enslaves those we hope to free.'

'It can't be denied that it has a certain splendour, my lord.'

'It's beguiling all right. So is a blue pit-spider, a gold ring-serpent or a pride of barbcats. This is just as beautiful, and more deadly than all of them put together.'

'It does have one advantage, sir, in that it's likely to bleed the magic in these parts, and reduce the amount available to the defenders.' Sephor gestured at the settlement with a gloved hand.

'You forget how irrelevant that is to us.'

The aide grinned. 'Of course, sir. Silly of me.'

'As I said, Sephor, have faith.'

'What are your orders, sir?' Wellem enquired.

'I see no reason to change our customary method. The defenders must be given the chance to lay down their arms.'

'The negotiators were sent out in advance, my lord, with the usual offer.' He stared at the barren area in front of the settlement below. A small group of riders was heading their way. 'I think that's them returning now. Sephor, you have better sight than me.'

The young aide cupped his eyes with his hands. 'Yes, it's them. The leader's holding a pennant. It's . . . red.'

Zerreiss sighed. 'As I feared. When will they learn that there doesn't have to be bloodshed?'

'They're terrified of you, my lord,' Wellem said. 'They must have heard the stories about you being merciful, but somehow they don't think it applies to them. All they take on board is that you're a conqueror. We've seen it before.'

'Or they have a greater fear of their masters than of me. Another case of better the devil you know.'

'Professional fighting men don't easily abandon their posts, sir. And rarely on the word of a warlord they know little about. It's not to be wondered at that they'd make a stand.'

'The contrary thing,' Sephor commented, 'is that inside a week I'll wager half of them will be riding with us. Empire soldiers or not.'

'Another irony I'm not blind to,' Zerreiss came back. 'If there was one thing it was in my power to alter, it would be the human cost of our campaign.'

'How do we proceed, sir?' Wellem asked.

'Bring the army into plain sight, and let the siege engines be seen. Show them what they're up against. Then we'll give them a final opportunity to surrender with honour. Failing that . . .'

'We fight.'

'Not before I've tilted the odds in our favour. There's still a chance we can avoid a slaughter.'

'You'll do it now, sir?'

'There's no point in waiting.'

Experience had taught Wellem and Sephor that there was no need to leave their master's side when he performed the deed. Nevertheless, they did. It seemed prudent to stand well away in the face of such awe-inspiring power.

As word spread from the hilltop and down through the

ranks of Zerreiss's army, they fell silent, too. The drums were stilled. Even the horses and oxen grew quiet, if restive.

Standing on the hill's summit, focused on the besieged settlement, the warlord raised his arms.

And the change began.

7

Winters were slightly more temperate in the west, but that didn't mean Merakasa, the sprawling capital of Gath Tampoor's empire, escaped being touched by cheerless weather. Indeed, the city was suffering a harsh winter in Gath Tampoorian terms, with acerbic winds and unremitting snowfall.

But it took more than low temperatures and driving sleet to dampen the populace's enthusiasm for displaying their status. In Merakasa, as in most of the supposedly civilised world, status equated to wealth. And for those who possessed it, the flaunting of riches meant the conspicuous expenditure of magic.

As in many other things, an element of fashion dictated what was considered stylish in sorcery, and one way this showed itself was in seasonal magic. The glamours conjured for winter reflected that season, or at least the rituals and folklore associated with it, so that at any given time dozens of likenesses of Jex Rime could be seen flying above the city. Jex Rime was a mythical spirit who dispensed gifts during the solstice festivities. He rode an open sky carriage, pulled by twelve pure white lizards, all of whom had names every child knew by heart. Now and then a set of lizards, carriage and benign occupant would flare into nothingness as their magic expired, or their owners grew bored with them.

At street level, bulky animate men, supposedly made of snow, lumbered along the pavements, beaming kindly smiles with lips of coal. Depending on the spell, they could be made to melt at a fixed rate. It wasn't unusual to see them wading on stumpy legs, delivering cheery waves with handless arms. Critics of the empire's increasing decadence pointed to the fact that most people found this very amusing.

On chic lawns, small armies of doll-sized ice pixies waged war with icicle swords for well-wrapped dinner party guests. When struck a mortal blow, the pixies shattered into a thousand crystalline fragments – the wounded merely shed icy pearl tears.

Smart landaus passed, drawn by purple reindeer. Frostbarbs, hardy mountain cousins of the more familiar barbcats, appeared on leafy avenues, their usually white fur striped or polka-dotted. Patinas of unseasonable flowers broke out on the walls of mansions. Glamour archers loosed ghostly arrows that winged harmlessly through living targets. Geese sang, giants walked cobbled lanes, hoary stardust fell on heaving pavements.

But gaiety and hedonism didn't hold sway in every part of the city. In the rundown quarters, elaborate magic was most often used as an instrument of control, or as state weaponry. Recent unrest added to the air of repression. Alive to the reality of a resistance movement previously thought negligible, and following the example set in the Bhealfan colony, the authorities were bent on rooting it out. This made swathes of Merakasa dangerous places to be.

At the centre of the city was an extensive enclave, sanctuary of the empire's rulers. Flags bearing Gath Tampoor's fire-breathing dragon emblem flew from its tallest towers. Its gates and lofty ramparts were heavily guarded by conventional forces and glamoured defences. It was a place outsiders were seldom invited to enter, and a summons to do so was rarely welcomed.

A woman stood on a high balcony. Her age would be hard to guess, beyond the fact that she was evidently very old. She tried to hide the fact with face paints, hair dyes and other artificial aids, but only succeeded in giving herself an appearance verging on the grotesque.

Empress Bethmilno, the twenty-fifth of her ancient line so named, wielded more power than anyone else in the whole of Gath Tampoor.

She shivered and came back into the stateroom. 'I'm cold,' she complained, moving towards a massive ornamented fireplace. 'I remember a time when variations in temperature meant nothing to us, no matter how great.'

'Things change, grandmother,' her companion said. Like all members of her inner circle, he was a blood relation, though an impartial observer might think he looked curiously old to be one of her grandchildren.

'Not always for the better,' she replied tetchily, warming her hands at the blaze. 'Look at the disorder that's sweeping through our streets.'

'Isn't that simply the current expression of grievances that have always been with us?'

'It's change,' the Empress insisted, 'and for the worse. Not that long ago our subjects wouldn't have dared bear arms against us.'

'We can deal with it. Look at the success Laffon's CIS and the paladins have had against these people on Bhealfa.'

'How successful was it if a pack of them got away to that damned pleasure island? We've allowed them a stronghold from which to spread their contagion.'

'Or neatly concentrated them. All the better to eradicate them.'

'The sooner we do that, the happier I'll be. We've allowed

the rebels too much latitude as it is. It sets a bad example.' She came away from the fireplace and seated herself. 'But that's not all that's changed. Disruptions to the energy grid are growing more frequent and stronger. That really does worry me. Rebels we can put to the sword. What's happening in the matrix isn't so easily corrected, even if we knew what the defect was.'

'I admit that's a problem of a different order, grandmother. But surely with the expertise we've built up over so long –'

'You'd think so, wouldn't you? But there are few precedents. This isn't the first time the matrix has been prone to disturbance, though the last was many years ago and we had some idea then of what caused it. There are no indications this time. I can't help feeling that the current upheaval portends something.'

There was a knock on the door, followed by the entrance of a retainer who announced a guest. The Empress waved the servant away.

'That will be Talgorian. You may set the timer, then leave us.'

A large hourglass sat on the mantelpiece. Her grandson upended it. The fine golden sand began to flow.

As he went out, a younger man was ushered in.

Andar Talgorian was of middle years. He was lean and vigorous, wore a stylishly barbered beard and dressed in the latest courtly attire. In keeping with his role as the Imperial Envoy to Bhealfa, he sported his air of diplomatic calm like a second skin. In truth, it wasn't how he felt. He found it irksome to have been recalled to the capital so frequently in recent months, and his annoyance was heightened by the prospect of an audience with Bethmilno. Being in her presence always made him anxious.

'Your journey here was comfortable?' she began.

He gave a deep bow. 'Tolerably, thank you, Excellency.'

She indicated a lower chair for him.

'I trust I find you in good health, ma'am,' Talgorian ventured, sinking into the cushions.

'Tolerably.'

Her slightly mocking use of his word was discomfiting. He maintained a bland smile.

'I'll come straight to the point, Ambassador,' the Empress continued. 'Some of the recent developments in Bhealfa have been gratifying to us. The revolutionaries have suffered a severe blow, and inroads have been made in restoring proper respect for our authority.'

'Thank you, Highness.' He felt uneasy. Experience showed that a compliment often came before a fall.

'However, certain aspects of what's been happening in Bhealfa are less pleasing.'

'Majesty?'

'A number of the traitors were allowed to escape to other shores. And it appears that a hardcore of rebels is still entrenched in the principality. This is not satisfactory.'

'With respect, Highness, the security forces, local and imperial, have responsibility in these matters.'

'Be assured I'll be making the point to them too, Ambassador. But the issue we're discussing now is the diplomatic corps' part in this. Your job is to convey our wishes to the relevant agencies. It seems there has been a lack of liaison in that respect.'

He thought this unjust, but refrained from voicing an opinion.

'No efforts must be spared to eradicate these rebels,' she went on. 'You'll work more closely with the CIS and the paladins on it. This is my will, as you'll make clear to any who question the policy. Is that understood?'

'It is, Majesty.' If she believed the security forces were being too soft, Talgorian didn't agree. Again, he held his peace. He valued his head too much.

'Good. As for the so-called Diamond Isle . . . well, it leaves us with a mess to clear up.'

'Indeed, ma'am.'

'Though it may not fall entirely on Gath Tampoor's shoulders.'

'I beg your pardon, Excellency?'

'We know that Rintarah's been plagued by insurgency as much as we have, and some of their troublemakers fled to the Diamond Isle too. As they currently have more protectorates in that region than we do, they might feel compelled to act. We'd be content if they so decided.'

'I'm . . . surprised, Majesty. We've always regarded Rintarah as being prime suspects in stirring up the insurgency.'

'I now have reason to doubt they're behind more than a small percentage of it. As are we, against them. Indications are that the Resistance is largely self-directed.'

Talgorian was adrift. 'Not long since, you spoke of possible war with Rintarah, and –'

'Nothing's changed,' the Empress returned sternly. 'Our differences remain. I'm simply stating that our aims aren't necessarily incompatible. We share a common interest in stamping out this canker.'

'You're suggesting some kind of cooperation might be possible, Majesty?'

'I didn't say that. My view is that, in the event, we wouldn't stand in Rintarah's way. The important thing is that the insurgents be eliminated. Particularly as we have reason to believe they might be aligned with a force that could . . . inconvenience us.' He wanted to ask who, but she ploughed on. 'We must be conscious of the greater picture. The empires have mutual interests beyond the rebels. Events should be seen in that context.'

'Do you have anything particular in mind, Majesty?'

'News is coming in of attacks on our far north outposts.'

'I've heard nothing about that, ma'am.'

'We have our sources.' She meant the matrix. A subject he was ignorant of, as were all but her inner circle. 'Reports are vague at the moment, but naturally our first thought was that Rintarah was behind it. But we've learnt that their settlements have been attacked too. That, and certain features of the attacks, lead us to wonder if another might be to blame.'

'Zerreiss.' He all but whispered the name.

'I give you credit here, Talgorian. You were one of the first to appreciate the threat this warlord might pose. The suspicion has to be that he's expanding his dominance, and in attacking both empires perhaps he hopes to create even more bad blood between us. Should he and the rebels link up, we could be facing a major irritant. Can you see why it wouldn't be in our best interests to obstruct Rintarah if it chose to oppose him?'

'I can, Highness. Though it's a strategy not without risks. If Rintarah and Zerreiss come to an accommodation, what's to stop them forming an alliance against us?'

'He's unlikely to reach an understanding with them or us. The man has the instincts of a conqueror, not an appeaser. He'd see the empires as natural enemies.'

'So the expedition we sent into his region, that we haven't heard from –'

'Must be assumed lost due to his actions, yes. Rintarah's too, for that matter.'

'That alone would constitute an act of war, Majesty.'

'I'm aware of the rules of engagement, Ambassador. Not that we need be burdened by such niceties.' She glanced at the sand-timer on the mantelpiece. The grains were running out. 'We've aired these topics sufficiently for now, and other affairs will shortly require my attention.'

'Of course, ma'am.' He made to rise.

'Stay where you are. This audience is not quite over.'

Talgorian lowered himself back into the chair, a sheepish expression on his face.

'I have something else to convey. It concerns the Bhealfan domestic situation, and a task I wish you to handle personally.'

'How may I be of service, Excellency?' He said this with some trepidation.

'We have spoken many times about Melyobar's behaviour. It's no secret that he's a tremendous drain on the protectorate's resources, and he brings authority into disrepute and ridicule.'

'His eccentricities are well known, it's true, Majesty. But the Prince is essentially harmless.'

Bethmilno didn't look amused. 'How do you know?' She didn't wait for an answer. 'Our spies tell us something untoward is occurring at his court.'

'There are always strange goings on in his circle, ma'am.'

'Exactly. He's beyond control, and it isn't a situation we can tolerate any longer. The time has come to put an end to his antics. He's to be relieved of his position, and direct rule imposed. We have that in all but name already, of course, but now the situation will be made plain.'

Talgorian was stunned. 'It's a sweeping change, ma'am. A major constitutional adjustment of that nature would require –'

'It necessitates no more than my word. I didn't bring you here to argue fine points of civic law. I am the law. Gather whatever force you feel necessary and remove him from office. I'll see to it that the militia cooperates fully, as will the paladins.'

'But . . . what do we do with him once he's overthrown, ma'am?'

'We are not insensitive in that regard. He is, after all, of royal lineage, though of no relation to my dynasty, fortunately. He'll be transported here and allowed to live out his days in comfort, if not the extravagant luxury he's been accustomed to.'

'I feel bound to say that a move like this could antagonise the populace even further, Excellency.'

'Does Melyobar still have a following?'

'No one could deny that his personal following has diminished, Majesty.'

'There you are then.'

'But what he represents –'

'He represents only his own unpredictable spirit. The example he sets as a figurehead has nothing to commend it. Whatever your feelings in this matter, I expect you to do as I say.'

'Excellency.' He bowed his head in acquiescence. 'It was only my desire to remind your Highness that the Prince has always been seen as indispensable to our diplomatic strategy in Bhealfa.'

She fixed him with a hard gaze. 'Graveyards are littered with the corpses of indispensable people, Ambassador.'

8

The graveyard was dusted with snow. Freezing winds raked the bleak headstones and made the gaunt trees shiver.

A small crowd of dignitaries stood before a newly erected monument, a grandiose affair of polished stone three times the height of a man. It took the form of an obelisk, with a black marble apex and a flowing, gold-leaf inscription carved on its face. Above the inscription was an engraved coat of arms showing a rearing white horse, one of the emblems of the paladin clans. Bouquets of flowers were heaped at the obelisk's base.

Two uniformed figures, draped in cloaks, detached themselves from the crowd and discreetly withdrew, taking a path leading to the cemetery's exit.

'A moving speech, if I may say so, sir,' offered the younger of the pair.

'You may, Meakin.'

'I'm sure your uncle would have appreciated your eulogy, and the memorial.'

'Perhaps. But if I knew Ivak he'd have preferred being in the old burial ground, out on the periphery.'

'Where High Chiefs are traditionally laid to rest.'

'Yes. But I'm damned if I'd put him in that decaying bone-yard. No one ever goes there these days. I certainly don't intend ending up in it myself.'

'New leadership, new traditions, eh, sir?'

'It's past time a fresh broom swept through the clans,' Devlor Bastorran replied, 'and I'll be wielding it.'

Bastorran, recently installed Clan High Chief of the paladin order, was impeccably turned-out, as was both his custom and that of the clans. His black hair was styled in a close military cut, and his dress uniform always looked freshly pressed. The immaculately tailored tunic he wore was scarlet, which distinguished the paladins from any other fighting force, and bore the various insignia of his exalted rank.

He was a man who harboured few regrets. Certainly he felt none in respect of how he'd gained his present position. To his way of thinking, speeding up the succession by clandestinely arranging his uncle's murder was a small price to pay.

At around twenty years old, Bastorran's aide was his junior by more than a decade. He was blond and clean-shaven, and though Lahon Meakin's duties were basically administrative, physically he could have passed for a fighting man. Unlike Bastorran, he wore a black tunic. Triple red piping at its wrists, and a circular red patch on the left breast, told the world he served the clans while not born a clansman. The lack of a suitable bloodline meant a limit to how far he could rise, but further advancement was of no concern to Meakin. His ambitions lay elsewhere.

As they trod the gravel pathway, Bastorran's slight limp was apparent, a constant reminder of his greatest humiliation.

'I feel as though a chapter has closed with the paying of this final tribute,' he said, tilting his head at the monument they were leaving. 'The end of one era and the beginning of another.' He seemed lost in reflection for a moment. 'But dwelling too much on the dead neglects the business of the living.' He was back to his normal brisk efficiency. 'Any news of the woman?'

'I'm afraid not, sir.'

If the aide was expecting a rebuke, it didn't come.

'So it appears that she had help from the Resistance?'

'Almost certainly, sir. She could hardly have got away without it, particularly given her condition.'

'Well, she'll have little joy in their company.'

'Should we step up the hunt?'

'No. Keep her on the list of most wanted. Otherwise you can scale it down.'

'The man she was with wiped out practically a whole patrol, sir.'

'I know that, Meakin. And it'll go on the balance sheet for when we have our reckoning with them. For now there's no point wasting resources looking for one man. As to the woman, she's served her purpose. She had nothing else important to tell me. I'd already loosened my leash on her, in fact. That's how she gave us the slip in the first place.'

Meakin was impressed by a rare show of culpability in his superior. 'Naturally I wouldn't presume to ask about this woman's identity, sir . . .' He saw Bastorran's quick, suspicious glance. 'But I'm intrigued as to why anyone would betray their own like that.'

'Love.'

'Sir?'

'Love, along with the application of pressure that played on her dotish affection. She thought she could regain something it was never really in my power to give her. Nor would I have done so, even if I could. People are slaves to their emotions. It makes them weak. Exploit them properly and there isn't anything they won't do.'

The road was in sight, with its fleet of waiting coaches and milling guards.

'Anything else I should know about?' Bastorran asked.

'Mostly routine matters, sir. Nothing too pressing. Oh, Aphri Kordenza was in touch again. She wants to see you.'

'That damn woman's proving a nuisance.'

'I'll make your excuses, sir. Keep her out of your way.'

'No. I'll take care of the meld. She could still be of use to me. Have her come in to headquarters some time tomorrow.'

'Very good, sir.'

They were through the gates now. As they neared their waiting carriage, Meakin spotted someone hurrying their way, cape flapping.

'That looks like Commissioner Laffon, sir.'

'So it is.'

They waited for the head of the Council for Internal Security to catch up with them. A man of perhaps sixty, Laffon was tall and skeletally thin, with slightly hunched shoulders. Completely bald, he had rangy, bird-like features, accentuated by a hook nose. His lips were thin to the point of non-existence, and his deep blue eyes hinted at a sharp intelligence.

'I'm glad I caught you,' he called out, panting faintly as he approached.

'Commissioner,' Bastorran greeted him.

'Excellent eulogy, High Chief. Quite moving.'

'Thank you. If, er, that was all you wanted to say, I trust you'll forgive me if I don't linger. I have matters that need –'

'I'd appreciate a moment of your time. I've one or two things to discuss, and a possible piece of news.'

'Then perhaps you'd care to ride with us?'

The trio climbed into the carriage. It pulled away, and two other carriages fell in, one ahead, one behind, containing an armed escort. Mounted paladins rode at the front of the convoy, making sure the streets were clear.

Laffon said, 'I'm pleased to tell you, Bastorran, that

preparations are in hand for the new series of raids on the insurgents. My people are ready whenever you are.'

'That's gratifying, Commissioner. But it's hardly news.'

Laffon smiled. 'News, in the sense of hard facts, is a flexible term, as I'm sure you're aware. What I have is a deduction based on intelligence, and a rumour.'

'Let's have the deduction first, shall we?'

'I think Reeth Caldason's on the Diamond Isle.'

Meakin reckoned his master did a good job of disguising his fury at mention of the Qalochian's name.

'I suspected as much,' Bastorran replied.

'Really? I was under the impression you were expending a lot of resources searching for him here in Bhealfa.'

'It's necessary to explore all avenues, Commissioner. Anyway, what makes you think that's where Caldason is?'

'We've had reports both of his departure from these shores and his presence on the island. Or at least someone bearing an uncanny resemblance to him.'

'I'm not surprised he's run away. Any man who could stab another in the back, as he did to my beloved uncle, is nothing short of a coward. Why someone like that should have a special dispensation from our rulers is something I've never understood.'

'You know it isn't an exemption as such. It's more an instruction that he should be handled with particular care. I have no idea why these rules were devised, but our betters have their reasons, I'm sure.' Laffon shrugged.

Meakin wished he could ask what those rules were.

'Well, perhaps it's time to throw out these instructions pertaining to Caldason.'

'I've always believed they should be obeyed, given their source. But the murder of someone of your uncle's status changes things. I, for one, would be willing to petition our superiors to look at the policy again.'

'I'm obliged, Commissioner. The lifting of the restrictions would be pleasing to me. It's just a pity that, if your information's correct, Caldason's beyond our present reach.'

'He might not be.' Laffon eyed Bastorran.

'What do you mean?'

'The rumour I heard. There's talk of a fleet being sent to the Diamond Isle.'

Bastorran's eyebrows raised. 'You're sure? My information is that Gath Tampoor was holding back in hope of Rintarah dealing with the matter.'

'My source is good. I can only imagine that Gath Tampoor's worried about Rintarah getting an edge in that part of the world, and decided they should have a presence there too. No doubt we'll be informed officially soon, one way or another. Though I have to say it's a bad time of year for such a venture.'

'If this is true, the paladins are sure to be represented in the invasion force.'

'As indeed will the CIS. We suspect there are a number of felons out there of interest to us. Not least the woman I told you about, who's a known associate of Caldason. We both have scores to settle on that island.'

'If there's a reckoning to be had,' Bastorran declared, expression intense, 'I want to be there.'

'You'd go yourself?'

'Absolutely. I owe my uncle the task of exacting vengeance on his murderer. It's not something I'd see delegated.'

'Ah. A matter of family honour.'

'Family and the clans. A blood debt,' Bastorran replied coldly.

'And the opportunity to exact retribution for your own . . . indisposition at Caldason's hands.'

Bastorran flashed the Commissioner a hard look. 'The issue is clan pride, not personal revenge.'

'Of course, High Chief. But there's little we can do about the problem just yet. We can, however, continue our purge of the terrorists here.'

'We've broken their backs. It's only a question of time before we eradicate them entirely.'

'Perhaps. The rebel movement may be weakened, but it's still capable of causing havoc. Why, there's unrest even as we speak, not ten blocks from here.'

Somebody in the crowd threw a device.

Magical munition or conventional bombard, it made little difference to the effect. It fell just short of a line of shield-bearing militia, producing an intense flash, a loud explosion and an eruption of noxious smoke. The cloud dispersed to show several troopers ablaze, their uniforms splattered with glutinous burning oil. Comrades rushed forward to beat at the flames.

The crowd and the militia took to exchanging missiles – rocks, arrows, slingshot and the occasional spear flew. On both sides, men and women fell. Then a trumpet sounded, and as one the lines of militia parted and let through a detachment of charging cavalry. The disturbance was becoming a full-scale riot.

In a room on the upper floor of a nearby house, derelict and half burnt out, two people watched the confrontation. One was Quinn Disgleirio.

He took a peek through the window. 'That could take some time.'

Dulian Karr sighed and parked himself on a battered wooden crate. 'At least we were lucky enough to find this place to shelter in. I've never seen a conflict blow up so quickly.'

'We're living in volatile times. And it's going to get worse.'

Outside, the sounds of fighting swelled. Screams, shouts

and explosions could be heard, backed by the crowd's constant roar.

'Is there nothing we can do?' Karr asked.

'Only sit it out. I'm beginning to wish I hadn't agreed to undertake this reconnaissance with you. It's not as though we've gathered intelligence of any real importance.'

'I'm not dead yet, Quinn. The day I can't go out on a field trip is the day you can consign me to the Pastures of Sleep for real.'

'Do you still think we're right about trying to get more of us out to the island? Rather than staying here and making the best of it, that is?' said Disglierio.

'It was always the plan to get as many people over as possible, you know that. If things hadn't gone so terribly wrong we'd probably be there now.'

'But circumstances have changed, haven't they? The gods forgive me for saying it, but the Diamond Isle doesn't seem so much like a haven now as a rat trap. For all the restrictions here in Bhealfa, at least there's plenty of scope for hiding and hitting out at the occupiers.'

'True. But let's not fool ourselves. The best we can hope for if we stay here is to harass them. For myself, I can see the attraction of making our stand there.'

'You're an old romantic, Karr. My ideal would be to stay. But then, I'm a patriot. That's what the Fellowship of the Righteous Blade's all about, after all.'

'Then you're a romantic yourself, Quinn.'

Disgleirio smiled. 'Could be. I just hate the idea of surrendering my soil to a foreign power and scuttling off to a run-down pleasure resort.'

'Don't tell me you're thinking of not going?'

'No. I may be a romantic but I haven't lost my reason. There's a chance we could hold out there. And just maybe something will turn up to help us. Don't ask me what.'

'If we don't have hope, we have nothing.'

'I do worry that we couldn't possibly get all of our people out there. Choices are going to have to be made, and that seems cruelly unfair.'

'I know. Decisions of that kind are never easy. But that shouldn't stop those of us fortunate enough to have the chance.'

'We're talking as though reaching the island's going to be easy. This could all be academic.'

'It's a big ocean, Quinn. Short of a complete blockade of the Diamond Isle it's impossible to close every loophole.'

'That's what they'll do though, isn't it? Gath Tampoor, or Rintarah. They'll seal it tight as a drum and –'

'Perhaps. We have to hope we find a way of preventing that.'

In the streets below the commotion increased again. Karr rose to take a look. The security forces were fighting back with magic, and concentrated energy beams scythed through the crowd. Militia used glamoured stun batons to down protestors, against a background of dazzle charges and concussion rounds.

Karr resumed his seat, shaking his head sadly. 'It's not the way the noble art should be used,' he complained. 'They debase it.'

'You sound just like Phoenix. But we do the same whenever we can,' Disgleirio reminded him.

'In self-defence. There's a distinct moral difference involved.'

'I daresay that's the way they see it too.'

'Then they're barbarians. The occupiers and their collaborators both. They cloak themselves in a mantle of civilisation, but they're barbaric all the same. That's another difference, Quinn; between what they say and what they do.'

'By now you should be used to the way they employ

language as a weapon against us. Taking another's land is liberation. Suppressing the people's right to speak is freedom. Executing a patriot is an act of public order. And anybody opposing them is a terrorist.'

'What depresses me is how many believe it. Repeat a lie often enough and it becomes a kind of truth. Couple that with keeping the populace in ignorance and you have a situation where most citizens of the empire are happy to send troops here but couldn't find Bhealfa on a map.'

'They don't need to. They've swallowed the oldest propaganda trick in the book. All you have to do is tell people they're under threat and they'll let their rulers do anything they want, no matter how draconian,' Disgleirio said bitterly.

'And they call magic an arcane art. It's nothing compared to the subtle craft of deception.'

'As an ex-politician that's something you know all about, isn't it? But we shouldn't fall into the trap of blaming the citizens of either empire. They're as much victims as the rest of us.'

'Of course they are. But we can't do much about their salvation. What we can do is look after our own kind, diminished as our ranks may be. Small triumphs, Quinn. That's what we have to content ourselves with now.'

Disgleirio nodded. 'Tanalvah's a good example. Finding her was a piece of pure luck.'

'Ah, yes. If ever there was a case of someone more sinned against than sinning, it's that young woman. It would be nice to think we could bring about an improvement to her tragic life.'

'That's the way I see it. Tan's done nothing to harm anyone. She deserves a little happiness.'

9

Tanalvah spent the night thinking about death.

She thought of all the deaths she had been inadvertently responsible for, and of Kinsel's probable death. She thought of her own, and of how she might bring it about.

But what seemed appealing during the lonely watches of a sleepless night carried less certainty at dawn. She was with child, and two other children depended on her. Kinsel could be alive. And she had an abiding conviction that Iparrater, her goddess, would be even more wrathful if Tanalvah added suicide to her sins.

The balance was in favour of taking another breath, facing another day.

This day, in particular, held a prospect worth rising for. Karr had promised her that Teg and Lirrin would be collected from the temple Tanalvah had entrusted them to. The children would be joining her here, in the Resistance hideaway. Not the most appropriate place for youngsters, perhaps, but at least they'd be together.

Easing herself from her bunk, she let out an involuntary groan as gravity delivered a reminder of her condition. She felt giddy and nauseous, as she often did first thing, and spent a moment breathing deeply until the sensation faded. Stretching, she got some feeling back into her aching limbs. Then she pulled on a formless shift and slipped her feet into a pair of leather-topped clogs somebody had given her.

The room she'd been allotted wasn't really a room at all. It was essentially a cubicle carved from the living rock of the catacombs, twenty paces deep, twelve wide. A makeshift wall of timber frames and canvas blocked what would have been its open end, with a flap door similar to a tent's. Tanalvah suspected it was an ancient burial chamber that had been cleared of bones, but didn't like to dwell on the idea.

Some effort had been put into making it comfortable for her. The bed had a plump straw mattress, with several thick pelts to keep her warm. She had a chair and a couple of unfussy shelves for her few possessions. A woven mat covered part of the floor. Someone had even gone to the trouble of finding an old tapestry to hang by her bed, though it was too faded for its subject to be recognisable. Compared to other lodgings she'd seen in this place, it was luxurious.

Her cell, as she'd come to think of it, was lit by a single glamour orb. She kept it on permanently, which was outrageously lavish, and she had candles and lanterns to hand as back-ups. Without the orb the chamber would be in total darkness, and that she couldn't abide.

A small outcrop of stone resembling a plinth stood near the door, where a wash basin and pitcher rested. The temperature was surprisingly mild below ground, yet the water was still cold enough to shock her when she splashed it on her face. Next she took up a brush and began jerking it through the tangles in her hair.

Attending to mundane tasks gave her no rest from the fixations that lodged like a chunk of ice in her guts. She saw no way of reconciling what she'd done with Kinsel's pacifism. If he lived, how he could possibly forgive her? She marvelled at how stupid she had been to believe Devlor Bastorran's lies about minimal harm coming to the people she betrayed. She felt suffocated by the fear of what would happen to the children in her charge, and the one unborn, if she was exposed. And she felt that exposure was inevitable, because it was all she could do not to fall on her knees, confess and beg forgiveness.

The Resistance had offered her passage to the Diamond Isle. She didn't want to go. It was hard enough coping with the people here. Over there, Tanalvah would have to confront those who had been closest to her, who had befriended and protected her. Especially Serrah, whom she dreaded facing. But her terror of Bastorran, and the chance of falling into his hands again, made her almost as afraid of staying.

Now she understood why Serrah had once found the prospect of death so enticing.

Tanalvah steeled herself to leave her tiny stone cocoon and join the others. She knew she wouldn't be able to look any of them in the eye. Enduring their kindnesses, their pitying gazes and their sympathetic smiles was a torment. It was a wonder to her that they couldn't see the guilt written on her face.

She summoned her resolve, pulled back the flap and stcppcd into thcir world.

As usual, the caves were bustling, and just as predictably people began to stare as soon as they noticed her. She felt naked. The temptation to admit what she'd done, to scream it out and get it over with, was near irresistible.

Then a group approached through the parting crowd, two adults and a pair of children. Dulian Karr and Goyter, beaming at her, with Teg and Lirrin clutching their hands. The children broke away and flew to Tanalvah's outstretched arms.

For the moment, all her troubles were washed away by tears of joy.

*   *   *

No more than an hour's ride from the necropolis, in the heart
of Valdarr, another reunion was taking place, albeit one with
considerably less warmth.

Inside the forbidding walls of the Bhealfan headquarters
of the paladin clans, beyond a labyrinth of passages and
secured doors, an inner sanctum was located.

Within, Devlor Bastorran was granting an audience.

A kind observer might describe his guest as striking. Although
seemingly asexual, close examination would indicate that the
visitor was female. She was athletic in build, verging on bony,
and had fair blonde hair cut close to the skull. Her flesh was
as pallid as marble. She had thin, nigh on colourless lips and
startlingly large, pitch black eyes. Conjecture on whether she
was handsome or ugly was irrelevant; her appearance flouted
normal conceptions of beauty. And right now those features
were further contorted with anger.

'I'm sick of waiting,' she hissed, jabbing a finger at his
chest. 'We had a bargain, and you never said you'd be this
long honouring it.'

'We did. But let me –'

'I should have known better than to trust the word of a
paladin. You're lying bastards, the lot of you, for all your talk
of honour and agreements.'

'That's not –'

'Well, chew on this, Lord High Muckamuck: we're bound,
you and me. Chained together by what I did on your behalf.'
Her eyes shone with a cold intensity. 'There's a price for
my silence about that, Bastorran. When are you going to
pay it?'

'I thought today might be a good time.'

'What?'

'If you'd let me get a word in,' he came back through
gritted teeth, 'I was going to explain. As you say, we had a
deal. I'm ready to fulfil my part.'

Aphri Kordenza eyed him suspiciously. 'You'll do as you agreed?'

'Your magical symbiosis with your . . . companion will be made permanent. Don't look so surprised. Did you really think I wouldn't honour our pact?'

'How will you do it?' the meld asked, ignoring his question.

'In what my sorcerers tell me is the best way. With this.' He slipped a hand into his tunic pocket and brought out a flat, wafer-thin object that had hundreds of tiny runic symbols etched into its surface. It looked like terracotta, and sat comfortably in his palm. He held it out to her.

'How?' she repeated, weighing it.

'At the moment you maintain your symbiotic status by periodically refreshing the magic. I'm guessing you need to visit a wizard with the necessary skills every few weeks, to renew the spell.'

She nodded. 'And pay handsomely for it.'

'I imagine it isn't always easy finding a sorcerer willing to do the job, either. Given that your condition's legally dubious.'

'It's a moot point. There are so few of us melds the Law's tended to ignore the situation. But we're getting off the subject.'

'That thing,' Bastorran pointed at the artefact she was clutching, 'cuts out the middleman. It keeps you permanently connected to the magical grid, drawing all the energy you need to stay as you are. No renewal of spells, no more expense.'

'What do I do, swallow it?'

'Only if you want to risk choking. But it does go inside your body. Just under the skin of your left heel, to be exact. It's a simple surgical procedure that takes a couple of minutes. I have physicians standing by, and they're the best. My own, in fact. You look wary. There's nothing to worry about. You'll be given a soporific and won't feel a thing.'

'I don't need one.'

'I'm told there would be a certain amount of pain involved without it.'

'I prefer to stay alert.'

He raised his eyebrows. 'As you please. But I really think –'

'I hope you're being straight about this, Bastorran. Because if it's some kind of trick, everybody's going to know you for a murderer. I've left details of your uncle's death with a confederate, and if anything happens to me –'

'We both know you haven't, Kordenza. And even in the unlikely event of you knowing somebody you'd trust with that kind of information, whose word are people going to believe? That of the grieving head of the paladin clans or some shifty member of the criminal classes? Besides, it's in my interest that your powers be at their height.'

'Why?'

'I have another commission for you. One which will reward you generously. Have faith in me. Your suspicions are misplaced.'

She thought about it. 'All right. Curse me for a fool, but I'll take your word.'

'Good. I'd say we should shake on it, but frankly I'd rather not touch you.'

'The feeling's mutual.'

He indicated the door with an outstretched arm. 'Shall we proceed?'

'In a moment. I said *I'd* accept your word. I've somebody else to confer with.'

Bastorran was nonplussed, then realised what she meant. 'Oh. Aphrim.'

'Of course. We're partners, you know. In all things.'

'Very well,' he sighed, perching himself on the side of a chair and crossing his arms. He found the spectacle unedifying, yet it held a perverse fascination.

Aphri Kordenza demerged. She tugged herself to one side smartly and left an image of her form suspended in the air.

The outline resembled a woman-shaped burnished rope, as though a lasso trick had frozen. As Bastorran watched, Aphri's reflection manifested a swirl of bone, sinew, blood and flesh. For a second, all was shimmering and indistinct. Then it gelled and took on form.

The new arrival in Bastorran's study looked superficially like the first, but close scrutiny showed subtle differences. The figure was male. It could have been Aphri's twin, and dressed identically to her in leather jerkin, britches and high boots. But there was a sense of it being only approximately human.

An almost transparent, finely veined, glistening membrane connected Kordenza and her twin. Her body jerked. The moist film detached itself and was instantly absorbed by her twin, making an unpleasantly wet sound as it was sucked into his flesh.

They gazed at each other raptly.

'Did you hear all that, my dear?' Aphri said.

'I did.' Her companion's voice was a shade away from being natural; it had a jarringly hollow quality, confirming his glamour status.

'What do you think?'

'It's what we've always wanted. But can we trust him?'

Bastorran felt a flush of rage at being spoken about as though he wasn't there. But he held his tongue.

'We've been through that, Aphrim,' Aphri said. 'I reckon it's a chance worth taking. Just think, you'll have all the power you want for those lovely new weapons you've dreamed up. So, are we agreed?'

'If you think it best, darling, yes.'

She flew into his arms. 'Isn't it wonderful, Aphrim? We need never part.'

They came together and kissed. A lingering, passionate, all-embracing lovers' kiss. Bastorran saw it as something distasteful, and corrupt.

When they finally drew back from each other, a translucent, glutinous strand ran from Aphri's mouth to Aphrim's,
as though they were dogs playing tug with a grey silk scarf.
It could have been the same stuff as the membrane which
earlier linked them. When it snapped midway, each of the
twins noisily inhaled their half. The paladin averted his gaze.

He stayed silent until the couple disengaged, then cleared
his throat. They turned as one to look at him. 'Can we get
on with it now?' he asked.

'Yes,' they chorused, disconcertingly. 'Aphrim will be there,'
Aphri added, 'watching over me.'

'Then perhaps you'll reconsider your decision about the
palliative?'

'No. What affects one affects us both. As I said, we prefer
to stay alert.'

'As you wish.'

They began moving to the door.

Aphri shot Bastorran a curious glance. 'You mentioned a
new commission.'

'Ah, yes. One that I think you'll view more as pleasure
than work.'

'We always get pleasure from our work,' Aphrim assured
him.

'What is it?' Aphri persisted.

'You're looking for revenge,' Bastorran replied, 'and so am
I. And I don't want to have to go through official channels
to get it, as it were. Which is why I require your services.
But it will involve all of us taking a little trip.'

'What are you talking about?'

'I know where Caldason is.'

*He didn't know where he was. There was a sense of who he was,
a realisation of his essential identity and a certain cogency of brain
function, but he had no idea of the place he was being shown.*

There was a lot of snow. It was hard to make out the landscape because of it, except for the fact that he was in a rugged terrain. Emaciated trees broke the whiteness, their contorted branches silhouetting a menacing sky. Black mountains, summits snow-dusted, marked the distant horizon on three sides. A constant wind blew, swirling flakes. He knew it was bitterly cold, but couldn't feel it, which didn't surprise him.

His instinct told him that something of importance was happening in this wilderness.

An image came to mind, unbidden and forgotten until now. A very, very long time ago, when he was a child, he had been taken to see a wise woman. He couldn't remember who she was, or what she looked like, nor could he recall who took him, or why. But he did remember something she taught him; something which he took for granted in his waking life as a warrior, a life that seemed so remote and unreal to him.

What he learned on that far-off day was the principle of no-mind. A state more easily experienced than explained, no-mind was about attaining a goal without consciously trying. The emphasis was on 'consciously'. It had nothing to do with the desire to achieve the goal, everything to do with how. His teacher used the example of a man throwing a spear or loosing an arrow, and failing to hit the target. But success was achieved when he stopped consciously trying. In order to triumph, the will had to be sublimated.

Was that a real memory, or the memory of a dream? He didn't know. Nevertheless, he obeyed its meaning. Stilling his mind, he let go of his resolve.

Instantly, he began to rise. Soon, the contorted trees were below him, looking like splashes of dark oil against the blanket of white. As he rose he moved forward; onward and up in the direction of the mountain range he was facing. He was aware of even stronger winds, which would have chilled him to the bone had he any sensitivity to his surroundings. Soaring, he passed above flocks of hardy birds, their powerful wings working the frigid air as they travelled south. Then the great snow-smothered peaks were below him and he had his first view of what lay beyond.

He looked down into a wide valley, another mountain range marking its farthest edge. The valley was waxen with snow, and drifts piled high against its dun restraining walls. A frozen river ran along it; a burnished mirror shot through with spindly cracks. But what caught his eye, what drew him, was a habitation. A small city had mushroomed at the valley's base, and extended on either side of the river. Cutting through the buildings was a causeway, connecting the harbour with an extensive fortress at the town's centre.

At one end of the valley, near a pass that formed its only entrance, there was an open plain. Descending rapidly, he saw the aftermath of mayhem there: many bodies, of men and horses, were scattered across the churned, muddy snow. Funeral pyres were burning. Prisoners sat huddled inside circles of spear-carriers, while groups of conquerors moved briskly about the battlefield, attending to the many tasks victory had brought them.

He was speeding along the length of the valley now, heading for the township and the castle it nurtured. Moving without deliberate volition, he flew above the port, where several ships were ablaze. Then a jumble of roofs passed beneath; thatched, wooden, tiled. There were streets, lanes, twisting alleys. Plenty of people were about, trudging dejectedly or herding the defeated. They carried loads, led cattle, pushed carts. Many simply wandered in a daze. But nobody saw him.

Ahead, the fortress loomed. He was moving so fast it looked as though he might be dashed against its colossal walls. But no sooner had the thought occurred than he began to slow.

The redoubt was rambling and multi-layered, the result of generations of over-building. It had a long terrace-cum-battlement situated high up as part of its frontage, and there was a single figure standing on it. At first, it was little more than a speck, but narrowing distance showed a man. Gazing at the view, his expression illegible, he had his hands laid upon the terrace's stone wall. Physically, he was completely unremarkable, and the way he dressed lacked ostentation. Yet there was something astonishing about him.

He was near enough to spit at the man, should he have wanted to, and now hung motionless in front of him. At first, the man seemed unaware of his presence, as everybody else had been. Then some kind of awareness came into his face, and he turned his head to stare.

The man's eyes were bottomless hollows.

He had no recollection of closing his own eyes. When he opened them again, he was somewhere else. The heights he'd ascended to before were nothing compared to this.

He floated in a starry firmament. The world lay far below, like an unfurled map, so large its edges curved away with distance. He saw all the realms there were, and the expanse of green-blue oceans separating them. One large, northernmost landmass drew his eye. Deep in its interior, something flashed. A pinprick. The flicker of a struck flint. It grew, a fleck of vivid crimson against russet. The stain spread, its tendrils seeping across the land, and into others. As it moved further, it flowed more rapidly. Whole segments of the terrain were coloured by it; regions, countries, continents.

The tide was red, like blood, or perhaps it was light. The qualities of both resided in it. Strands probed, joined with others, filled in to engulf another patch of brown or green. Its very progress seemed to add to its own momentum, as though a pillar supporting a temple roof had toppled and caused an entire row to fall, each one upon the next. But this was no temple. It was a world. A world being swallowed by blood and light.

Perhaps he should have felt bad about it.

He didn't.

10

'You saw the world drowning in blood and it seemed *benevolent*?'

'That's not exactly what I said.'

'It's near enough, Reeth. But the way you explain it, it doesn't sound particularly benign.'

'I didn't say I understood what I saw. You asked me how I felt about it, and I told you.'

Serrah snuggled deeper into the warmth of their bed. The window was ajar and the dawn's feeble, wintry light coloured the sky.

At last she said, 'It has to be Zerreiss, doesn't it? The man in your dream.'

'He didn't wear a label round his neck.'

'But it's logical, isn't it? Everything you've described indicates it was the warlord you saw.'

'You wouldn't have taken him for that. I never set eyes on a man so . . . ordinary before. Not handsome, but not ugly. Not tall, not short; not thin or fat; neither old nor young. He was like a pot taken out of the kiln too soon. Just completely . . . commonplace.'

'He doesn't sound the way you expect a warlord to look.'

'But that's it. Despite his appearance, there was something . . . I don't know, something about him that meant I didn't doubt he was a leader. I can't explain.'

'And he saw you?'

'It felt that way.'

'How common is it to have people in your dreams recognise you, Reeth?'

'I wouldn't say he recognised me. He was aware of me, I think. And no, it never used to happen until these recent dreams, or visions, or whatever they are. In fact, these new ones are taking over. I hardly ever have the old visions anymore; the ones that seem to be about me as a child.'

'Poor darling. Something new to torment you.' Serrah rested her head against his chest. His arm came up to enfold her. 'Could it be his doing? Zerreiss's?' she wondered. 'Is he making it happen?'

Caldason shrugged. 'Who knows what he's capable of? But why should he?'

'That's anybody's guess.' She sat up again and stretched a hand to the clutter on a small table by the bed.

'You're restless.'

'I'm surprised you're not. If I had the sort of experiences you're having I'd be in a complete state.' She hefted a water bottle and drank. 'Like some?'

He took it and quenched his own thirst. 'I'm used to them. Though the new ones are a puzzle laid on a mystery.'

'Right.' Serrah straightened, business-like. 'Let's go through it.'

He sighed. 'You think I haven't, a thousand times?'

'Two heads and all that. Humour me on this. You've been having these . . . let's settle on visions, shall we, for want of a better word? You've been having them how long?'

'Long as I can remember.'

'And we're agreed that what they show is you? Scenes from your early days, so to speak?'

He nodded. 'It took me a long time to figure that out. Which makes me feel pretty stupid, frankly.'

'You're not stupid, Reeth.' She leaned over and planted a kiss on his cheek. 'Anybody would be thrown by something like that.'

'It was the last thing that occurred to me. That they were about me, I mean. Too close to it, I suppose.'

'All right. I don't imagine we're going to get to the bottom of how these visions come to you. But maybe we could think about some of the things in them.'

'How do you mean?'

'Who was the old man you kept seeing? Who was it that came close to killing you when your people were massacred, and how did that lead to your present part-immortal state?'

'Yes, well, again I've thought about that a lot.'

'And your birth, Reeth; the vision you had about coming into this world and your mother dying. Though I think you punish yourself about that unnecessarily. It's not the child's fault if their mother dies birthing them, you know.'

'Perhaps.'

'There's no perhaps about it, my love. You can't blame yourself for something that isn't your doing. Believe me, I know. It's a lesson I think I've learned about Eithne, though it's taken me long enough.' Caldason didn't answer, so she carried on. 'The old man was obviously a guardian of some sort. He risked himself to protect you. But why?'

'That's a bigger question than the how, isn't it? Why am I being shown these things? What's their purpose?'

'Does there have to be a purpose? Is there a reason the sun comes up every day or the birds sing? Maybe it just *is*.'

'A lot of people believe these things happen because the gods will it. It's what Tanalvah would say, isn't it?'

'Is that what you're saying? You think the gods are responsible for what's happening to you?'

'An honest answer would be I don't know. I'm not even sure what I think about the idea of gods.'

'Hmm. So, you got one set of visions that plagued you for years, and they have to do with chunks of your life history. And they tie in somehow with the fits of rage you suffer. Right?'

'They're often connected. Though not always. The berserk I had during the last pirate raid, for instance. No visions that time.'

'Now there are new visions, but they're different, and they have something to do with Zerreiss.'

'We don't know that.'

'It's a good bet. And you're still getting the rages with these new visions, and –'

'Where's this getting us?'

'I don't know. Maybe nowhere. But I like getting things straight in my mind. As I said, the visions have changed but you're still berserking. And now you're perhaps being noticed by somebody in them.'

'Can you draw any conclusions from all that?'

'No. Beyond the obvious fact.'

'Which is?'

'Magic. That has to be the link.'

'I always assumed I was under some kind of hex, so that comes as no big surprise.'

'Pretty powerful magic though, don't you think? Unlike anything I've come across. Not to mention that whoever's responsible hasn't lifted the charm on you in over seventy years. That seems an awfully long time to pursue a vendetta without some kind of payoff to it.'

'The curse, or whatever it is, is a payoff in itself. Whoever was responsible for my state had the satisfaction of knowing I'd suffer for a very long time.'

'It doesn't make sense, Reeth. No ordinary human would live long enough to savour your pain. Unless you've been cursed by successive generations of wizards. Or else . . .'

'Go on.'

'Or else there are others like you. People with incredibly extended life-spans for whom centuries mean nothing.'

'We know at least one. Phoenix. He's in his hundredth year, remember.'

'That's different. An exceptional case. He had access to a little bit of Founder knowledge that made it possible.'

'Maybe he isn't the only one. Who's to say there aren't caches of their lore in other hands? Hell, I'm going to be looking for the Founder's knowledge trove myself.'

'Which, of course, raises the question of whether somebody else has already found it.'

'You know how to brighten my day, Serrah.'

She grimaced at him. 'Having said that, I don't think anybody has.'

'How can you be so sure?'

'I can't. But remember what Phoenix himself said, and Karr: if the Source had been discovered we'd have seen the effects of it all around us. Whoever had access to it wouldn't stop at merely extending their lives; they'd be running things by now. Or we'd all be dead.'

'Perhaps they simply haven't mastered it.'

'After seventy years? I don't think so. In fact, I don't buy the whole hex thing, not really. I mean, what kind of curse is it that bestows something like immortality on the victim? Yes, I know that as a gift it's been a two-edged sword for you, but you get my point. I reckon we're looking at something quite different to an enemy's enchantment. Though I'm damned if I know what.'

Caldason smiled. 'I think you're beginning to see it isn't a problem given to easy solutions.'

She had to smile back. 'I didn't expect to solve it in five minutes. Dolt.'

He laughed. 'Really? I would have thought any self-respecting problem wouldn't dare defy you.'

'You cheeky . . .' She snatched up a pillow and battered him until it split, releasing a cloud of tiny feathers.

'Reeth,' she said, plucking feathers from her lips and adopting a more serious tone, 'is Kutch sharing these latest visions with you?'

'He picked up on the first one or two. But it seems to have stopped since he quit his spotter training.'

'There it is again: magic. There's a link here somewhere. I'd swear these things connect.'

'I've not been able to figure out how.'

'We should talk to Kutch. You never know, he might come up with something. Some clue or –'

He took her in his arms and gently nibbled her ear. 'All right. But let's do it later, shall we?'

Their lips met.

In one of the Diamond Isle's remotest parts, at its eastern tip, sheer cliffs acted as a natural barrier to assault from the sea. At the cliffs' top, on a stretch of grassland, there stood an assembly of chalets, a relic of the island's days as a pleasure resort. It was here that the handful of Covenant sorcerers who had escaped Bhealfa chose to congregate, alongside the few wizards already in residence. A centre for retreat and meditation, the spot was universally respected as the island's only private place.

The cabins were dilapidated, and around them the snow had been trodden to slush. A small stand of trees acted as a windbreak, but in their wintry, denuded state the protection was minimal. Overall, the impression was cheerless.

One hut stood well apart from the rest. The snow

surrounding it was near pristine, bearing only a few sets of footprints, and all its windows were shuttered.

Inside, Kutch Pirathon was finishing a study session with his surrogate mentor, who this day had eschewed a magical disguise. He appeared as he was; elderly, white-haired and furrow-faced.

'And you're sure you haven't experienced any of Reeth Caldason's visions lately?' Phoenix asked.

'No,' Kutch repeated, irritated at the old man's persistence. He slammed shut the hinged book he'd been perusing. 'And I don't lie about these things. That was something my master always insisted on.'

'Then he taught you well. Don't be offended, boy. I'm pressing you only because it's important.'

'As I said, we stopped sharing visions a couple of months ago.'

'When you gave up spotting.'

'Yes.'

'And dreams? What about those?'

Kutch looked reticent. 'Well . . .'

'What was it your master always insisted on?'

The youth sighed. 'Occasionally, in dreams . . . yes, there's a connection. But not often, and nowhere near as powerful as the visions I used to get. It's not a problem, but . . . I thought stopping my training as a spotter would free me.'

'Well, it seems it mostly has, as you say yourself. But I suspect some link between you and Caldason will go on as long as you practice magic of any kind.'

'Oh.' He was deflated. 'That's a depressing thought.'

'Because you think that means you're forced to make a choice? Between your friendship with Caldason and your devotion to magic?'

Kutch looked up hopefully. 'Doesn't it?'

'I think you're misunderstanding me. The link will go on if you continue with magic, though it may be possible for us to dampen its effect on you. But nothing you do, including abandoning the craft, will make any difference to Caldason, if that's what you were hoping. His entanglement with magic is beyond any action you take.'

'But that seems so unfair. Reeth hates magic.'

'I hate rain, but that doesn't stop me getting wet.' He added more soberly, 'Use your common sense, boy. Caldason's feelings in the matter are of no more account than a condemned man's opinion of the rope he's hanged with.'

'Can't you do anything for him?'

'Our efforts have proved futile. Now his hopes reside in the Source, assuming he can find it, and if what's left of Covenant can decipher it. Neither of which will be easy.'

'Then we have to do all we can to help him find it.'

'Indeed. Because if he fails, only one other way of breaking his bonds remains.'

'What's that?'

'His death.' Phoenix gazed steadily at Kutch.

'But he can't be killed.'

'You know that's not true. His condition is one approaching immortality, not immortality itself. Ending his life would be difficult, but not impossible.'

'You aren't making me feel very happy about this, master.'

'It's not my job to ensure your happiness. But your survival does concern me. Which is why I needed to know the extent of your connection with Caldason's visions.'

'My survival? How could a glimpse of Reeth's visions possibly –'

'Are you ignorant of the potential destructive power of magic, despite all your studies? Caldason's harnessed to some aspect of the potent art even we don't understand. Remember what I told you about my Covenant brothers who were killed examining an exposed energy channel? This business with Caldason could prove just as fatal for you.'

'We're all going to die in this place anyway,' Kutch muttered.

'Perhaps.'

'So wouldn't it be better to be doing something about that, rather than –'

'There's nothing we can do, beyond aiding our defences as best we can. I suppose I could try to have you smuggled off the island. It might work.'

'No. I . . . I'd prefer to take my chances here, with the people I know.'

A slight smile creased Phoenix's ancient lips. 'If that's what you want. But the point I'm trying to make is that neglecting your studies doesn't help Caldason, and it certainly doesn't help you. It's a shame you had to abandon spotting, given how rare a gift it is. That apart, you have a talent for the craft, and you're bright enough to achieve full sorcerer status, if you work at it. Don't throw that away.'

The boy brightened. 'You really think so?'

'I'm not given to empty flattery.'

'I'm so pleased to hear you say that. There have been times lately when I've kind of wished I'd followed the path Varee took.'

'Varee?'

'My brother. He left to join the army when I was a kid.'

'Ah, yes. Well, I'm glad you didn't. It would have been a loss to the Craft.'

'Thanks.'

'And would have greatly disappointed your master, I don't doubt.'

'Yes, I think Domex would have been upset. But I'm pleased you've got confidence in me, Phoenix. It means a lot to me that you'd –'

'Ssshh.'

'What?' Kutch whispered.

'Someone approaches,' the wizard replied in an under-tone.

'I don't hear any –'

Phoenix waved a hand, silencing him. Kutch strained to listen. He heard nothing at first, and doubted the sorcerer's senses. Then he wondered at them. Very faintly, the sound of horses' hooves could be heard. As they grew louder, the wizard moved to a window and peered through a crack in the shutter.

'Nothing to worry about,' he said. 'It's friends.'

He went to the door and opened it, Kutch at his side. A blast of cold air slapped their faces.

Two riders were approaching, travelling fast, urging their mounts on with cuffs from the reins. One was Caldason, bent low into the cutting wind, cloak billowing. Serrah rode along-side, barley hair flowing free.

They arrived in seconds, their steaming horses kicking up clods of frozen earth as they were curbed. Caldason and Serrah quickly dismounted.

'Reeth, Serrah,' Kutch greeted them. 'What are you doing here?'

'Well, we set out to talk something over with you,' Serrah told him. 'But events seem to have overshadowed that.'

'What are you referring to?' Phoenix asked, less than amused by the interruption.

'Come and see for yourself,' Caldason said.

They donned cloaks and followed him. He led them away from the cluster of huts and to the cliff's edge.

'There.' He pointed out to sea. Two ships were nearing the island, their purple sails swelling.

'Another attack!' Kutch exclaimed.

The pirate galleons hoisted black flags and began a tack for a less daunting shore of the island.

Serrah let out a weary breath. 'Here we go again.'

11

A small battle raged across a myriad droplets of quicksilver.

Each shimmering bead reflected its own fragment of the event. They showed mobs sweeping through ruined streets, throwing stones, fighting, commiting arson. There were hordes of civilians clashing with uniformed, baton-wielding men at barricades. Magical discharges flashed like searing lances, setting people ablaze.

The pewter gobbets coalesced, mingled, became a shiny liquid. Then the fragmentation occurred again, and other, similar events unfolded. Gutted buildings, rampaging crowds, looting, cavalry charges and arrests. Repeatedly the fluid turned through its cycle, flowing, reforming, displaying scenes of civil disorder. Bodies littering city squares, prisoners herded into carts at sword-point, and roadside executions.

The hoary substance through which the drama played out, bubbling and seething, filled the bed of a smooth-walled pit. Two men stood at the polished handrail surrounding this cavity, looking down at the ever-changing vista. They wore fine robes of glamoured fabrics that coursed with colours and subtle patterns.

Both men were old. Cosmeticians and face glamours had

alleviated their appearance to some degree, but not convincingly. The smoothness of skin and abundance of hair proved frauds on close inspection.

Elder Felderth Jacinth, the single most feared man in the empire, was marginally the older. But it was a near-run thing as to who was the grimmer.

'Enough,' he decided, slicing the air with an easy gesture.

The images in the pit dissolved; the not-quite liquid fell back to churning and grew quieter.

'Do you still think this unrest is of little account, Rhylan?' the Elder asked.

His brother seemed less ruffled. 'Let's not get this out of proportion; it's not as bad as the visualisations suggest. The disturbances are restricted to isolated pockets.'

'But they shouldn't be happening at all.'

'Our system's too well ordered to allow such disobedience to persist for long. Besides . . .'

'What?'

'Besides which the greater part of the masses are bound to be restrained by their devotion to us.'

'Please, Rhylan, let's not stretch credulity too far.'

The Elder turned away from the pit and its faintly sulphurous fumes, followed by his brother.

They walked into the main body of an enormous, windowless chamber. It was fashioned from exquisite marble, and a score of pillars rose gracefully to a high, vaulted ceiling. An abundance of glamour orbs bathed the room in a soft glow. In keeping with old ways, the routes of subterranean power channels were marked out with coloured pigments. Red, blue, green, gold, a mesh of lines cut across the chamber's floor.

Shaped like a shield and large enough to support a chariot and team, a table occupied centre stage. Clusters of the power lines ran to its sturdy legs, infusing the oak with magical essence to invigorate those who deliberated there, and to make vibrant the motif imprinted on the table's surface. So that the emblem of empire – an eagle in flight against a backdrop of lightning bolts – was imbued with pseudo-life. The eagle soared, working its powerful wings as lightning crackled all around.

Upwards of twenty members of Rintarah's Central Council were seated at the table. Had an ordinary citizen been admitted, which they never were, they would have noticed that the men and women present bore an obvious familial resemblance. Blood, rather than egalitarianism, had always determined the Council's composition. An onlooker would also have been struck by the fact that the majority in attendance were very old.

Felderth Jacinth took his place at the head of the table. Rhylan made for the last vacant seat.

'Some of you, including my brother here, feel that our current public order problems are no more than a passing nuisance,' the Elder began without preamble. 'I disagree. What we're seeing on the streets of Jecellam, and throughout Rintarah, may not be widespread, but it is significant.'

'More important than the unrest we've weathered in the past?' a sceptical relative asked.

'Yes, and for two reasons. First, we have something new in the mix: the Diamond Isle. From the moment dissidents from here, and from Gath Tampoor, were allowed to reach it, it kindled hope in the radicals' breasts. The wretched place is a beacon for every malcontent, troublemaker and revolutionary.'

'But we're talking about a relatively tiny number of people,' Rhylan argued.

'Which wouldn't ordinarily concern us too much,' the Elder agreed. 'But that brings me to the second factor, and one which I shouldn't have to spell out. The Qalochian.'

'Ah yes, a problem that should have been dealt with long ago.'

'Had we been able to settle our differences about him, it would have. Now we have him entangled with the dissidents, and that's like throwing oil on smouldering embers.'

'Aren't we in danger of exaggerating Caldason's importance?' another sceptic wondered.

'That argument's devilled us for far too long,' the Elder replied. 'If we forget his genesis, and his potential for harm, we do so at our peril.'

'I agree,' a female councillor interjected. 'Caldason and the alienated ones are a volatile mix. There's no question that action's overdue.'

'But we don't even know if he's aware of his latent capabilities,' Rhylan responded, 'let alone about to exercise them.'

'There you have it: we don't know,' Felderth Jacinth said. 'Are we prepared to take that risk?'

'We need no persuading of the man's latent menace,' someone else assured him. 'It's the methods about to be employed that trouble many of us.'

There were supportive murmurs. Almost half the people at the table nodded agreement.

'As we've permitted this situation to escalate to crisis point,' the Elder told him, 'we're left with little option.'

Rhylan spoke for the doubters. 'But joining forces with our deadliest rivals? That strikes many of us as an extraordinary state of affairs, brother.'

'We are not joining forces with them. Achieving a joint goal would be a more accurate description.'

'Whatever you call it, it's totally unprecedented.'

'Desperate times demand desperate measures.'

'Maybe so. But are you honestly saying that the situation on the Diamond Isle is beyond the capability of Rintarah's armed forces? Why do we need Gath Tampoor?'

'We don't. Militarily, of course we're perfectly able.'

'Then why this . . . alliance?'

'Gath Tampoor is preparing to act whatever we do, and politically it makes sense for them. They have to demonstrate to their subjects that dissidence won't be tolerated. If we act differently we leave ourselves open to accusations of weakness, which would only give sustenance to our own rabble-rousers.'

'The argument does have merit,' a supporter murmured.

'I repeat that this is not an alliance,' the Elder continued. 'It's a question of mutual self-interest. Necessity makes for strange bedfellows, and no matter how profound our differences, the only issue of any import is survival.'

That brought down a pall of silence.

The Elder waited a beat, then explained, 'There need be no concerns that our dealings with Gath Tampoor have in any way compromised us. Such exchanges as have occurred were at the highest level, and our position was made plain. There can be no misapprehension on their part that we're offering concessions of any kind.'

'That's reassuring,' an opponent uttered with less than total conviction. Then he added, 'What exactly do we know about the security situation in Gath Tampoor's sphere?'

'If anything, they're suffering more than we are. But then they do have some notoriously troublesome colonies, Bhealfa being a good example. Which was Caldason's birthplace, of course.'

'Hmmm. And the rebels? Do we know their disposition?'

'Less clearly than we did. They've been decimated and many of the survivors are scattered, which makes intelligence-gathering all the harder. Not that it was ever easy planting spies in their ranks.'

'Yet we had one informer amongst them with access to their upper echelons.'

'Yes, and they proved a useful source. But contact was broken just when some very interesting information was starting to come through. We don't know what happened to that informer. Our suspicion is that they perished at the hands of Gath Tampoor's security forces during their cull.'

'Ironic,' Rhylan observed.

His brother nodded. 'Indeed.'

'Of course, the informer might simply have changed allegiance.'

'What do you mean?' the Elder asked.

'It's a reasonable supposition that Gath Tampoor also had a highly placed source in the so-called Resistance, else they wouldn't have been able to strike at them so hard. Perhaps it was the same person.'

'That's possible. It's also largely irrelevant now. Our only concern is Rintarah's internal security, and we know that although crippled, the rebels still pose a threat. Which brings us back to the action I intend taking.' A clamour broke out. The Elder raised a hand to silence it. 'For those of you who waiver on this, let me add another factor.' He turned and pointed to the pit. It was an intentionally dramatic gesture. 'We all know that strange things have been happening to the energy mesh. My fear is that the disturbances will grow worse unless immediate steps are taken to trace their origin.'

'You can't be suggesting a connection, surely?' Rhylan exclaimed. 'What possible relation can there be between the rebels and the matrix?'

'I don't know. But it takes little effort to imagine a potential link between it and Caldason. Nor should we overlook Zerreiss.'

'The warlord? Being cautious is a commendable trait, brother, but don't you think you're going a bit far? What does he have to do with the picture you're painting for us?'

'Perhaps nothing at all. Or he could be the lynchpin in this affair.'

'Oh, come on, Felderth –'

'Hear me out. We know he's carving a domain for himself in the northern wastelands, and that alone makes him a threat. Then there's the question of the mission we sent to investigate his activities, and the one Gath Tampoor dispatched. There seems little doubt both have been lost, and the chances are it was Zerreiss's doing. If Caldason, the rebels and Zerreiss united we could be facing a much more formidable menace than a mere handful of traitors.'

'If. It's not our way to talk ourselves into a panic over hypothetical possibilities. What would they have in common?'

'A hatred of the empires seems a good enough impetus to me. Zerreiss certainly has no respect for us or Gath Tampoor; he's attacked both our colonies with equal zeal. He might see a benefit in joining with our enemies. And I suspect that's how Gath Tampoor sees it, too.'

'This is all supposition. Where's the proof?'

'I've no hard evidence. But I do have something I think is heavily circumstantial.' He took a parchment scroll from his robe and placed it on the table. 'Recently, I noticed an anomaly. The last three or four occasions when the matrix became agitated occurred on what seemed to be significant dates. When I checked I discovered the upheavals coincided with Zerreiss's conquests. I set our officials to compiling a list of his victories and major battles, and when they took place. Every one of them tallied with a disturbance in the matrix. It's all there.' He nodded at the scroll.

Rhylan picked it up. 'And this is indicative of what, exactly?' His tone held an uncertainty that hadn't been there before.

'Again, I don't know. But there's a definite correlation. And with each conquest he makes, with each step nearer our sphere of influence, the disturbances grow stronger.'

'There's no doubt about this?' his brother said, studying the scroll.

'None.' The Elder addressed them all. 'Don't you see? We

have something here that's unprecedented. If there's the slightest prospect of it affecting our position we're bound to act. We've survived as long as we have by anticipating threats, and stamping down hard at the first sign of any opposition to our power. Ask yourselves this: what do we have to lose by taking action, bar a few lives amongst the lower orders? Inaction, on the other hand, could prove disastrous.'

Largely favourable murmurs rose from the Council.

'I propose we vote on this,' a supporter suggested.

'Those in agreement with military action as outlined,' Jacinth said, 'raise your hands.' He scanned the table. 'And against?' There was a quick reckoning. 'The ayes have it.'

But only just.

Rhylan got up. 'A word on behalf of the naysayers, brother?'

The Elder nodded.

'There's wisdom in what you've told us, as usual. But I know you'll respect the reservations some of us have. In recognition of that, I'd like to suggest a rider to the Council's decision.'

'Of course.'

'We should be kept fully informed at every stage of this operation.'

'Naturally, that goes without saying.'

'And in the event of any mishap, any hint that this enterprise was misconceived, a further vote shall be taken with a view to instantly recalling our forces. The outcome of such a ballot to be absolutely binding.'

'You ask no more than that which would have been freely given, Rhylan. So be it.' He rose. 'There are busy days ahead and we all have our tasks. Unless anyone else wishes to speak . . . ? Good. Then I suggest we adjourn and go about our business.'

The Council dispersed in whispering groups.

But the brothers lingered, and, as one, moved back to the pit.

The Elder gestured, reactivating the silvery mass. Visions came again. Views of the streets, squares and parks of Jecellam, once the most orderly of all capitals, now fraying at the edges.

Snow had begun to fall. It dusted the shoulders of dissenters and enforcers alike, and tempered unlawful fires, but it did nothing to quench the passion for justice.

At a silent command from the Elder, the empire's largest port came into focus. A great invasion fleet was at anchor there. Lines of stevedores chained provisions from hundreds of wagons jamming the dockside, while battalions of harbour marshals swelled the crowd, making preparations for the embarkation of a waiting army. Ships were so numerous they queued out into the bay; a seemingly endless prospect of nodding masts and fluttering sails.

And beyond, the vast expanse of a heaving ocean.

12

Flying the colours of the freebooter alliance, around a dozen ships lay at anchor within sight of the Diamond Isle.

The small fleet's number had recently been reduced. Not through the attrition of warfare, but a cause less predictable, and one that left fury in its wake.

On the deck of the largest vessel, Kingdom Vance vented his anger.

'Three ships! Three damn ships, and two score men!'

'So you said,' Kinsel Rukanis told him.

Vance turned from the rail and faced the singer. 'You find this amusing?'

'Instructive would be a better word.' He was shivering from the cold, and found little protection in his threadbare garments.

'Instructive? The only lesson I draw is that a bunch of turncoats switched sides.'

'Have you thought why?'

'Why?' There was genuine menace in his tone. 'Because they're cowards!'

'Isn't it possible they deserted because they realised the futility of what you're trying to do?'

'That's just another way of saying they're spineless. I'm better off without scum like that.'

'Or could it be that they saw the justice of the rebels' cause?'

Vance laughed cynically. 'They're fools as well as lily-livered if they think that. They deserve each other.'

'You surprise me, Captain. I thought you'd feel an affinity with the rebels, given they stand against the authorities.'

'Then you think wrong, singer. I've no love for the empires, but at least you know where you are with them. They've got power, and don't have any scruples about using it. I can respect that. The only thing of any account in this world is what you can grab with your own two hands.'

'If that's what you truly believe, I'm sorry for you.'

'Save your pity for yourself, Rukanis. And think on this. The people on that island chose to leave their homes and come here. By doing that they deprived us of a land of our own. That makes them my enemy.'

'Who's being self-pitying now? You chose your way of life. Were you forced into piracy? Did somebody hold a blade to your throat? No. Make an accommodation with the islanders, Vance, as your deserters have. End this lunacy.'

'You come out with that refrain as regularly as any of your airs, and I'm growing tired of it. There'll be no truces or climb-downs. And the ones who ran out on me are going to pay for it when I take that island.'

'If you take it.'

Lightning swift, Vance swung his fist into the side of Rukanis's head. It was a savage blow, and the singer would have fallen if he hadn't been standing with his back to a mast. His cheek instantly reddened. A dribble of blood seeped from his swelling lip.

'You're forgetting the nature of our relationship,' Vance hissed, his face close. 'Prisoner and captor, not equals. You're not somebody I take advice from.'

Rukanis spat blood on the deck, then met his gaze. 'Is hearing the truth really such an unfamiliar experience for you?'

The pirate made to strike him again, but hesitated, and finally stayed his hand. 'To hell with it.' He turned away, leaving Rukanis to dab at his mouth with a shirt cuff. 'It's only a question of time before I get what I want,' Vance promised. 'And you're going to help me.'

'Anything happening?' Serrah asked, squinting at the group of ships lying well offshore.

'No.' Caldason offered her the spy tube. 'See for yourself.'

'Not much point looking at nothing, is there? Come on, we can't do anything here. We've got plenty of eyes on them.'

They resumed their walk along the compacted spine of the sandbank. The wind was raw, and they felt its chill despite their hooded fur topcoats and fleece gloves.

'You know, I still find it hard to believe,' she said.

'The pirates?'

'Yes. When they came in flying white flags I thought it was another trick.'

'Darrok was convinced of it.'

'Perhaps he was right.'

'Planting vipers in our midst, that kind of thing? I doubt it. Too obvious. But they'll be kept under guard until we're sure.'

'Says something about morale under Vance if that many changed sides, doesn't it?'

'All it tells us is that forty-three of his cohorts were disheartened enough to desert. It doesn't necessarily weaken Vance. If anything it makes him more dangerous.'

'How's that?'

'It's going to fire him up all the more; give him another reason to hate us and want this island. And now his ranks have been purged of waiverers he's got a stronger force to send against us.'

'Well, at least we got three more ships because of it. Talking of which . . .' She nodded ahead.

They overlooked a cove the islanders used as a small harbour. A two-masted, square-rigged ship was anchored in the shallows, and half a dozen smaller craft were moored at a makeshift jetty.

'It's a brig,' Caldason announced.

'You're an expert on ships all of a sudden, are you?'

He smiled. 'Er, no. It was the one that brought me over.'

'Thought it seemed familiar. Is it big enough for the voyage you have in mind?'

'Darrok says it is. Actually, it has to be. We don't have an over-abundance of ships to spare, you know.'

'What about one of the galleons the pirates came in?'

'They're fighting ships; we need them here. The brig's built for speed, not sea battles.'

'But you don't know what might be defending the Clepsydra. A warship could be –'

'We can only work with what we've got, Serrah. Besides, the faster the ship the quicker the journey. Getting back as soon as possible is a real consideration if this place is going to be blockaded.'

'You still think it will be?'

'It's what I'd do if I was either of the empires. Isolate the infection.'

'Maybe we should just use all the ships and get everybody out of here.'

'And go where? Our options are limited, to say the least. No, it's this island or nothing.'

'Course it is.' She reached for his hand. 'But whatever happens, at least we'll be together. Now I'm getting all sappy, damn it. Why do you let me get into such a state over these things?'

'Me? I didn't even –'

'Look! Isn't that Zahgadiah and Pallidea? On the landing stage? Let's get down there.'

They began their descent.

Once brief greetings had been exchanged, Darrok had news.

'We've learnt something interesting from the defectors,' he explained, 'and I think it'll give you some heart.'

'So spit it out,' Caldason said.

'Vance is holding your friend Rukanis.'

'I knew it!' Serrah exclaimed. 'How is he? Did they know?'

'Being Vance's prisoner's never going to be a pleasant experience, and naturally he's suffered some knocks. But he is alive.'

'You don't know what a relief that is.'

Pallidea, hand resting on the edge of her lover's hovering dish, voiced caution. 'Perhaps you shouldn't get too excited. There's more.'

'Tell us.'

'I said it would give you some heart,' Darrok answered. 'The not-so-good news is that Vance and his alliance think they can use Rukanis as a bargaining chip. To get us to give up the island.'

'We'd never trade,' Caldason said. 'They must know that.' He noticed the look on Serrah's face. 'Well, we wouldn't. How could we? And Kinsel would be the first to understand that this whole venture's worth more than the fate of one individual.'

'Vance wouldn't,' Darrok told him. 'Even if he did, what's a man's life to him? He'd see it as worth a try.'

'What does he intend doing?' Serrah asked.

'We don't have any details, but you can bet it'd be to the point, and brutal. Hand over the Diamond Isle or watch your friend burn to death in a cage hanging from a yardarm. That's the way Vance operates.'

'We've got to do something to get Kinsel out of this, Reeth.'

'Yes.'

'And soon. Right away. Before we set off on this voyage you're planning.'

'Of course. Though I'm not so sure about the we, Serrah.'

'We've been through this. I'm going with you. You promised.'

'It could be dangerous.'

'Then why are you going in this thing?' She jabbed a thumb at the brig. 'If the journey's dangerous you should be using a warship, and a bigger crew.'

'I told you. It's because –'

'Good. That's settled then.'

'Serrah. If you thought about this for just a minute you'd see –'

Darrok cleared his throat loudly. 'Don't mind us. But some other time might be more appropriate for this, don't you think? Besides, company's arriving.'

A cart drew up at the end of the jetty. Phoenix was driving, with Kutch at his side. The boy scrambled down and sprinted to the others, leaving the magician to secure the horse.

Serrah met him with, 'Guess what, Kutch? Kinsel's alive.'

'We heard. Great, isn't it?'

'It is if we can get him out of Vance's clutches,' Caldason said.

'Can we?'

Phoenix caught up, panting slightly. 'It's a good question. Do we have a plan?'

'We've only just found out,' Caldason informed him.

'I'll call a special session of the Council for this afternoon,' Darrok suggested. 'We'll get something thrashed out then.'

Caldason nodded. 'All right. But let's not turn this into a talking shop. We need to act quickly.'

'There'll be a decision today, I guarantee it. Meantime, don't go doing anything on your own account. Understood?'

'As if I would.'

'He means it, Reeth,' Serrah assured him sternly. 'I'm all for rescuing Kinsel as soon as we can, but going off half-arsed isn't the best way.'

'I'll do nothing on my own. But there's a limit to how long I'll hold to that. For Kinsel's sake, and mine. I'll not wait forever if it means delaying the voyage much longer.'

'As we can't decide anything about Rukanis's fate for a couple of hours,' Phoenix said, 'we'd be best employed assessing the preparations for your expedition.'

'That's why we're here,' Darrok reminded them. 'For my part I've scrounged enough provisions to last you about two weeks, Reeth. Though it was the devil's own job getting the Council to part with them. And the victuals are nothing fancy. It's iron rations, and you'll have to stretch 'em. There's an issue of warm clothing too, given you'll be heading northward.'

'What about the skipper?' asked Caldason.

'The same one who brought you out from Bhealfa; Rad Cheross.'

'Good. And the crew?'

'Mostly his own, and all volunteers. A little over a dozen, which I'm told is a bit tight but sufficient to run a vessel like this.'

'Anything else I should know?'

'Only that there'll be a small consignment of gold on the ship. Not a fortune exactly, but it could be useful in case you have to bargain for . . . whatever it is you might find.'

'Gold? I thought the Resistance's coffers were empty.'

'They are.'

'This is your own money?' Caldason raised his eyebrows.

'I've never seen you look bashful before, Zahgadiah,' Serrah told Darrok.

'Shut up,' he replied, his cheeks colouring.

'It seems you're growing more partial to the cause every day,' Caldason said.

'It's on loan. I expect it back if you don't use it.'

'That's generous. Thank you.'

'Don't go all mushy on me, Reeth, I couldn't stand that. Just look after my damn gold.'

'As far as the sorcerer fraternity's concerned,' Phoenix volunteered, 'we'll be supplying some magical protection, and a small armoury of munitions. Not a lot, but as much as we can spare.'

'Appreciate it,' Caldason responded. 'Though I feel happier with a good length of tempered steel any day.'

'You don't know what you're going to meet out there. You're searching for Founder artefacts, remember, and we have no real idea what might be defending them. You need all the safeguards you can get.'

'Who's going to be on board to handle the magic?'

'I'd like it to be me. Unfortunately that's a little too much for the Council to swallow. They say I'm needed here to direct the island's magical defences. The same goes for the other sorcerers we have, given how pitifully few our numbers are.'

'So who, then?'

'Kutch.'

'Whoa. That's a hell of a responsibility for the boy. No offence, Kutch.'

'I can do it, Reeth,' the apprentice protested. 'Phoenix has been training me. You said I could go anyway, so I might as well make myself useful. I can help keep us out of trouble.'

'And who's going to keep trouble from bothering you?'

'I will,' Serrah stated. 'I'll keep an eye on Kutch; you concentrate on the search.'

'Got it all worked out, haven't you?'

'Yes. You know how scarce resources are. It's a miracle we got the Council to agree to this venture at all. The trade-off is that you've got to take what's on offer, like you said about this ship.'

Caldason grinned. 'Looks like I haven't got much choice.'

'Too right. Live with it.'

'I hate to inject a note of hard reality into this,' Phoenix interrupted, 'but you do realise this is probably all academic, don't you?'

'I know it won't be easy,' Caldason said, his attitude sobering.

'Let's look at exactly what that means, shall we? Covenant, and some other scholars of the noble art, believe the ancients left a store of knowledge which we call the Source, although it's unlikely that's what the Founders themselves called it. Assuming it's a reality and not just conjecture, we don't know what it is or if it survived.'

'I've heard all this.'

'It bears repeating. We think the Source is connected in some way to the Clepsydra. Not that we really know what that is either. We have a hunch, which we dignify by calling it a theory, based on incomplete fragments of Founder lore open to many interpretations, as to roughly where these mysteries might be hidden. We have no idea what might be defending them. And if the Source should ever be discovered we're far from certain we could understand it, let alone make use of it.'

'Those sound like the kind of odds I'm used to.'

Phoenix frowned. 'There's no call to be flippant about this, Caldason.'

'I was never more serious. However slim the chance, for me and for what's left of the Resistance, I'm going to take it.'

'Very well. In which case I can perhaps offer a little help in narrowing down the possible location you seek.'

Using his forefinger, the wizard swiftly drew a shimmering

rectangle in the air, then made a hand gesture. The oblong began to fill with colours and shapes before clarifying to an expanse of blue-green overlaid with innumerable specks.

'This is the area of the ocean where we suspect the Clepsydra isle's located,' Phoenix explained. 'Over the past few months my colleagues and I have been extensively researching such records as we have to try and pinpoint the site more accurately. We haven't met with complete success. Far from it. And let me caution you again that what we're doing is highly theoretical and could be wrong-headed. But we believe we can reduce the options . . . so.' He touched the glamour map near its top right-hand corner, where the specks were most numerous. Instantly, the chart dissolved, to be replaced by a close-up of the section he'd indicated. The specks had grown to blobs with more definable, irregular shapes. 'Our best guess is that what you seek lies within this cluster.'

'That's, what? Forty, fifty islands?' Caldason estimated.

'Approximately, yes. Still a sizeable number but nowhere near the hundreds making up the entire group.'

'How big are they?' Pallidea wondered, gazing at the floating chart.

'The largest are no more than about a tenth of the size of the Diamond Isle. The majority are much smaller, and some are little more than rocks. Which may have some bearing on your search, Reeth, if we were to assume the very smallest are the least likely locations. But of course, not knowing what form the Source or indeed the Clepsydra takes, we can't necessarily make that assumption.'

'Well, it's some help I suppose,' Caldason said.

'I'll see that your skipper has a copy of this,' Phoenix promised. He waved his hand. The map faded to golden embers, and died, leaving a sulphurous whiff in the brittle air.

'Things seem to be progressing well,' Darrok judged. 'At

this rate you'll be able to set off pretty soon, Reeth. Or at least once we've done something about Rukanis.'

'I should have asked before, I suppose, but I hope my absence won't hinder your being able to deal with the pirates.'

'I think we'll manage without you for a while,' Darrok responded dryly. 'After all, I've been defending this place for quite a few years already. Without any outside help.'

'Ouch,' Serrah mouthed.

'Besides,' Darrok went on, 'I've unfinished business with Vance, as you know, and I think it's something I'd rather like to settle personally.'

'That I can understand,' Caldason granted.

'So I reckon the best thing we can do now is –'

'What the hell is that?' Serrah pointed inland.

They all looked to a patch of level grassland beyond the beach. A strange contraption was slowly making its way across the sward. It was an open wagon, unremarkable in itself, except that it lacked shafts or a horse to pull it. Somebody clad in blue robes sat in the driver's seat, but with their hands in their lap, having no need of reins.

'Ah,' Phoenix said. 'That's Frakk, a sorcerer who escaped here from Bhealfa. An independent; not a Covenant member or anything.'

'But what's he doing?' Serrah wanted to know.

'Testing a very ingenious idea. A carriage powered by magical essence. In fact, he could be the only person who fled here not out of conviction but pique.'

'What?'

'He tried to get various people interested in it back in Bhealfa. He even approached the paladins with the contraption. Apparently demonstrated it for the Bastorrans themselves, no less. They treated it as a joke and subjected him to public humiliation, and very nearly a whipping. He was so outraged he threw in his lot with the Resistance and brought the idea to us.'

'It's weird.'

'But clever,' Darrok said. 'One of those notions that seems so simple you wonder why nobody thought of it before. Phoenix here has been helping with some modifications.'

'Yes,' the wizard confirmed. 'It used to run on a store of magical energy carried on board. Now were getting it to run by drawing its motive force directly from the power grid.'

'I thought it was original enough to warrant the allocation of some resources,' Darrok explained.

'It's certainly original,' Caldason agreed, watching as the device bumped across its muddy field. 'But what are we going to use it for?'

Darrok shrugged. 'Damned if I know.'

13

Much of the easternmost region of Bhealfa consisted of meandering rivers and scrubland. For Prince Melyobar's court, travelling above ground, the terrain was irrelevant, but it presented many problems for the innumerable camp followers trailing the flying palaces. As a consequence, the court was forced to slow down.

While any diminution of pace was guaranteed to make the Prince nervous, for Devlor Bastorran and Lahon Meakin it came as a small relief.

They sat in the back of a carriage being driven at speed across the inhospitable landscape. The mud-splattered carriage bumped and rolled, throwing them about in their seats and rattling their bones.

'Damn the man!' Bastorran cursed.

'Sir?'

'Melyobar. I go through this wretched performance every time I'm obliged to meet him.'

'You've been granted an audience before, sir?'

'Several times, when I accompanied my uncle. It was always a farce.'

'But this time's different, isn't it, sir? Your first meeting with His Highness since you became High Chief.'

'And it's only happening now because I can't put it off any longer. If protocol didn't demand it, I wouldn't be here at all. You look shocked, Meakin. Find my attitude disloyal, do you?'

'Er, no, sir. That is . . . well, a little surprising perhaps.'

'I'm as devoted to the institution of monarchy as the next man. More so than the Prince, I'd venture. Be honest, you can't pretend you don't know the stories about him.'

'There are always rumours, sir, and admittedly most of them are odd.'

'Everything you've heard about Melyobar is true, and more. He isn't a patch on the old King, Narbetton. And be warned: you will not, of course, address the Prince of your own volition. Should he speak to you, be brief and circumspect in your answers. You smile, but this is a serious matter.'

'Sir.' Meakin's demeanour was instantly solemn.

'The man has some . . . let's say unusual notions. Showing disrespect for them, or gods forbid, questioning them, is more than an indiscretion; it's downright dangerous. So keep your mouth shut and follow my lead.'

'Yes, sir.'

They bumped over a particularly deep pothole. Bastorran swore vehemently under his breath. Meakin leaned to his window and gazed at the hovering palace. Its enormity was astonishing. It led an unruly procession of lesser, but still massive, floating structures that blotted out the sky.

'Ever seen it before?' Bastorran said.

'Once. When I was much younger, sir. With my mother and brother, and from a distance. But I've never forgotten it.'

His master gave an offhand grunt, uninterested, and muttered, 'You'll be seeing it much closer soon enough.'

If the airborne convoy inspired wonderment, what was happening below stirred a different kind of awe.

Their carriage bounced along in a torrent of humanity. As far as they could see on all sides a kind of insanity was on the hoof: an incalculable number of wagons, coaches, traps, gigs, landaus and carts thundered across the land. Like sea-going craft they traversed an ocean of uniformed and civilian mounted riders, and far to the rear of the wheeled conveyances and charging horses a multitude of people strained to keep up on foot. The scene was reminiscent of a free-for-all land-grab or gold rush. Except the aim was to keep pace with the spectacle passing overhead.

'Ah,' Bastorran said, 'here's our escort. Hold on. The ride's about to get even rougher.'

Meakin looked out at the chaos on his master's side, but could make no sense of it, let alone identify any kind of escort. Then a particular contrary movement caught his eye. A carriage not dissimilar to their own was edging towards them through the human deluge. As it weaved their way, Meakin could make out a royal crest on its side, and the palace guard uniform the driver wore.

'They're experts at negotiating this rabble,' Bastorran explained. 'I hope you're fit, Meakin.'

'I think so, sir.'

'You'll need to be. Ready yourself.'

The royal carriage drew alongside. Its driver and Bastorran's exchanged shouts that were impossible to hear above the din. Then the door of the carriage opened. Inside, another uniformed man beckoned. Bastorran opened his own door, letting in a blast of cold air.

'Come on,' he said. 'And don't linger if you value your neck.'

The paladin grasped the hand stretching from the other carriage and jumped.

Meakin eased himself across to the open door. He looked out, trying to ignore their speed and the bedlam all around. Bastorran was yelling at him from the second carriage and beckoning. A hand was extended. Meakin reached for it and leapt. A dizzying second later he was across and deposited on a seat by a grim faced Captain of the Guard.

'Well done,' Bastorran congratulated him coolly. 'But don't relax just yet. We still have the pleasure of getting on board the palace itself.'

They pulled away from the paladin carriage and soon lost sight of it in the galloping confusion. Their new carriage sliced into the crush, handled skilfully but totally without regard for the safety of others. Riders who got in the way were downed and trampled. Wagons swerving to avoid the carriage crashed into each other, shattering axels and shedding passengers. There were collisions and runaway horses.

'I must say this does have a certain exhilarating quality to it, eh, Meakin?' Bastorran enthused.

'Um, yes, sir.' He was trying to stop himself being hurled from his seat.

After what seemed an age they were in the shadow of the royal palace, its massive base sliding along above them at three or four times the height of their carriage.

'What now, sir?' Meakin asked.

'Not too many more indignities to go,' Bastorran replied caustically.

The officer who'd sat silently facing them went to open the door nearest the palace. The carriage began undertaking a series of complex manoeuvres. Within minutes they were beside a wooden platform suspended from the palace by a complex arrangement of stout ropes.

'Over we go,' Bastorran instructed.

They stepped onto the rocking platform, grabbing the handrail to steady themselves. Immediately the carriage moved away. The platform hung for a moment, swaying, then began to be hoisted up. Knuckles white on the rail, wind beating at his face, Meakin looked to the scene unfolding below, but even from his elevated position he couldn't see an end to the camp followers.

Perhaps a hundred feet up the edifice they arrived at a wide terrace. Here they were met by a contingent of guards, escorted to an ornate entrance and into the palace proper. They were then lightly searched; a humiliation Bastorran endured in scowling silence. After that they were shepherded through a maze of eccentrically decorated passageways and made to climb a seemingly endless succession of staircases.

Walking yet more lengthy corridors lined with grotesque statues, and hanging back from their escort, Bastorran whispered, 'What do you think? You can speak freely. But keep your voice down.'

'It . . . it's . . .'

'Insane?'

'I was going to say vast, sir.'

'That's part of the insanity.'

Going through a set of reinforced doors, they emerged onto broad battlements.

'And we're still only a quarter of the way,' Bastorran said, pointing up at the looming pile above them. 'You can see why I enquired after your fitness.'

'I can, sir.'

Making their way across the ramparts to another section of the palace, they passed a dozen full-sized catapults, standing in line.

'These are new,' the paladin commented.

'Their defences certainly seem comprehensive, sir.'

'Yes,' Bastorran replied thoughtfully. 'But why catapults? They're siege engines; hardly the most ideal of defensive weapons.'

'Perhaps it's another of His Highness's . . . eccentricities,' Meakin ventured in an undertone.

'Probably. I should know better than to be surprised at anything he does.'

They were led back inside the building, through more passages and up further flights of stairs. At last they were shown into an anteroom and left to wait.

Bastorran seated himself, and motioned for his aide to do the same.

Meakin cleared his throat. 'I wonder how –'

Bastorran nudged him in the ribs and indicated the ceiling. A brass coloured spy glamour hovered there.

'– how long it'll be before his gracious Highness consents to see us,' Meakin finished lamely.

'There's no way of knowing.'

They were settling into an awkward silence when a lackey entered and guided them into the Prince's reception suite.

It was a long, elegantly furnished room. At its far end, Melyobar occupied a throne mounted on a dais. He wore a red, ermine-lined cape, though the effect was somewhat diminished by a grubby shirt, dusty breeches and scuffed, mud-splattered boots.

Bastorran bowed. Meakin took his lead and bobbed low too. Raising a languid hand, the Prince waved them closer.

'Your Royal Highness,' Bastorran opened. 'Thank you for seeing me.'

The Prince managed a vacuous nod. His eyes flitted to the paladin's companion. 'Who?'

'My aide-de-camp, Highness. Lahon Meakin.'

'Lahon?' Melyobar repeated, a look of confusion on his face. 'Devlor, surely? And he's your aide now, High Chief?'

'Highness?'

'I thought your nephew was your heir,' the Prince

explained with some exasperation. 'Certainly something more than merely your aide.'

Realisation dawned on Bastorran. 'I fear we're at cross purposes, sire. My fault entirely. I am Devlor, Lord High Chief of the Paladins. You're thinking of my late uncle, Ivak.'

Melyobar blinked at them, like a myopic trying to focus. 'Late?'

'Sadly, sire, yes. My uncle passed on some months ago, the victim of a notorious radical. You were informed at the time, Majesty.'

The Prince sighed. 'Another triumph for him.'

'With all due respect, Your Highness, I hardly think the assassin's deed could be termed a triumph.'

'Assassin? I suppose he is, in a way. The great slayer is a kind of ultimate assassin. Yes, I like that.'

Bastorran and Meakin exchanged glances; the former one of vexation, the latter puzzlement.

'Apologies, sir,' Bastorran said, 'but I misconstrued your meaning. You're speaking of Death, naturally.'

'Of course I am. Who else? The grief over the loss of your uncle has obviously skewed your senses.'

'Yes,' the paladin replied as best he could between clenched teeth, 'that must be it.'

'What a pity your uncle couldn't have modelled himself on my own dear father,' Melyobar suggested, 'the only person in history, so far, to defy the Reaper's dominion. Truly a shining example to the rest of us.'

'Indeed, sire.'

'So, why are you here?' the Prince asked brightly.

The change of topic and mood almost stumped Bastorran. 'I'm here to be officially recognised as the new Clan leader, Majesty.'

'To receive my blessing.'

'Er, yes. In a way. It's a formality, of course, but –'

'And what kind of leader will you be?'

'What kind, Your Majesty?'

'As compared to your late uncle.'

'I would hope to emulate all his best qualities, Highness. Though in some respects I'm departing from his style of leadership.'

'How?'

'One of my Uncle Ivak's many virtues was that he had too much heart, Your Majesty.'

This came as a surprise to Meakin, but naturally he kept silent.

'Commendable as this quality was,' Bastorran went on, choosing his words carefully, 'it had the regrettable effect of encouraging Your Highness's enemies.'

'He was soft on the terrorists?'

'I'm not certain that was his intention, sire, but it's how his actions were perceived.'

'Whereas your policies will be firmer.'

'Considerably. I'd go so far as to say that under my leadership recent events might have taken a very different turn.'

'You would have prevented this exodus of rebels I've been told about?'

'I take it Your Royal Highness is referring to certain anti-social elements escaping justice by fleeing to the Diamond Isle. It was hardly an exodus.'

'But how would you have stopped it?'

'Simply by ensuring that there were no rebels to escape, Majesty. Unlike my uncle, and, if I may say so, certain other decision-makers in the security services, I would never have tolerated these traitors' existence in the first place.'

'It seems we share a similar view, High Chief.'

'I'm pleased to hear you approve, sire.'

'Oh, yes. If a fire rages, cut down the trees it feeds on.'

'Precisely, sir.'

'My father often says that the best way to catch a fish is by draining the sea.'

It struck Bastorran and Meakin that this was an odd analogy, quite apart from Melyobar's use of the present tense, but both dutifully nodded.

'I wonder how they dealt with him during the Dreamtime?' the Prince said.

'Your pardon, Majesty?' Bastorran replied.

'Death. Would he have walked the land in those days?'

They realised he was drifting again.

'I have no idea, Majesty,' the paladin ventured. 'Hasn't Death always been in the world?'

'He must have been, mustn't he? I mean, if he wasn't, the Founders would still be here, wouldn't they?'

'Yes, I suppose that's –'

'It's a sobering thought, isn't it? Even the mighty Founders, subject to his whim. It goes to show how worthy an opponent he is, doesn't it?'

'As you say, Highness.'

Something like clarity seemed to inform the Prince's features. 'Still, it's all irrelevant now, of course. Or about to be.'

'Sire?'

He gave them a smile that was almost impish. 'You'll see.'

14

It had been snowing hard in the northern wastes. Zerreiss's army was forced to halt, and even the warlord himself, usually a patient man, had grown restless. But as night fell on the third day, the snow finally died down.

In the warlord's tent, bathed by the soft glow of oil lamps and candles, Zerreiss stood by a hide map on an easel.

'Finally ending here,' he concluded, pointing to a spot on the chart.

'But what you're suggesting doesn't make up the time we've lost, sir,' commented Sephor, the younger of his two closest aides. 'In fact it adds a significant amount of time to the original plan.'

'I'm aware of that. But can it be done, logistically? Wellem?'

'It's not impossible, but it'll need a great effort and a lot of preparation. You're talking about taking the bulk of the army to sea for the first time, and the practicalities of that are complex.'

'But that was always our intention.'

'Yes, chief, but not this soon in the campaign. The number of ships we'll need –'

'That's why I propose taking port cities here, here and . . . here,' Zerreiss said, indicating sites on the map.

'Even if we captured every vessel in all three locations,' Sephor noted, 'which assumes the defenders wouldn't move or torch them, we still wouldn't have all the ships we need.'

'Then we'll build more. We have the manpower, and the skills.'

'Would we have the materials?' Wellem asked.

The warlord turned to his map again. 'There are forests here and here. Not too far to haul timber from, assuming the weather's kind to us.'

'You've heard this before, chief, but I'm worried we'll spread ourselves too thin. You're proposing three sieges to take place more or less simultaneously, and what could be a massive boat-building programme. That's in addition to the forces needed to guard the places we've already conquered.'

'But recruitment continues apace,' Zerreiss told him. 'There's always a net gain. Everywhere we go, they flock to us.'

'Faster than we can train or equip them.'

'The best training they can have is in the field. It's how I got mine. And remember that most of the men we're attracting to the cause are military anyway. They're not tyros.'

'Sir,' Sephor ventured awkwardly, 'you've told us what you want to do, but you haven't said why.'

A second passed before Zerreiss answered. 'I had another dream,' he explained. 'I was standing on the terrace of a fortress. The very fortress we conquered not a week since. In my dream I stood there, as I did on the day we took it, surveying our victory. And I saw him again.'

'The same man you've dreamt of before?'

'Yes. If they can be called dreams.'

'What happened?'

'Happened? Nothing. Well, nothing and everything. You look at me strangely, my friends, but that's the only way I can express it.'

'Do you have any idea yet who this man is?' Wellem asked.

'I'm no nearer knowing that than when he first invaded my sleep.'

'And you're still sure he's a real person? Not . . . forgive me, sir, but not your mind's fabrication?'

'I've no doubt he's real.'

'Then maybe you should consider yourself the subject of a magical attack,' the old campaigner stated matter-of-factly.

'I don't think you need worry yourself on that score. Whoever this man might be, I don't think he's a sorcerer. Though I sense there is a connection to magic in some way.'

'Isn't that a contradiction, sir?'

'Am I not a contradiction myself, Wellem? Why should this man be any less of an enigma?'

'But what has he to do with your new instructions, sir?' his younger aide wanted to know.

Zerreiss smiled. 'Trust you to bring me back to earth, Sephor. No, don't be embarrassed; I need pulling to the point sometimes. Simply put, he's the reason for my fresh orders.'

'You'd change your plans, the whole direction of the campaign, because of somebody you've dreamed about, sir?'

'Not so much change as accelerate.'

'But why, sir?'

'I sense he's nearer, physically, than he was. Don't ask me how I know. Or why I, of all people, should start to believe in unexplained intuition. I only know that if there's a chance of being in this man's presence, I should take it.'

'What do you think you might gain from that?'

'Have I ever steered you down a wrong path?'

'No, sir,' they answered in unison.

'Then trust me now, as you have in the past.'

'It's not that,' Sephor assured him. 'We just want to under-stand.'

'So do I. That's what I've been trying to say.' He sighed. 'The best way I can put it is that he has a . . . significance.

And I can't help feeling it might tie in with a particular thought I've long been haunted by.'

'Sir?'

'Could there be another like me?'

It was obvious the notion had never occurred to his aides. Sephor recovered first. 'We've always thought of you as unique, sir.'

'I have, too. Or rather, I feared it. My whole life I've wondered if I was alone in possessing the talent. And if I am, why? Why me? I hoped there were others, but as the years passed that hope withered. But suppose I'm not exceptional. Can you see what that would mean?'

'Allies?' Wellem offered.

'More than that. I didn't choose the gift I carry, and sometimes the burden of it seems hard to bear. How much easier it would be if there were others to share the effort.'

'I've never doubted your abilities, sir.'

'I know. But it feels a bit different from my side.'

'You have us,' Sephor assured him, 'and not just us; there are thousands now who believe in you and want to support you.'

The warlord laid a hand on the young man's shoulder. 'And I'm more grateful for that than I can say. But there's something even you can't give me. For all your loyalty and trust, you can't empathise. Not truly. You can't know what it's like to be alone the way I am. If you could, you'd understand why I have to find him.'

In Bhealfa, too, there was a temporary respite from snowfall.

Not that weather conditions affected the number of people thronging the streets of Valdarr, or the attendant magical surges. But it certainly made the citizens' daily lives more miserable as they traipsed through slush and skidded on icy sidewalks, and it snarled up traffic.

Andar Talgorian's carriage, travelling to paladin head-quarters, took nearly an hour to make a journey that should have lasted minutes. Unsurprisingly, he arrived in a dejected mood.

Nodding the diplomat to a chair, Bastorran asked, 'So, how was Merakasa?'

Mindful that Commissioner Laffon was present, and aware he currently enjoyed favour with the Empress, Talgorian replied cautiously. 'It was a pleasure to meet with Her Royal Highness, as always. But I must confess I find the prospect of the imminent military action somewhat depressing.'

'Nonsense,' Bastorran snorted. 'It's exactly the right response to the situation on the Diamond Isle. I only regret it hasn't happened sooner.'

'War should always be the last resort.'

'We've reached the last resort.' He handed Talgorian a goblet of wine. 'What would you have done, talk them to death?'

'If you mean do I think there's still time to reach a nego-tiated outcome, the answer's yes.'

'My late uncle often said that you were a peacemonger. He meant it kindly, I'm sure.'

'I prefer to see myself as pragmatic,' Talgorian countered. 'And it seems to me that talk has to be a better option than spilling blood.'

They exchanged frosty smiles.

'I agree with the High Chief,' Laffon chipped in. 'If you negotiate with these people you only give them credence.'

'Surely they already have credence in the eyes of our su-periors. If they didn't, why send a costly expeditionary force against them?'

'Because force is what they understand. It just proves my point.'

'The Commissioner's right,' Bastorran said. 'And we should

be as ruthless with them at home as I trust we're going to be overseas.'

'Is it possible to be more brutal than we already are?' Talgorian wondered.

It was Laffon's turn to adopt a feigned smile. 'If I didn't know better, Ambassador, I'd think you were sympathetic to these malcontents.'

'No one is more opposed to public disorder than me, Commissioner. I merely query the methods we're using to deal with it.'

'Whatever our view of the coming conflict,' Bastorran said, raising his glass, 'I'm sure we can all agree to toast the mission's success.'

Eyeing each other, they drank.

Talgorian was the first to lower his glass. 'I hope it goes without saying that the Diplomatic Corps stands ready to offer whatever help it can to both your organisations in this expedition.'

Bastorran gave a hollow laugh. 'Forgive me. But there's hardly much use for the service of diplomats once hostilities begin.'

'Then perhaps you can help me.'

'What do you mean?' Laffon said.

Talgorian finished his wine and waved away a refill when Bastorran offered him the carafe. 'Tell me, have either of you seen Prince Melyobar recently?'

'As it happens, I have,' Bastorran replied.

'How did you find him?'

'I don't think it would surprise any of us if I said . . . problematic.'

'As unpredictable as usual, in other words.'

'Yes. But Melyobar's state of mind is hardly news. Why do you ask?'

'Her Royal Highness has decided that the time has come to take steps as far as the Prince is concerned.'

'Steps?' Laffon echoed.

Talgorian produced two folded parchments bearing the Empress's personal seal. 'These should explain everything.' He handed one to each of them. As they tore them open he added, 'You'll see that Her Majesty requires the paladins and the Council for Internal Security to cooperate fully.'

Bastorran read quickly, then looked up. 'You're in charge of this operation?'

Talgorian nodded.

'Why you?' Laffon wanted to know.

'It's not for me to question the Empress's decisions. But perhaps she thought the CIS and the paladins would have enough on their plates. And strictly speaking it is a diplomatic matter; after all, Melyobar is constitutionally Bhealfa's sovereign.'

'Naturally I bow to Her Majesty's wisdom on the matter. In fact, I expect to be summoned to an audience with her myself quite soon. No doubt she'll expand on her wishes then.'

'In the meantime you have what you need in that letter.'

'I'm pleased the Prince is finally going to be dealt with,' Bastorran declared. 'Something should have been done about the man long since. When are you going to tackle him, Ambassador?'

'I'm not sure yet. It's obviously a delicate situation and needs to be handled discreetly.'

'I wouldn't leave it too long if I were you. The last time I was at the palace I saw something rather curious.'

'Oh? Stranger than usual, you mean?'

'Point taken. I don't know if it fell into the category of abnormal or not, seeing as we're talking about Melyobar. But he's installed a battery of siege catapults, and it looked as though the fortifications had been beefed up even further. I can't help wondering why.'

'As you say, curious. But I don't intend storming the place. I'm thinking of a more tactful approach than that.'

'What are you going to do, reason with him?' Bastorran came back acerbically.

'Essentially, yes. But I'm not so naive as to think he'll appreciate Her Majesty's proposal. Which is why I'll need a robust escort to accompany me. And I think it should consist of personnel from different services, given the sensitive political nature of the operation. We'll need to liaise on this.'

'It'll have to be large if he decides to be uncooperative.'

'I don't think it'll come to that. It's not as though the empire intends making a prisoner of him; he'll be treated as an honoured guest.'

'You might have a job persuading him of that. Don't underestimate his liking for power. After all, no one's ever tried restraining him before.'

Any response Talgorian might have made was pre-empted by a rap on the door.

'Come!' Bastorran snapped.

Lahon Meakin stuck his head into the room.

The paladin glared at him. 'I told you we weren't to be disturbed!'

'I'm sorry, sir, but something's come up.'

Bastorran rose, mumbling apologies, and joined his aide in the corridor.

'This had better be important, Meakin,' he hissed.

'We've news of a disturbance on the streets.'

'Is that all? You should know better than to bother me about such a –'

'This is something different, sir, and I think you'll want to attend to it personally.'

15

Somebody was running along the street, smashing windows with a chain.

A roadblock of wagons sealed one end of the road, manned by dour-faced militia. At a distance, an angry mob faced them. Every so often, people ran forward to lob stones. Houses and a shop burned and no one was trying to put them out. Behind the barricade, mounted troopers were arriving.

Sheltering in the mouth of a nearby alley, Quinn Disgleirio and a pair of Righteous Blade members watched the confrontation.

'What started it?' Disgleirio said.

'There was a raid on a local house,' one of his companions explained. 'The militia were heavy-handed, as usual, and this crowd gathered.'

'It doesn't take much to set off a riot these days,' the other added.

'Well, we don't need it,' Disgleirio told him. 'There's enough oppression on the streets without inviting more.'

'Can't see us stopping it now,' the first Bladesman reckoned.

'No. But we can try to limit the damage.'

There was uproar at the roadblock as uniformed riders

moved through the crowd, laying about them with clubs and sabres.

'Looks like we're too late,' the second Bladesman said.

The fight quickly turned into a rout. People scattered, pursued by baton-wielding militia, and the first of the runners were approaching the alley where Disgleirio and his men sheltered.

'Chief?' one of his companions queried.

'Protect as many as you can.'

They stepped into the slush-covered street, drawing their swords.

The stream of fleeing protestors was turning into a flood. Some were cut down by the cavalry chasing them; others fell, to be trampled by the charging horses.

Disgleirio and his men fanned out, three rocks in the current of panicked humanity.

'Stand firm,' he instructed, 'and watch your backs.'

A screaming woman dashed past, two militia on her tail with blades in their hands, but they lost interest in her when they saw the trio of Bladesmen. Disgleirio left his comrades to deal with the troopers. His attention was on a cavalryman sweeping along the street, lashing out at fleeing citizens.

The Bladesmen and the militia engaged. Those trying to escape gave them a wide berth as two frantic duels spilled from the pavement into the road.

Disgleirio concentrated on the trooper's galloping horse. As it drew level he slashed at the rider, hewing the man's leg. The rider cried out and tumbled from his saddle, hitting the ground heavily and bouncing several times on the cobbled surface before coming to rest. His horse bolted into the jostling crowd.

But Disgleirio had no time to enjoy his luck. Another group of militia was sprinting his way. He turned back to his men just as one downed his opponent; the other had already triumphed and stood over his prone adversary.

'More!' Disgleirio yelled, jabbing a thumb over his shoulder. 'Cluster!'

At his command they swiftly came together in a well practised manoeuvre. They formed a circle, shoulders touching; sword in one hand, dagger in the other. A formation some called the Porcupine. When the fresh group of law-enforcers arrived, hotfoot, they faced a defensive ring bristling with steel barbs, but as they outnumbered the Bladesmen two to one or more, they thought to overwhelm them.

One of the militia fell immediately, lung punctured. Another reeled away bearing the yawning gash of a knife stroke. A third toppled with his chest perforated.

Odds thinned, the Bladesmen abandoned their huddle and set to in a general melee. A quick and bloody round of swordplay ensued, the participants huffing steam in the chill air. In short order, two more foes suffered lethal strikes. The remaining pair of militia, lightly wounded, took to their heels.

The Bladesmen caught their breath, sweat freezing on their brows.

'They'll be back with reinforcements,' Disgleirio panted. 'We can't do much more here. I think it's time to –'

'What is it, chief?'

'Who is that?'

They followed his gaze.

A slim, lithe individual with cropped fair hair had appeared on the street. He or she – it was impossible to tell which – was armed, and attacking people seemingly at random, whether they had weapons or not.

'Is it a glamour?' one of Disgleirio's men asked.

'I don't know what it is. But I'm going to find out. You two get yourselves clear.'

'But, chief –'

'We're taking a risk just being here. Now do as you're told!' He began jogging towards the apparition.

As he approached he got a clearer look at the figure, and decided that on balance it was female. He also saw that she had a somewhat alarming countenance, with unusually large, intense eyes set in a face so pale he thought she might be ailing. But there was nothing feeble about the way she lashed out at anybody within reach.

When he was just short of a sword's span from the woman, Disgleirio stopped. He took in the litter of corpses and groaning wounded.

'Yes?' Aphri Kordenza said. Her tone was casually irritated, as though addressing a bothersome vagrant.

'Who are you?'

'A concerned citizen. What of it?'

'Are you with the militia?'

'Do I look like I am?'

'Then why are you doing their dirty work?'

'Because it pleases me.'

'Murdering innocent people gives you pleasure?'

'You talk like a priest. If you don't like it, try stopping me.'

'That was my intention.'

'Then why didn't you say so in the first place? I can't abide idle chatter.'

She moved so fast it was all he could do to fend off her first blow. The second and third came as swiftly. And she had strength as well as speed; her strikes jarred Disgleirio to the bone. Driven back, he was forced on the defensive, parrying her blade but unable to attack. Her skill and agility shook him. He was a master swordsman, but she was easily his match.

Pulling himself together, he began to rally. He even got in some offensive strokes. But the more he picked up, the greater the woman's onslaught. Her passes were increasingly vicious, and landed with ever more accuracy. Disgleirio deflected them, and paid her back in kind, though it took all his expertise. He was holding his own but making no headway.

As they fought, he noticed another strange thing about the woman. Whenever she lifted her left foot there was a glimmer of light beneath her heel. At first he thought he'd imagined it, but then she had to leap to avoid one of his swings, and he saw an arc of tiny blue sparks flowing between the ground and her foot. It made him think she was magically vitalised in some way, but he was too preoccupied to dwell on it.

They continued battering and weaving, narrowly avoiding shrieking passers-by and riderless horses. The woman's movements were so fluid it was hard for him to connect with her blade, never mind land an effective blow. He felt leaden-footed by comparison, and feared he was about to take a lethal hit.

Suddenly he wasn't alone. His companion Bladesmen appeared and ploughed into the fray. The woman was unfazed. If the look on her disquieting face was anything to go by, she actually relished the challenge. She widened her attack to engage the newcomers, her blade playing against theirs fast and firm. The rattle of steel was unabated as they dodged and twisted, seeking an opening. Then she cleaved flesh.

One of the Bladesmen staggered, a hand to his chest, blood pumping through splayed fingers. He went down, beyond help.

Disgleirio cried out. His remaining companion powered into the woman. Unblinking, she glanced away his blade and laid open his arm, wrist to elbow. He howled and withdrew.

'I told you to get out of here!' Disgleirio roared, shoving him aside.

The wounded man lurched clear, clutching his gushing arm. Disgleirio swung back, ready to resume the fight.

The woman had gone. He scanned the street, trying to distinguish her slender form in the milling chaos. Then he caught sight of her. She was standing in the wide entranceway to an abandoned building on the opposite side of the road. He began elbowing his way towards her. But with a dozen paces to go, he froze.

In the doorway, a bizarre scene unfolded. The woman stepped smartly to one side, leaving an impression of her shape etched in the air. Rapidly, the outline filled. Bones, viscera, organs, arteries and veins appeared, then a casing of flesh. The blank face of her double took on features, which as they clarified strongly resembled the woman herself, though on closer inspection they displayed a more masculine set. Finally, clothes formed, identical to the garb the woman wore. The resultant being could have passed for her twin brother.

The doorway where the pair stood was gloomy, so it took Disgleirio a few seconds to notice something else. Some kind of fine web connected the twins. It was moist and gelatinous, and Disgleirio couldn't shake the thought that it was a monstrous afterbirth. As he watched, it split and was instantly absorbed into the woman's body.

He had never seen a meld before, but knew he must be looking at one now.

The twins exchanged affectionate smiles, and in unison walked out into the street. Curiously, both of them seemed to have a slight limp.

There were less people about, the bulk of the mob and their pursuers having moved on. But there were still enough to make Disgleirio worry for their safety.

His fears were justified.

The twins were staring at him. She made a comment Disgleirio couldn't hear, and they laughed. Then she started to march his way. At the same time, something remarkable happened.

At first, her twin didn't move. Then slowly, with all the ease and lightness of a child's kite, he rose from the ground. When he reached the first storey of the building, he levelled, stretching his arms and legs out straight. The next second he was slicing through the air.

Quinn ducked. The glamour-twin swooped over him, just clearing his head. But the attack he expected didn't come. Instead, the man swerved and flew down the street. He made for a knot of protestors nursing their wounds, diving at them. When they saw him coming, those who were able tried to scramble out of the way. The glamour-twin puffed his cheeks and spat a gout of flame which enveloped many of the crowd. The stragglers ignited, turning into fireballs, blundering and screaming. Their tormentor turned and made for another bunch of people further along who, seeing what had happened, were trying to outrun him.

Disgleirio watched in horror, to the extent that he momentarily forgot the woman. Then a movement caught his eye. She was almost upon him, charging, sending her sword in a great swipe that he had to jump aside to avoid. Their blades collided and the duel restarted.

Meanwhile, the glamour-twin soared over cowering bands of citizens, raining fire down on them. A buggy ploughed through the scene, the driver desperate to escape. The twin disgorged a spume of flame at it, and carriage and driver went up like tinder. The spooked horse, towing a blazing funeral pyre, surged in panic. With a grinding crash the buggy overturned, spilling its grisly load. The horse galloped on, dragging the burning remains and scattering onlookers.

Somebody loosed an arrow at the airborne man from an open window. His fiery breath charred the bolt before it hit. Veering, he headed back. Another arrow skimmed his way, but it was sufficiently off target for him to ignore. He turned his wrath on the archer, huffing flame through the open window and converting him to cinder. The room blazed, venting oily black smoke.

Disgleirio was only dimly aware of the slaughter. He was embroiled in a swordfight he was beginning to think he couldn't win. The woman's stamina never seemed to flag, confirming his instinct that she was replenishing her vigour magically.

They fought on, each seeking a chink in the other's guard. Had either of them been a lesser talent the game would have been over long since. As it was, Disgleirio feared her staying power would be the decisive factor.

But as they fenced, he formed an impression. He could have been deceiving himself, but he got the feeling she wasn't finding him as easy a mark as she thought. Self-deception or not, it gave him heart. His pace went up a notch. He dared to hope.

In the event, his determination wasn't put to the ultimate test. He became aware of a vibration underfoot. It soon translated to the sound of thundering hooves. A large body of riders was approaching. His opponent heard it, too, and as though obeying some silent signal, they disengaged and backed away from each other.

Other sounds began to overlay the hoof-beats. Shouting, screams, the pounding of boots on cobbles. Disgleirio and the woman turned towards the source. Several hundred people were running their way, chased by a contingent of cavalry wearing the distinctive scarlet tunics of the paladin clans.

A handful of lead runners darted past Quinn and his adversary. More and more followed, until they were engulfed by a torrent of terrified people. Disgleirio lost sight of the woman, and after a moment resisting the tide he joined the stampede. All was chaos. He was carried along in a sea of frightened faces and bellowing voices. His shins were kicked and his ribs elbowed. He was jostled and shoved.

Somebody grabbed his arm and held on tight. He struggled violently, then saw it was the wounded Bladesman he'd ordered away. Following his lead, half dragged, he fought his way across the pugnacious flow of humanity. They eventually broke out onto a less densely packed stretch of pavement. The Bladesman hauled Disgleirio across it and into a gap between two decrepit shanties.

'Thanks,' he panted.

'I know you told me to leave, chief, but –'

'Forget it. It's a good thing you didn't.' He glanced at the bloodstained, makeshift cloth binding the man's arm. 'How is it?'

'I'll live. What the hell was that flying thing, chief? And the woman?'

'I think we ran into a meld.'

'I thought they were a myth.'

'Apparently not.' Disgleirio looked out at the passing crowd and the paladins harassing them. 'We can't do anything here. Best to get away.'

His companion nodded. 'Er, what's that, chief?'

'What?'

'Your tunic.' He pointed.

A scrap of paper was half stuffed in Disgleirio's pocket. He took it out and unfolded it. There was writing on it, in block capitals. They read: INVASION OF DIAMOND ISLE IMMINENT. EXPECT MORE RAIDS ON RESISTANCE HERE.

'What is it?' the Bladesman asked.

'See for yourself.' Disgleirio showed him the note.

'Where did it come from?'

'I don't know. It must have been . . . somebody in the crowd.' He scanned the street again, puzzled.

Two blocks away, sheltering in the entranceway to a stable, Aphri and Aphrim were locked in a lingering kiss.

'We can't loiter here, my love,' she whispered, gazing deep into his barren eyes.

He nodded. There was something in that simple gesture which could have been interpreted as sadness.

'Soon,' she promised.

He shrunk in her embrace, not in stature, but mass. His body joined with hers. She drank him.

Aphri stretched, and belched.

Someone tapped her on the shoulder. She spun around, drawing her sword.

'What the hell do you think you're up to?' Devlor Bastorran demanded.

She relaxed and let the sword slip back into its scabbard. 'Just keeping my hand in.'

'Fool. Do you have any idea the risk you're running brawling in public like this? Not to mention forcing me to be seen with you.'

'You worry too much. We were only disposing of a few malcontents. You should be grateful.'

'Grateful be damned. We're perfectly capable of dealing with this rabble without your help. I want you out of here.'

'All right, all right. I'm going.'

'Oh, no, I'm not taking your word for it. You're leaving under escort. I'll have my aide go with you.' He looked around. 'Where the devil is the man? *Where's Meakin?*' he yelled at two lieutenants twenty paces distant. They shrugged and shook their heads. 'Well, find him!' he bellowed. The pair scurried off.

'It's wonderful,' Aphri told him.

'What is?'

'The new state I'm in. The connection with the grid. I've never felt so powerful.'

'I know,' Bastorran said. 'But do me a favour, Kordenza. Save it for Caldason.'

16

Sluggish winter tides lapped the Diamond Isle's shoreline. The sky was overcast and the air raw.

There was activity everywhere. Lookouts haunted cliff tops, guards patrolled the seashore, civilians were coached in spear and sword. Fortifications and defensive lines were being erected throughout the island.

Several score men and women toiled on a beach in the shadow of the terraced fortress, some working with long-handled spades while others knelt, busying themselves with trowels. Carpenters hefted stacks of narrow timber planks. Braziers, cauldrons and anvils were scattered about the place.

Two well wrapped figures watched from a nearby promontory.

'What are they doing?' Kutch said.

'Being inventive,' Caldason replied. 'That's something human beings are pretty good at when their backs are to the wall.' He pointed at the people digging. 'They're using the sand to make moulds for arrow heads, spear tips, even some sword blades. The metal's heated in the kilns over on that side, and they use the wooden blocks to carry the cauldrons. It's crude, but effective.'

'Don't we have enough weapons already?'

'We can't have too many in a situation like this. And some you can't easily retrieve once you've used them, like arrows. You have to assume they're single use. So we've set a target of turning out twenty thousand arrow heads.'

Kutch whistled. 'That's a lot.'

'It's nowhere near enough. Think about it. Say two hundred archers use fifty arrows each and that's half of them gone. We could get through that many in one engagement.'

'It doesn't sound much when you put it that way.'

'It's the same with the number of people we have to defend this place. But don't get me started on that.' Caldason turned away from the scene. 'If we get a move on we can make supper at the redoubt. What do you say?'

'I'm starving.'

'Good. Let's go.'

They had use of a small, two-wheeled farm cart, with a mare to pull it. As most of the island's roads were ill-kept, many of them little more than trails, the going was bumpy.

Five minutes into their journey they saw a work gang felling a small wood close to the road.

'We seem to be cutting down an awful lot of trees,' Kutch said.

'All those arrow heads need shafts,' Caldason reminded him, 'and we have to have bows and spear shanks. Not to mention fuel.'

'What if we run out of wood?'

'Whether it lasts depends on how long we're holed up here. Actually, timber's abundant. I'm more worried about victuals. Water's all right; we have wells. But food could be a problem. Darrok built up a store of dried goods, but there's not a lot in the way of fresh produce, particularly in winter. There's fish, of course, though the waters are getting too dangerous for that.'

'You still think there'll be an invasion?'

'Nothing's made me think otherwise.'

'Can we hold out?'

'Truthfully?'

'I always expect you to tell me the truth, Reeth.'

'Of course. Then . . . probably not.'

'Oh.'

'But that's on paper, so to speak. As I said, people can be inventive when they're up against it. They can be incredibly brave, too. And all sorts of things could turn the tide in our favour.'

'Like finding the Source?'

'You know I've got hopes pinned on that for myself, but we shouldn't rely on it to save us. We don't really know what it is, and I might not find it.'

'You've always been one for going against the odds, Reeth.'

Caldason smiled. 'Maybe. But I try to be prepared when I do it. Talking of which, I wish you'd let me teach you some sword craft.'

'I'm not sure I'm really cut out for that.'

'Anybody can pick up a few pointers, and you're young and reasonably fit. I'd feel better if you had some basic self-defence skills, given what's coming.'

'Well, perhaps you could teach me a few essentials. But I think magic serves me better.'

'Force of arms is more likely to be the deciding factor in defending the island. Magic might not be much use.'

'They'll be using it against us, won't they? We have to have a way of countering that. You've such a strange attitude to the Craft, Reeth. On the one hand you hate magic, and on the other you look to it for salvation.'

'Only because I've no choice. But we're not talking about me, we're talking about what's happening here. I've been in a lot of conflicts, and most of them have been settled with blades, not magic.'

'Magic shapes our world, Reeth. It can do stupendous things. That was something I first saw when I wasn't much more than a baby.'

'What did you see?'

'Melyobar's flying palace. I was with my mother, I think. I can't remember. But I've never forgotten the palace. It must have been . . . I don't know; a long way off, and the sun was setting behind it, brilliantly red. It was fabulous.'

'I can imagine that would leave a mark on a child.'

'So much so that when Master Domex came to take me away I wasn't so unhappy about it. I mean, I hated leaving my mother and everything, but I thought we'd be making palaces fly.' He grinned. 'It wasn't quite like that, of course.'

'I remember a time before the palace was built. Actually saw it under construction if I recall.'

'I keep forgetting how old you are, Reeth. It must be weird having memories going back that far.'

'You might have far-reaching memories yourself one day,' the Qalochian replied dryly, 'if you're lucky enough to live to an old age. But if your best example of what magic can do is a madman's folly —'

'It isn't. I'm just saying it can do astonishing things.'

'Like subjugating the population? Stupefying them with illusions? Corrupting their values?'

'That's not magic's fault. It's the people who use it. In the same way you'd use the Source for good if you found it.'

'And how are you going to change human nature?'

'I think people can be good if they're given the chance.'

'There are always the bad, Kutch, no matter what you do.'

They were arriving at the redoubt. The renovation and fortifying work on the stronghold was almost finished, though scores of people still laboured there.

Caldason drew the cart to a halt. As they climbed down, he added, 'The truth is I prefer the honesty of blades. Magic's too damned complex, apart from anything else.'

'Not once you're attuned to it,' Kutch told him. He looked around and spotted a small pile of logs. 'See.' His hands performed an esoteric gesture. He gazed intently.

One of the logs shuddered slightly. A corner lifted. Then the log rose from the heap and hung in the air. Kutch moved his outstretched finger. The log aped it, swaying from side to side as though floating on agitated water. A second later it dropped back onto the pile with a dull thud.

From the look on Kutch's face it had been a physical effort. He turned to Caldason and beamed.

'Impressive. But it's hardly going to stop an invasion fleet, is it?'

Caldason headed for the fortress's cavernous entrance. Kutch followed, seething.

A wide central corridor bisected the building's ground floor. The door they were making for, near its far end, led to a dining hall. Before they reached it, they heard raised voices close to hand. Familiar voices, coming from a room they were about to pass. Reeth and Kutch exchanged a look. Caldason opened the door.

'. . . and I say there's no justification for it!' Serrah raged. She saw them come in and stopped.

Darrok was there, his disc perched on a bench. Pallidea stood beside him.

'Reeth,' Serrah said. 'Good. You'll back me on this.'

'Back you on what?'

'That.' She nodded at a large open chest sitting on a table.

He walked over to it, Kutch in tow. The chest was crammed with fist-sized cloth pouches. One had been slit. Inside was a quantity of tiny, almost translucent, bluish-white crystals.

Kutch was puzzled. 'What is it?'

'Ramp,' Caldason said.

'Yes, fucking ramp,' Serrah confirmed, near incoherent with anger. 'It's Zahgadiah's.' She glared at him.

'What's going on, Darrok?' Caldason said.

'Nothing anybody need get worked up about.'

'Really?' Serrah hissed dangerously. 'How do you figure that?'

'I'm not denying it's mine. Or the island's, strictly speaking.'

'I knew you'd been a rogue in your time, but I thought even you'd draw the line at dealing in this shit.'

Darrok held up a hand. 'Hear me out,' he grated. 'I don't like it any more than you do. But the fact is I inherited it. Well, more accurately it came as one of the assets when I bought the island.'

'Assets? This stuff killed my daughter!'

'I know, Serrah, and I'm sorry about that. But you have to understand the nature of the Diamond Isle. People paid fortunes to come here. Or they used to, in its heyday. In exchange they expected to indulge in whatever experience took their fancy. Ramp was one of the things they wanted. But I never offered it. They had to ask.'

'But it's illegal.'

'Not here. Ordinary laws never applied to this place because we've always been outside any state's jurisdiction. The only rules were the ones we imposed ourselves. Actually, I guess that's why some guests wanted ramp. You know, the allure of something they couldn't safely get at home. For most it was plain curiosity.'

'That's how it started with Eithne.'

'She was a child, Serrah,' Darrok replied gently. 'I'm talking about adults. People mature enough to make their own decisions.'

'It's a fine distinction. And it's not one my old employers back in Gath Tampoor made. For all their many faults, they had no tolerance for ramp traffickers. Fighting those people was part of my job, remember.'

'Do you know where ramp came from?'

'Came from? What do you mean?'

'It's not a natural substance, you must know that. It consists of a number of natural ingredients, but it has to be processed. Manufactured. Who do you think first did that? Do any of you know? Reeth?'

'No idea.'

'Nor me,' Kutch added gravely.

'Criminal gangs,' Serrah said. 'The same people who make the stuff.'

'I was part of a criminal gang,' Darrok reminded her. 'Not that we had much to do with narcotics, despite being pirates. But I know ramp didn't come from the criminal underworld.'

'Where, then?' Caldason asked.

'One of the empires.'

'What?' Serrah exclaimed.

'Some say Gath Tampoor, others blame Rintarah. Perhaps it was something they both came up with independently. I don't suppose we'll ever know.'

'I don't understand,' Kutch admitted. 'Why would anybody invent such a horrible thing?'

'As a weapon. A covert munition in the war between the empires. It was designed to disrupt the enemy's population and weaken morale; to encourage criminality and corrupt institutions. Not to mention diverting resources to deal with it.'

'But that's wicked,' Serrah said.

'Since when was morality a strong point for either empire? In its twisted way, it was a brilliant idea. Nobody could deny the damage it's caused. But it was stupid, too. For all their cunning, the empires didn't foresee it getting out of control. They didn't anticipate it seeping into the lives of those who served them. Or affecting their own children, come to that. That young man whose death you were accused of, Serrah. What was his name?'

'Chand Phosian,' she whispered. 'The Principal-Elect's son.'

'Phosian, yes. He was killed by ramp, indirectly.'

'And through that my eyes were opened and I came to the Resistance.'

'Ironic, isn't it?'

'If what you say is true, they killed Eithne as well, as surely as if they plunged a blade into her heart.'

Darrok nodded. 'If you needed further proof of the evil the empires do, there you have it. It doesn't matter if it was Rintarah or Gath Tampoor.'

'How do you know all this?' Caldason wondered.

'When you live outside the law you occupy another world. You get to see and hear things ordinary folk don't. I was told the story about ramp many times, by people whose word I relied on. I even spoke to old hands who claimed that in the early days, when ramp was first appearing, they were offered it as contraband by government agents. I'd no reason to disbelieve them.'

'She didn't stand a chance,' Serrah murmured, eyes misting. 'It's so damn addictive.' Caldason slipped an arm around her shoulder.

'There might be a reason for that, beyond its narcotic properties,' Darrok offered. 'It could be just a myth, but it was rumoured that some kind of spell was built into its formula, to make users crave it more.'

Caldason glanced at Kutch. The boy looked away, reddening.

'When I found this,' Serrah said, indicating the chest, 'it all came back. Eithne. Everything. What I'm hearing now isn't making me feel any better. You've got to destroy it, Zahgadiah.'

'I can't do that, Serrah.'

'Why not?'

'Because we might need to use it as a kind of weapon ourselves.'

'What the hell does that mean?'

'You know what ramp does to someone taking it. Increased strength, stamina, aggression. It turns people into fearless . . . beasts. For a while, anyway. I heard some Resistance members in Bhealfa took it during the cull, out of desperation. If it comes to the last resort here, I think it should be available for those who want it.'

'If I'm going to go down fighting I'd rather do it without that muck in my head.'

'So would I. But I can't deny it to anybody who feels differently. And in some circumstances it just might turn the tide.'

'So what are you going to do, dole it out to everybody?'

'No. It's a last-ditch thing. It'll be there if things get hopeless. Along with a stock of poison I keep, for any who prefer that.'

'You paint a very charming picture of our prospects.'

'I'm just trying to be realistic about what might happen.'

'It stinks, Zahgadiah, and I don't like it one bit.'

'This isn't the time to argue amongst ourselves,' Pallidea suggested.

'You don't say much,' Caldason told her, 'but it usually makes sense.'

'Hear, hear,' Darrok added. 'I'm sorry you feel the way you do, Serrah, and I understand why. But this is something the Council's agreed on, too. So let's drop it, shall we?'

'Do you agree with this, Reeth?'

'Whatever you or I think doesn't make much difference, Serrah. It's been decided.'

'Is that all you've got to say about it?'

'We're not in a normal situation. Everybody on this island

could be heading for death. Who are we to dictate how they face it?'

She sighed. 'Well, at least get the damned stuff out of my sight.'

'I'll have it moved,' Darrok promised. 'It'll be hidden. And hopefully it'll never be needed.'

'I think we have something more positive to discuss, don't we, Zahgadiah?' Pallidea said.

'We do. Reeth and I have worked up a plan for rescuing your friend Kinsel.'

'How are you going to do it?' Kutch asked.

'Good question. Let's discuss it while we eat, shall we?'

17

'So you think it was the same meld Reeth and Serrah encountered?' Karr said.

'How many can there be?' Disgleirio replied. 'But it shook me, I can tell you that. I've never faced such strength in an opponent, or skill. And she took the life of one of our best men, which is something I'll not forget in a hurry.'

'She was aiding the militia?'

'Well, in the sense that she was attacking civilians. But I don't think she was working with the authorities. More like a freelance.'

'But not some kind of maverick, apparently. At least, Reeth didn't think so. He suspected a connection with the paladins.'

'Whoever she's aligned with she did a lot of damage out there today.'

Goyter stuck her head round the door, a familiar, determined look on her face. 'Come on, you two, eat. I won't tell you again.'

Karr smiled wryly. 'I think we'd better do as she says. The wrath of a meld's as nothing compared to hers.'

Disgleirio had to grin. He knew it was at least half true.

They filed out of Karr's tiny makeshift study. The ex-Patrician walked stiffly, but try as he might to hide the pain, he couldn't disguise his eyes. Disgleirio pushed from his mind the thought that their leader, his friend, had death written on him.

A spacious side chamber in the catacombs had been given over to a dining area. Half a dozen long, sturdy benches almost filled it. But most people had eaten by this hour, and only a handful lingered over their meals. Karr and Disgleirio chose seats at an unoccupied table.

Once they'd settled, the Righteous Blade man said, 'But the really strange aspect was the business with her foot. I reckon she was drawing magical power directly from the grid. Have you ever heard of such a thing?'

'Actually, yes, though it's rare. When I was a young man there was a case that caused quite a stir. It was a minor member of the royal family; a cousin of the King or Queen. I don't recall which. Anyway, he was ailing. Had some kind of wasting disease the healers couldn't deal with. Somebody came up with the idea of rejuvenating him by linking him directly to the magic source.'

'Did it work?'

'For a while. But it only postponed the inevitable. Tragic, really.'

'It sounds costly.'

'Oh, yes. The meld you tangled with must be very wealthy, or have rich patrons. Not to mention access to the magical know-how.'

'I wish Phoenix was here to ask about it.'

Goyter arrived with a tray. She placed food in front of them, and a jug and goblets.

Karr nodded his thanks. 'Where's Tanalvah?' he asked her.

'With Teg and Lirrin. I'll try to have her join you. She still looks a wreck, poor thing. What's wrong with your food?'

He stared at his bowl disdainfully. 'Nothing,' he sighed.

'You can't expect hearty banquets, Dulian, not when you

have your health to think of.' She moved off, tray under her arm.

'Hearty banquet,' Karr grumbled. 'Chance would be a fine thing. They feed you slop when you come into this world and again when you're getting ready to leave it.' He glanced at Quinn's plate. 'Not that yours looks much more appetising.'

Disgleirio was going to counter his comment about leaving the world, but decided to ignore it. He knew Karr had no time for platitudes. Instead he said, 'I'm amazed they get regular meals organised at all.'

'Yes, the quartermasters and cooks do a miraculous job. I'm turning into an old grump, Quinn.'

'Not you.'

Karr tried a spoonful and made a face. 'Tell me about the note you got.'

Disgleirio put down his goblet. 'I've got it here.' He dug the piece of paper out of his pocket and handed it over.

Karr squinted. 'Hmmm. That's hardly news. It's no secret that the Diamond Isle's probably going to be attacked, or that our operation here is vulnerable.'

'Yes, but why should somebody go to the trouble of telling us that unless they have inside information? Whoever it was took a hell of a risk getting this to me. I reckon it's genuine, but who's responsible, or why, I can't imagine.'

'We still have supporters, including people who want to help us without getting too involved.'

'How many know I'm in the Resistance?'

'Good point. But it would have been a reasonable supposition simply because you were trying to defend innocent people from the militia. Nevertheless, I agree we should take this note at face value.' He handed it back. 'I'll get a warning out to all our cells.'

'Suppose the note's referring to a raid here, at headquarters?'

'I have to assume that no matter how good the informant's knowledge, they don't know about this place. It's too well kept a secret.'

'Isn't that what we were saying before the betrayal?'

'I'm not being complacent, Quinn. I'll certainly order an even greater level of security. But the truth is that having to move our HQ again would be too much of an upheaval, particularly when we're so close to activating the new plan.'

'We should speed up the schedule.'

'I'm not sure we can; everybody's working flat-out as it is. It might be different if there were more of us.'

'Then what about passing word of this warning to the Diamond Isle?'

'We'll try, but you know how hard it is getting anything through to them. If the authorities aren't already nullifying message glamours, they soon will be. Anyway, the islanders aren't stupid. They don't need us to tell them they're in an incredibly exposed position.'

Tanalvah appeared, walking with the slow, slightly rolling gait of a heavily expectant mother. She looked drained. Disgleirio got up and dragged out a chair for her.

'Where are the children?' Karr asked.

'Sleeping,' Tan replied, expelling a weary breath. 'Who did you say was in an exposed position?'

'We were talking about the Diamond Isle,' Disgleirio explained.

'Though we were only stating the obvious, I'm afraid,' Karr added. 'It's not exactly a revelation that those on the island are in a hazardous state.'

'At least they don't have a traitor in their midst,' Disgleirio muttered, 'as far as we know.'

Tanalvah coloured. She was sure their eyes were on her. Then Goyter turned up with her meal, and fussed over her for a moment. Tanalvah prayed that the distraction would make them forget the subject.

'We all feel bitter about the betrayal, Quinn,' Karr said. 'But we have to let it go. It's history now.'

'Not if the traitor's still in our ranks.'

Tanalvah's heart sank again.

'If they were, why haven't there been further betrayals?' Karr reasoned. 'Why haven't they finished us?'

'Perhaps they're biding their time.'

'It would have made sense to hit us while we were weak and disorganised. That didn't happen. To my mind, that means whoever was responsible fled or died.'

'Pushing your pet theory again are you, Dulian?'

'Yes. I still think there's a good argument for it having been Kayne.'

Tanalvah lifted her gaze. 'Who?'

'Mijar Kayne,' Disgleirio answered. 'Dulian's referring to an unfortunate episode that we in the Righteous Blade aren't particularly proud of. Kayne was a rogue. He used his position to enrich himself, mainly by demanding money to protect people we were already sworn to defend. And we think he might have sold low-level intelligence to the authorities.'

'What happened to him?'

'Something that's very rarely occurred in the history of the Brotherhood; he was expelled. During the slaughter that followed the Great Betrayal he was killed in a skirmish with paladins. While looting, typically. We were looking for him ourselves at the time. It was a toss up as to who put him to the blade first.'

'And that's why there's been no further treachery,' Karr said. 'A dead man can hardly indulge in perfidy.'

'He was greedy and vain, but petty criminality doesn't make somebody a traitor on that scale. I don't think it was Kayne.'

Karr looked to Tanalvah. 'You're not eating, my dear.'

'I've no appetite.'

'You must keep up your strength, you know.'

'Yes.' But she made no effort to touch her food.

'These aren't pleasant matters to dwell on, particularly for someone in your condition. Forgive us.'

'No, I . . . I'm interested.'

'Well, we have some news you might find a little more cheering. We've nearly completed preparations to try to reach the Diamond Isle. I'm not saying it would be easy getting there, but we have a plan that –'

'Everyone's going?'

'No. Unfortunately we had to be selective. But those staying behind never intended going to the island in the first place. Or else they've volunteered to stay in the hope they'll have an opportunity in future, if things settle down.'

'How many are going?'

'As many as a ship will hold. It could be a couple of hundred, depending on the vessel. But we'd do our best to make you comfortable and –'

'You're asking me to go with you?'

'Of course.'

'I can't.'

'We understand you'd be concerned for your safety,' Disgleirio said, 'and for the children's. But everything possible would be done to protect you all.'

'I can't go,' she repeated.

'Taking you somewhere so potentially dangerous must sound insane to you, Tanalvah,' Karr added. 'But we've reason to believe things are going to get worse here. At least you'd be with friends on the island.'

'It's not that. I don't want to go.'

They were confounded, and it showed.

'I don't mean to sound ungrateful,' she told them, 'but I can't leave.'

Disgleirio recovered first. 'Why?'

'If . . . when Kinsel gets back, he'll come here, to Bhealfa.'

'Tan . . .'

'I know what you're going to say, and I don't care. I put my trust in Iparrater. The goddess will protect him and bring him back to us.'

'Your faith's admirable,' Karr responded gently, 'and it gives you strength. But you have to be realistic. It could be that Kinsel won't –'

Tanalvah got up, awkwardly, knocking over a glass. She pushed away Disgleirio's helping hand.

'Kinsel will look for me and the children here,' she repeated obstinately. 'Where else would he go?' She began to move away.

Disgleirio would have followed, had not Karr grasped his arm. 'Let her be,' he advised. 'She needs time.'

'For what?'

'To come to terms with the fact that Kinsel's lost to her.'

Kinsel Rukanis couldn't sleep.

There was nothing unusual about that in itself; he'd had no better than a few hours of rest on any night since being sentenced, but he dared to hope this night might be different. On some obscure whim, Vance had ordered him taken from his filthy berth in the bowels of the ship and given his own cabin. True, the door was locked and guarded, and Kinsel couldn't stray far from his bunk due to his ankle being chained to it. All that notwithstanding, his new surroundings were luxurious compared to what he'd grown used to. But sleep was still elusive, despite his exhaustion.

His emotions constantly surprised him. Why should he expect to sleep, given his circumstances? Why suppose he would ever sleep again? Or live to do so, come to that. He began to feel selfish for wanting something as natural as sleep.

Everything seemed so much worse in the middle of the

night. Not that things were really any better in the daytime, but during the hours of darkness defences were down. Skin was somehow thinner, fears more pressing. It was when hopelessness triumphed, and the thought of self-destruction took on an allure.

There was no cheer to be had from the cabin. It was spartan to the point of bleakness, containing little more than the cot he occupied, and that was bolted to the floor. The only light came from the three-quarter moon, its frail beams entering by way of a minute porthole.

It was quiet. All he heard was the creaking of the ship at anchor, and the pacing of the guard on the other side of the door. The man was either taking his sentry duties seriously or just trying to keep warm. In any event the measured tread of heavy boots on weathered planks was mesmerising.

Kinsel lay staring at the low timbered ceiling, listening to the rhythm of the guard's footsteps and trying not to think. He counted the paces. Eight steps took the guard to the limit of his territory, then there was a pause, some shuffling, and eight steps back. Kinsel didn't find it a comfort exactly, or relaxing, but it did have a kind of consoling quality. Perhaps because it gave him a tenuous connection to another human being, even though the guard had no friendly intent.

So he listened, totted up the footsteps and kept his mind as blank as he could.

One . . . two . . . three . . . four . . . five . . . six . . . seven . . . eight. Pause. Shuffle. One . . . two . . . three . . . four . . . five . . . six . . . seven . . . eight.

Kinsel remained in his sleepless state for an indefinite period of time, lulled by the tempo of the stranger walking outside.

One . . . two . . . three . . . four . . . five . . . six . . . seven . . . eight. Pause. Shuffle. One . . . two . . . three . . . four . . . five . . .

The sudden termination was like a slap in the face. An affront to his reality. He was so startled he instinctively sat up.

There were new sounds. A scuffle, and what might have been a muffled cry. Then the thud of something weighty meeting the deck, followed by a more distant commotion, of men running and shouting, and the chiming of steel. He drew up his knees and hugged them protectively, straining the chain that bound him.

The door rattled, the handle shook, and a hammering began. Kinsel held his peace, not knowing if calling out would be wise or not. He wrenched at the chain, uselessly.

The hammering gave way to a concerted battering. Not a fist now; something metallic. The door shuddered in its frame, and with a crash, the head of an axe burst through. Several more blows followed, sending splinters flying. Kinsel ducked.

The door gave. It flew inward, whacked the wall and bounced half closed again. Somebody shouldered their way in. His appearance was hidden by the gloom, but a moonbeam struck the double-headed axe he was clutching, glinting the steel.

'Kinsel?'

Rukanis thought he recognised the voice, but didn't trust his senses and stayed mute.

'Kinsel?' The man moved forward, catching enough of the meagre light from the porthole to show his features.

Kinsel fought disbelief. He wanted to speak, and only croaked. Gulping a breath, he tried again. 'Reeth?' It came out as a rasp.

Caldason stood over him. 'You took some finding,' he said.

'Reeth?' Kinsel repeated, gaping. 'Is it really you or am I dreaming?'

'It's no dream. But it'll turn into a nightmare if we don't get you out off this ship, and fast.'

'But how did —'

'Questions later, all right?' He took in the singer's wasted frame and haggard face. 'Hell, Kinsel, you look rough.'

'Yes. I expect I do.' His eyes welled. He began to shake.

Caldason laid a hand on his shoulder, squeezing. 'Steady. It's going to be all right; I'm getting you out of here. Can you walk?'

'Yes. Well . . .' He nodded at the chain securing his ankle.

Caldason went to the foot of the bunk and swung his axe at the wooden upright. The blade sliced through in a single stroke, and he pulled the chain through the loop on Kinsel's anklet. 'We'll get that off later. Up you come.' He helped him stand.

The noises outside grew wilder.

Kinsel wiped the back of his hand across his eyes. He looked dazed. 'You're not alone?'

'No. But we're nowhere near the size of Vance's crew.' Rukanis visibly tensed at mention of the pirate's name. 'We don't have too far to go. Can you make it?'

'I'll cope.'

'Good. Let's move.' He went to take the singer's arm.

'There's no need. I can do it alone. Really.'

'You're sure?'

'Just lead me. But, Reeth . . .'

'Yes?'

'Tanalvah. And the children. How . . . how are . . . ?'

'They're fine.' Caldason had no way of knowing whether they were or not, but felt a judicious lie was in order. 'You've no need to worry about them. Just concentrate on doing as I say.'

Caldason checked that the way was clear and they moved out of the cabin. The door opened directly onto the deck where a stiff, cold wind blew. Kinsel shivered. Caldason unhooked his cloak and wrapped it round the singer's shoulders. Kinsel didn't protest.

The body of the guard was slumped against the wall in a gathering pool of blood. Kinsel stared, but said nothing.

'Keep going,' Caldason urged.

Kinsel walked falteringly, like a man who'd been kept in a confined space for too long, which in many ways he had.

As they moved away from the cabins and towards the main deck, they saw a handful of men. Beyond them, a larger group were engaging some of the pirate crew.

'They're with us,' Caldason said, signalling to the nearer group.

Two of the men peeled off and jogged to them.

'Where's Darrok?' Caldason wanted to know.

'Amidships,' one of them answered.

'I want you to go with these men, Kinsel.'

'But, Reeth –'

'You can trust them. They'll take you down to a boat we've got moored alongside. Do as they say. They'll take care of you.'

'What about you?'

'I'll be along. Soon.'

'Why not now?'

'There's something I have to do first. Look, there's no time to discuss it, all right? You'll be fine.' He turned to the two men. 'Look after him.' They nodded and moved forward to take charge of Kinsel.

The singer allowed himself to be led towards the stern. Caldason watched them go, then ran forward. When he was near the end of the cabin block, he stopped dead.

Two brawny pirates had rounded the corner ahead. They were well armed and bent on mayhem. The second they saw him, they charged.

He would have preferred meeting them with his swords. But they were sheathed. His only option was the axe, and he had it swinging before the first man reached him. Skidding to a halt just beyond the axe's sweep, the pirates hung back until it hit the apex of its swing. Then they darted in, forcing

Caldason to retreat. But he had the axe moving again instantly, blocking their assault.

They came on in a pincer movement, hacking at him from left and right. He parried them, muscles straining as he worked the heavier weapon. The exchange grew ever more frenzied, the fury of his opponents rising.

Frustration bred rashness, and one of the pirates got too close. Caldason offset the man's blade with a heavy blow, following with a swipe that wrong-footed him. Then he swiftly brought the axe over in an arc, shattering the pirate's skull. A puppet with its strings slashed would have fallen no quicker.

The second pirate, stunned by his comrade's fate, scuttled clear. But wrath got the better of caution, and he made to rush into battle once more. Caldason lifted the axe well over his shoulder and hurled it with all his strength. Spinning through the air, a speeding ring of wood and steel, it pierced the man's chest, the force of the strike sending him tumbling, lifeless.

Caldason looked back along the deck and saw Kinsel being helped over the rail. He left the axe embedded in the corpse and moved on, drawing a sword.

The group of islanders he joined amidships had dealt with their opposition. The bodies of perhaps a dozen pirates were scattered around. Caldason was about to ask after Darrok when he appeared, swooping in on his glamoured disc.

'Did you find him?' he asked.

'Yes.'

'And?'

'He's alive, but he looks a mess.' Caldason indicated the bodies. 'There are more than this, surely?'

'We had a stroke of luck. Look over there.' He pointed at a large grille set in the deck some way further along. 'But I wouldn't get too close if I were you.'

Caldason trotted to it, and saw that the hatch had been

secured with a chain and heavy lock. As he approached he heard a din rising, and when he leaned over to look, a roar went up, and cutlass tips jabbed through the grille. He pulled back, but not before seeing several score pirates in the hold.

Darrok glided in to hover beside him. 'Most of them were sleeping below decks when we got on board, and we managed to keep them there. I wouldn't count on it lasting much longer though.'

A determined pounding shuddered the grille, underlining his point.

'What about the rest of the ship?'

'Cleared. Except for the wheelhouse block.'

'And that's where Vance's cabin is?'

'Underneath the bridge, yes. At least, it always was, and the defectors from his crew confirmed it. I've kept it well guarded. We haven't tried going in there yet.'

'Then it's time we did. Let's get Vance sorted and get out of here.'

'I've been waiting to hear that for a long time, Reeth.' He yelled orders at the waiting islanders, telling them to be ready to evacuate the ship. More than a few of the men looked disgruntled.

They set out for the wheelhouse, Caldason walking next to Darrok's gliding dish.

'Why the long faces back there?'

'Some of our men wanted to finish off those below deck, too,' Darrok said. 'They think we're losing an opportunity by not putting them to death.

'Maybe they've got a point.'

'I can't bring myself to order the killing of men in a situation like that.'

'After what they did to you?'

Darrok eyed him darkly. 'Oh, don't get me wrong; I hate them. But there's a difference between meeting a man in a fair fight and spearing fish in a bucket. I like to be able to sleep nights.'

'As it happens I see no honour in it myself. Though I'd do it if I had to.'

'I'd have to be pushed pretty hard. But I've no such compunction about Vance. Besides, I'll be cutting off the serpent's head. The pirate alliance will fall without him.'

They got to the wheelhouse at the stern. The bridge itself was occupied by islanders, and guards dotted the deck.

'Well, that's it,' Darrok said, indicating a single door under the bridge.

'You'll never get your disc through there.'

'I will if I tilt it. Don't look at me like that. If I slide off onto my arse I'm still going in. I've waited too long for this reckoning.'

'All right. But let's get the door down first. Don't worry, you've got first crack at Vance. What do you intend doing with him, by the way?'

'Cutting his throat's a temptation. But I'll call him out. He can face me in single combat.'

'What if he won't?'

'If he sees it's his only option, he'll face me. I'll tell him you'll let him go if he wins.'

'You think I'd do that?'

'That's your decision. I'll be past caring.'

'Thanks,' Caldason came back dryly. 'Hold on.' He beckoned to a couple of the men guarding the area. 'We need to get through that door,' he told them. 'Can you improvise some kind of battering ram? Good. And get a few more people to help use it. Go!'

They ran off.

'What kind of a fight is it going to be with you in that thing?' Caldason said, nodding at Darrok's dish. 'Gives you a bit of an advantage, doesn't it?'

'You really think having no legs is an advantage in a duel? I don't care. I just want to get to grips with the man. Anyway, fuck advantage; he owes me.'

'Your decision.'

The sound of chopping drifted to them.

'Of course, there might be more in there than just Vance,' Caldason reckoned.

'We can deal with it,' Darrok replied dismissively. 'Where are they with that ram?'

'They're coming.'

A party of six or seven men staggered into view, carrying a stout wooden spar.

'What is it?' Caldason called to them.

'We found a damaged mast in a lumber-room near the prow,' a muscular islander explained. 'Should do the job.'

They lined it up in front of the door.

'Sure there's no other way out of there?' Caldason said.

Darrok shook his head. 'Just a porthole about the size of Vance's head. I'd pay good money to see him try to get through that.'

'Stand by then.' He gave the signal.

The ram crew took a run at the door. A tremendous crash rang out. The door stayed closed.

'Again!' Darrok bellowed.

The ram pounded the door a second time. Still it held. They didn't wait to be told to try again, and the third impact broke through, leaving the door in splinters. Caldason dashed forward. He ducked into the entrance, sword raised, the rammers crowding in behind him.

The cabin was large, and although poorly lit, no one seemed to be there.

A grand, elaborately carved bed stood against one wall. Beneath its brocaded silk sheets was the outline of a figure, which Caldason approached cautiously. Blade poised, he reached down and tore away the covers.

'Gangway!'

Darrok manoeuvred his flying dish through the doorway. Tilting at a perilous angle, he just managed to scrape through.

'Well?' he said, arriving beside Caldason.

'Just this.'

The thrown-back sheets revealed a couple of shabby flour sacks, stuffed with straw.

'Shit,' Darrok muttered dejectedly.

'Looks like our information wasn't entirely up to date.'

'I should have known better than to think he'd be caught this easily.'

'There'll be other times.'

'I was keyed up for this, Reeth. Ready to pay the bastard back, you know?'

'You'll get your shot. But right now we need to leave.'

They went back on deck.

Darrok produced a cloth satchel. Inside was a quantity of the rust-coloured powder called dragon's blood. He placed it, open, at the base of the ship's main mast. Then he lashed a clay water bottle above it, stoppered neck downwards.

'This is going to sink the ship?' Caldason said.

'There's nowhere near enough for that. But it'll act as a useful diversion.' He took a small rubber vial from his pocket. 'Vitriol. A smidgen of this on the bottle stopper will burn through in a minute or less. Then the water hits the powder and . . . boom.'

'What about them?' Caldason pointed at the hatch set in the deck. The pirates trapped below could still be heard clamouring.

'I suppose we've got to give them a sporting chance. Haven't we?'

'I'll gladly kill any of them we meet in other circumstances.'

'I'll take that as a yes. If I do this, can you . . . ?'

'All right. But make sure our people are off first.'

Darrok bellowed the evacuation order and men began running towards the rail. 'I'll hold off until you get to the grille. But it won't do to linger, Reeth. The rate the vitriol works at is unpredictable.'

'Right.'

'You'll need this.' He handed Caldason an iron key. 'And get clear of that hatch fast. Those crewmen aren't going to be in a happy mood when you free them.'

'Just be sure to wait for me.' He sheathed his sword and jogged off.

Darrok watched Caldason reach the hatch. Then after checking everyone else had gone overboard, he carefully opened the vial.

Caldason was on hands and knees, scrabbling for the chain and trying to avoid the swords thrust through the grid. He managed to get hold of the padlock and inserted the key. There was a sudden movement at the edge of his vision as Darrok's dish took off, heading out to sea. Caldason turned the key and prised apart the arch of the lock, then he was up and running.

The hatch cover burst open behind him, and a flood of howling men poured out. As he ran for the ship's rail an arrow whistled past his head. Another missed him by an even narrower margin. He heard the sound of many boots, thundering in pursuit. The rail was just ahead, and he leapt, skimmed it with his heels and went over the side.

There was what felt like a long drop, followed by the impact of freezing water and seconds of swirling confusion.

Hands were hauling him out. They dragged him aboard a large rowing boat, an old whaler with seating for twenty rowers. Somebody threw a blanket around his shoulders and he was guided to an empty bench. Kinsel sat closest to him, swathed in a blanket and wearing a glazed expression.

Arrows zipped into the water all around the boat, a few
burying themselves in its timbers. One sliced through the
thigh of a rower, at which several men took up bows and
began firing back.

Then Darrok swooped in, scattering the pirates on the ship,
buying the whaler time. Skipper Rad Cheross was at the
rowing boat's helm. Rows of thick metal tubes had been
attached to the stern and sides, their forward ends hammered
shut. Cheross sat by a makeshift valve.

'I hope your friend Phoenix was right about this!' he
shouted at Caldason. 'Oars up! Hold on to something!' He
turned the valve.

Sea water flooded the tubes, meeting the dragon's blood
packed inside. The boat shuddered violently. For an infinite
moment everyone on board fully expected to be blown to
pieces. Instead the vessel lurched forward, plumes of flame
jetting from the tubes.

The craft moved faster and faster, its nose raised, and the
passengers were thrown back by gravitational force. At the
helm, Cheross struggled to steer a straight course.

An explosion sounded at their rear as a fireball rose from
the pirate ship. The central mast was ablaze and panicked
men could be seen running on deck.

A ragged cheer went up from the whaler. Then Darrok's
dish flew in from above, keeping pace with the speeding
boat. Ahead, the outline of the Diamond Isle loomed against
the night sky's blue velvet.

The whaler kept up its velocity, swift as an arrow. Caldason
was pummelled by wind and drenched with icy spray, yet
couldn't help feeling exhilarated. And he wasn't alone.
Grinning, he turned to his companion.

Kinsel was sobbing.

18

A wing of the redoubt was used as an infirmary. But due to Kinsel's state he was put by himself in a room nearby. In the corridor outside, Caldason and Darrok waited.

'I've only seen your friend once before,' Darrok said, 'at the concert I mentioned, years ago. So I can hardly compare now with then. But to me he seems a shadow of the man he was.'

'You'd be right. I just hope it's only his body the last few months have left their mark on.'

'He should be grateful he came away from Vance alive. That's quite a feat in itself.'

'You should know,' observed Caldason.

'Something else I know is that Vance is going to want retribution for this. He must be spitting blood.'

'No change there, then.'

'And I missed my chance to repay him. That rankles.' Darrok's floating dish rocked, as though shadowing its master's agitation.

'The way things are going, you'll get another crack at him.'

'Assuming a fleet from one of the empires doesn't arrive first.'

'That would solve the problem, wouldn't it?'

'Not quite in the way I hoped.' Darrok glanced at a window opposite. A pink dawn was breaking. 'Can we hold out,' he wondered, 'if an empire moves against us?'

'They will, be sure of that. Whether we can hold them . . . well, that might be down to the Source, and we've chewed that over often enough.'

'Forget the Source. I don't want to sound negative, but we can't count on you finding it. There's no way we can hold off an invasion just by force of arms, is there?'

'I think you know the answer to that. We could delay things, at best.'

Darrok sighed. 'I would love you to have said something else.'

A door banged and the sound of running feet reached them. Kutch and Pallidea arrived.

'Is it true?' Kutch blurted, panting. 'You rescued Kinsel?'

'We got him, yes,' Caldason confirmed.

'Great! How is he?'

'Kinsel's been through a pretty rough time, Kutch. That's bound to take its toll.'

'He's not mutilated or dying or anything, is he?'

'No. But he's low physically, and his spirits are down too.'

'Is he going to be all right?' Pallidea asked.

Before anyone could answer, the door to Kinsel's room opened. Serrah and Phoenix came out.

'How is he?' Darrok said.

'Malnourished, ill-treated and depressed,' Serrah replied. 'Just about what you'd expect, in fact.'

'He's very distraught,' Phoenix added. 'I've given him a powerful sleeping draught. He'll be out for some time yet.'

'We couldn't get him to say much on the way back here,' Caldason told them. 'How was he with you?'

'Confused,' Serrah answered. 'We have to remember that

a lot's happened while Kinsel's been away. Not just to him, to all of us. He'd been told about the migration here, but not much else. But he had only one real concern.'

'Tanalvah.'

'Yes. Tan and the kids. I couldn't bring myself to tell him we've no idea how they are.'

'I couldn't either.'

'But we have to assume they're all right, Reeth, and we've got to get word to Tan about Kinsel. We owe it to her.'

'How? Getting messages off this island hasn't exactly proved easy.'

'I might be able to help with that,' Darrok offered.

'Really?' Serrah said. 'What do you have in mind?'

'Just a little something I've been keeping by. I'll check to see if it can be done.'

'It's not another accelerated boat, is it?' Caldason ventured, adding, 'Which, by the way, was a brilliant idea, Phoenix.'

The sorcerer nodded, modestly.

'That's not something we're likely to repeat,' Darrok said. 'We can't be so lavish with dragon's blood in future.'

'Pity. It might have come in handy on my trip.'

'You'll have to rely on conventional means. We need the powder here.'

'Since when were you so enthusiastic about magic, Reeth?' Serrah wanted to know.

Kutch looked as though he was about to make the same point.

'I'm not so dim as to ignore something that could speed the journey,' Caldason said. 'But that's as far as it goes. I wouldn't use magic by choice.'

'So you're thinking of setting out soon?' Serrah asked.

'I said I wouldn't go until we did our best for Kinsel. That's done. There's nothing to keep me now.'

'So when are we going?'

'The next day or two.'

'That soon?'

'You don't have to come, Serrah. You or Kutch. In fact, you know how I feel about –'

'No. I'm still coming.'

'Me, too,' Kutch put in.

'This is all very well,' Phoenix pronounced. 'But what do we do about Kinsel?'

Like the proverbial iceberg, Prince Melyobar's court showed only a tenth of itself to the world. Not physically, but in terms of the hierarchy of functionaries, servants and labourers needed to service it. Naturally, the bottommost echelons of the pecking order consisted of menials, toiling at jobs those higher up would rather not think about, let alone undertake.

Two such workers, holders of the rank of private in the Palace Guard Auxiliary, had one of the more onerous tasks. Their duties took them to the lowest depths of the palace, to ignored and feared zones where the court's less salubrious business was conducted.

This chilly dawn they walked dank corridors that were badly lit and unheated, so that the winter cold seeped through lichen-covered walls.

'Just one from last night, Nechen,' the older of the duo declared. He was brawny and grizzled.

'Thank the gods for that,' his slightly younger, marginally less grizzled and brawny companion replied. 'I hate it when we have a heap of 'em first thing.'

'There'll be more as the day wears on, you can count on that.' He hawked and spat. 'Damn, but the air down here plays havoc with my tubes.'

'Their number never goes down though, does it, Welst? I mean, when did we last have a day without any?'

'It's in the nature of this place. There's bound to be a steady stream, given the Prince's way of doing things.'

'Yeah, but –'

'Ours is not to reason why,' Welst cautioned. 'We do as we're told. Unless we want to end up down here ourselves. And not walking about, if you get my drift.'

'Well, I wouldn't mind being assigned to other duties, I can tell you that,' Nechen said. 'This kind of work has a way of getting a man down.'

'The best chance we have of that is by doing this job well.' He gave his companion a penetrating glare. 'And by not complaining.'

They trudged on in silence, their footsteps echoing in the bleak stone corridors. At length they rounded a bend and came to a set of heavy doors. A gaggle of guards sat on benches beside them.

The sentries knew the privates well, and waved them on without formality. One of the watchmen rose and took a huge bunch of keys from its hook. The doors were unlocked, emitting a throaty creak as the guard pushed them open.

Beyond lay a further labyrinth of corridors, housing the palace's dungeons. The turnkey led the way, and several minutes later they arrived at a particular door. A stretcher was waiting for them, propped against the wall outside.

'It's in there,' the jailer announced. He leaned forward and undid the door, then backed off. 'You'll find this one's a bit . . . ripe. I'll, er, leave you to it.' He scampered away.

'As usual,' Nechen muttered. 'Leave it to the poor bloody infantry. Let's get it over with, shall we?'

Welst laid a restraining hand on his companion's shoulder. 'Not so fast.' He dug out a couple of grubby face masks. 'We're supposed to put these on, remember.'

'If we must,' Nechen sighed.

They tied on the cloth masks, covering their mouths and

noses. Welst plucked a torch from its bracket and pushed open the cell door. Even with their masks, the odour was overpowering. It was pitch black inside, so Welst held up the brand, casting light. Things scuttled into the shadows.

'Well, there he is.' He nodded at the bunk, the cell's only piece of furniture.

A body was sprawled face down across it, knuckles touching the floor on one side, feet on the other. They approached, crunching over rank straw.

'Good clothes,' Nechen said. 'Must be an aristo. Wonder what the poor sod did to warrant the Prince sending him down here.'

'Perhaps he used the wrong teaspoon. Like I said, ours is not to –'

'Yes, yes, I know.'

'Come on, we haven't got all day. Turn him over.'

'Why me? Isn't it your turn?'

'I did it last time,' stated Welst.

'No, you didn't. It was me yesterday, too. Why do I have to –'

'Just do it. The quicker we get this done, the quicker we're out of here.'

Nechen sighed and rolled the corpse. 'Gods, he's in a bit of a state, isn't he?'

'Been lying here more than a few days, I reckon. Go and get the stretcher.'

'It's my turn for that as well, is it?'

Welst shot him another look.

Fuming, Nechen stumbled out of the cell. Welst watched him go, then bent to the body. Quickly, he searched the man's clothing. All he found was a few coins, and a glamoured locket bearing the animated, smiling likeness of a woman. The locket was too risky, so he stuffed it back. Grumbling at the poor pickings, he slipped the coins into his pocket.

'What was that?' Nechen said, dragging the stretcher in.

'Nothing. Just . . . just saying a prayer for the poor wretch.'

'Really? Oh, that's nice. I never had you down for the sentimental type, Welst.'

'Yes, well, I've got hidden depths.' He added briskly, 'Let's get on with this, shall we?'

They lifted the body, dumped it on the stretcher and threw a filthy blanket over it. Then they manoeuvred their load through the door.

The guards at the sentry post held their noses as they went past.

A lengthy journey stretched before them, back along winding corridors, up and down flights of steps, through numerous doors. Yet for all the thousands who populated the palace, they met few other people.

In a long, completely deserted corridor, dimly lit by glamour orbs, they put the stretcher down and stopped for a breather. Propped on a ledge, Welst took out his clay pipe and began thumbing dark, coarse tobacco into its bowl.

'What do you think they're doing with them up there?' Nechen wondered.

'The stiffs? Damned if I know. And I'm not sure I want to.' He struck flint and lit the pipe, puffing acrid clouds. 'If you're wise, you'll not take too obvious an interest yourself.'

'It's a rum do though, isn't it? What with that and the damned zoo we took aboard.'

'That I can sort of understand. Our betters like exotic pastimes.'

'Smelly beasts that have to be fed, when they could have glamours? Makes no sense to me.'

'Who can fathom the rich?' Welst's pipe billowed pungent fumes.

'And all this going on when there's unrest everywhere in the country.'

'In that respect we're in the best place. There's probably not a safer billet in the world.'

'Since when was Melyobar in this world?'

'Ssshh. Walls have ears,' Welst mouthed. He knocked out his pipe. 'Come on.'

They hefted the stretcher with a grunt and continued their journey.

The worst part was the stairs. They had to climb seven floors just to reach what passed for ground level. Their destination was twice as far.

At last, after much struggling and cursing, they reached their goal. It was a section given over to the sanctums and workshops of the small army of magicians serving the Prince. As one of the palace's more sensitive areas it was well guarded, which meant another quarter of an hour spent negotiating security checks.

Finally standing at the entrance to the chamber they sought, Welst rapped his knuckles on its oak door. Almost immediately a spy-hole slid open and they were scrutinised. The door opened and they were ushered in by a minion, who motioned to them to put down their burden and wait while he went for a superior.

Despite having been inside many times before, Welst and Nechen never ceased to be intrigued by the activity there. The room was cavernous, with much of the floor space taken up by benches where numerous sorcerers toiled. Their work surfaces were strewn with flasks, retorts, herbs and powders, and clusters of mysterious apparatus whose function was impossible to guess. Apprentices moved among the benches, supplying their masters' needs.

Stacks of cages lined the walls, but too far away for whatever occupied them to be seen. There were rows of great iron vats mounted on furnace hearths, their unknown contents bubbling loudly. The entire chamber was suffused by a misty fug, and perfumed with aromas sweet and foul.

A blue-robed adept appeared. He was young, for a sorcerer, and clean shaven. The preoccupied expression he wore could be mistaken for stern.

Welst greeted him with a deferential dip of the head. 'Mage Okrael, sir.'

Nechen, always awkward in the presence of his elders, made do with a slipshod salute.

The sorcerer acknowledged them with a distracted nod, his eyes on the stretcher. 'Do you know how this one met his end?' he asked, kneeling to pull back the blanket.

'Nobody said, sir,' Welst replied.

'Very well. Bring him over here.'

They lifted the stretcher and followed him, weaving through the bustle. No one took much notice. Okrael led them to a table and they deposited the body on it. The wizard began a cursory examination.

'No obvious signs of disease,' he muttered. 'I'd say he died of brutality and simple neglect. Poor devil.' He looked troubled.

'Then he'll be fitting your purposes, sir?' Nechen ventured.

'Probably not. But that isn't really your concern, is it?'

'No, sir.'

'Thank you, gentlemen. That'll be all.'

'Sir.'

They turned and left, taking the stretcher with them while the sorcerer beckoned a couple of novices to strip the body.

Outside, Welst said, 'That mage needs to harden his attitudes a bit.'

'You think so?'

'Doesn't do to get too involved with the deceased. Not in this place.'

'Where to now, Welst?'

'Back down. Chances are there'll be another for us by now.'

Making their way to the inevitable staircase, they were passed by four auxiliaries pushing a large open cart containing a dead camel.

One of the men knew them. 'The Prince's going to be none too pleased about this,' he remarked in an undertone as they went by.

The detail pushed their cart towards the same door Nechen and Welst had just come out of.

'See?' Nechen said. 'Glamours don't peg out like that.'

'They do if you run out of coin,' Welst reminded him.

Their return trip took them close to the Prince's quarters, the most heavily defended section of the palace. Suspicious glances and twitchy sword hands discouraged lingering, and Welst and Nechen hurried on with their descent.

Beyond the hard-faced sentries and watchful sorcerers, through the steel gates and glamoured booby-traps, lay Melyobar's private chambers. Behind a particular reinforced door, protected by enchanted locks, rested the not quite dead, not quite living body of King Narbetton. Beside the bed, his son sat stiffly.

'And now they tell me this Talgorian's coming here,' the Prince complained. 'The Ambassador, father. Yes, him. Was I consulted? Did anyone ask my permission? No. Nobody listens to me. Anybody would think . . . What? I have no idea why he's coming. No one's had the courtesy to tell me. Yes, it is absolutely outrageous. What's that?'

He listened, head tilted, fingers on temples.

'I'm not sure I agree, father. My inclination is simply to refuse him entry. It's not as though there's any official business that . . . Why should I let it go ahead? I understand the need for caution, but . . . Hmm? Ah, yes. I see.'

Melyobar pondered the King's counsel. 'You're right,' he decided. 'He can come. Whether he leaves is another matter. And as you say, soon that won't matter. Nothing will.' He bent to listen again. 'Yes, very close. But I take your point. The sooner it gets underway, the better.'

He rose. 'Thank you, father. As ever, your guidance has proved most valuable. Pardon? Yes, of course I'll keep you informed.'

The Prince backed away respectfully, then turned and left the room.

On exiting, his entourage fell in. Eight hand-picked body-guards, a personal secretary, a manservant, a scribe, a senior mage, the mage's apprentice, a healer, two message-carriers, and a pair of baton-wielding vanguards to ensure his way was clear. The usual complement of personnel.

He stated his destination and the mob moved off with him cocooned inside.

It didn't take them long to arrive at the sorcerers' quarters. As they approached the very door Welst and Nechen had used earlier, it opened and the sorcerer Okrael stepped out. Seeing the procession bearing down immobilised him, but he had the presence of mind to bow.

'Just the man,' Melyobar puffed, winded from the short trip. He let his entourage scrutinise the wizard for imposture, then waved them aside.

'Sire,' Okrael greeted him uneasily.

'How goes the work? Are we on schedule?'

'It's progressing well, Majesty. Only . . .'

'Yes? There are no hold-ups, I hope?'

'No, sire. It's just that . . .'

'Spit it out, man!'

'It's dangerous.'

'I know that.'

'I mean, sire, it presents a danger to everyone, not just

whichever enemy Your Highness may choose to turn it on.'

'This isn't the first time you've dared to question the workings of the project, is it . . .' The Prince blanked.

'Okrael, sire.'

'. . . is it, Okrael?'

'I wouldn't presume to question anything, Highness. My only concern is the safety of our own people.'

'Do you presume to think I'm unconcerned about the well-being of my subjects?'

'No, sire, of course not.'

'Don't force me to question your loyalty, wizard. You're a very small cog in the wheel I have turning here. It'll spin as well without you.'

'Yes, Majesty.' The colour had gone out of Okrael's face.

'There's no reason why what you're creating shouldn't be effective?'

'No, sir.'

'And the work is going well, you say?'

'There have been no hitches, sire.'

'Good. Then there shouldn't be a problem about speeding up the timetable.'

'Sire?'

'You adepts have spent far too long on this. I'm minded to set a date for deploying your handiwork.'

'May I ask when, Your Majesty?'

'I'm thinking that around the time of the new moon would be suitable.'

'That's . . . just a few weeks, sire.'

'Yes.' Melyobar's face cracked into a gleeful grin. 'Wonderful, isn't it?'

19

The sun hadn't risen high enough to burn off the mist clinging to the ocean.

Despite the hour, the quayside was buzzing with activity. Three ships were at anchor; one was the packet that had brought Caldason to the Diamond Isle, the others were similar sized vessels. A line of men chained provisions to them.

Further along the quay, five people were gathered: Caldason, Serrah, Kutch, Darrok and Pallidea.

'Do you really think this is going to work?' Serrah said.

'It should,' Darrok replied. 'It cost me a small fortune.'

'Then it's good of you to contribute it.'

'I was keeping it for emergencies. I guess that's what we can call this.'

'How will it know where to go?' Caldason wondered. 'The Resistance are hardly going to be using the same hideouts, are they?'

'It'll be attuned to a person, not a place. As I said, it's a top-quality glamour.'

'Who's it going to search for? Karr?'

'With the best will in the world, he wasn't in good health when we last saw him. So I thought we'd go for someone younger, fitter; and in a position to pass on the message. Quinn Disgleirio seemed a good choice.'

Caldason nodded. 'Makes sense.'

'Ironic, though,' smiled Darrok.

'Why?' Serrah asked.

'I don't think Disgleirio's overly fond of me.'

'He's a traditionalist,' Caldason explained. 'Not the kind to approve of somebody with a reputation like yours.'

'He wouldn't be the first to think ill of me. It goes with the territory.'

'So what are we waiting for?' Serrah said.

'Phoenix. This isn't the kind of glamour anybody can prime. It needs a sorcerer.'

'He'll be here,' Kutch volunteered. 'He was finishing off his studies when I saw him earlier.'

'Well, I wish he'd get a move on.' Darrok shivered. 'It's damn cold out here.'

'You won't freeze,' Caldason told him. 'Here he comes.'

A wagon arrived, depositing Phoenix. He swept up to them with the vigour of a much younger man, robes whipping in the wind.

'You have it?' he said without preamble.

'Here.' Darrok held out a cube on the palm of his hand. The cube was reddish, and made of no easily recognisable material, though it most closely resembled a soft wood. Its surfaces were inscribed with intricate symbols.

Phoenix took it and cupped it in his hands, as if warming wax. When he opened his hands, it was malleable. He produced a thin black strand and began gently working it into the softened material.

'What's that?' Caldason said.

'A lock of Disgleirio's hair,' the sorcerer replied.

'That was something you just happened to have, was it?'

'I've quite a collection of body-sheddings from Resistance

members – hair, nail clippings, flakes of skin – against an eventuality like this. It ensures the glamour homes in on the right target. I can see what you're thinking, Reeth. Don't worry; I haven't got anything of you filed away.'

'Glad to hear it.'

'Now, if you don't mind . . .'

They fell silent while Phoenix continued with his preparations. Once he had the strand of hair embedded, he conjured a spell with hand gestures and a short bout of chanting.

'It's ready,' he said, holding up the cube between thumb and forefinger.

'You've lodged the message?' Darrok asked.

'Of course.' Phoenix looked slightly offended. 'Just as you dictated it.'

'Then let's get it done, shall we?'

Phoenix went to the edge of the quay. The others followed, Darrok gliding in on his silver dish.

'Ready?' The wizard said.

'Do it,' Caldason told him.

Phoenix tossed the cube into the grey water lapping the dock. There was an eruption of bubbles, and colours flashed beneath the waves. Slowly, a bulk rose out of the water.

It proved to be the upper part of a marine creature. Blue-black and sleek, it had whiskers and an elongated snout, while its hands were paddle-shaped, and its eyes large and dark as coal. It vaguely resembled a cross between a seal, a dolphin and an otter. The pseudo animal stared at them.

'Go!' Phoenix ordered.

The beast sank and turned at the same time, flowing gracefully. It circled once, moving like a knife through the water, then swerved and headed out to sea. They watched until it dived and disappeared.

'Gods speed,' the sorcerer muttered.

Darrok floated his dish away from the water's edge. 'That's

that. It'll either get there or it won't. We may never know either way.'

'That's a cheery thought,' Serrah said.

'Just the truth. I suggest you forget about it. You've got plenty to occupy you this morning.'

Caldason glanced at the ships. 'How's the loading going?'

'Let's ask Cheross, shall we?' Darrok directed his disc towards the crowd of stevedores. The others tramped along behind.

As they walked, Phoenix fell in beside Caldason. 'I've been meaning to ask,' he confided in an undertone, 'how are the visions?'

'I'm still getting them.'

'Are they of the same nature?'

'They seem more to the point, whatever the point might be, and they're usually shorter. Why?'

'I can offer you a draught that could alleviate their effect. Something that might put you in a deep, non-dream state.'

'Could. Might. What am I, Phoenix, a rat for testing your potions on?'

'I only make the reservations because we're talking about you. An ordinary man would succumb to the draught. With you, there's no telling, but it's worth trying. It wouldn't harm you whether it blocks the visions or not.'

'Whatever I get isn't dreams, so I can't see how the depth of my sleep would make any difference. Besides, I don't want them blocked.'

'You don't? After all you've done to be rid of them?'

'Since they started changing in character they've become more interesting than vexing to me.'

'And there speaks the man who loathes magic so much.'

'Of course I'd rather be without them. But it seems there's some kind of meaning in what I see.'

'I thought you couldn't understand the visions,' said Phoenix.

'I'm not saying I can, only that they're trying to convey something. And they have an incredible vividness, as real as being awake.'

'You know, there's an old sorcerers' adage that goes, "Who's to know which is real, our waking lives or our so-called dreams?" The Craft has always believed that the realms of the unconscious communicate with us. So maybe these visions *are* telling you something.'

'You make it sound as though I'm causing this to happen myself.'

'Are you saying you aren't worth listening to? That you'd turn a deaf ear to your innermost fears and hopes?'

'None of it's coming from me, Phoenix. This is from outside.'

'Then I won't try to persuade you about the draught. If you're sure.'

'I'm sure.' Kutch and Serrah were walking well ahead, with Darrok in the lead, Pallidea at his side. 'Right now,' Caldason said, keeping his voice down, 'I'm more concerned about the boy. Do you think he'll be able to handle this voyage?'

'Kutch's young and inexperienced. He can be rash. But you of all people should know that he has heart and spirit. Above all, he has a natural affinity with the Craft. I think he'll cope.'

'It's putting a lot on his shoulders.'

'Weren't you even younger when you had to face the world on your own account? Nevertheless I take your point, and to be on the safe side I've had glamoured detection devices installed on board. Kutch's aware of this, and knows how to interpret them.'

'What do these things detect, exactly?'

'In essence they're a crude form of the ability Kutch has naturally. They detect magical activity. That could prove useful in your search.'

They arrived at the crowded end of the quay at that point, ending any further questions Caldason might have. When he saw them, the packet's skipper, Rad Cheross, hurried over.

'How's it going?' Darrok asked him.

'We're not far short of being ready, which is a relief as I'd like to use this mist for cover while it lasts.'

'When do we leave?' Caldason said.

'An hour, maybe two,' Cheross reckoned.

'Think we'll have any problem slipping by Vance's ships?'

'It's a big ocean. They can't be everywhere. Fortunately the packet's fast, should we run into trouble, and having a couple of decoys helps.'

'How much do we have in the way of provisions?' Serrah wondered.

'Enough for a month. A bit more if we ration. But that's it, unless you like fish. There's nothing else in the parts we're going to.'

'I'd hope to be nowhere near as long as that,' Caldason told them.

'Suits me.' Cheross glanced at the loading work. 'Excuse me, will you? I want to keep on top of this.' He turned away.

'Well, it seems to be going to schedule,' Darrok said. 'Anything we've overlooked, anybody? Speak now or it's too late.'

'My only worry's leaving Kinsel so soon after his rescue,' Serrah admitted, 'particularly given the state he's in.'

'He'll be fine with us,' Phoenix promised. 'The care he'll get will be just as good whether you're here or not.'

'We'll all be keeping an eye on him,' Pallidea added.

'Put it out of your mind, Serrah,' Darrok chipped in. 'Concentrate on getting the job done and yourselves back here.'

'Thanks, Zahgadiah. We will.'

'Right, I'm going to see if I can hurry things up.'

'Anything we can do?'

'Just don't go away.' He tilted his disc and stretched a gloved hand. 'Pallidea.'

His lover deftly climbed aboard. The saucer rocked gently, then shot off.

Sensing that Caldason and Serrah could use a moment alone, Phoenix took Kutch aside for a last-minute pep talk.

'What's the cut-off point for this trip, Reeth?' Serrah said.

'What do you mean?'

'We've never discussed how long it's going to go on for.'

'You heard Cheross. There's only enough food and water for a month.'

'That's too long to be away from this place and you know it. And I wouldn't put it past you to make us eat fish and drink rainwater if you had to prolong it.'

'Phoenix has narrowed things down to a specific number of islands, which should save some time.'

'Yes, about fifty of them.'

'A little more than that, actually.'

'What worries me is that if you don't find what you want you'll just go on looking indefinitely.'

'I won't do that, Serrah. There is a cut-off, and we'll both know it.'

'I'm not trying to dampen your enthusiasm. You know that, don't you? I just don't want you to be too disappointed if this doesn't work out.'

'I'm used to disappointment.'

'Not in all things, I hope.' She smiled.

Darrok returned at speed, alone this time, and hovered in front of them. 'Seems they'll be finished in under an hour, so be ready. And let's have no tearful farewells, shall we? I can't stand 'em.'

*   *   *

Two hours later they were well underway, far enough out to make the island a black ribbon on the horizon, with grimy white seagulls the only relief from steel-grey ocean and sky. The mist was clearing.

At the stern rail, Caldason, Serrah and Kutch watched as the two decoy ships disappeared around the island's east and west headlands.

'I can't believe we're actually going at last,' Kutch said.

'I should think Reeth's even more pleased,' Serrah replied. 'Aren't you, love?'

'It's good to be on our way,' Caldason agreed.

'You could be a little more enthusiastic about it.'

He smiled, mildly. 'I'm just tired.'

'You do look bushed. Take a nap. There's nothing you can do here.'

'Maybe I will. You'll call me if –'

'What's going to happen in the next couple of hours?'

'Vance could happen. We're not clear yet.'

'If we get our throats cut I'll be sure to wake you. Now get some sleep.' She leaned over and kissed his cheek.

Caldason nodded, heavy-eyed, then turned and made for their cabin.

It was part of the crew's modest quarters below decks, and tiny. Once inside, he didn't even bother kicking off his boots, simply unbuckling his scabbard, laying it aside, then stretching out on the bunk.

The second his head touched the pillow, he flew.

Far below lay the ocean, drab and choppy. The packet ploughed through it with ballooning sails, looking as fragile as a child's toy in the vast expanse. He travelled at a greater speed than any sea-going vessel, so that in an instant he passed the ship, then left it behind.

Drawn northward, on the same course as the packet, his velocity increased. He soared into piercing airstreams, yet was untouched by them, as though invisibly cocooned. And he was unaware of the sting of ice crystals when he sliced into low clouds.

He covered an enormous distance but glimpsed no other craft. At least, that's how it seemed. His speed was such that something as minuscule as a ship was easily overlooked in that immense ocean. He was likewise oblivious to land masses. Although he thought he saw, just fleetingly, a canopy of dark shapes hugging the surface of the ocean. Some were the size of islets, others no more than specks, and there was a profusion of them. They could have been the island group the packet was bound for; they were gone so quickly it was impossible to tell.

He began to slow, but not for any apparent reason. There was no land in sight. Beneath him, wind-driven waves caressed the sea with foaming fingers, just as before. Soon he moved no quicker than if he were swimming under his own muscle power.

At length he noticed something. In the sky, some distance ahead, there was what he took to be a black cloud, which appeared to be expanding, growing darker. Then he realised it was coming his way. As it approached he could see that it consisted of hundreds of individual dots, each moving of their own volition. The nearer the dark throng got, the more defined its constituent parts became, but it had almost reached him before he recognised what it was.

The cloud arrived and a world of frenzy engulfed him. All was wildly fluttering wings and ruffled feathers, beady eyes and spiky beaks, as a deafening, shrill cacophony battered his ears. He was in the eye of a storm, the centre of a blizzard of terrified creatures.

Suddenly it was over. The birds were well to his rear, a swirling miasma of flapping dots again. But more flocks were coming his way. And like the one he had passed through, they had an unnatural aspect: they were made up of different types of birds.

There was turmoil in the ocean, too. Huge schools of fish could be seen, swimming hard just below the surface. Fish of many kinds, from the smallest fry to large predators. Animals which, like the birds, would never normally group together, except in the face of some overriding common purpose.

This was no migration. The birds and the fish were fleeing from something.

A glint of light showed further north, against the far-off horizon. It grew in size and intensity until it replicated the rising sun. Then its flame spread to the sea, as though burning oil had seeped onto it. A fiery tidal wave rolled towards him, carrying shapes within it, Looking down from his elevated position he tried to make out what they were.

He thought he saw a glowing angelic host. Or perhaps a demonic horde. Then he came to see that it was a fleet, a thousand vessels or more, bathed in flame.

A man stood at the bow of the leading ship. A man he knew, though they had never met. A man who possessed an extraordinary power.

Their eyes locked, and he understood.

The warlord was coming.

20

It took several days for Darrok's aquatic glamour to reach Bhealfa's shores.

At the coast, the glamour nosed its way into the mouth of an estuary and entered the island's river system. Other fish shunned it, or perhaps they couldn't see it. And as it had no need for rest and sustenance, nothing obstructed its journey through the wintry waters.

Following its charm-induced instincts, the glamour went unerringly to the branch of the river serving the capital. But having achieved Valdarr's main port, it could no longer fulfil its mission in its present state, so a transformation was triggered.

There was turbulence, erupting bubbles and bursts of light. A different creature broke the surface of the water and rose out of it, dripping wings spread wide.

The bird was something like a raven, though not enough like one to convince anybody. But as it was about to enter a city swarming with glamours it was unlikely to be noticed. Soaring high, the illusion circled, alert for psychic scent. Then it knew its path, and set off at speed.

The sector neighbouring the docks was mean, all narrow

winding lanes and rowdy inns. Here the throb of magic was weak, and the militia patrolled in mobs. Acres of dour warehouses ruled the manufacturing district. The adjacent cattle-yard marked out its corrals with multi-coloured glamour orbs. Commerce shaded into residential districts, unremarkable suburbs lit by the prissy blush of respectable magic. They gave way to wealthy sectors, where the illumination of sorcery was at its most extravagant.

The pretence of a raven flew on.

Rich quarter or poor, the city's infatuation with magic was unabashed. Emporiums of illusion catered for the well-off, while lesser clientele were served by humble charm shops and dubious street vendors. The glamoured gambling dens did brisk business, with hex-powered fortune wheels and cards that turned of their own volition. In the smart parlours of fashionable couturiers, living mannequins modelled the latest gowns. On the streets, the needy rummaged for scraps.

The raven homed in on a safe house, ready to tell its tale and die.

On the opposite side of the city, an hour or so after the glamour's demise, wintry sunlight bathed the Pastures of Sleep. No such luxury existed in the catacombs beneath; only man – or magic – made light pushed back the gloom there.

A single charmed globe gently lit one particular chamber. Within, two sleeping children shared a cot, while Tanalvah sat on the only chair, head in hands. Had she sobbed, it would have been quietly, for the sake of the children, but she had reached a place beyond tears.

Teg and Lirrin were all that had stopped her from confessing. Her terror of what might become of them, and of the child she carried, was the remaining brake to her admission of guilt. But under the weight of the secret she carried, her thinking had changed. How could she subject them to life with a murderess? What kind of existence would they have when she might be exposed at any time? Above all, how could she live with herself after what she'd done? And loathe as she was to accept it, underlying everything was a growing acceptance that Kinsel was lost.

She slowly rose, stifling the groan brought on by the familiar stabbing pain in her lower back. Leaning with some difficulty, she lightly kissed each child, then she turned and shuffled from the cell.

There were people about, as there always were, day and night. Some nodded or waved. She didn't notice. A short walk took her to the great central hollow at the heart of the complex of tunnels. Karr and Goyter were cosseted in a corner, occupied with paperwork. Tanalvah made her way to them.

Karr saw her and called a greeting.

'Everything all right, Tan?' Goyter asked.

'Can I join you?'

'Of course,' Karr said. 'Nothing's wrong, I trust?'

'I've something important to tell you.'

Goyter was concerned. 'Whatever is it, dear? You look terrible. Here, do as Dulian said and sit down.'

Tanalvah sank onto a chair.

'Are you ill?' Karr wondered.

'I'm fine.' She took a breath. 'No, I'm not.'

'So you are sick?'

'It's not that. I . . .'

'I hope you know that you can share your problems with us, Tanalvah.'

'All I need you to do is listen. And try to forgive me.'

'Forgive you? Whatever for?'

'Just hear me out.' She took in their confused, expectant faces. 'The way you see me . . . the way you think I am . . . it's wrong.'

'I don't understand.'

'Please, Dulian. This is hard for me. I have to tell you . . .
tell you . . . it was me who –'

Somebody was shouting. A figure emerged from one of
the tunnels at speed and ran towards them.

'It's Quinn,' Goyter said. 'I wonder what's happened now.'

Disgleirio arrived, breathless. 'Good, you're all here together.'

'We were having a private conversation with Tanalvah,'
Karr told him, piqued at the interruption. 'So unless your
news is urgent –'

'It is,' Disgleirio panted. 'With respect to Tan, I think that
what I have to say is much more important.'

'Really? And what might that be?'

'Kinsel's alive.'

'What?' Tanalvah whispered. The colour bled from her
face.

'It's true. He's alive, and he's on the Diamond Isle.'

Deathly pale, Tanalvah swayed, looking ready to faint. The
others clustered around. Disgleirio took her shoulders,
steadying her. Goyter fanned her with a sheaf of documents.

'Here, drink this.' Karr held a cup of water to her lips.

She sipped from it. 'I'm all right,' she managed. 'I just . . .
I'm sorry . . .'

'How do you know this, Quinn?' Karr demanded.

'A glamour; a pretty fancy one. It carried a message from
Darrok.'

'What did it say?'

'Not a lot. Apparently Kinsel was rescued from pirates.'

'Pirates? Gods. How is he?' Karr asked.

'The message said only that he was alive.'

'I said Iparrater would protect him,' Tanalvah stated softly.
'I knew the goddess wouldn't forsake us.'

Karr squeezed her trembling hand. 'And your faith seems
to have been vindicated, my dear.'

'How does this make you feel about coming to the Diamond

Isle now, Tan?' Disgleirio asked. He was grinning.

She looked dazed for a second. 'I'll go. Of course I'll go.'

They were all beaming at her.

'And I'm sure we'll find that Kinsel's just fine,' Karr assured her.

'When do we leave?'

He laughed. 'As soon as we can.'

'You were trying to tell us something, Tanalvah,' Goyter reminded her. 'Before Quinn arrived.'

'I . . . It was nothing. Nothing at all.' Her moment of joy was corrupted. It all came flooding back. The only crumb of consolation was that she now had a chance to make her peace with Kinsel before the end. An end she knew was inevitable.

'Well, if you're sure,' Goyter said. Her expression seemed a little guarded.

'I'm sure.'

'You look sad.'

'Do I?'

'This is a shock for you. Your feelings are bound to be confused. Just remember that we're here for you.'

'I will. Thank you, Goyter. Now I really must tell the children.' She made to stand.

Goyter stretched a hand and restrained her. 'That can wait for a moment. Get your breath.'

Reluctantly, and with a sigh, Tanalvah sat again, though all she wanted was to be alone.

'Did the message say anything about the others, Quinn?' Karr asked. 'Reeth, Serrah, Kutch . . . ?'

'No, nothing at all.'

'Let's hope that's a case of no news being good news,' Goyter observed.

'Keep up your guard!'

'That's easy for you to say.' Kutch backed off and lowered his sword. 'You're used to this, I'm not.'

'All right,' Caldason conceded, 'we'll take a break.'

They were on deck, and wandered over to sit on a couple of barrels. The weather had grown noticeably colder the further north they travelled, and the ocean wind had a stinging edge.

'I'm sweating,' Kutch complained, wiping a sleeve across his forehead.

'I'd expect you to be. Combat's a strenuous activity, particularly if you're not used to it. Your arms and legs should be aching, too.'

'You bet they are. I don't think I'll ever make a fighter, Reeth.'

'No, you won't.'

'Oh.'

'But we're not trying to turn you into a master swordsman. We just need to teach you some basic self-defence techniques.'

'I still reckon my best contribution's going to be with magic.'

'You'll find that hard with a blade in your guts.'

'Er, true.'

'It's up to you. But I'd feel better knowing you had some skills to protect yourself with.'

'I want to learn, Reeth. It's just . . . well, to be honest, the thought of facing somebody with a sword for real frightens me.' Kutch reddened and studied his boots. 'I feel like a coward.'

'Good.'

'Eh?'

'People think behaving bravely means acting without fear. It doesn't. True courage is when someone acts despite their fear. You're not a coward, Kutch. I've known you long enough to recognise that.'

The boy smiled, half proudly, half abashed. 'Thanks, Reeth.

I don't feel very brave, I can tell you.'

'Start to worry if you do. Anyway, I think we've done enough for today. If you want another session tomorrow, just say.'

'I will. I mean . . . yes, please. And I'll try my best next time.'

'Our best is all any of us can give. How are you faring with your duties as ship's sorcerer?'

'Actually, there's not much to do. I regularly cast the detection spells Phoenix taught me, but that's about it.'

'Have you come up with anything?'

'No. Nothing except the background emissions from magic that are always present. Though there's less of that way out here, of course.'

'Background emissions?'

'All the magic being conjured in the world leaves a sort of residue. It's around us all the time.'

'And you can . . . sense it? How? Through these detecting spells or your own spotting talent?'

'A bit of both, I suppose. The training Phoenix gave me heightened my natural awareness of it, and that hasn't gone away, even though I stopped the exercises.'

'How does it . . . What's the word? How does it seem to you?'

'That's hard to explain. It's a bit like . . . like a piece of music being played quietly in another room. Or a whiff of honeysuckle on a summer breeze.' Kutch grinned. 'Only it's not really like that at all. You'd have to practice the Craft yourself to understand.'

'Then I'll stay ignorant.'

'I wish you weren't so antagonistic towards magic, Reeth. Knowing you disapprove of what I do makes me feel uncomfortable.'

'It's true I'd rather you weren't doing it. I'd prefer nobody to be doing it. But in rejecting magic I'm not rejecting you, Kutch. I hope you know that.'

'Yes, I do. But magic has benefits, Reeth. It brings so much good to people.'

'I could argue with that.'

'You're a special case.'

'Am I? What about those who can't afford it? Or suffer because of it? Are they special cases, too? If so, there's a hell of a lot of them.'

'I'm not saying things are perfect. But that's the fault of the system we live in, not the Craft.' He held up the rapier he was still clutching. 'It's like this sword. It can be in the hands of a tyrant or a freedom fighter. The sword has no say in it.'

'Pity there are so many more in the hands of tyrants then, isn't it?'

'You know what I mean, Reeth.'

'Yes. Though I think the logic's questionable. But you're overlooking the fact that I'm letting magic aid this voyage. That shows my mind's not totally closed, doesn't it?'

'It's a start, I suppose. But I'd like to see you grant that magic can do lots of positive things.'

'You'll never get him to agree with that, Kutch.' Serrah had arrived without them noticing.

'Maybe not,' Kutch replied, 'but it's worth trying.' He stood. 'I promised Phoenix I'd keep up with my studies, so I'd better make a start.'

'Don't be too late getting your head down,' Serrah cautioned. She took his seat on the barrel.

'I won't. Oh, the sword.' He made to give it back.

'It's yours,' Caldason told him. 'Get used to wearing it.'

'Really? Thanks, Reeth.' He sheathed it and left smiling.

When he was out of sight, Serrah said, 'Think that's wise?'

'Would you go without your blade?'

'Me? Hell, no. I'd feel naked. But he's just a boy.'

'I can't remember how many different weapons I'd owned before I was his age,' Caldason said.

'You come from a warrior race; it was expected of you. He's always been a bookish kid.'

'Then it's time he learnt to look after himself. Particularly with what's coming. And he's nearer man than child. Did you notice how he's starting to argue back?'

'He is fighting his corner more than he did. And yes, you're right; he should be armed. For all the good it's going to do him,' Serrah said.

'Do I sense a note of defeatism?'

'You know the odds. We'll be lucky if any of us on the Diamond Isle come out of this alive. Assuming it hasn't already been overrun when we get back.'

'This is a way of asking how much longer our trip's going to take, isn't it?'

'You know I'd feel happier on the island, doing what we could to defend it.'

'If we find the Source –'

'Yes, if. If we find it, if we work out how to use it, if we get back in time, then perhaps it could fend off an invasion. We can't pile all our hopes on a myth, Reeth.'

'Is that what you think?'

'Of course I hope it isn't. But don't you think there might be just a hint of gold at the end of the rainbow in all this? Quests usually occur in wordsmiths' stories or fairytales, Reeth.'

'What are you saying, that we should turn back?'

'You know I'm not. And I'm no less hopeful about the Source than you are, despite what you might think. But we never put a real limit on how long this is going to take. I'd like to have one.'

'I promised you we wouldn't be out here any longer than

we had to be. Why the sudden urgency?'

'That last vision you had. You saw Zerreiss coming. Shouldn't that ring alarm bells for us?'

'You're assuming the vision's prophetic.'

'Do you doubt it?'

He shook his head. 'No, I don't.'

'Then maybe it isn't too smart to be sailing into his path.'

'He's a long way off. I . . . knew that, in the vision. We could be done before he gets here.'

'It's the "could" that worries me.'

'Look, it won't be much longer before we get to the island group. We should be sighting them any time now, in fact.'

There was a cry from the lookout in the crow's nest.

'This is just too much of a coincidence,' Serrah said.

'That's not landfall. It's something else.'

They got up. A ship could be seen, well off from the prow. It was triple-masted, and looked sizeable, even from a distance. Caldason and Serrah hurried forward.

Rad Cheross was at the bow, studying the ship through a glamoured spy tube.

'What is it?' Serrah asked.

'That's an empire vessel,' the skipper told them.

'Which?'

'Rintarah, from the markings.'

'Is it an attack?' Caldason said.

'I don't think so. The rigging's set wrong, and I can't see anybody on deck.'

One of Cheross's crewmen appeared on the bridge with a pair of hand flags and began signalling.

They let a few minutes pass, maintaining their speed and course.

'No reply,' the Captain reported, lowering the spy tube. 'I reckon it's adrift.'

Kutch arrived. 'What's happening?'

'We're not sure,' Serrah explained. 'Could be a ship in trouble.'

'Can you try probing for magical activity, Kutch?' Caldason suggested.

The ship was nearer now. It looked becalmed. The Rintarah eagle emblem was plain to see on the mainsail.

Kutch closed his eyes and concentrated, knuckles white on the guide-rail.

'Anything?' asked Caldason.

'Nothing,' Kutch reported. 'But I'm not sure there would be from this distance.'

Cheross raised his spy tube again. 'So what do we do?'

'Get us over there,' Caldason said.

They crossed in the packet's largest lifeboat. Caldason led the boarding party, accompanied by Serrah, Kutch and nine of Cheross's crew. Reeth got one of the crewmen to hail the vessel, but there was no response.

'Picking up anything, Kutch?'

'No, Reeth. Not a thing.'

'All right.' He addressed them all. 'We're all going aboard, bar you.' He nodded at the helmsman. 'This could be a trap, so we need to get on fast, and I want weapons drawn when we reach the deck. If there's any sign of trouble we go on the offensive. Everybody clear? Good. Let's do it.'

The lifeboat bumped against the hull of the Rintarahian ship. Grappling hooks were tossed and ropes secured. Caldason and Serrah were the first up. Unused to such physical activity, Kutch went last, helped by a crew member.

On board, all was silent, save for the drifting ship's creaking timbers.

Caldason split the party into three groups. Four men were sent on a sweep, prow to stern, while four others were told to check below decks. He took Serrah and Kutch to the wheelhouse block, where the Captain's quarters were located.

At the first door they came to, he paused. 'You stay here while we look inside, Kutch. If you sense anything hostile, shout out.'

'I will.'

'And if it comes to a fight, try and stay clear.'

The boy nodded.

Caldason tried the handle. It was unlocked. He kicked open the door and went in fast, with Serrah right behind him.

They found themselves in an unremarkable cabin. The bunk was unmade, and there was a certain amount of everyday clutter. A quick search showed nothing out of the ordinary.

The next cabin was very much the same. An unsheathed, discarded sword, lying by an open clothes trunk, was the only sign of anything amiss.

Kutch went with them when they entered a third, much larger room, evidently the officers' mess. It had a long oak table, and wall racks holding tankards and earthenware crockery. Several chairs had been overturned, and there was broken glass underfoot. The table was a jumble of plates and cutlery, as though a meal had been interrupted. Hunks of stale bread and platters of rancid meat attested to the fact.

Caldason dipped his finger into a goblet of wine and touched his tongue with it. 'Sour,' he announced.

'What happened here?' Serrah wondered.

'I don't know. But it was quick, unexpected.'

The leader of one of the search parties came in. He was full-bearded and burly, with a ruddy face that spoke of years at sea. There was a thick, leather-bound book under his arm. 'The ship's completely deserted,' he reported.

'Any bodies?' Caldason asked.

'None we could see.'

'Signs of violence?'

'Not exactly.' He looked around. 'More like in here. As though everybody dropped whatever they were doing to answer an alarm or something. Down below, in the crew's quarters, the hammocks are still strung. You'd never get that in a well-run command, least of all an empire ship, unless something untoward occurred.'

'What's that?' Caldason said, indicating the book.

'We found it up by the wheel. It's the Captain's log.' He handed it over.

Caldason unceremoniously swept aside some of the detritus on the table and laid it down. Flipping pages, he came to the last, brief entry. 'This is dated months ago.'

'What does it say?' Serrah asked.

'Just routine stuff. The weather, a note about some provisions being low, that sort of thing.' He turned to the sailor. 'Do you know what these numbers mean?'

The man leaned in. 'They give the ship's position on the day this entry was written. If I read it right, they've drifted a hell of a long way.'

'Where were they?'

'Much further north. Very much further.'

Caldason and Serrah exchanged a look.

'You know what this ship is, don't you, Reeth?' she said. 'It's the expeditionary vessel Rintarah sent to investigate Zerreiss. Gath Tampoor sent one too, according to the Resistance.'

'I think we can assume that met a similar fate.'

'Yes, but what? What happened here?'

Caldason looked to the apprentice. 'You've been very quiet, Kutch. Can you help us on this?'

'What I'm spotting doesn't make sense. Or rather, what I'm not spotting.'

'I don't understand.'

'Neither do I. Remember what I said earlier, about there

being minute particles of magic everywhere, all around us? There are none here.'

'So?'

'You don't get it, Reeth. There are *none*. It's like the atmosphere, the very fabric of this ship, has been . . . cleaned. There's not the slightest trace of magic. On a ship that would have had a full complement of sorcerers and used the Craft in all sorts of ways.'

'That's significant?'

'Significant? Reeth, it's impossible.'

21

Where rival empires competed for dominance, foreign policy was often a euphemism for armed conflict. At any given time, territory was contested, rebellions were being quelled and unruly populations subdued. Occasionally, actual wars were waged between the empires, fought on their behalf by client states, but they were rarely, if ever, referred to as such. They were represented to the public in the guise of tiny nations pluckily struggling for freedom against enemy aggression. Whatever the terminology used to sanitise these clashes, one reality was constant. There were casualties. And while the warring parties had made destruction a fine art, little attention was paid to helping its many innocent sufferers.

Outrage at this spawned a popular movement. Its pioneers were women; the mothers, wives and sisters of victims. One offshoot of this essentially pacifist grouping was the Daughters of Mercy. Also known as the Star Network, for the golden sunburst that adorned the organisation's uniforms and transportation, the Daughters were a charitable association of volunteer healers. An exclusively female initiative to begin with, its remit was eventually widened to include male helpers, but the name was kept in honour of its origins.

The Daughters of Mercy refused aid to no one, civilian or military, of whatever side. Bringing succour was their only purpose. They endured hostility and suspicion, and they had their martyrs, but over the years they came to earn the respect of almost everyone. So it was commonplace for their members to accompany armies into battle, or, as today, a fleet sailing to mount an invasion.

The armada leaving from various of Bhealfa's ports, numbering several hundred ships, was just one colony's contribution to a greater Gath Tampoorian fleet. Perhaps half a dozen Star Network vessels went with them. One of the hospital ships, adorned with yellow starbursts, kept as far from the majority as possible. Scrutiny was something it couldn't afford.

'Well, we joined the fleet without too much trouble,' Disgleirio said. 'So far, so good.'

'We haven't left Bhealfa's territorial waters yet,' Karr reminded him. 'There are plenty of opportunities for being found out before we make our move.'

They were wearing fake uniforms, the star motif on chest and back. Their view consisted of nothing but ships.

'Do you think it's going to work?' Disgleirio asked.

'It has to. There's little point in us arriving with the fleet. We've got to outpace it. Fortunately this ship's designed for speed; war fleets aren't. The trick is slipping away unnoticed.'

Goyter came to them. She wore the feminine version of their garb, the golden stars bright against the white cloth of her jerkin.

'Quinn,' she said. 'I've been looking for you. They could use your help with the guard duty rota. A little supervision wouldn't go amiss, if you know what I mean.'

Disgleirio nodded. 'I'll get it sorted. If you'll excuse me?'

'Go ahead,' Karr told him.

When he'd gone, Karr asked Goyter how Tanalvah was.

'Resting, along with the children. Though there's precious little peace and quiet below decks, given the number of people we've crammed in.'

'We'll let them up as soon as we're clear of the fleet,' Karr assured her. 'Tell me, what do you make of Tan's mood?'

'It still swings a lot. She's either ecstatic or depressed, and tearful in both states. But it's only to be expected, I suppose, given what she's been through. I asked her if she'd had second thoughts about coming with us, seeing as we're heading for a war zone, and what with the children and everything.'

'I can guess her answer.'

'Yes, she's hell-bent on getting to the island. But it worries me, Dulian. I mean, it's all right for us; we're old. But do we have the right to drag a young, pregnant woman and two children into this mess?'

'It has to be her decision. But I know that if I still had a partner I'd like to be with them at a time like this. Wouldn't you?'

'Oh, yes.'

'I'm sorry, Goyter. You must be thinking of Brek.'

'It's a rare day when I don't.'

'How long is it now?'

'Since they killed him? Three years, four months and getting on for two weeks. And yes, of course I'd love him to be here. So I'm doing the next best thing and going for both of us. It makes it feel less like Brek . . . died in vain, I guess.'

'Your man didn't die for nothing. He gave his life fighting repression. There can't be too many better ways.'

'That's what I keep telling myself. Now stop it. You're making me morose, and I'd rather eat glass than play the grieving widow. Besides, you're looking glum enough for both of us. What's up?'

'I'm uncomfortable about using the Daughters of Mercy as our cover.'

'I thought we went through all that. It's a brilliant idea, Dulian. I can't see how we would have had a chance of getting out of Bhealfa otherwise.'

'But what if it goes wrong and rebounds on them? They're decent people. And there are those in the empires who'd jump at a chance to discredit them.'

'Sometimes we have to do things we'd rather not, if it's for the greater good. Worrying about it serves no purpose. It's too late now. It's done.'

'I suppose you're right.'

'You know I am. So what else is on your mind?'

'Isn't it obvious? Look at the size of this fleet. A sledge-hammer to crack a nut, if ever I saw one. The prospect is that we're sailing to almost certain death, and taking a hell of a lot of others with us.'

'As you said about Tanalvah, it's their choice. We all know what we're getting ourselves into. And there's something that you, of all people, should never lose sight of.'

'What's that?'

'There's always hope.'

The Bhealfan armada consisted of ships of many different classes. One category was owned by paladins, and such was the power and wealth of the clans that they were virtually a fleet within the fleet. The leader of their contingent, only two arrow-shots from the disguised Resistance vessel, was an especially grand flagship. On its bridge, well away from the steersman and other crew, two figures gazed out to sea.

'You know, we've never been on a ship before,' Aphri Kordenza admitted.

'Really?' Devlor Bastorran made no attempt to hide his indifference.

'What's the protocol? I mean, are we expected to follow navy rules or something? Not that there's a chance we would.'

'There's only one rule for you aboard this ship: behave yourself.'

Her dark eyes flashed dangerously. 'Selves,' she corrected. 'Selves. I do hate it when people don't take us seriously as a couple.'

'As far as this voyage is concerned, you are not a couple. You're simply you. I don't expect to see your . . . other half at any time. I'll thank you to keep his visitations strictly confined to your locked cabin.'

'Aphrim isn't going to like that.'

'Tough. We're part of an invasion fleet, not a pleasure cruise. I don't need the complication of you and your friend running amok on this trip. Keep your head down until we get there.'

'Then what?'

'Then you can let rip. There'll be plenty of sword fodder on the Diamond Isle.'

'That's just a snack. What about the banquet?'

'Caldason's the main reason I'm making this journey.'

'And you'll let us take him?'

'We'll see. You'll certainly play a part in his death.'

'We want the main role,' she came back petulantly.

'You'll get what circumstance hands us. If you're in a better position to kill him than I am, you've my permission.'

'But you're looking to do it yourself, aren't you?'

'He owes me a debt of honour.'

'He owes us too, remember!' Her eyes flashed viciously.

'Some might consider it presumptuous,' Bastorran replied coldly, 'that you should equate the honour of the head of the paladin clans with whatever passes for it among paid assassins.'

She swelled her hollow chest. 'We have our pride.'

'Swallow it. For this to work you have to do it my way.'

'I don't know why you bothered bringing us along at all.'

'Because I need somebody to help get my . . . our revenge on Caldason. Someone with your special skills. An ally I can trust.'

'Because we're implicated in your uncle's death too, you mean.'

'Keep your voice down!' Bastorran hissed, glancing around anxiously. 'You're more than implicated in that matter, and don't you forget it. And don't ever, ever mention the subject again. If you do, I'll make you wish you were never born. Both of you.'

'So much for equality between partners in crime,' Kordenza sniffed.

'As far as this mission goes, you're an employee. Do as I say and you'll be a well-paid one, in addition to the gift I've already given you. Plus you'll have the chance to get even with the Qalochian. Is that really so onerous?'

'Suppose not.'

'But foul this up and you'll regret it. Don't make the mistake of thinking I wouldn't have that thing torn out of your foot. Slowly.'

Kordenza sulked for a moment, then said, 'I thought your bald friend was supposed to be here.'

'What?'

'Tall, skinny. Bosses some spy unit.'

'Respect for your betters isn't a strong point with you, is it? I assume you're referring to Commissioner Laffon.'

'That's him. The creepy one.'

'You're obviously unacquainted with the expression about how people who live in houses made of glass shouldn't cast rocks.'

'Pardon?' She looked confused.

'Forget it. The Commissioner was recalled to Gath Tampoor at the last minute, if it's any of your business.'

'How irritating for him.'

'Yes. Particularly as he also has a personal interest in someone who could be on the Diamond Isle. As a matter of fact, I agreed to assist him in that regard. You can help.'

She eyed him suspiciously. 'Can I?'

'I think you'd be eminently suited to the job. Laffon wants us to capture a certain rebel.'

'We specialise in termination, not taking prisoners. Why the leniency?'

'The person in question's wanted back in Gath Tampoor. She was once a member of the security forces herself, so there's a political element. She needs to be interrogated, and something like a trial would be expedient, in terms of public opinion.'

'Who is it?'

'Actually, it's quite possible you know her. Laffon believes she's associated with Caldason. That means she could be a path to Caldason, of course.'

'Now that is interesting. Tell us more.'

'I can do better than that; I can show you. My aide's approaching with everything you need.' He indicated the lower deck with a prod of his thumb. Lahon Meakin marched their way, carrying something under his arm. 'Here's a chance to practise your new found discretion,' Bastorran added mordantly.

Kordenza shot him a dagger look.

Meakin climbed the stairs, and gave a deferential head bow. 'From Commissioner Laffon, sir.' He held out a sizeable leather wallet, tied with red ribbon.

Bastorran snatched it. 'This is the suspect's CIS file,' he told Kordenza as he unwound the ribbon.

Discreetly, Meakin retreated a step or two.

'Here.' The paladin slipped a thin, square object the size of a palm from the wallet. He handed it to her.

Kordenza stared at the swirling, milky surface until it coalesced. A face appeared, projecting out from the surface of the slate, and began to slowly turn, until the whole head had been shown. Then the face grew a miniature body, gradually revolving as though on a potter's wheel.

'Familiar?' Bastorran asked.

'Oh, yes. Laffon's right; she was with Caldason. And we owe her a spanking.'

'She's to be captured, remember. Though a little damage in the process would be quite acceptable.'

'What's her name?'

Bastorran held up the wallet. The stitched label bore copperplate writing that read, 'Serrah Ardacris'.

22

'*Twelve fathoms!*' The crewman gathered the chain, ready to cast it again at the skipper's command.

'When do we start worrying about the depth?' Serrah asked.

'At a fathom or less,' Cheross told her, 'if we take possible submerged outcroppings into account. And the currents in these parts are particularly treacherous, which is why seafarers don't come here.' He nodded at the crewman to take another measure.

The packet had entered an area of the ocean dotted with barren islands, many little more than rocks jutting from the freezing waters.

'Now we're here,' Serrah said, turning to Caldason, 'exactly how do we go about finding what we want?'

'If I'm being completely honest, I'd have to say I don't really know.'

'There's a surprise.'

'*Ten fathoms!*'

'But we should be able to narrow things down a bit through a process of elimination,' he went on.

'What are we eliminating?'

'Well, it seems reasonable that the Clepsydra isn't going to be on one of these tiny islets.'

'Why not? We don't know what the Clepsydra is, let alone the form it might take.'

'To figure this out we have to make guesses about where to start.'

'Guesses?' she repeated witheringly.

'Eight fathoms!'

'Assumptions, then. There are hundreds of islands in this group. We can't search all of them. So we have to concentrate on the most likely, and mass is a logical way of sifting them.'

'But that means scouring the whole group for islands of the right size. That alone could take weeks.'

'Not necessarily. There was something I noticed on the maps of this place Phoenix showed me. And the Captain can confirm it. Rad?' Caldason looked across at him.

'There's an old myth attached to this area,' Cheross explained. 'Well, not so much a full-blown myth, just a story. It's said two gods were warring with each other, and one of them . . . I can't remember which; it doesn't matter . . . one of them took up a mountain and flung it at the other. Only it missed and fell to earth here, in the ocean. The waters being shallow, the mountain shattered and its fragments became the island group.'

Serrah frowned. 'How does that –'

'When you see the charts,' Caldason said, 'that's what it looks like. As though a great big rock was dropped from the sky and shards flew off it. The largest islands are at the centre of the group. Most of them, anyway. The rest get smaller the further they are from the core. So the first thing we do is head there, and as this is a dense cluster, it shouldn't take too long to reach the centre.'

'Hmm. So what's your definition of a big island, seeing as

we know nothing about the Clepsydra? How big is big enough?'

'Some of the larger islands have vegetation, and fresh water springs. That might be a clue about where to look. But we'll set a minimum. Say . . . anything large enough to sit a small village on,' Caldason replied.

'How many fall into that category?'

'A couple of dozen,' Cheross volunteered. 'Maybe more.'

'That's ridiculous,' Serrah complained. 'How do we narrow it down?'

'I'm hoping Kutch's spotting talent might help,' Caldason replied.

'*Five fathoms!*'

'So that's the plan, is it? Look for the biggest rocks and hope the boy can solve the riddle?'

'It's all we've got. Along with these.' He tapped his forehead.

'I don't want to add to your worries,' Cheross interrupted, 'but take a look above. A storm's brewing. We could be in for a bumpy ride.'

Rain hammered down from the night sky. The ship rolled and pitched. But they still moved, inching through the muddle of islands.

Caldason, Serrah and Kutch clustered under the bridge block's overhang, seated on crates. They wore furs for the cold, hoods for the rain.

A clattering water bottle rolled towards them across the sloping deck. Caldason trapped it with his boot. He squinted into the ocean mist. 'At least the rocks seem to be getting bigger.'

Serrah stuffed a strand of wet hair back under her hood. 'I should hope so, after all day and most of the night.'

'Get some rest, both of you,' Caldason suggested. 'You don't have to stay here.'

'I thought we weren't that far from the core,' Kutch said.

'We're not. But the weather's slowed us to a crawl.'

'I think I'll stick with it for a while,' Serrah decided.

'Me too,' Kutch agreed.

'Suit yourselves.'

A moment passed in damp silence.

'Reeth . . .,' Kutch began.

'Yes?'

'I think . . . I think I can sense something.'

Serrah and Caldason straightened, weariness cast off.

'What is it?' Serrah asked.

'It's nothing specific, and I wasn't sure at first. But . . . I can feel an increase of magical discharges. Like mild pins and needles.' He grinned at them, half afraid.

Serrah laid her hand on his arm. 'You mean greater than you normally pick up as background noise?'

'Oh, yes. Lots.'

'Shouldn't you cast one of Phoenix's detection spells?' Caldason suggested.

'I don't think I need to. Then again, it could help with location.'

'Best to try,' Serrah said. 'Is there anything we can do?'

'No. I just need a little quiet time.' He started to get up.

She hung on to his arm. 'Kutch, are you certain about this?'

'Pretty much. At any rate, something's going on. Let me check.' He ducked into the rain, hurrying across deck with his head down.

Dawn was beginning to break. The sun's rim pierced the horizon, turning it cherry red.

'Perhaps this won't take as long as we thought,' Caldason remarked.

'You be careful with that boy, Reeth,' Serrah came back sternly. 'Keep him from harm.'

He was stung. 'Do you think I'd let anything happen to him if I could help it?'

'If you could help it, no. But we haven't a clue what we're dealing with. Who knows what's guarding the Source?'

'It wasn't my idea to have Kutch on this voyage. Or you, come to that. But now you both are, I'll do everything in my power to look after you.'

'I can look after myself, thanks very much.'

'Will you look after me too, then?'

She smiled. 'Buffoon.' Her tone softened. 'Of course I know you wouldn't willingly put Kutch in danger. Sorry.'

He slipped his arm around her. 'Forget it. We're all on edge.'

'It's because he's so young and vulnerable. When I look at him I can't help thinking of . . .'

He had to say it for her. 'Eithne.'

She nodded. 'I failed her. I won't do the same to Kutch.'

'You didn't fail her. Let go of the guilt; you can't bear it forever.'

'That's strange advice from somebody carrying so much himself,' she replied gently.

'We both wear our pasts like millstones. But what we're heading for could help us cast them off.'

'Don't put too much hope in the Source, Reeth. Chances are you'll be disappointed.'

'Then I'll be no worse off than I am now. Better. I've got you.' He made to kiss her cheek. She turned and waylaid his lips.

After a moment, she said, 'Do you really think we've a chance of finding the Clepsydra, and whatever the Source may be?'

'I wouldn't have set out if we didn't. Though granted it's a slim chance.'

'Do you reckon it's going to be guarded?'

'We have to assume it will be. But you know all this, Serrah. Why the inquisition?'

'I like to understand what I'm getting myself into, believe it or not.' She paused for a second. 'And I suppose I want convincing. No. Reassuring. I need to be reassured that what we're doing makes some sense.'

'I'm not certain I'm the one to do that. But I think this makes as much sense as anything we've done.'

'That isn't saying a lot, Reeth.'

'No,' he agreed, 'it isn't, is it?'

They laughed.

The packet kept moving, slowly, through lessening rain. Dawn was in full flush now, though its light was dismal. The islands they passed, dark bulks rising out of untrustworthy waters, grew larger.

Kutch hurried back, his breath white steam.

'Learn anything?' Caldason said.

'I didn't bother casting more than a couple of the spells, but they confirmed the high level of magic around here.'

'What about the direction it's coming from?'

'There are no specifics on that. The atmosphere's so saturated, it's hard even for a clever spell to locate,' Kutch said, frowning.

'Isn't it logical that the origin of all this magic is going to be at the centre of the island group?'

'Logic doesn't necessarily come into it. The magic could as easily be coming from the outskirts as the heart. It could be a speck of land or one of the biggest islands. It could be coming from a number of islands. The size or location doesn't really matter; it's the nature of the magic that's important. Mind you, having said that . . .'

'You do think it's coming from the core?'

'Yes.'

'So do I.'

'I sense it,' Kutch said. 'What are you basing your feeling on?'

Caldason shrugged. 'Just a hunch.'

Serrah stared at them, pensively.

'So we start at the centre and work our way out?' Kutch asked.

'Sounds like a plan,' Caldason told him.

Cheross was passing, looking as wet and tired as the rest of them. 'It'll be a couple of hours before we reach the inner group,' he said. 'You should try to get some sleep.'

Less than two hours later, and scarcely refreshed, they gathered again at the prow. The morning light was insipid this far north, and the air was desperately cold, but at least it had stopped raining.

The packet was anchored near an island. It had sheer cliffs and granite peaks, and they could see a stretch of pebbly beach.

'Do they have names?' Serrah asked.

'The islands?' Cheross said. 'Not that I know of.'

'I wonder if the Founders gave them names,' Kutch reflected.

'Why wouldn't they?' Caldason asked.

'Some scholars think they developed a culture that went beyond words and images as we understand them. Perhaps the Founders felt no need to label the world the way we do.'

Cheross shook his head. 'A world without names? That'd be chaos.'

'They had a different way of looking at things.'

Serrah chimed in with, 'Clepsydra's a name, isn't it?'

'Yes, but we don't know if the Founders coined it,' Kutch explained. 'There are very few words in our language inherited from them, and they're all contentious.'

'What are you saying? That they didn't have words for anything at all? Cheross is right; that would be chaos.'

'Not to the Founders. Anyway, I'm not saying they didn't have words for some things. Perhaps they named what had particular significance for them. The scant evidence they left, the fragments of their knowledge, seem to back that.'

'What does it look like? This evidence they left.'

'Well, it isn't in its original form. These scraps, which is all we're really talking about, have been copied many times over the centuries. We've got them on paper; we don't know what their original form would have been. As to the language . . . well, language probably isn't the right word. The Founders' writings are a mixture of symbols, mathematical allusions and . . . magicky stuff.'

'Your use of the correct technical terms must make Phoenix proud.'

They all laughed, though there was a nervy edge to it.

Kutch was red-faced. 'I just didn't want to bore everybody.'

'We know,' Serrah mouthed kindly.

'The Founders might not have left names for these islands,' Caldason reminded them, 'but they could have left something else.'

'Like booby-traps,' Serrah offered, sobering.

Caldason nodded. 'If the prize is as important as a lot of people think, it'll be guarded. The question is, with what?'

'Magic,' Kutch stated matter-of-factly. 'We're talking about the Founders, remember.'

'What form could it take?'

'Who knows?'

'Would it still be potent after all this time?' Serrah wondered.

'I can't answer these questions,' Kutch admitted. 'All I can do is try to detect any magic with evil intent.'

'With all this other background magic going on?'

'I've been trained to filter it out. Besides, it's of a different nature. The textures vary.'

'As to the matter at hand,' Cheross said, 'we'll keep a skeleton crew here and send the majority of the men with you.'

'Thanks,' Caldason replied, 'but no. All we need is a rowing party to get us over there.'

'But surely, in the face of –'

'I don't want to put your crew in greater danger. And unless any of them happen to be master wizards, or have a spotting talent like Kutch's, there's not much they can do to help us. Whatever's out there, Serrah, Kutch and I are going to be looking for it alone.'

'Every member of my crew would gladly volunteer to go with you.'

'I know, and we're grateful. If we need them, they can come later, when we're certain everything's clear, but we take the initial risk.'

'And you're sure this is the island?' The Captain nodded at the looming rock.

'We can't be sure,' Kutch replied, 'but this is where the magic feels strongest.'

'Let's not get too carried away,' Serrah cautioned. 'The very first island we land on? And the most conspicuous? It's unlikely to be that easy.'

'We have to start somewhere,' Caldason told her. 'And I've got an instinct about this island too.'

She gave him a curious look, but said nothing.

'I'll arrange to have you taken across right away,' Cheross announced. 'Once you've disembarked, the boat will wait for a couple of hours. If you need us after that, we'll come at your signal. But if we've heard nothing from you after twelve hours, this ship sails back to the Diamond Isle.'

Caldason nodded. 'Fair enough.'

'Then let's get things moving.' Cheross turned away to give out orders.

'All right, you two?' Caldason asked, keeping his voice low.

'I'm fine,' Serrah replied.

'I'm quite excited,' Kutch admitted.

The crew were scattering to various tasks, and the noise level went up a notch.

'It could be an idea to take some extra weaponry along,' Caldason suggested.

'Against magic?' Serrah said.

'That might not be all we run into.'

'I'm taking a set of throwing knives, along with a couple of my usual blades,' she said, eyeing him. 'If that's not enough, nothing will be.'

'What about you, Kutch? Can I persuade you to carry another weapon?'

'I already do, Reeth.' The boy slipped a hand into his fur jerkin and brought out a dagger. 'Recognise this, Serrah? You gave it to me the day we got out of Bhealfa.'

'I'd forgotten it. You didn't have to use it that day, thank the gods. But be prepared to.' She looked to Caldason. 'What about supplies? Are we going to load ourselves down with those, too?'

'A canteen of water each and a little hardtack. Not much point in taking more.'

'You don't expect us to be there very long?' Kutch supposed.

'We'll return soon, or we'll be dead. Either way, there's no sense in burdening ourselves.'

They were called. The boat had been lowered, and its eight rowers waited. Caldason led Serrah and Kutch to the rail, where they collected water pouches. Then they descended rope ladders to the bobbing craft.

Their journey across was short, and the sea had settled down, but they were tense, expecting some kind of ambush or trick to foil them. Although the biggest of the group, the island was of a modest size. Serrah, the urban dweller, would have described it as being equivalent to nine or ten city blocks. Kutch would have seen it in terms of so many fields for ploughing. To Caldason, its widest point corresponded to three good spear throws.

There were cliffs at one end of the island, and a couple of modest rocky crests further inland, but basically it was flat, with shingle beaches fronting most of its shoreline.

They landed without incident. The rowers were thanked and left on the beach. Caldason, Serrah and Kutch could feel the crew's eyes boring into their backs as they set out.

Out of the men's hearing, Kutch said, 'The magic . . . I can feel it. It's very intense.'

Serrah shot him a concerned glance. 'Are you all right to go on?'

'Yes. Yes, I'll be fine.'

They came to the top of the beach. Over a ridge, where they couldn't be seen by the nervous band of rowers, lay a scrubby plain.

'Which way?' Serrah wondered.

Reeth and Kutch pointed simultaneously, and unerringly. North. Towards the interior.

'Well,' she said, 'that seems fairly clear.'

'It's where the magic's coming from,' Kutch explained.

Caldason said nothing.

As they travelled, the scrub gave way to grass, and bushes and trees started to appear.

'You wouldn't have thought vegetation could take hold in a place like this,' Serrah remarked.

'It's the magic,' Kutch told her. 'There are very strong energy channels running through these islands. They bring fecundity, particularly where one or more cross. Haven't you noticed how mild the temperature is?'

'Now that you come to mention it –'

'What's that?' Caldason said.

In the undergrowth there were fragments of whitish stone.

'Could be a path of some kind,' Serrah decided.

'It's the remains of a road,' Kutch confirmed, 'and it looks really old. What sort of stone is that?'

'One I've never seen before,' Serrah replied, excavating it with the toe of her boot. 'If it is a road, it seems to start about here; and it's going the same way we are.'

They followed it. The landscape became increasingly lush, and the air warmer. Bizarrely, trees were in leaf, and there was an abundance of unseasonable wild flowers.

At length, they saw the road's destination. It terminated at a tall outcropping, and there was an opening in the rock. Not a natural fissure, of the sort leading to a cave, but a cut entrance, large enough to comfortably drive a wagon through. If there had ever been doors, they had rotted away long ago.

A jumble of debris was scattered around the outcrop. As they approached, they could make out fallen pillars, broken plinths, and what might have been the remnants of an arch.

'This looks like the way into a temple or something,' Serrah said.

'It's hardly a place to hide anything,' Caldason agreed. 'All it lacks is a sign.'

'Perhaps whatever's in there wasn't hidden,' Kutch ventured.

'What do you mean?'

'We've assumed that the Clepsydra, and the Source, were deliberately concealed. But maybe they weren't so much hidden as just . . . left. Abandoned.'

Serrah was doubtful. 'And no one's come here before us and found them?'

'What if we're the only ones who can see this?'

'That doesn't make sense, Kutch. I'm not a spotter, and neither is Reeth.'

'Forget my spotting talent. Suppose us being able to see this place is a function of Founder magic.'

'I don't understand.'

'Maybe we were meant to find it.'

'How could that be?' Serrah's brow wrinkled.

'As I said, they didn't think like us.'

'We're jumping to conclusions,' Caldason said. 'Serrah could be right; somebody might have got here first. Let's check the place.'

They stood in front of the entrance, gazing at a pitch-black interior. Kutch and Serrah took out small glamour orbs, and Caldason spent a few seconds patting pockets before producing one himself. Then they stepped inside.

A musty smell hit them. The dust of ages. Twenty or thirty paces in, they came to a set of broad stairs that swept down into deeper darkness. Clutching the hilts of their swords, they warily descended.

One hundred and thirty-five steps later, they arrived at a level, and ahead of them was a wall that didn't quite reach the ceiling. There were two doorless entrances in the wall, to right and left.

'Which one?' Caldason wondered.

'Give me a leg-up,' Serrah told him. Boosted to the top of the wall, she peered in, holding out her glamoured orb. She saw more walls, and passageways that zigzagged. 'It's a labyrinth.'

'How big is it?' Caldason asked.

'I can't see its end. It's too far, too dark. But in the distance . . .'

'Yes?'

'There's a kind of glow. That's all I can make out. Watch yourself, I'm coming down.'

'How do we handle this?' Caldason said. 'If there are traps in there or –'

'Excuse me,' Kutch interrupted. 'We're assuming things again. It looks as though this was some kind of public place, a memorial or something, not a secret to be defended. You know what mazes are for? They're a path to enlightenment, a map of higher states of consciousness. It's a symbolic journey, not a trap or a barrier.'

'So what do you suggest?'

'I'm not saying we shouldn't be ready for trouble, but let's try walking it the way the Founders would have. As pilgrims or adepts, or however they thought of themselves when they came here.'

'We just walk it?' Serrah said. 'Is there any special way of getting through?'

'The tradition with labyrinths is to take left turns on the way in, right turns coming back.'

'That sounds vaguely impossible.'

'It's as good a plan as any,' Caldason decided. 'So we go in by the . . . left door?'

'The right,' Kutch corrected. 'Think about it.'

'I'm trying not to,' Serrah told them. 'It makes my brain hurt.'

Caldason went first, but most of the paths were wide enough for them to walk abreast. The shimmer of their glamour orbs lit walls, floor and ceiling of a uniform whitish-grey and unwavering evenness.

'It's so smooth,' Serrah muttered, skimming her fingers across a surface. 'What is it?'

Caldason shook his head. 'No idea, but for all its smoothness it has friction. Have you noticed how the floor slopes, yet we're not sliding down it?'

'I have,' Kutch replied. 'We're going deeper. And it's a lot warmer, too.'

'How does the magic feel to you?' Serrah asked him.

'It's . . . heady. Definitely building.'

They took yet another left turn.

'Is it my imagination,' Serrah said, 'or is it getting lighter down here?'

Kutch wiped the back of his hand across his sweaty forehead. 'We're close now.'

'Ssshh.' Caldason had a finger to his lips. 'Do you hear that?'

Serrah strained to hear. 'There's something.'

'What do you think? Flowing water?'

'No. It's too . . . slithery.'

They carried on. The light grew brighter, the air hotter. They turned, turned, turned again.

The labyrinth abruptly ended.

They faced a wall. It had a single entryway carved into it, identical to the one they came in by. Beyond it was light, unidentifiable sound, and the weight of an awesome presence. Each of them felt it.

Caldason moved forward, drawing a sword. Serrah did the same and made to follow. She looked to Kutch, saw the expression on his face, and waited. Smiling, she pocketed her orb and offered him her hand. He took it, squeezing hard, and they joined Reeth.

For a second, the three of them hesitated at the threshold.

Then they went through.

23

The Bone Temple at Earth's End. Gazall's bridge over Teardrop Valley. The five remaining towers of Akhom-Behtz. The statues of Crae and Fornarr at Dragon Spine Mountain. All were chilling partly because they were colossal, and size is naturally intimidating.

However, it was mainly their great age that was disturbing. It had something to do with the eons they'd weathered, and the countless mortals they'd outlasted. As though, like vampires, they drew into themselves the life essences of short-lived things to prolong their own mono-lithic existence. It was as if they imbibed the detritus of the ages; every windblown particle of human skin, every stray hair, every speck of sweat or drop of shed blood, absorbed.

Kutch, Serrah and Caldason felt that dread. They knew the terror of vast antiquity, and of gigantism, a feeling compounded by the fact that what they were looking at was imbued with such a sense of otherness.

The maze had led them to a massive cavern. It was brightly lit by sorcery, though no glamoured orbs were apparent; the light seemed to bleed from the yellowish rock itself. The air was perfumed by a mingling of aromas, sulphur being the strongest by far.

Big as the cavern was, a single artefact utterly dominated the space. It was the size of a mountain peak, and seemed to be fashioned from the living rock, along with a commingling of other materials that might have included steel, quartz, zinc, ceramics, and even gold. The great broad face of the edifice was adorned with unknown symbols in vivid colours that kept their brilliance despite the passing of countless ages.

Much more striking was a dowel, wide as a mature tree, long as a street, suspended from the upper reaches. It was similar to a pendulum, but appeared to be stationary. Closer scrutiny showed that it must have moved, imperceptibly slowly, from a point on the far left towards a corresponding point on the far right. A green symbol marked its start and a red symbol its terminus, which the pendulum's tip had almost reached. The whole contrivance was attended by a deep, rhythmic throb that massaged the soles of their feet.

'I don't know what I thought the Clepsydra would be,' Serrah whispered, 'but I never imagined it like this.'

Seen head on, the relic looked as though it sat on an islet. It gave that impression because a small river ran the length of its base, flowing between openings on opposite sides of the cavern. But it was no ordinary river. The liquid was quicksilver.

It didn't run straight from one aperture to the other. On the way, the pewter stream fed itself to the Clepsydra, as water pours through a mill. Sluggish, glutinous, it made a pulpy sound as it slipped into artfully carved ducts.

'No wonder it's stood for so long,' Kutch said, awestruck. 'It draws directly from magic's chariot. The amount of power involved – I wouldn't go too near, Reeth. This level of energy's really dangerous.'

Caldason didn't reply. He looked distant.

'Reeth?'

Serrah went to the Qalochian and grasped his arm. 'Reeth!'

He came back into focus. 'What?'

'You were away there.'

He shook his head to clear it. 'It's hot down here, and the magic . . .'

'It's pretty overwhelming,' Kutch agreed.

'All I can feel is the heat,' Serrah said. 'Here.' She handed Caldason her water pouch.

He took a long drink and seemed better for it. Then he turned to Kutch. 'So what do you reckon? What is this thing?'

'I think the scholars were right; it's a timepiece.'

'Measuring what?' Serrah asked. 'Hours? Days?'

'You have to think on a much larger scale than that.' He was gazing up at the thing. 'Look at the symbols.'

'You understand them?'

'Mostly, no. But one or two are in remaining Founder fragments, and we think we know what they mean.' He pointed. 'See that one? At the beginning of the pendulum's track?'

'The one that looks like a figure eight with a billhook through it?'

'Yes, the green one. It means . . . well, it means a lot of things, but chiefly something like birth or beginning. One interpretation is "seed"; another's "Spring", or "a well".'

'Not too difficult to interpret, then,' she said.

'No. It's fairly obviously a starting point. All those other symbols the pendulum's passed on its journey presumably mark important stages or events.'

'Events in what? Somebody's life?'

Caldason had been taking this in silently. Now he spoke. 'All of our lives.'

'What do you mean?'

'Kutch is beginning to understand. Aren't you, Kutch?'

The apprentice nodded. He was pale, despite the heat.

'Don't keep me in suspense,' Serrah complained. 'What is it?'

'That symbol right at the top, in black and orange,' Kutch explained hesitantly, indicating an image the size of a wagon wheel. 'It's the Founders' glyph for all. Everything.'

'And by everything . . .'

'Scholars believe it meant just that; the whole thing. The world.'

'I still don't —'

'Look where the pendulum is now,' Caldason said. 'You see? Where the tip of the arrow's pointing? I'd put money on what that symbol means.'

'It's end,' Kutch confirmed. 'Not death exactly, because the Founders didn't seem to have a symbol for that. But "cease", "expend" and "ultimate" all fit. It's a symbol we always see in relation to the Founder concept of the Last Days.'

'Oh, great,' Serrah exclaimed. 'We come looking for help and find the world's about to end. Assuming the Founders knew what they were talking about.'

'They were an extremely perceptive race,' Kutch replied.

'It doesn't follow that they were right about everything. I mean, if they were so clever, how come they aren't still around?'

'I suppose even the Founders weren't infallible. But they had the most advanced civilisation the world's ever seen. They could have been right about this.'

She sniffed dubiously and studied the pendulum. 'What do you think that means in terms of time? How long do we have left?'

'This thing was designed to measure eons. So who can say? Centuries? Weeks?'

'More likely weeks than centuries,' Caldason said.

'How do you figure that out?' Serrah asked.

'Because we've arrived here at just this time.'

'That sounds very mystical for you, Reeth.'

'It . . . feels right.'

Kutch nodded in agreement.

'You're saying we were somehow meant to be here at this time?' she pressed.

'I don't know what I'm saying, only that being here now seems a kind of . . . fit.'

'Getting here as the world's due to end is good timing?'

'As you said; maybe they were wrong about that.'

'But you think something's going to happen?'

'I'm hoping we'll find the Source.'

'We're all hoping that. It's why we came, remember?' She took in the vastness of the cavern. 'So where is it?' There was a trace of mild derision in her voice.

He shrugged. 'Perhaps Kutch's spotting talent . . .'

'I don't think I can,' the boy confessed.

'I thought you were trained to filter things out,' Serrah said.

'I was. But this place is so saturated, it's impossible.'

'We don't have a plan then.'

'Yes we do,' Caldason corrected. 'The oldest one in the book. We search.'

'Where?'

'This cavern might not be all there is down here.' He nodded towards the rock wall furthest from the Clepsydra, where shadows were deepest.

'Fine by me. This thing gives me the creeps; I'll be glad to get away from it.' She turned her back on the dreadful, pulsating mechanism.

They set out. As they neared the wall, they activated their glamoured orbs. The outlines of several tunnels could be seen, darker than the surrounding gloom.

'Which one?' Kutch asked.

'We could split up,' Serrah suggested.

Caldason shook his head. 'Not wise.'

'Hey,' Kutch said, 'look at this.' He was scraping at the dusty ground with the sole of his boot. 'I hadn't noticed it before.'

Serrah gazed down. 'What is it?'

'A marked energy line.' He'd revealed part of a dark blue stripe, still vivid after an eternity.

'Here's another.' She exposed a patch of yellow.

'Nothing surprising about that,' Caldason decided. 'The Founders started the tradition, didn't they, Kutch?'

'Hmm, it's thought so.' He was preoccupied with clearing the dirt.

Between them, shuffling about, they uncovered half a dozen or more. Red, green, orange, purple, criss-crossing the cavern's base and slicing into the Clepsydra.

'At least three run straight from that tunnel,' Kutch pointed out.

Caldason took a look. 'So let's go that way.'

'As a system for finding something,' Serrah protested, 'this is crazy. You do know that, don't you, Reeth?'

'Got a better idea?'

She hadn't.

They moved towards the opening, orbs held out and weapons ready. The entrance they'd chosen was generously sized, easily wide and tall enough for them to pass through comfortably, but they felt no ease as they went in.

They found themselves in a tunnel that turned sharply to their right. As it progressed it slanted, taking them gently but decisively deeper. When the path levelled, a few hundred paces on, it opened out and led into another chamber. This was large, but nowhere near as huge as the one above.

Everything here looked natural, unlike the unknown substance the maze was fashioned from. Stalagmites and stalactites bristled like serpents' teeth, and there were stone hillocks and granite arches. Tunnel mouths riddled the cavern.

In places, the rock resembled grey frozen waves, as though it had flowed before hardening. The air was fusty.

'I wonder how far this all goes on for,' Serrah said.

'Could be miles,' Caldason reckoned.

'So how do we go about searching?'

He turned to Kutch. 'What do your senses tell you now?'

'The magic's less oppressive, but it still feels like a blanket. Though . . .'

'What?'

'It seems a little weaker in that direction.' He nodded.

'All right. Come on that way.'

Serrah caught his arm. 'Should we be going the way Kutch senses less magic?'

'We're going the way of difference. It's all we've got at the moment.'

They fell in beside him and moved in the direction Kutch had indicated. Tramping the irregular floor, they were aware of the humidity and the unmoving air.

Then Caldason stopped and held up a hand. 'Feel that?'

A cool draught blew gently from a nearby tunnel.

It caressed Serrah's cheek. 'So we go in there, right?' She viewed the prospect sourly.

'Yes, let's keep following our hunches.'

'I think you mean your hunches, Reeth.'

They entered the shaft. It was narrow and winding, and it reminded Serrah of why she shunned enclosed spaces. However, eventually it opened into yet another sizeable cavern, not unlike the last.

'How many more?' Kutch wondered.

Serrah shushed him.

There was a rushing noise. The light from their orbs threw back the glint of a subterranean river. At first they thought it was more quicksilver, but it proved to be water, and it was cold, despite the sultry atmosphere.

Serrah knelt on the bank and scooped a little with her palm. The taste was intensely brackish and she spat it out.

'What did you expect,' Caldason teased, 'honeyed wine?'

She rose and looked about. 'This is hopeless, Reeth. We could wander around down here forever.'

'Perhaps we should be a bit more methodical about it,' he conceded.

'It'd make sense to have some kind of system. Maybe we could –' A sound cut her short. Then she caught a movement on the edge of her vision. Something darted into one of the tunnel entrances.

Caldason saw it too. 'Stay with Kutch!' he yelled, racing off.

'Like hell! Come on!' She dashed after him, dragging the boy with her.

Caldason sped into the tunnel, with Serrah and Kutch pelting in close behind. They ran headlong, navigating twists and tunnel splits. Their giant shadows were grotesque against the craggy walls.

Serrah could hear Kutch breathing hard behind her. She saw Reeth's back, some distance ahead, but he was drawing away. She was losing sight of him.

Caldason wasn't sure what he was chasing. The figure was lithe, and moving fast. It obviously knew these tunnels well, judging by the fluidity with which it traversed them. He began to think it was going to get away.

No sooner had the thought occurred than the figure came to grief. It tripped, tumbled, fell. He put on a burst of speed, hoping to get there before it found its feet.

There was a collision. A tangle of limbs. He was struggling, fighting with something wild, feral. Something that scratched and spat with sharp teeth and raking nails. A mass of black hair.

He had hold of a girl. He thought it was a child at first,

then realised she was a young woman. Slimly built, perhaps half-starved. And she had a knife. Its curved blade flashed. He caught her wrist and arrested its arc. Although her frame was slight, she was strong, but no match for him.

Further along the tunnel they'd been running down there was a stirring. Pinning the frenzied girl, Caldason looked up. Someone approached in shadow. A voice sounded. He couldn't make out what was said, but the girl heeded. She let go of her knife and went limp.

Caldason hardly noticed. He could see the figure clearly now as it slowly approached, and was transfixed.

Serrah and Kutch arrived, panting. She had her sword drawn. He clutched his dagger.

'What is it?' she said. 'Who . . . ?'

Caldason wasn't listening. He was staring at the new arrival.

He had no recollection of ever meeting him, but he knew him well. He'd seen him a thousand times before.

It was the old man who lived in his dreams.

24

An observer could have mistaken them for a tableau of wax mannequins.

Then Serrah said, 'What the hell's going on, Reeth? Who are these people?'

Caldason said nothing.

The old man took a hesitant step forward, a look of consternation on his face. 'Reeth? Can it be?'

Caldason slowly rose, ignoring the girl he'd been pinning down. She scuttled away, scooping up her knife, and dashed to the old man. Blueberry-eyed and her hair bedraggled, she stood defiantly at his side, blade at the ready. She was scrawny and dirty, and dressed in brown rags.

The old man was no better outfitted, in tattered, rough-woven cloth. He was liver-spotted, and his beard was white. 'Reeth?' he repeated. 'Is that really you?'

'Don't you recognise me?' Caldason whispered, finding his voice at last.

The old man gently shed the girl's protective arm and moved into the light.

His eyes were milky and disfigured, and unmistakably blind.

'My gods,' Kutch let out.

'There are three of them,' the girl explained, glaring at the outsiders. She addressed the old man exclusively, as though the others couldn't hear or understand. Her voice had a surprising purity, despite its harsh tone.

'Thank you,' he responded. To the rest, he added, 'You must excuse Wendah; it's been a very long time since either of us knew company.' He took another few paces until he stopped by Caldason's outstretched hand. 'May I?' he asked. Taking the Qalochian's silence as consent, he reached up and touched Caldason's face, his fingers gently tracing its contours. 'It is you. I thought . . . I feared you were dead.' He threw his arms around him.

Awkward in the embrace, Caldason replied, 'And I was never sure you actually existed.'

The old man backed off, his ruined eyes moist. 'Being muddled about the past, not remembering, that's only to be expected, given what you've been through.'

'One thing I do seem to know is that you looked exactly the same. You haven't aged a day. What are you doing here? And what happened to your sight?'

'We have much to discuss, Reeth. There's a great deal to be explained, and your friends, these people with you, they must be confused.'

'You bet,' Serrah assured him. 'This particular friend wants to know what the hell you two are talking about. Starting with where do you and Reeth know each other from?'

'From my dreams,' Caldason told her.

'Your what?'

Kutch and the girl looked no less taken aback.

'As I said,' the old man intervened, 'there's a lot to be explained. And I've been expecting someone to come, looking for answers.'

'You have?' Serrah said. 'Why?'

'For the last couple of years there have been disturbances in the essence powering the Clepsydra, and in the device itself. In recent months it's grown much stronger. Something had to happen.'

'Is there someplace we can discuss this?' she asked. 'Somewhere out of these tunnels?'

'Of course.' He addressed the girl. 'It's all right, Wendah.' His hand unerringly found the blade she held, and gently turned it aside. 'We must offer our guests such hospitality as we can.' After a second's hesitation, she put the knife away. To them all, the old man said, 'Come. It's not far.'

He set out, lightly clasping the girl's shoulder. She glanced back, scowling at them, and it seemed to Kutch that she paid particular attention to him.

The procession negotiated a series of tunnels, with attendant sets of perplexing bends and twists, then they entered a low-roofed grotto. Within, a large, cleverly placed flat stone concealed the entrance to a hollow. They squeezed inside.

The cave was ample in size and lit by wax and oil. Sufficiently so that Caldason, Serrah and Kutch disabled their glamour orbs. What the light showed was an ordered jumble. Mismatched bedding, and crates used as furniture. Crab shells for dishes, and chipped pots. A crudely made bow, propped in one corner, along with a bundle of coarse arrows. Driftwood and cast-offs, adapted to the necessities of survival.

'Our abode,' the old man announced, 'such as it is. Try to make yourselves comfortable.'

'You live here?' Kutch exclaimed.

'If you can call it living.' The old man seemed breathless. He put a hand to his brow and looked pained.

Serrah was concerned. 'What's wrong? Can we do anything?'

'Thank you, no. I'm constantly . . . in discomfort.'

The girl, still eyeing their visitors suspiciously, helped him to a chunk of rock vaguely resembling a throne. He sank onto the makeshift seat with a relieved sigh.

She took a cracked cup and fetched some water from a nearby cask. Then she squatted beside him, watchful.

'Do take your ease,' the old man repeated. He drank, his hands trembling slightly.

Kutch and Serrah perched amongst the clutter. Caldason sat on a barrel.

The old man said, 'I never thought to –' He stopped himself, smiling thinly. 'I was about to say I never thought I'd see you again, Reeth. Not in this world. It seems I was right about that.' A fleeting reverie occupied his face. 'I'm a poor host,' he decided. 'You must think me ignorant for not even asking your friends' names.'

'No,' Caldason replied. 'Nobody's slighted. This is Serrah Ardacris; and our friend, Kutch Pirathon.'

The 'our' told the old man all he needed to know about Reeth and Serrah's relationship. 'Wendah,' he introduced, squeezing the girl's arm, 'friend and dependable companion. She acts as my eyes, in a very real way. Been with me here since she was a child.'

'How did that come about?' Serrah wondered.

'She was the sole survivor of a shipwreck. Most vessels avoid this place; many of those that don't, come to grief. Everything you see here was salvaged from wrecks.

'Do you remember my name, Reeth?' he asked abruptly.

The Qalochian was caught off-balance. He shook his head, discomfited.

'Praltor Mahaganis,' the old man supplied. 'Does that mean anything to you?'

'No. Or rather . . . perhaps. I don't know. Sorry.'

'Don't worry about it now. It'll come.'

'How do you survive in this place?' Serrah said.

'We have rainfall for drinking water, much of the surface

vegetation's edible, if bland, and we catch fish. Occasionally we dine on fowl. Wendah's pretty handy with bow and sling-shot, though not in your league, Reeth. And there's flotsam and jetsam to pick over. But tell me about yourselves. How do you come to be here?'

'The Source,' she told him.

'Ah.' If the answer surprised him in any way, there was no sign. 'Why do you seek it?'

'It's possibly our only hope. How much do you know about what's happening in the outside world?'

'Very little. We've been here a long time.'

'The Resistance has given up inciting revolution against the empires,' she recapped, 'and tried to establish a dissident state. But the scheme was betrayed and it's near to collapsing.'

'There's an organised resistance?'

'Exactly how long have you been here?'

'Most of Reeth's adult life.'

'How did you come to this?' Caldason asked, indicating their squalid surroundings.

'You don't know what you are, do you?' the old man countered. 'Of course you don't; we'd all be aware of it if you did.'

Caldason was baffled. 'What on earth are you talking about?'

The old man waved the question aside. 'What do you remember? Of your days with me, that is.'

'It's not so much memories as . . . dreams of that time. You were training me in the martial and mental skills I'd need. Equipping me to survive. I owe you my life.'

'It was the least I could do.'

'How so?'

'I'm in your debt.'

'You've got it wrong. I'm in yours.'

'Perhaps you wouldn't feel that way if you knew the truth.'

'What truth?' Serrah interrupted tetchily. 'You hint at rev-
elations, but –'

'Reeth's people were massacred by mine,' Mahaganis
declared bluntly. 'I think that qualifies as a debt, don't you?'

No one spoke, until Caldason recovered his disbelieving
tongue. 'You've been stuck here too long,' he said quietly.
'It's given you delusions.'

'It's not a fantasy, Reeth, and there's no pleasant way of
putting it: my blood tried to exterminate yours. I would have
told you long since, except events tore us apart.'

The colour in Caldason's face was sapped. 'If what you say
is true, that means you're . . .'

'A paladin,' Serrah finished for him.

Mahaganis nodded. 'I was born to the clans. And into their
leadership ranks, moreover.'

Caldason was on his feet, his hand going to his sword
hilt. Wendah put herself between him and the old man,
whipping out her knife. Then Serrah was there, clutching
Caldason's wrist and trying to calm him.

'What do you think you're doing?' she demanded.

He looked through her, and she feared he was about to
go into a berserk – in which case none of them stood a
chance.

Kutch joined in and did his best to placate the Qalochian.
Slowly, they got through.

'The Reeth I know doesn't pick fights with blind men,'
Serrah reminded him, 'or with girls.' She eyed Wendah, who
maintained her defensive stance.

'All right,' Caldason said, pulling himself together. 'It's all
right.'

They steered him back to his seat on the barrel. The girl
backed off.

'I don't blame you, Reeth,' Mahaganis told him. 'I deserve
your wrath, on behalf of my kin.'

Caldason raised his head. 'None of this makes sense.'

'I know,' the old man replied, not unkindly. 'So consider the facts.' He paused, gathering his thoughts. 'Hard as it is to believe these days, the clans were once honourable. They prided themselves on defending the weak against the rapacious. But like so many others in this world, they fell into corrupt ways.'

'And you didn't.'

'I stood against their growing treachery, their cruelty. My own people, mind you. My own people.' Bitterness rose like bile, and as quickly abatcd. 'What they did to your tribe, and what they wanted to do to you, was the last straw. I felt morally bound to help you escape that fate. In return, they put me here.'

'This was your punishment? Exile?'

'Did you think I came to this island willingly?'

'Why didn't they just kill you?' Kutch asked, agog.

'To make me suffer the more for my defiance. That and a certain awe for my rank. The clans tend to dote on their leadership.'

'Things have changed a bit in that respect,' Serrah dryly informed him.

'No amount of depravity on their part would surprise me,' Mahaganis stated soberly. 'Anyhow, I was dislodged, my faction purged. After I aided Reeth, they finally caught up with me, which is how I came to be here, nurse-maiding an orphaned child and the Source.'

'So it does exist.'

He wore a pained expression. 'Oh, yes.'

'Where is it?' Caldason demanded, rising again. '*What* is it?'

The old man lifted a mollifying hand. 'Your patience still needs work, Reeth. It was always a virtue that eluded you.'

'The Source could be decisive in what's going on out there, Praltor. It could be the salvation of a lot of people, me included.'

'It could also be your damnation.'

'At least don't deny us that choice.'

'But it doesn't just affect you, does it? The repercussions could be enormous. Its power is . . . beyond words. Just being near it can be destructive.'

'Neither of you seem to have suffered too much by it.'

'Really? All right then, Reeth; if you want it so badly, take it.'

'Where is it?' Serrah asked. 'How do we find it?'

Kutch had been watching silently. He said, 'I know.'

'You do?'

'I can feel it.' He nodded at the old man. 'It's him.'

Caldason stared. 'What?'

'The boy's very perceptive,' Mahaganis noted approvingly.

'Are you all going to start talking gibberish again?' Serrah wanted to know. 'Because if you are . . .'

'Kutch here asked why my enemies in the clans didn't simply kill me and have done with it,' Mahaganis reminded them. 'It was partly because of my station, but that paints far too benevolent a picture of them. They actually spared my life in order to torment me further.'

'What have your sufferings to do with the Source?'

'What do you suppose the Source to be, Reeth? A store of knowledge, yes; but what about its form? A grimoire, perhaps? A whole library? Hoards of papyrus, or clay tablets? Over the eons since its accumulation by the Founders it may well have been all those things. But it's something much more nebulous than that. Essentially, the Source is an occult system, a concept. And I've come to believe it's something much more than that.'

'Such as?'

'The Source is some kind of embodiment of magic. I think it's . . . sentient.'

'That's a hell of a conclusion to draw,' Serrah responded. 'What's your evidence?'

'Tell them what they did to you,' Wendah blurted out.

Everyone was thrown for a second by the usually silent girl's sudden outburst. Then Mahaganis spoke.

'As punishment for aiding Reeth,' he said, 'and for turning my back on the paladins, they infused the Source here.' He laid a finger against his temple. 'In my mind.'

'And they put out his eyes with fire,' Wendah added, 'to make his torment worse.'

'That was a masterful touch of sadism,' the old man remarked, almost admiringly. 'It left me with nowhere to look but inward. So all I glimpse, permanently, is the quintessence of Founder evil; and the squirming, putrid life force in which it's suspended. You ask me for evidence. I have the testimony of my own, unblinking inner eye. For all practical purposes I am the Source.'

Another silence, broken this time by Serrah. 'We have people back on the island who can help you,' she promised. 'Magicians, scholars –'

He shook his head. 'The clans couldn't master it, for all their resources, and they would dearly have loved to. Respect to your sorcerers, but what chance would they have?'

'If it's so powerful,' Kutch asked, 'why did the Founders leave the Source to be discovered? Why didn't they destroy it, or at least hide it better?'

'Perhaps whatever catastrophe overtook them was too swift. But I suspect the real reason is because even the Founders couldn't better it. My feeling is that it can't be understood and, as long as magic fuels it, it can't be destroyed.'

'That's a cheerful prospect,' Serrah returned mordantly.

'There's nothing joyous about any of it,' Mahaganis informed her. 'Unless you count the fact that the magic locked in my head has kept me going far beyond my natural lifespan. But that can be a mixed blessing, can't it, Reeth?'

Caldason ignored that, and posed a question of his own.

'You still haven't told me why the clans targeted my tribe for butchery.'

'Your kin were irrelevant, except insofar as they might have protected you. Or at least they were of no consequence to the client who commissioned the slaughter. You were the only real target.'

'Why? And who –'

'There are some things you're ready to hear, others not.' He was massaging his forehead. 'We've spoken enough about all this for the moment.'

'Have we? Have we really? I'm not a child anymore, Mahaganis. I don't need to be sheltered and lied to.'

'Not now, Reeth. I don't feel too good.'

'To hell with that. Answer me.'

'Leave him alone!' Wendah demanded. 'Can't you see he's ill?'

'Would it hurt him that much to tell me?' Caldason's temper was rising.

Serrah caught his arm. 'What are you going to do, Reeth, beat it out of him?'

Caldason sighed. He regarded the frail old man and the emaciated girl at his side.

'No,' he said. 'What we're going to do is get you two out of here.'

25

While not especially built for speed, the Daughters of Mercy hospital ship was compact and sleek, and capable of a good rate of knots. Fortunately so, for no sooner had the island been sighted than trouble struck.

An insipid sun at their backs, a brace of privateers bore down on the disguised rebel craft. Shortly, a second pair arrived, the other edge of an intended pincer.

The Mercy ship put on speed. From port and starboard, further pirate galleons closed in, canvas swelling, prows carving the chill water. On board the infirmary craft the order went up to jettison all surplus cargo, and crates, chests and casks tumbled overboard. Lightened, the quarry surged.

A race ensued, the hospital ship trying to reach friendly climes before the pirates blocked its path. It was a close run. The hunted vessel beat the tightening blockade by a nose, and now it was a chase, the loner battling to outpace a small fleet even more determined to prevent it making shore.

Then a new set of ballooning sails was spotted, moving out from the island itself. A flotilla hove into view, equal in number to that which the pirates had mustered. And though ramshackle and makeshift, it put them to flight.

So it was that Dulian Karr and the dregs of the Resistance came to the Diamond Isle.

For Karr and Goyter, Quinn Disgleirio and a few hundred others, it was a time of joyous reunions.

For Tanalvah Lahn it was an experience of quite a different order.

In the shadow of their great tiered fortress, the islanders allowed themselves a brief period of rejoicing, for all that their situation looked hopeless. There were celebrations, some revelry, and cups raised to fallen comrades. But Tan was insensible to all that and had no part in it. In any event, Karr arranged for her to be taken to Kinsel without delay, while Goyter cared for an exhausted Teg and Lirrin.

Tanalvah was put into a carriage bound for the central redoubt and made as comfortable as possible, given her condition. She endured the short, bumpy journey in a mixture of anticipation, confusion and fear, and too soon found herself delivered to the island's grim-walled fastness of last resort.

A small, wood-panelled chamber, sparsely furnished, was hastily made available. Its windows had been boarded for defence, so it was lit by candles and a lantern, despite the daylight outside. Tan was installed on the only decent chair, and her beaming well-wishers withdrew.

She was grateful for the room's half light. Its shadows gave her haven, a veil to hide her shame. The silence was less welcome. It meant she had only her thoughts for companionship, and she was loathe to be in that company.

On the voyage over she had determined to be rid of her intolerable burden once and for all, and to confess, but only to Kinsel. There were many whose forgiveness she craved, but none as greatly as his. So, much as she longed to see him, she dreaded the prospect in equal measure.

Alone with her dark reflections, time dragged interminably.

Perhaps a minute passed, perhaps an hour, before there were sounds in the passageway outside. Footfalls. A loose board creaking. The soft rattle of the door handle.

Tanalvah got up, awkwardly, meaning to move to the opening door, but she could do no more than stare at it, blood pounding in her ears.

Then he was there, outlined by the frame.

She was shocked by his appearance. He'd lost weight and looked haggard. He was hollow-eyed and his complexion was pallid. Kinsel was equally as shaken at seeing her, and by how heavy with child she was.

They stood numbly, taking in their respective states, until, as though at an unspoken command, and as one, they flowed into each other.

They hugged, caressed, sobbed. Finding their voices at last, their tearful outpourings would have seemed nonsensical to an eavesdropper. When some kind of coherence came, they mouthed endearments and devotions, and spilt their fears.

At length, eyes glistening, they drew back from each other, hands linked.

Kinsel smiled, nodding at the swell of her belly. 'Look at you. You're twice the woman you were.'

'And you've been wasting away.'

'Nonsense. I'm better for it.'

She gave a laugh that sashayed into a wheezing sob. 'I didn't think I'd ever see you again.'

'I was afraid I'd lost you, too.'

'And the baby. Our baby. I didn't think –'

'I know.' His arms were round her again. 'It's all right,' he soothed. 'We're back together. Tell me about Teg and Lirrin. They're well?'

She nodded, moist eyes blinking. 'They're fine. Growing so fast. Missing you.'

'I can't wait to see them.'

He talked on, supportive and affectionate, making her feel good in a way no other man ever had, so that any thought of confession began to fade. It could wait until later. Tomorrow, perhaps. Why spoil this?

'. . . and our friends from Bhealfa?' Kinsel was asking. 'Dulian, Quinn –'

'They're all right,' she replied a little brusquely, less than pleased to be reminded of the Resistance. Then she checked herself, her mind turning to other faces. 'What about Serrah, and Reeth and Kutch?' she said. 'I didn't see any of them when we landed.'

'Reeth finally got his way and went off in search of the Clepsydra. Serrah and the boy went with him.'

Tan was relieved that they weren't on the island. She wasn't proud of the feeling, but it seemed trivial in light of her greater crime.

'You were wrong about him,' Kinsel told her softly.

'Who?'

He smiled. 'Reeth. You doubted him. But he was the one who freed me.'

That was more than she could bear. Gratitude and guilt swept over her. 'I feel ashamed,' she said.

'Don't be silly,' he gently chastised. 'What have you, of all people, to be ashamed about?'

'I misjudged him.'

'You made a perfectly rational assessment of Reeth's character, based on the little we knew about him. Misjudgment's not a major sin, Tan. But that isn't important now. All that matters is that we've been reunited. We can start anew, be happy again with the children and –'

'It'll come to grief.'

'There's no need to be so pessimistic, my love. We've been given a second chance. Let's seize it while we can.'

'A Gath Tampoor battle fleet's on its way here. And for all I know, Rintarah's sending one, too.'

'You're sure?' Kinsel looked shocked.

'We barely outpaced it.'

'We always knew it would be dangerous here,' he said, collecting himself. 'But whatever comes, at least we'll be together.'

'You don't understand,' she whispered. 'We may never have –' Pain creased her face and she gave a silent gasp. Her hands went to her abdomen.

Kinsel was alarmed. 'What is it?'

'Nothing. Just . . . a twinge.'

He helped her back to the chair. She sank into it with a sigh.

'Shall I get a healer?' he asked, tightly clasping her hand.

'No. I'm . . . I'm all right.'

'What's happening, Tan? Is something wrong?'

She managed a feeble smile. 'Not wrong, my love; natural.' She placed his hand on her swollen belly. 'It means it won't be long now.'

Serrah took a sharp intake of breath. Grimacing, she clutched her stomach.

Caldason said, 'You all right?'

'It's just a . . . stitch or something.'

'Sure?'

'It's nothing, Reeth.' She straightened, the pang fading. 'Probably the lousy rations we've been eating.'

'You look pale.'

'So do you. None of us are exactly at our best after weeks in this tub. I don't know how regular sailors cope with it.'

'We should be back on the Diamond Isle soon.'

'I can't wait.' She returned to gazing at the dismal horizon.

They were on deck, well bundled against the cold, and the packet was rolling in the current. Not brutally, but enough to make the footing uncertain for land dwellers. A light spray fell constantly.

Fifteen paces away, sheltered by a sailcloth awning, Kutch sat with Mahaganis and Wendah. The blind old man wore a stoic expression, while his young companion, finding her tongue at last, was engaged in an earnest, whispered conversation with Kutch.

'They seem to be getting on well,' Caldason noted a little icily.

'Since they realised what they have in common, yes,' Serrah replied.

'Which is?'

'You've not been paying much attention lately, have you, Reeth? Apparently Kutch and the girl have a similar power. It's a magic thing. You wouldn't be interested.'

'Seems you know more about what's going on than I do.'

'Only because I'm actually talking to them.' She nodded Mahaganis's way. 'The old man's getting under your skin, isn't he?'

'He won't tell what he knows. About me.'

'You should be grateful to him.'

'I am. I owe him my life, but I question his motives.'

'I think you're wrong to. If he's holding anything back, it's to protect you.'

'I don't need protecting.'

'You did when you were a child.'

'The man was a paladin, Serrah. Can you imagine how that makes me feel?'

'Whatever he was, didn't he make amends by defending you? Or are you saying he's beyond redemption?'

Caldason brooded on that for a quarter minute, then came back softer with, 'How are you feeling now?'

'I'm fine,' she said, grateful to be reminded that she had someone who cared. 'Come on, let's join them.'

'You go ahead. I'll just –'

'Slink away and sulk? Life's too short, Reeth. I mean literally. Remember the Clepsydra. If it really does indicate some
kind of apocalypse, we've no time to waste. In getting things
sorted, that is.'

He accepted her hand, and a tad reluctantly allowed himself
to be led.

As they approached the group, Kutch and Wendah got up
to leave.

'Nothing personal, I hope,' Serrah remarked.

Kutch looked embarrassed. 'Oh . . . no. Of course not. We
just –'

'I understand,' Serrah smiled. 'Off you go.'

The boy nodded gratefully, and Wendah briefly relaxed
her customary surliness. As they passed, Kutch deftly plucked
something from non-existence and gently propelled it Serrah's
way. The glamour was in the likeness of a radiant, single-
stemmed flower. Its bloom was a kaleidoscope of stunning,
ever-changing colours, and it gave off an exquisitely sensual
perfume.

The flower hung in the air, revolving slowly for Serrah's
enchantment. Then Wendah turned her head, puffed her cheeks
and blew at the glamour. It fragmented into thousands of
golden, cart-wheeling sparks that danced back to nothingness.

Serrah was delighted. Caldason seemed less amused.

Kutch and Wendah headed for the stern, engaged in
discussion.

'The young have such reckless vitality, don't you think?'
Mahaganis said, as though he'd seen what had happened.
'Just like you as a youngster, Reeth.'

'My youth was a bit out of the ordinary, if you recall.'

'Granted. But I think there are similarities. You and I had
something in common, in that we were outcasts; and they
have a bond too.'

'So I heard. Not that anybody's explained it to me.'

'It's unlike you to neglect intelligence gathering,' the old man rebuked. 'I understand Kutch is a spotter. Rare as that is, Wendah happens to have a similar talent. It's good for them both, I think, to find another like themselves.'

'She can see the magic, or whatever it is spotters do?'

'In a way. What she does subtly differs from spotting. You might call it accessing.'

'What's that?' Serrah asked.

'He's talking about accessing the Source,' Caldason said. 'That's right, isn't it, Praltor?'

'Yes. But don't get too excited. Wendah's ability in that respect is very limited.'

'But you can connect with this thing you say is inside you?'

'Connect's too strong a word. Any direct link would be more than a human could bear. I'm not sure a legion of first-rate sorcerers could safely plumb its depths.'

'So what do you draw from it?' Caldason persisted.

'I don't draw anything,' Mahaganis retorted, anger flaring. 'It's the exact opposite. What Wendah allows me is a defence.'

'Defence?'

'Some ease of the pain. A shield against this torment in my head. Her talent's nothing compared to the power of the Source, but it's kept me sane.'

'I don't understand. And shielding you against what?'

'Where Kutch only sees, Wendah . . . obstructs. She has the ability to deflect magical energy to some extent, and she's used that gift to help guard my reason. As to what she's guarding me from; have you any idea of the Founders' malevolence? What am I saying? You of all people should appreciate that.'

'There you go again,' Caldason grumbled, 'implying something without being specific.'

'Let's just say we're both labouring under our own singular curses.'

'No, let's not say that. How about the truth instead?'

'There are some things you're not prepared to hear just yet.'

'I'm not a child anymore, Praltor. You don't have to look out for me or worry about my feelings.'

The old man said nothing.

'Did whatever you're hinting at have anything to do with the way we parted?' Caldason pressed. 'Because I've no memory of how we went our separate ways.'

'As I said, your recollection's bound to be patchy.'

'Why?'

'It was a difficult time. There were battles, skirmishes –'

'What happened to split us?'

'We got to the point where there was little more I could do to help you.'

'You're lying.'

'Reeth!' Serrah exclaimed. 'Show some respect.'

'No,' Mahaganis told her, 'he's right. The fact is, Reeth, that I . . . left you.'

'You did what?' she said.

'He could look after himself by then, believe me. And there were circumstances.'

'What kind of circumstances?' Caldason demanded, his voice dropping and edged with menace.

'I'd come to fear you,' the old man confessed.

'You were afraid of me?' The Qalochian was genuinely taken aback. 'Why?'

'For what you are. And for what you're capable of.'

'More riddles. Just once, could you have enough respect for me to explain what you mean?'

'Reeth, I . . .'

'Please.'

Mahaganis sighed. 'Very well. But you must try to under-
stand what I'm going to say, and to keep a grip on yourself.'
'Tell me.'
'It's your ancestry that worries me.'
'My being a Qalochian, you mean?'
'No.'
'Well . . . what, then?'
'What frightens me, Reeth, is your Founder blood.'

26

The pit was a simmering cauldron. In its depths a hoary, foaming stew effervesced.

'It's getting worse, brother.'

Felderth Jacinth nodded. 'Further justification for the action we're taking, if such were needed.'

'Even action as unprecedented as this?'

'In the present situation, Rhylan, any step is justified.'

'There are many on the council who have doubts about that.'

'Not a majority, I think. And the dissenters have no real alternative to offer.'

They resumed staring at the gummy, silverish liquid churning at the pit's bottom.

'I've never seen it so agitated,' Rhylan said.

'Nor have I,' the Elder confessed.

'Which makes me wonder if concentrating on this rebel horde on the Diamond Isle could be to the detriment of our response to the warlord.'

'They're one and the same, effectively. We're not neglecting any threat Zerreiss presents, but equally we need to deal with the dissidents. Bearing in mind the danger of them joining together, tackling both carries the same weight in my mind. In any event, you've left your objections a bit late,' Felderth said pointedly.

'It's not an objection. Just an observation.'

'Well, my observation is that we have no choice but to follow the course I've chosen.'

There was another moist eruption in the pit. Energy flushed through the tinted power lines that criss-crossed the floor of the immense chamber. Its angry vigour lit up the great council table, setting the Rintarah eagle emblem crackling. And, for all the Jacinth siblings knew, the surge carried on to sear through the channels running beneath Jecellam's bustling avenues.

'We're making history, Rhylan,' Felderth remarked.

'That's what worries some people.'

'How so?'

'Your critics see this as some kind of capitulation to Gath Tampoor. At the least they regard it as moving closer to them, which would be unacceptable, of course.'

'There's no danger of that. How often must I say it? We're simply acting together on this occasion because it suits us both.'

'And you don't see the risk of setting a precedent?'

'That won't be allowed to happen.'

'How can you be so sure? Because if you're wrong about this, brother, it could place a strain on the veracity of your leadership.'

'You're saying there could be some kind of rebellion? A coup? It would be the first time in our history if there was.' The Elder seemed totally unconcerned.

'I'm not suggesting anything so dramatic. But there are factions on the council who would welcome an opportunity to obstruct your rule, as you well know.'

'They'll come round when they see us emerging stronger from this crisis.'

'Many are mindful that the council's most important function, the duty that overrides all else, is to ensure the continued survival of our kind.'

'You think I'm unaware of my responsibility? If any other than you had implied negligence in that respect, Rhylan, they'd have felt my wrath.'

'I'm implying nothing. But you know the argument. By the very act of seeming to aid Gath Tampoor, we potentially weaken our own security.'

'But they're equally aiding us. It's a trade-off. In the end it doesn't change the balance; it just rids us both of an irritant.'

'And what happens the next time a threat appears? Do we cooperate with the enemy again, and slowly erode the differences between us? Indeed, brother, some believe that's your aim.'

'They can believe what they like,' the Elder said coolly. 'But note that, despite the unpopularity of my stance, the council didn't vote against it.'

'As you say, they have no alternative to offer. And perhaps . . .'

'Yes?'

'Perhaps they intuit a deeper motive on your part.'

'Which is what?'

'That once Gath Tampoor has ceased to be of use to us, we'll be in a better position to take advantage of their naiveté. A blow has added weight when struck under a supposed truce.' His conspiratorial smile was returned. 'Though of course I appreciate that a leader's intentions can't always be plainly stated.'

'Indeed. I daresay Gath Tampoor's ruler has similar problems. Speaking of which . . .'

'Yes, of course; it must be almost time.' Rhylan backed off a couple of paces.

Felderth carried out a series of subtle hand gestures, a conjuration directed at the heaving contents of the pit. It proved resistant to his command and carried on its unruly bubbling.

'Do you need help, brother?' Rhylan asked.

A look of intense concentration knitted the Elder's brow. 'I think I have it.'

The pewter liquid quietened, save for a pattern of ripples stirring its surface. In seconds the disorder calmed and an image appeared. It sharpened into a face, then the face took on distinctive features.

The likeness of Empress Bethmilno came into focus.

'Greetings,' Jacinth intoned. 'It's been a long time.'

'Let's get straight down to business, shall we?' the Empress replied coolly.

'That's my intention,' the Elder came back.

'I don't expect us to forget old enmities, bearing in mind how deep they run. But for the moment we need to liaise on matters of importance.'

'My sentiment entirely,' Felderth concurred.

'Very soon our fleets will rendezvous. Yet we've managed to get this far without settling the extent of our cooperation. This must be made clear.'

'I agree that we need to set parameters. I suggest we keep this alliance –'

'Temporary alliance,' Bethmilno corrected.

'As you say. I suggest this transient alliance be restricted solely to the original objectives. Simply put, we cooperate without let until those aims are achieved. Then, at an agreed point in time beyond that, normal hostilities between our states can resume.'

'That would be acceptable. Though, of course, the temptation to take advantage of the period between triumph and the ending of our pact could prove strong.'

Rhylan said nothing. His eyes flicked between the Empress's image and his brother's stern features.

'It may be a temptation for Gath Tampoor,' Felderth declared loftily. 'Rintarah, on the other hand, honours its promises.'

The Empress snorted. 'I won't dignify that with a response. Other than to say that we have a mutual interest in survival, as our history attests. We'll have to trust in that when it comes to honouring pledges.'

'I'm not sure I infer your meaning.'

'Then I'll be transparent. Any premature aggression would invite the full strength of Gath Tampoor's military capability. Let that be a buttress to our agreement.'

'And I can offer a similar assurance as far as Rintarah's forces are concerned.'

'I see we understand each other, Elder.'

'Clarity is always my goal, Majesty.'

'There remains only the matter of when our provisional union should come to an end.'

'Shall we say forty-eight hours after the eradication of the targets?'

Bethmilno thought about it, trying to see if agreement gave the opposition any kind of advantage. 'All right,' she decided. 'Word will be sent to our fleet commanders.'

'And to ours,' Felderth replied, raising a hand.

The link was broken. Bethmilno's image dissolved.

The Empress watched as Felderth's likeness fragmented and disappeared into the glutinous liquid.

The throne room in her palace at Merakasa was dimly lit and virtually deserted. Several representations of the empire's dragon emblem decorated the chamber, and the most prominent, occupying a sizeable wall, throbbed with magical vitality. The Empress came away from the hollow where the quicksilver simmered and turned to the only other person present.

'Why do we need Rintarah, grandmother?' he asked. To an eavesdropper, the use of her familial title might have seemed bizarre, given that he was an old man himself.

'We don't. Our presence will stop them making common cause with the rebels or Zerreiss against us. It's all about expediency.'

'So we'll betray them?'

'Of course. Just as soon as they've ceased to be of use.'

'There are some stirrings around the court about all this.'

'Stirrings?'

'About the wisdom of cooperating with the enemy.'

'I've just made clear exactly what that cooperation amounts to.'

'Yes, but there's talk about whether you've got your priorities right.'

Bethmilno adopted an aggressive tone. 'You're questioning them?'

He shook his head. 'I wouldn't dream of it, grandmother. But there are those who express concern about developments other than the rebels.'

She nodded cannily. 'You're referring to the Clepsydra.'

'Yes. Is it true that it's been discovered?'

'It was never really lost. We always knew approximately where it was, but we hadn't bothered locating it. It's only come to light now because our agents were shadowing a Diamond Isle ship, which led them to it.' She smiled in a self-satisfied manner.

'And is the Clepsydra really indicating an . . . end point?'

'It wasn't far off doing that the last time I saw it. And that was a very long time ago.'

'Are you saying we have nothing to fear, grandmother?'

'I'm saying I doubt the Clepsydra's veracity. Because for all the skill with which it was created, it's stood unattended for an age. There have been numerous shifts in the earth's crust during that time, not to mention extremes of weather. Changes that could impair its function, and it goes without saying that it's beyond the capability of any alive now to repair it.'

'What of the so-called Source? If the rebels found that, too –'

'Again, a groundless concern.' The Empress was growing impatient.

'But its power,' her grandson ploughed on regardless. 'Wouldn't it be an appalling weapon in enemy hands?'

'Only hands capable of using it. The rabble has no more understanding of how to master an artefact from what they call the Dreamtime than a dog knows how to drive a carriage. If we thought otherwise, we would have sought out and destroyed the Clepsydra long ago.'

'I repeat, grandmother, that it's the Source which causes most concern.'

'And I say again,' she replied tetchily, 'that they have no hope of drawing on it. In any event it seems it's been put beyond their reach, thanks to a bit of inventive maliciousness on the paladins' part. Stop fretting'

'I'll try. So, how do we proceed?'

'First we annihilate the rebels. Then we destroy the warlord. There's nothing complicated about it,' she assured him.

'It's simple,' Zerreiss repeated patiently. 'All I'm ordering is a diversion, and not an enormously big one at that.' He indicated a spot on the hide map pegged up in front of them. 'From here to around . . . here. It'll put just a few days on our schedule. A week at most.'

'With respect, sir,' Wellem said, 'it's to do with practicalities.' He jabbed his thumb sternward. 'Redirecting all this is no small task.'

Their flagship was at the head of a massive fleet, consisting of a singularly ill-assorted collection of vessels; captured, commandeered and hastily built. Most were troop carriers, decks jammed with combatants and lashed-down war engines. Accompanying supply craft, laden with provisions, moved low in the freezing water.

'Apart from re-plotting our course,' Wellem continued, 'the distribution of rations would have to be adjusted. That and a dozen other problems make it a logistical nightmare.'

'I'm aware of all this,' Zerreiss replied, 'and the difficulties aren't nearly as daunting as you make out, old friend. But I appreciate your efforts to save me from myself, as you see it.'

'Sir, I would never –'

The warlord raised a hand to silence him, adding good-humouredly, 'Of course you would. But this detour has great implications for our struggle.'

'To a rock in the middle of the ocean, occupied by radicals? Do we need allies that badly?'

'This isn't about recruiting, is it, sir?' ventured Sephor, the warlord's younger aide. 'It's about him, isn't it? The man in your dreams.'

'I've not made a secret of it,' Zerreiss confirmed. 'Nor do I take strategic decisions based on hunches or intuition. You know that. Yet I strongly feel that heading for that island, meeting that man, are prerequisites for everything else we have to do.'

'I don't pretend to understand,' Sephor admitted, 'but I trust your instinct in this, sir. You've never steered us wrongly before.'

'And I don't intend to start now,' Zerreiss assured him.

'You know we won't be the only ones heading there,' Wellem reminded them. 'Our intelligence says at least one empire fleet's moving into those waters.'

'It's a good point,' Sephor reckoned. 'For the first time we'd be engaging the full force of imperial might head on.'

'Have faith in me,' the warlord said. 'We've been preparing to take our message to their civilised world for long enough. It's time we met.' He fixed them with his cool, steady gaze. 'Signal the new course.'

It was often said that the gods had some curious ideas about the deployment of their human progeny. While sceptics saw this as pure chance, and believers viewed it as divine intervention, both agreed that the disposition of players in the great game of life frequently displayed a savage irony.

So it was that this vast stretch of water hosted another ill-assorted troupe, also bound for the Diamond Isle.

'Drink in the sight,' Devlor Bastorran said. 'You're witnessing a momentous event.'

'Is that so?' Aphri Kordenza yawned into the back of her hand theatrically. 'Just looks like a lot of boats to me.'

'Ships,' the paladin corrected.

'Boats, ships; they're only boring things that happen to float.'

'You've no sense of history.'

'Aphrim and I have something more important: a sense of self-preservation.'

'Then perhaps you should take more interest in what's going on around you.' Bastorran gazed at the meld distastefully.

'We take in enough to ensure our security. Everything else is surplus to requirements.'

'It really doesn't concern you that we're part of something no living eyes have seen before?'

'No. And we think it doesn't matter to you either. We reckon you're like us; when it comes down to it, you're only interested in the Qalochian and getting your own back on him.'

'Wiping out the rebels has its appeal, too,' he said thoughtfully.

'Sure, but even that's not personal like Caldason, is it?'

'I've never denied it. At least, I've never denied it to you.'

'Then don't give us all this history in the making shit, Bastorran.'

He held her gaze. 'If you've got any ideas about getting to him first and depriving me of my revenge, freak, you'll be history yourself. Both of you.'

'You've no worries on that score. We'll be contenting ourselves with cutting rebel throats, and hunting down the Ardacris woman.'

'Who's to be kept alive, remember. I promised Laffon I'd deliver her for interrogation.'

'You're no fun at all, are you?'

'I only said she'd be fit for questioning. I didn't say anything about her being whole.'

'That's some consolation, I suppose.'

'Helping bring about Caldason's death should provide further solace for you. So long as it's me who strikes the final blow.'

The symbiote brightened. 'That is something worth looking forward to. Aphrim's going to be absolutely —'

Someone discreetly cleared their throat. They turned to see Bastorran's aide approaching.

'What is it, Meakin?' the paladin snapped.

'Begging your pardon, sir, but the Captain sends his compliments and asked me to let you know that our fleet and Rintarah's are about to officially rendezvous. Up ahead, sir.' He held out a glamoured spy tube. 'You might find this useful.'

Bastorran grunted and snatched it.

'Amazing sight, isn't it, sir?' Meakin ventured. 'History in the making.'

'Quite,' Bastorran returned crisply.

Kordenza rolled her eyes skyward.

'The Captain also said that we should be in sight of the Diamond Isle in less than a day,' Meakin added.

'And not a minute too soon,' the symbiote mumbled.

On all sides, the sea was hidden by uncountable numbers of vessels of every conceivable kind. Forests of bobbing masts blotted out the horizon.

Ahead, the two stupendous fleets were merging, aglow with magical radiance.

27

'Talk to me, paladin, or get ready to swim the rest of the way!' Caldason had Praltor Mahaganis by the scruff of his neck up against the brig's guardrail.

Serrah barged between them. 'Reeth! Calm down.'

'Out of the way.'

'You know you don't mean it.'

'Don't I? Take a look at my face and say that again.'

'Let him be.' Her tone was deliberate and threatening.

'No,' Mahaganis declared, 'Reeth's right. I should never have held anything back.'

They ignored him.

'In case you hadn't noticed, Reeth,' Serrah said, 'we have a fucking enormous enemy fleet threatening to block our path!'

On their starboard side an apparently limitless number of ships were approaching. They were some distance away, but the leaders had enough of a lead to cut off the brig, and soon.

'This isn't exactly the time for a history lesson,' she added.

'It might be the only time we have left,' Caldason told her.

'He's right,' Mahaganis said, a weary, resigned edge to his voice. 'You should know everything.'

Kutch and Wendah came running. The skipper, Rad Cheross, and a couple of crewmen were close behind.

'What's all the fuss?' Kutch panted.

'What are you doing to him?' the girl demanded angrily. From the look on her flushed face she was ready to pitch in.

'It's all right, Wendah,' Mahaganis assured her. 'No one's trying to hurt me.'

'He is.' She scowled at Caldason.

'No he's not,' Kutch said. 'Reeth wouldn't do that.'

'Wouldn't he? He's a killer, isn't he?'

Caldason let go of the old man.

Serrah placed a hand on the girl's shoulder. 'Kutch is telling you the truth, Wendah. Nobody's going to be harmed. Now let's all just be calm, shall we?'

Cheross stepped forward. 'You might like to take this somewhere private. You're in our way.' He nodded towards the closing fleet.

'Is there anything we can do?' Serrah asked.

'Not unless you've sailing skills you haven't told me about. The best thing you can do is to leave us to it. Get yourselves to the mess, you'll not be disturbed there.'

'Can we outrun them?'

'We've a fair chance. But I'm making no promises. Be ready to defend the ship if I have to give the order.'

'Against all those?' Kutch blurted.

'It won't come to that,' Serrah promised. 'We're stopping Rad doing his job. Let's go.'

She led them away. Wendah took the old man's arm and guided him, with Kutch at her side. Caldason trailed behind. The deck was slick with spray, and a stiff wind blew constantly. They were glad to pile into the ship's largest cabin, and took seats at the long oak table it housed.

Kutch said, 'What is going on, Reeth?'

'You know what Praltor said about me having Founder

blood. You can't make a statement like that then refuse to elaborate. I need to hear the rest, and now, while there's still time.'

Wendah's eyes widened. 'Before we die, you mean?'

'Reeth means in the time left before we get to the island,' Serrah lied, flashing him a hard look. 'Don't you, Reeth?'

'That's right,' he replied after a pause. 'I should have said.' He turned to Mahaganis. 'Tell me what you meant about Founder blood. Please.'

'Yes. Hmm, a drink first, if someone would be so kind.' Wendah poured him watered wine from a jug. He smiled. 'Thank you, child.' Finding her hand, he squeezed it, then drank, finally thumping down the cup with resolve. 'What I told you, Reeth,' he stated, 'was no lie. Founder blood flows in your veins.'

'How can that be?' Kutch wanted to know. 'The Founders died out millennia ago.'

'That's where you're wrong.'

'Are you mocking us?' Caldason said. 'Or is senility addling your brain?'

'Neither,' Mahaganis replied. 'I was never more serious.'

Serrah raised a mollifying hand. 'This is just plain confusing, Praltor. Start at the beginning, can't you?'

'All right.' He took another sip of wine and composed himself. 'Nobody knows how or why the Founders lost their dominance. All we do know is that they had a remarkable civilisation, most of whose achievements are beyond our comprehension. The Founders were once the undisputed rulers of the world, then fell from grace, or were toppled, and their kind became extinct. At least, that's what most people think.'

'You're saying otherwise?'

'Oh, yes. Whatever cataclysm brought down the Founders, it didn't wipe out all of them. I don't know how many survived, or whether their descendants are disparate individuals or organised in some way. I suspect the latter. I think they exist as some kind of secret society, perhaps in a far land, away from prying eyes and –'

'You know this for a fact?' Serrah couldn't keep the scepticism out of her voice.

'Where and who they are can only be supposition, but I do know they exist because I was protecting Reeth against them. However they dispose themselves, they're powerful enough to imperil anyone else who stands in their way.'

Caldason fixed him with a level gaze. 'You say I have their blood. So why would I need protecting from them?'

'Preserving the purity of their race is one of their highest ideals. You were the first example of a half-breed, or at least the first who lived that I heard of. Their blood courses in your veins, but that doesn't make you one of them. It makes you something obscene in their eyes, something to be destroyed.'

Caldason said nothing.

Serrah asked, 'How did Reeth come to have this mixed parentage?'

'As the result of a union between his Qalochian mother and a Founder-descended man. I don't know if love was involved on either side or whether it was just a dalliance. I don't know if your mother knew her lover was a Founder. I do know that he broke one of the strictest Founder taboos in laying with her. She died in childbirth, as you know, quite possibly because their race and ours weren't meant to interbreed. But her death wasn't enough for them. Reeth had to be eliminated too, as an abomination in their reckoning.'

'You were there at my birth,' Caldason remembered. 'I saw it in a vision.'

'Yes. I'd freshly deserted the paladins. The corruption had eaten deep into the clans and I was one of those who got

out. I stood with the Qaloch, as others did, to oppose the
persecution and injustice your people faced. As much of the
maltreatment came from the paladins, from my blood, my
duty lay in trying to rectify that wrong.'

'You knew about these Founder offspring by then?'

'Only because of my association with your people. As the
native inhabitants of Bhealfa, their lineage was age old, and
their path had crossed with the Founders' many times in
the past. In fact, I suspect Qalochians were used as a pool
by the Founders. There were wise folk in your tribes who
knew the truth. No one believed them, and they grew to
be circumspect.'

'A pool?' Serrah queried.

'I think that, now and again, Qaloch women were used to
pleasure Founder males. As they've always been subject to
bigotry, and widely feared because of their martial reputation,
Qalochians were a good choice. Very few cared what happened
to them, and even fewer would have listened to their
grievances.'

'What an awful way to exploit people. These Founders
sound complete shits.'

'It must have been a very convenient arrangement for
them,' Caldason said, a cold wrath barely restrained. 'What
happened to change things?'

'It came to a head with your mother's pregnancy,'
Mahaganis replied. 'I believe that was an extreme rarity,
unprecedented, perhaps. As I said, our races were not
intended to procreate. That was when the clans were
contracted to wipe out the Qaloch, to be sure of killing
you. It took no great leap of imagination to realise that
Founder descendants were the clients. The paladins, to their
shame, didn't know or didn't care where the money came
from.'

Caldason, as a rule so hard to read, was visibly shaken.

'They wanted my death so badly they'd massacre my entire race?'

'That's how jealously they defend their blood. I know it's hard to take, and how easy it must be for you to feel guilty about your people's fate, but it's not your fault, boy. You have to get that through your stubborn head if nothing else.'

'But why should it be so important to them?' Serrah wondered. 'Why did Reeth have to die? It seems such a harsh punishment for breaking a taboo. There has to be more to it.'

'All cultures have their prohibitions, including ours,' the old man reminded her, 'and some of the empires' punishments are pretty draconian.'

'Maybe . . .' Wendah muttered in a small, uncertain voice, then stopped, looking uncomfortable.

They were all surprised to hear her speak. 'Go on, dear,' Mahaganis cajoled. 'What did you want to say?'

'Only that . . . well, it might not be just about some rule being broken.' She gave Caldason a wary sidelong glance. 'Perhaps they hate him because they fear him.'

'The same thing occurred to me,' Kutch threw in.

'What's your meaning?' Mahaganis said.

'Is it because Reeth's half Founder that he's lived so long?'

'It must be. In the same way that the Source has prolonged my own life.'

'And like Phoenix.'

'Who?'

'Someone we know,' Serrah explained, 'who's also lived beyond his time through Founder magic. Sorry, Kutch; make your point.'

'I was going to say, what does it mean to have Founder blood? Apart from living longer.'

'It would explain Reeth's visions,' Mahaganis told him, 'and the apparent link he has with the warlord, Zerreiss. Though I've no idea why.'

'They seem like symptoms,' Kutch reasoned. 'I was wondering whether, if you share their blood, do you share their powers?'

'The Founders weren't human. Some scholars think they might have been like us once, long ago, but developed into something beyond our state. Who knows what breeding with them means?'

'Suppose it gives some magical power or ability they don't want to share? Something that might be dangerous to them.'

'I can . . . see something in Reeth,' Wendah contributed, adding unnecessarily, 'with my talent.'

'What can you see?' Caldason asked, less than kindly.

She blinked at him, as though trying to penetrate a haze. 'I can't explain. Something I've never seen before.'

'You haven't had contact with that many people,' Serrah reminded her.

'That's true. But it still feels strange.'

'What about you, Kutch?' Serrah asked.

'I gave up spotter training because I couldn't cope with what I was picking up from Reeth, remember. So I suppose that kind of confirms it.'

'No, it doesn't,' Caldason objected. 'You're all making a hell of a lot of assumptions about me. What about the alternative?'

'What alternative?' Mahaganis said.

'That whatever ails me has nothing to do with Founder magic.'

'What else could it be?'

'I don't know . . . a curse laid on me by an enemy perhaps, or –'

'A curse unlike any ever seen before? Oh, come on.' Mahaganis grimaced. 'You're looking for explanations when the truth's staring you in the face. Nobody can blame you for not wanting to accept any of this, but whatever troubles you was inherited from your father, and he was of the Founder race.'

'What knowledge do you have of him? Did you ever meet?'

'No, and I've no idea what became of him. Perhaps he suffered the ultimate punishment. We don't know how they'd treat one of their own in this kind of situation. But . . .'

'What?'

'I have no proof but, having learnt how the Founder descendants operate, and from what I gathered from Qalochians who survived the great massacre . . .'

'Don't start being coy with me again, old man.'

'I think he was the one who tried to kill you.'

There was a knock on the mess door. Rad Cheross entered. 'We've outpaced the enemy fleets, just, and there's no sign of pirates. I guess they're keeping clear for obvious reasons. Barring mishaps, we'll reach the Diamond Isle in an hour or two, just ahead of the empires. Be ready to disembark fast.' He didn't wait for comments.

Caldason got to his feet.

Serrah was anxious for him. 'Reeth?'

'I need some air.'

He headed for the door and she followed. Understanding their need for privacy, the others stayed where they were.

On deck, Caldason went to the rail and gazed at the colossal armada that glowed on the horizon. The sky had grown darker.

Serrah slipped an arm around his waist. 'How are you feeling?'

'I've learnt that my mother died birthing me, my father tried to kill me and my race was all but exterminated because of me. What would you think my feelings were?'

'Complicated?'

He smiled despite himself. 'I can always rely on you for a little gibbet humour.'

'Sometimes it's all we've got.' Her features hardened. 'You know, I'm sceptical about some of what Praltor said in there.'

'Such as?'

'Mainly, this idea that the Founders are still around as some kind of secret society. I'm not sure I buy it. He said himself that it was supposition. I never came across a hint of it during my time with the CIS, and dealing with covert groups was my job.'

'There was a lot the CIS kept from you.'

'Yes. But if there's some kind of truth here, I don't think Praltor knows all of it.'

'Are you also sceptical about whether I've got some malign Founder canker inside me?'

'I . . . don't know, Reeth. But I'm inclined to think that in that respect the old man could be right.'

'I was afraid you'd say that.'

She shrugged. 'Actually, most of this is academic. Don't look at me that way. It's academic in the sense that it doesn't help us now, does it? I mean, take a look at what's coming.' She nodded in the direction of the invasion fleet. 'What does any of this matter when the chances are we're sailing to our graves?'

28

They got into port safely, but only just ahead of the combined fleets' vanguard. With the enemy ships standing offshore, and arriving in ever greater numbers, reunions were passionate but necessarily brief.

Frantic preparations were underway. Warriors ran to defensive positions. Arms were being distributed and guardposts manned. Hundreds streamed to the nearly completed fortress, churning the frozen ground to mud.

'Did you hear?' Serrah yelled as they pushed their way along the crowded quayside. 'Tanalvah's here!'

'I heard,' Caldason told her. 'Apparently Karr and Disgleirio made it too, along with a few hundred others from Bhealfa.'

'Talking of which . . .' She nodded at a wagon drawing up.

Disgleirio was driving, with Karr at his side. They were transporting a group of defenders who quickly dismounted and sped to their duties. Disgleirio helped Karr to clamber down and the pair approached.

'Thank the gods,' Karr exclaimed. 'I was beginning to fear we wouldn't see you again.'

'You don't get rid of us that easily,' Serrah replied as they hugged.

'Though you might have jumped from the proverbial frying pan into the fire,' Disgleirio observed, offering Caldason his hand.

'I've always enjoyed a little warmth,' the Qalochian told him.

'Well, things look set to get hotter around here any time now.'

'We heard that Tan's on the island,' Serrah said.

'Yes, and we have Quinn to thank for bringing her back into the fold,' Karr explained.

'Is that so? Well done, Quinn.'

The Righteous Blade man merely smiled, a little bashfully.

'And how's Kinsel?'

Disgleirio was glad to shift attention from himself. 'He's doing well physically.'

'Which implies ways in which he's not doing well,' she returned.

'His ordeal's left marks on him you can't see straightaway. Understandably.'

'Where's Darrok?' Caldason wanted to know.

'He's supervising defences on the other side of the island,' Karr said. 'As to the others . . . Ah, here's Phoenix now.'

The elderly wizard was marching through the press, accompanied by a couple of acolytes almost obscured by his fluttering cloak. 'Welcome back!' he rumbled. 'How did your mission fare?'

'It turned out . . . interesting,' Reeth answered.

'Nothing ever goes simply with you, does it, Reeth? So you didn't see the Clepsydra?'

'Oh, we saw it all right.'

His eyes widened. 'What about the Source?'

'We found it.'

The wizard looked like a child who'd been handed a large bag of sweets then locked in a toyshop. 'Gods, Reeth! What

form does it take? Was it defended in any way? Did you
have to – I don't like your expression. Have you brought
something to help us or not?'

'Perhaps.'

'Best not to tease him, Reeth,' Disgleirio cautioned.

'I'm not trying to be awkward. It's just . . . I don't know.'

'Where is it? Show it to me,' Phoenix insisted.

Caldason thrust a thumb in the direction of the brig's
gangway. Kutch and Wendah were making their way down
it, leading the obviously blind Mahaganis.

Phoenix was puzzled. 'They have it?'

'Kutch will explain. And the girl, her name's Wendah,
shouldn't be messed with.'

'I hate to break this up,' Disgleirio interrupted, 'but we
have an invasion to repel.'

All around, the atmosphere was growing increasingly frenzied. More people were rushing by, many beachward, while
defenders arrived on horseback and in carriages. People were
chaining crates and barrels.

'Reeth, Serrah; we need you. Badly,' Karr said. 'We haven't
many with your skills and experience. I want to put you
both in charge of warbands.'

'Whatever we can do,' Caldason responded. 'But in these
initial stages, we want to be freelances, going where needed.
We think we can be more useful that way.'

'All right. Though what you call initial stages might not
last too long if they throw everything at us in one go.'

'All the more reason for us not to be tied down to any
one detail. And if they have any sense they'll test our defences
before committing their entire force. They can't know what
we might have in reserve.'

'No, but they can guess.' Karr turned to the sorcerer.
'Phoenix, do what you can with whatever it is Reeth's brought
back. If you can make some kind of weapon out of it –'

'We can't promise anything like that, particularly with time so obviously short. But we'll do our best.'

'I can't ask more of you than that.'

'I want to see Tanalvah,' Serrah declared.

'She's all right,' Disgleirio assured her, 'and so are the children. There's no need to worry about her.'

'I'm sure she is. But I'd still like to see her.'

'She's over in the redoubt with Kinsel,' Karr explained. 'Perhaps you could make yourself useful and bring them back here to the fortress.'

'What was the point of building the central redoubt if you don't intend using it?' Caldason asked.

'It's been a bone of contention while you've been away. How it should be best used, I mean.'

'I suggest you put all those incapable of fighting up there; the old and feeble, the young and the sick. Allocate a minimum number of the fit to defend it. That'll keep the invaders guessing at the garrison's strength, and if we're overrun, maybe the enemy will show mercy to the non-combatants.'

'Where does that leave Tan and Kinsel?' Serrah wanted to know.

'By rights, with the non-combatants. But maybe we should leave the choice to them.'

'Tan's got to be near her time by now. The safer she is, the better.'

'Safe just became a practically meaningless term in these parts,' Disgleirio reminded her.

'Then I'm going over there now. Coming, Reeth?'

'I need to stay here and take a look at the defences. Do you mind?'

'You do that.'

'I could take you in the wagon,' Disgleirio offered. 'I need to be in those parts anyway. And I could bring you all back, if that's needed.'

'Fine.'

'But don't linger,' Caldason warned them. 'We've no way of knowing how long a reprieve we've got before the attack starts.'

Serrah kissed him. 'See you back here.'

She and Disgleirio ran for the wagon and clambered aboard.

Hardly was the port out of sight than Serrah felt tiny cold pinpricks on her face. She looked up to see snowflakes swirling in the chill air.

'Oh, great.' She pulled her coat tighter.

'Bad weather could actually be to our advantage,' Disgleirio reckoned. 'To the invaders this is unknown territory. The prospect of having to take it in a blizzard could slow them down quite a bit.'

'Do you always try to wring something positive out of every situation?'

'Not always, though I tend to the more dire things get. Surely that's better than the alternative?'

'So how dire do you think our situation is at the moment? Come on, Quinn, you know you don't have to hold back for my sake.'

'It's as bad as it gets, short of us all having swords at our throats, which is something we should expect in the not too distant future. They have so many ships we're going to find ourselves stretched to breaking point covering all possible landing places. Man for man, we're probably outnumbered twenty to one. Barring some miracle, I'm afraid the best we can hope for are honourable deaths.'

'That's a pleasant prospect.'

'You asked.'

They passed columns of armed men trudging towards the coastlines, and long strings of asses laden with weapons and supplies. Warning beacons were being lit on surrounding hill-tops and the more distant cliffs.

Twenty minutes later the towers of the central redoubt came into view. Here, too, all was movement and bustle.

'Want me to come in with you?' Disgleirio asked. 'Because otherwise I can be doing a few urgent things and come back for you in, say, no more than an hour?'

'You get on then, and thanks.'

'Remember the room where Kinsel was when you left? You'll find them two doors farther on.'

The guards knew her, and waved her through the heavy, half-open gates.

There was commotion inside too, but once she got to the redoubt's interior things were a lot quieter. Walking an echoing corridor, she came to the door Disgleirio had indicated, and found it slightly ajar. She knocked lightly, and without waiting for an answer, went in.

Tanalvah sat in an overstuffed armchair, draped in blankets and with her feet on a stool. She seemed to be asleep. Serrah thought she looked pale, and a little too gaunt for an expectant woman.

The room was sparsely furnished, and would have been austere if not for the log fire roaring in its spacious hearth, which gave off a mellow aroma of pine and vanilla. A small table held the remains of a meal, largely uneaten, and several wooden toys were scattered across the floor's bare boards. There was a door to an adjoining room, left partially open, through which soft voices could be heard.

A woman sleeping, the homely if spartan scene; it struck Serrah as incongruous, given what was happening outside.

Tanalvah's eyes opened.

For a second, she gave the impression of someone who thought they were dreaming.

'Tan,' Serrah whispered.

Tanalvah's eyes widened. Even more colour drained from her face, and she started to struggle to her feet.

Serrah came forward. 'No, no, stay where you are, Tan. It's me. Serrah.'

'Serrah,' Tanalvah repeated, the word devoid of any emotional content.

Kneeling, Serrah embraced her. She kissed her cheek. It was cold, and Tanalvah was stiff, almost rigid, to the touch. 'I'm so glad you made it through,' Serrah said.

'I'm . . . glad you did, too.'

'I've confused you, coming in here when you're barely awake. Sorry. But I couldn't wait to see you.'

Tanalvah looked as though she was about to say something, but just stared.

Serrah hadn't thought their reunion would be like this, but she reminded herself of everything her friend had been through, and made allowance.

To her relief, the uncomfortable silence was broken. From the next room, Kinsel swept in, accompanied by an excited Teg and Lirrin.

'I thought I heard . . . Serrah!'

'Hello, Kinsel.' She let herself be enveloped by his hug. Then she succumbed to the children tugging at her skirts and stooped to fuss over them.

When calm descended and the children had quietened, Serrah got her chance to ask, 'How are you, Tan?'

The answer was tearful. 'Fine. Just . . . fine.'

Serrah and Kinsel exchanged brief, meaningful looks.

'Your time must be soon,' Serrah said.

Tanalvah nodded.

'She's tired.' Kinsel stated the obvious. 'We're doing what we can to take some of the load off her. Aren't we, kids?'

The siblings nodded solemnly.

'They've all been wonderful,' Tanalvah sniffed. 'I don't deserve it.'

Kinsel took her hand. 'Don't be silly, my love. You deserve the best of everything.'

'And how are you faring yourself, Kinsel?' Serrah asked, hoping to move things away from the maudlin.

'Well, I'm still trimmer,' he grinned.

'So I noticed.'

'Forgive me, I've not asked; how did the mission go?'

'Weirdly. I'll fill you in on that later.'

'How's Reeth? And Kutch?'

'We all got back safely. And I think Kutch might have his first sweetheart.' Serrah smiled at him.

'Really? Who?'

'Somebody we came across on our voyage. Hopefully you'll meet her soon.'

'Poor kids. Brought here at a time like this.' He stole a glance at his own adoptive pair. 'We've not heard a lot about what's been happening today. Can you tell us what's going on out there?' His eyes said, be circumspect, for the children's sake.

'Something we've been expecting for some time. The empires have arrived, in force.'

'Empires? Both of them?'

'They've combined their fleets and seem to be acting together.'

'They think we're that much of a thorn?'

'Apparently so, and that's why I came. Well, I came because I really wanted to see you all, of course, but also to ask how you felt about moving to the fortress.'

'The fort?' Tanalvah said, looking alarmed. 'Do I have to?'

'No. I mean, it's not an order or anything. But you could be safer there.'

'Aren't we safe here? I thought this place was a stronghold too.'

'It is. It's just that the thinking is it might be better to concentrate all the noncombatants up there, and keep this place for the defenders so they – Tan?'

Tanalvah's face twisted and her body writhed.

'Tan? What's the matter?'

'What is it, my love?' Kinsel said.

'It's . . . all right. Just . . . just another . . . spasm.'

Kinsel took a cloth and dabbed her moist brow. The children looked on, fretful.

'You're getting these often?' Serrah asked.

'Couple of . . . times a . . . day.'

Serrah had the ignoble thought that this was rather conveniently timed, then immediately felt ashamed for entertaining the idea. 'If you're getting contractions, maybe this isn't the best time to move you.'

'Tanalvah's all right,' Kinsel told the children. 'There's nothing to worry about. Now come on, it's time you got some sleep.' He shepherded the complaining youngsters back to their beds. 'I'll be right back,' he mouthed.

Serrah turned to Tanalvah. 'Sure you're all right, Tan? Because you don't look too brilliant, to be honest.'

'I'm all right. Really. I would prefer to stay here though.'

'I suppose you won't be any less safe here than anywhere else on the island. And there should be some proper medical attention available, though under the present circumstances there's going to be competition for it. But you really ought to think about sending the children to the fort. It's where they stand the best chance.'

'We don't want to be parted again, whatever the reason.' Kinsel had returned. 'We've discussed it.'

'I won't try arguing with you. But let me know if you change your minds. We might still be able to get you up there, as long as you don't leave it too long.'

'We understand,' he said.

There was a sound like rolling thunder.

Tanalvah looked alarmed. The children appeared at the door again, hands clasped anxiously.

'It's all right,' Kinsel said. 'There's nothing to worry about.'

The children ran for Tanalvah.

Serrah and Kinsel moved to a window, away from the others. There wasn't much of a view, and all they could see was the lowering sun.

'What the hell was that?' Kinsel whispered.

'I think it was the start of a war,' Serrah said.

The sun was going down. It would be a cold evening, and an eventful one.

'I'm surprised it took them this long to open hostilities,' Disgleirio said.

'This is just a skirmish to test our strength,' Caldason replied. 'It's only a preliminary.'

'Not for the poor devils giving their lives out there.'

They were holed-up in a defensive ditch on a rise overlooking the port and bay beyond. A few hundred others were strung out along the dug-out's length, clutching weapons, awaiting their time. It was very cold, and would have been colder had a light snow not been falling.

At sea, a handful of Diamond Isle vessels were engaging a group of invader craft. The islanders, hopelessly outnumbered, proudly flew the rebels' green scorpion insignia. Their antagonists sported dragon and eagle emblems in roughly equal number, testifying to the unholy alliance of empires.

To Caldason's surprise, and regret, Rad Cheross had taken his little brig into the conflict. It was already paying for its bravery. Tilting at an unnatural angle, sails askew and smouldering, water lapped at its decks.

Glamour cascades pounded timber. Ships burned, and some collided, casting men overboard. Others were embroiled in gory melees as they battled to repel boarders. There was a cacophony of fighting and dying, the sounds of rent oak and magical reports drifting across to the silent onlookers.

Similar clashes were going on all around the island. Their primary purpose, as far as the empires were concerned, was to destroy as many ships as they could, making escape impossible. The defenders reasoned that as their small, disparate fleet was likely to be lost anyway – they could hardly drag the craft inland for protection – they might as well sell them at a price in blood, even if that was a modest cost to the invaders.

Some craft were fired and sent out crewless to ram and ignite enemy ships. The twilit sky was beginning to turn ruddy over the coasts.

'This isn't going well for us,' Caldason said.

Disgleirio took a swig from his flask, then offered it. Caldason shook his head. 'It's buying us time. They expected to do no more.'

'I hope we're using it wisely.'

As he spoke, several detachments of islanders jogged into view, ready to strengthen the line. Many were Righteous Blade members, the backbone of the island's defences.

'I think so,' Disgleirio said. 'How long before they try coming ashore, do you think?'

'Now the fighting's started, I'd say sooner rather than later. And this area's going to be a shambles.'

'We won't be sticking around for that. We'll hinder them as much as we can, then cut and run.'

'Have a direction in mind?'

'Straight back inland, the bulk of us. We've an ambush or two planned to slow them further, then we basically scatter and strike as bands. There are bound to be some set piece confrontations, like here on the beach for example, but in the main we intend avoiding them. Guerrilla methods, as you said.'

'What about the fort? Is it sealed yet?'

'All but a couple of well guarded entrances for stragglers. Damn, that reminds me. We need to get those sorcerers moved.'

'Who?'

An unusually intense flash bathed the trench in scarlet light for a second, as a series of booms swept in from the sea battle.

Disgleirio blinked. 'Phoenix and some of his Covenant people. They're over at the Ferrymen's Inn, by the end of the quay, with the old man you brought back and Kutch and the girl. I don't think they're going to be sufficiently clear if we start getting landings.'

'I'll get 'em out.' Caldason rose to leave, adding, 'If Serrah comes back –'

'I'll be sure to keep her here for you.'

Caldason nodded and set out at a dash.

His sprint took him past a crowd milling portside, waiting for orders, and more columns of defenders bound for the shore. They seemed pitifully small in number. He pushed on, huffing steam.

The sorcerers' faction and their attendant aides were spilling from the tavern's doors, such was the attraction of the Source. He elbowed his way in.

Phoenix was to be found in a back room from which most were barred, a prohibition no one felt inclined to impose on Caldason. Praltor Mahaganis was there, stretched out on a couch and apparently asleep. Kutch and Wendah were present too. Several Covenant adepts, engaged in preparing aromatic concoctions or note-taking, made up the party.

'Not much to report yet, I'm afraid,' Phoenix announced as the Qalochian barged in. 'We've barely begun.'

'It's fascinating, Reeth,' Kutch said. 'Phoenix plans to try drawing out something of the Source using a form of deep hypnosis, the inhalation of certain herbs and –'

'You have to get yourselves out of here.' His tone left no room for doubt, and the chamber fell instantly quiet. 'And any of these sorcerers not directly involved with your work, Phoenix, are needed to defend the island.'

'We're trying to do our bit here, Reeth,' the elderly wizard argued. 'Any interruption of our efforts is only going to delay the possibility of our coming up with something that might help us all.'

'I know, and I have a vested interest in it too, remember. But we can't guarantee the safety of this place.'

'We thought we'd have much longer before –'

'Not from the way things are going out there. Our sea defences, such as they are, aren't proving too much of an obstacle. Pick the help you need and get yourselves and Praltor to one of the fastnesses in the interior. Do it now. If you loiter, the enemy's going to be on us.'

A buzz began. The sorcerers started gathering their para-phernalia and packing their books. Caldason pushed his way to Kutch and Wendah.

'I want you to go with them,' he said. 'You'll be safer in the interior with Phoenix, and I'll try to get to you as soon as I can. Failing that, I'll send somebody. All right?'

'Things are really that bad?'

'And about to get worse. I've always tried to be honest with you, Kutch. What's coming is going to be frightening and more destructive than you can imagine. I want you both to stay as far away from it for as long as possible.' He noticed that Kutch and Wendah were holding hands, and added, softly, 'Look after each other. Being with someone helps the fear.'

Caldason was due for another surprise. Wendah moved to him, stood on tiptoe and planted a kiss on his cheek. Before he could say anything, a kind of chant rose. It took him a moment to realise that it was his name being repeated by successive voices, and getting nearer as the message spread his way. He was being summoned.

Giving Kutch's shoulder a squeeze, he worked his way back to the outer doors. Outside, in the cold night air, people were pointing for him to see. A disc was diving from the sky, its metallic surface reflecting the multicoloured explosions originating seaward.

In seconds it was hovering in front of them. Darrok sat in its hollow, Pallidea at his back, her crimson hair streaming.

'Welcome home, my friend,' Darrok growled. 'You'll forgive me ignoring the formalities but we have a situation and I could use your help. The first landing's just taken place.'

29

A harsh wind and eddying snow. Heavy, wet sand underfoot. Clashing steel and the cries of dying men.

They fought on a beach in semi-darkness. Two groups, one
from the sea, the other defending the land, brawling ankle-
deep in freezing waves. Above, a crescent moon beginning
to show, and the brittle pinpricks of stars.

Caldason cracked an opponent's skull, then spun to pierce
another's chest. The void he created was quickly filled by a
further pair, looking to down him. He proved a disappointment. The first took a slash of steel across his throat, while
his crony yielded to a punctured lung. Still the intruders
came, uniforms ill-assorted, looming out of the dusk like
murderous phantoms.

Glamour phantoms mingled with the raiders too, as confusion sowers; part of a parallel conflict raging between the
small number of sorcerers present. A quarrel that saw blazing
flashes of magical vitality exchanged, and men falling with
blistered cavities in their chests.

The band Caldason had joined was at best half the size of
the invaders', and not overburdened with skilled fighters.
But they had the edge in ferocity, born of desperation, and

they had Darrok aggravating the enemy with his diving disc. And so the landing party was slowed, checked, and finally forced to withdraw.

Darrok swooped down to join Caldason, arriving as the Qalochian took up a discarded spear and lobbed it at a fleeing seafarer's back. The rest of the islanders' band was in hot pursuit of the retreating invaders, many of whom were already scrambling into boats.

'If there had been more of them,' Darrok said, 'I'm not sure we could have held.'

'There are.' Caldason nodded seaward. 'Plenty . . . out there.' He scooped up a handful of moist sand and wiped clean his gory blade. 'This was just a spat.'

The beach was littered with corpses. Those of the enemy bore tattoos of both dragon and eagle, revealing the extent to which the supposedly rival empires were working together.

'Never thought we'd see something like this, eh?' Darrok remarked.

Caldason pointed. 'Look at that one. And there.' The dead he indicated weren't in uniform; at least, they weren't in the same kind of uniforms as the majority.

'Pirate garb,' Darrok confirmed.

'Vance's men?'

'Of course. I wondered how long it'd take him to make a pact with the bastards. No doubt his reward's the privilege of looting what's left of this place.'

'It's spitting in the ocean as far as our situation's concerned. We were already massively outnumbered.'

Darrok seemed preoccupied with his grievance. 'This is something else I owe Vance for, and if I ever get a chance to pay him back –' He stopped and gazed at the sky.

'What is it?' Caldason said.

'Friendly, I hope.' A flying object was approaching from

inland, and pitching their way. After a moment, Darrok added, 'As I thought.'

It proved to be a bat, larger than any species known to Caldason. It had a wider than natural wingspan, and its black hide had orangey-yellow dappling, giving it the look of a predatory wildcat.

'Be back in a minute,' Darrok promised. He zipped off and met the creature, hovering before it. The bat hung suspended in the air, defying gravity despite no longer flapping its wings.

A commotion flared up at the shoreline, a last skirmish with the escaping invaders. As it died down, Darrok was hurtling back, the glittery remains of the spent message glamour dissipating behind him. His expression was grave.

'They're trying to get a squadron of land leviathans ashore. Our people are slowing them, but not much.'

'Where?'

'Not far from here. That sheltered cove further west. We'll start seeing the really serious landings now, Reeth.'

'And the enemy getting siege engines into play.'

'I've got something that could stop them.'

'You have?'

'But there's a problem with it.'

'Well, there it is.' Darrok floated beside the barn's large open doors, indicating what was inside.

It was an immense wooden structure, with uprights and cross-struts of sturdiest timber, and a single arm that could be wound back by use of spindles and pulleys, with a pouch attached to its end by thick leather straps. In essence, it was a slingshot, built on a huge scale.

Darrok glided over to the trebuchet and gave it an affectionate slap. 'They call it the Claw. That cradle's big enough to take rocks the size of sedan chairs, and the mechanism's powerful enough to fling them enormous distances.'

'Where did it come from?' Caldason said, cricking his neck to see the weapon's top.

'A few years ago I had a minor warlord and his extensive retinue as guests. When the time came for him to leave, it turned out he couldn't meet his bill. I got his people to build this by way of payment. I was thinking of Vance. I reckoned it might come in useful for defending the island.'

'So why isn't it out there somewhere doing just that?'

'The warlord was a lousy leader, but he had some great craftsmen on his payroll, armourers in particular. This thing's beautifully designed and built, and it needs only a handful of people to operate, but it takes scores to move it. Manpower or horses; we can't spare them.'

'Ironic.'

'You can say that again. We could do a lot of damage with this beauty, but I don't know how we'd get it where it's needed. And the frustrating thing is that it isn't that far. Any ideas?'

'No. That is . . .'

'What are you thinking?'

'That magician? What was his name?'

'Who?'

'The one everybody said was crazy.'

'You're not really narrowing down the field, Reeth.'

'Frakk.'

'Frakk?'

'You can't have forgotten. The wizard with the horseless carriage.'

Darrok snapped his fingers. 'Right, him. We were hoping to use his invention for ploughing fields or –'

'Or transporting things.'

'How would we do it? Practically, I mean?'

Caldason looked about the barn. 'You've got plenty of wheels here to fit on the trebuchet, or the makings. I guess

we'd attach one of his magic boxes to each wheel. Or axle?
I don't know, we'd have to work out the details.'

'It's a good notion, Reeth.'

'Do you know where this Frakk is?'

'He should be in one of the designated sorcerers' nests. I'll
find out.'

'Meantime, I need to find Serrah.'

'And we need you here to oversee this. I was hoping you'd
lead the detail that delivers the machine. Serrah's going to
be fine in the redoubt, believe me.'

'I'd like to confirm that for myself.'

'If it's any consolation, Pallidea's out there somewhere as
well, and I'd like nothing more than going to find her. We're
too stretched. They can look after themselves, Reeth. Our
job's trying to stop the invaders.'

'All right. But I'm going for her as soon as I get the chance.'

'Fair enough. Now let's get ourselves organised, shall we?'

Runners were dispatched to find Frakk, and a crew of
carpenters was brought in to work on the trebuchet. Rapidly,
the device was rigged with multiple wagon wheels.

As the work was being completed, Darrok received another
glamoured message. This time, incongruously for winter, it
came as a swarm of wasps that droned the tidings.

'Somebody at HQ's bored or desperate,' Darrok commented.

'What's the news?' Caldason said.

'We're holding off the landing west of here, just. But it's
taking too many defenders away from other fronts.'

'How many other landings do we know about?'

'Quite a few. But we'll have to leave them to somebody
else. Let's concentrate on our patch.' He turned in his
hovering disc and looked to the barn doors. 'Where is that
sorcerer?'

On cue, Frakk arrived, escorted by a small company of
fighters. He looked dishevelled and befuddled.

'Have you been told the plan?' Darrok asked without preamble.

'Er . . . yes. Well, the basics.'

'We've got to move this to the next bay,' Caldason said, nodding at the catapult. 'Is it possible?'

'Well, I've never tried moving anything this big before, but in theory it should work.'

'Do you have enough of your . . .'

'Energy cubes. Yes.'

'How would we control the thing, steer it?'

'With a wheel, like . . .' Frakk scanned the barn. 'Like that.' He went to a wagon wheel that had been left standing upright, and laid his hands on it. 'We connect it to the axle and it steers the load this way. Left . . . right. See?'

'What about starting and stopping?'

'Ah, that and regulating the energy flow is a magical function. It needs a sorcerer to control it.'

'Then you're coming with us,' Caldason decided.

Darrok didn't join the trebuchet party. With too many calls on everyone, they decided Caldason alone would be in charge. The group he took with him numbered just ten, including Frakk.

The Claw rumbled along ponderously, with the wizard steering, his knuckles white on the wheel. Caldason accompanied him, standing with an arm looped around one of the wooden uprights. The rest of the band rode on horses and an open wagon. It was evening by now, but they burned no lights.

The ships of the invasion fleets felt no similar need. They were lit up by oil, wax and magic, and glowed like a fairy-tale city. All along the shoreline there were fires and gaudy detonations.

'Can't we go any faster?' Caldason yelled.

Frakk swallowed and nodded. The trebuchet lurched forward.

They struggled to avoid potholes, and several times had to detour to evade steep inclines, but the power driving the wheels never faltered. Another half hour of bone-rattling saw them at their destination.

'Well done, Frakk,' Caldason told him.

The sorcerer reddened bashfully.

A crowd of defenders, deeply in need of heartening, cheered when they saw the trebuchet.

Most of the islanders were stationed on a sweep of ridges that looked down onto the bay, and commanded the only road. The bay itself was illuminated by spiked lanterns, bonfires and glamour orbs, making it almost as bright as day, which was a necessity for invaders trying to establish a bridge-head. Barges were transporting men and siege engines from ships to shore.

There were four or five land leviathans on the beach. Like moving houses, or more accurately, small fortresses, they held men, perhaps as many as fifty in the larger examples, and teams of horses. The latter were yoked to ingenious mechanical systems that produced the motive force. Each of the contraptions was iron clad, and probably spell protected. There was nothing magical about their means of propulsion, unlike the trebuchet, but their armoury included magical weapons of destructive ferocity. They moved slowly but were notoriously hard to stop.

The islander's main strategy was to rain arrows down on the beach. While it was difficult to see what else they could do, given their meagre arms, it was really no more than a hindrance.

Caldason had several of Darrok's men with him, members of the personal army that originally policed the Diamond Isle. Several had used the trebuchet, though not in anger. He put them in charge of operating it, and ordered the machine brought forward. Frakk didn't have to do a thing, since scores of volunteers heaved the brute into place. Its pitching arm was wound back and secured and the generous leather cradle was spread out. From the scrubby terrain, a rock was selected, big enough that it took eight men to move it.

'What's the target?' an operator wanted to know.

'That one.' Caldason pointed to a leviathan freshly unloaded and making its cumbersome way up the beach. 'And be ready to reload fast.'

The operators set to adjusting the Claw's alignment by spinning wheels and depressing levers.

'Fire!' Caldason yelled.

The arm went up and over so fast it was a blur. Its rock spun through the air in a great arc, plunging towards its target. People on the beach scattered as the projectile descended.

It missed.

The rock landed mere feet from the leviathan, felling a handful of warriors but doing no harm to the siege engine.

Caldason bellowed, 'Reload!'

The operators worked frantically to modify their settings. Arrows were winging up from the beach below, along with bolts of magical energy. The islanders replied in kind, though with less intensity.

'Fire!'

The trebuchet whipped off a fresh shot. This time, it reached its goal. It wasn't a direct hit, but in a way, something better. The rock struck the back end of the leviathan as it was negotiating a slope. The fortuitous angle, and the force of impact, flipped the tank as though it were a toy. As it lay on its side, men scrambled free, several leading wounded horses.

The islanders were quick to capitalise on their luck. They let loose a shower of flaming, tar-tipped arrows. Dozens streaked to the leviathan's exposed and vulnerable under-side, and almost immediately the machine was belching acrid black smoke and dancing sparks.

Flocks of arrows and sizzling energy beams again scoured the ridges. Once more, the islanders returned fire as best they could, and were cheered to see several invaders engulfed by flames.

'New target!' Caldason ordered, pointing.

They got off a couple more throws in fairly quick succession. The first was a dream hit, landing squarely on the roof of a vehicle with a deafening crash. For all its armour, the leviathan had little resistance to such a blow and was crushed to two thirds of its bulk.

Perhaps over-confidence accounted for what happened next. The second rock missed its objective by a considerable margin, though it did bounce into a wagon, wrecking it.

Looking for a fresh target, Caldason glanced out to sea. A barge was coming in, carrying two leviathans and a number of soldiers. He decided on a change of tactics.

'Could you hit that?' he asked the gang master.

'It's on the edge of our range. But we might make it if we use smaller rocks, and maybe we'd need to hit it more than once.'

Caldason told them to try.

In the event, the first shot scored well. By good fortune it came down on one of the few clear spaces on the barge's deck. A shattering of timber was followed by an erupting spume of water. By the time the trebuchet had been reloaded, the barge was going down.

The second volley was another hit. It didn't pierce the craft, as its predecessor had, but it did enough damage to hasten the sinking. The leviathans were sliding across the creaking deck, and men were jumping overboard. A cheer went up from the islanders.

Caldason organised teams to search out suitable rocks and transport them to the firing point in quantity. At the gang master's suggestion, they tried shots consisting of mixtures of smaller stones and debris. Falling like deadly hail, they were remarkably effective, not so much for harming the leviathans, but as a good way of keeping the enemy troops pinned down.

A couple of hours after arriving at the cove, and with his crew firing off a constant bombardment, Caldason decided he could leave. He handed over command of the trebuchet to the highest ranking rebel he could find, then took a fast horse. Looking back as he left, he knew there was no hope of doing more than slowing down the landings.

His route took him inland, so he saw nothing of fighting, but he passed plenty of islanders on their way to beef up the defences; and plenty more, the old, the sick and youngsters, heading for various refuges. All along the coastline, the sky was red.

Caldason arrived at the redoubt in the dead of night. No one hindered his approach, and he was let in as soon as he was recognised. Although he wasn't the only islander seeking shelter there, he was told most had made for the seafront fortress. He was given directions to the rooms Kinsel and Tanalvah occupied, and in the corridor leading to them, he found Serrah.

When they finished embracing, he briefed her on what had been happening, then asked, 'What's going on here?'

'There's a lot of activity but little actually occurring, if you know what I mean. Tan and Kinsel didn't want to go to the fortress, which might be just as well, because we've had reports of successful landings there. It's all pretty confused, but the place could already be under siege.'

He thought of the people he'd seen heading for the supposed sanctuary, and of Disgleirio, who was trying to protect it. In all probability their fate was already sealed. 'We always knew they'd get ashore. All our defences are predicated on guerrilla tactics, not the impossibility of keeping them off the island.'

'If there's enough of us left to fight. Have you seen those fires or whatever they are along the coast?'

'A lot of that's designed to fill us with fear and awe, remember.'

'I think I've got quite enough of both already, thanks.'

'Well, just bear in mind that if we're going to get out of this, it's by using our heads.'

'Are we going to get out of it, Reeth? Any of us?'

'Maybe with a miracle.'

'Oh, great.'

'Don't knock it; they happen. I met you, didn't I?'

She smiled and squeezed his hand. 'You're a base flatterer. You know that, don't you?'

'I only speak the truth.' He returned the smile. 'Tell me, how's Tanalvah?'

Serrah's expression saddened. 'She might be in the first stages of labour, or will be soon enough. I'm worried about her. She doesn't seem like the Tan we knew back in Bhealfa.'

'She's been through a lot.'

'That's what everybody says. It's more than that, Reeth, though I don't know what. It's getting Kinsel down, too, although he's too kind to admit it.'

'What about the kids?'

'Confused. Scared, of course. But holding up pretty well, all things considered. By the way, they've got Praltor here.'

'Here?'

'The Covenant people thought it was the safest place. After all, he's precious, isn't he? Might come up with that miracle we need.'

'Don't mock.'

'I wasn't. Not really. Kutch is here too, along with the girl.'

'That's a relief.'

'And Phoenix, of course. Oh, and Goyter's around. Directing things efficiently, as always.'

'Karr?'

'Overseeing defences at the main port, I heard. I don't know where Quinn is.'

'He was there too, last time I saw him.'

Neither of them wanted to say what they were thinking about the port area.

'I'd like to see Kutch,' he decided, 'and find out how things are going with Mahaganis. Where are they?'

'Not far. But wouldn't you like to look in on Tan first?' He hesitated, and she said, 'I know you've had your differences in the past –'

'Not on my side. She always seemed disapproving of me.'

'Wasn't there just a bit of ruffled feathers about your shared heritage?'

'We've got different ideas about what it is to be of the Qaloch, it's true.'

'Don't you think now might be a good time to bury the hatchet over all that?'

He nodded. 'I've nothing against the woman. Even if she does worship Rintarah's gods.'

'Yes, well, you can keep that opinion to yourself. Come on.'

She led him to the door of the apartment and knocked quietly. They heard a muffled invitation to enter. Inside, Kinsel greeted them, and was particularly pleased to see Caldason safely back.

Tanalvah was in a bed on the far side of the room, well away from the shuttered window. She still looked very pale. The expression she wore when she saw her fellow Qalochian was unreadable.

'How are you, Tan?' Serrah asked.

'I'm all right,' she replied, unconvincingly. Her eyes were on Caldason.

'It's good to see you,' he said.

'Reeth,' she whispered, lifting her hand to him.

It took Caldason a second to realise she wanted him to take it. When he did, lightly, her flesh was cold. She squeezed, her nails biting.

'I'm sorry, Reeth,' she breathed. 'So sorry.'

'There's no need –'

'Oh, but there is.' Her gaze was intense. 'Please forgive me.'

Caldason said nothing. After a moment she let go of his hand and slipped into an apparent drowse.

Kinsel came over and whispered a faltering apology.

'Don't worry about it,' Serrah told him. 'We know she's under a lot of strain. You all are. How are Lirrin and Teg?'

He nodded. 'Fine. Or as fine as we could hope under the circumstances. How are things going on the outside?'

'Mixed,' Caldason replied. 'The best you can do is stay put here with your family, and do as you're told if we have to evacuate.'

'Will it come to that? I mean, where could we move to?'

'I'm sure it won't,' Serrah assured him. 'Now you concentrate on looking after Tan and leave everything else to us.' She planted a kiss on the singer's cheek.

They made their goodnights in an undertone and slipped out.

Once they were sufficiently far from the door, Serrah said, 'What did you think?'

'She doesn't look much like a bonny mother-to-be, does she?'

'No. Something's definitely wrong, but the healers can't find anything specific. It seems obvious it's in her mind.'

'What does that mean?'

Serrah looked thoughtful. 'I suppose I'm agreeing with what you said earlier; she's been left low by her experiences. Melancholic. But she did try to make up with you.'

'Did she?'

'Yes. She was apologising for your past differences.'

'You think that's what she was doing?'

'What else?'

'Let's find Kutch, shall we?'

The Covenant sorcerers had been given a wing in the redoubt. On the way there, Serrah and Reeth ran into Goyter, who was looking for them.

After welcoming Caldason back, she said, 'Phoenix wants you. Apparently there's been some kind of breakthrough.'

They hurried to the wizards' quarters and were quickly admitted. In a large hall, full of tables stacked with the paraphernalia of magic, makeshift beds and a scattering of chairs, Phoenix greeted them. Then Kutch emerged from the jumble, beamed widely, and joined them. Wendah, always his shadow these days, was close behind.

'So what's happened?' Caldason wondered.

'The hypnosis and infusions and . . . well, the several techniques we were able to apply to Praltor, have paid a small dividend,' Phoenix explained. 'But as he's had the burden to carry I think it only right that he be the one to tell you about it.'

'A small dividend,' Serrah repeated. 'Not greatly significant then?'

'A small part of the wealth of knowledge the Source undoubtedly contains,' the elderly magician made clear, 'but a revelation in the normal course of things. Come, hear about it.'

They followed, intrigued. Phoenix took them to a

bedchamber, one of several lining a corridor off the hall, and Kutch and Wendah crowded in behind him.

Praltor Mahaganis looked tiny in the vastness of an imposing four-poster bed, but his complexion was ruddier, thanks to some nourishment and certain restorative herbs he'd been given. His sightless eyes had a vigour that was close to unnerving.

Wendah moved to sit on the bed beside him, their hands meeting.

'We have, you understand, come practically nowhere in terms of extracting any substantial material from Praltor's brain,' Phoenix said. 'I'm not sure we ever shall, particularly given the time restraints we're all labouring under now. But we have managed to unlock one segment, quite possibly as much by happenstance as intent, and released certain information into his conscious mind. Praltor?'

'It was as though a whole slew of memories appeared in my head.' There was a note of something like astonishment in the old man's voice. 'Which is absurd, because I couldn't possibly have been present at the events depicted. Yet I . . . see what I see, in my mind's eye, and it's wondrous and terrible, and I don't know if a mortal should be privy to such things.'

'Go on,' Wendah gently urged.

'I was wrong,' the old man confessed. 'I thought that Founder descendants survived as some secret cult, hidden away from the world. I could hope for so comfortable a truth.' He paused, massaging the bridge of his nose with thumb and index finger. 'The Founders were once something like us,' he resumed. 'That was an unimaginably long time ago, when even the stars in the sky held different patterns to the ones now. Theirs was a magical civilisation, like ours, except that they constantly originated and refined the sorcery, and didn't just consume it. Over an ocean of time these beings developed an ever greater expertise in the noble art. And through its use they evolved into . . . something else. Somehow they conquered material existence, or rather transcended it, and cast aside flesh and blood to exist in a non-corporeal state. They created a realm that was infinitely malleable, where their hearts' desires could be fashioned at will. This is what we call the Dreamtime, and it would have been utterly alien to us in every way. It's the place that you, Reeth, have visited in the visions that plague you; one of the heritages of your Founder blood.'

'I saw it too,' Kutch reminded them. 'I shared Reeth's dreams.'

'You did,' Mahaganis granted, 'briefly, because of your inherent spotting talent, and the training you undertook to bring it out. Magic draws magic, they say, and what Reeth carries intermingled with your gift, Kutch. I would expect the same thing to happen to Wendah if she spent appreciable amounts of time in Reeth's company, though your talents are different.'

'Are you telling us anything we didn't already know or hadn't guessed?' Caldason asked.

'Hear me out and decide. The Founders moulded existence to their own design. They even defied death, gaining immortality or something very much like it. You Reeth, and Phoenix and myself, have all had a taste of that, just from touching the hem of the Founders' gown, so to speak. You could say they created a kind of heaven. They certainly seemed to think so. But there was just enough of the beast in them still, a trace of the savage from the days when they were like us. And they did as savages will do and fell into dispute. They had two basic philosophies, opposing ways of reckoning with life, and a schism opened up. There was war in heaven. The upshot of all the destruction they wrought wasn't extinction, as you might expect, but a fall from grace.'

'I don't understand,' Serrah confessed.

'Simply that. They fell. The heights they'd attained were lost to them. Their towering triumphs slipped from their grasp. They were relegated to flesh again, which they found loathsome. But they still had power, and they survived, and their quarrel carried on. For ages the two groups have been locked in a death struggle like a pair of scorpions. They've battled each other with humans as their pawns, perpetuating their ancient war. Only now, fearing a tangible threat, have they finally reunited to preserve themselves.'

'Are you saying what I think you're saying?' Serrah said.

'The Founders didn't die. Nor do they survive as a line of mere offspring with watered-down blood in their veins. Aided by what was left of their magic, they founded the empires. And now they're coming to get us.'

30

The weather in most of Bhealfa was abysmal, and particularly along its eastern coast. High winds, driven snow and freezing sleet. No one should have been travelling, and sensible people weren't, particularly at night, but Prince Melyobar's court never stopped under any circumstances. Movement was its rationale, its reason for being. And in theory at least, it was better protected than other forms of transportation and more able to withstand bad weather.

None of that stopped Andar Talgorian cursing the Prince. Gaining entrance to the palace was difficult enough at the best of times. Getting aboard when the elements raged, in the dark, was nightmarish.

The envoy was accompanied by a detachment of hand-picked empire troopers. He had agonised about its size, but in the end decided that Melyobar's arrest would best be achieved by twenty experienced men. He also brought an approved sorcerer along, naturally. A larger company would have aroused suspicions and possible hostility. This more modest number could be passed off as a bodyguard for troubled times.

In any event, he intended the task to be carried out quickly and efficiently. He even dared to hope that many in the Prince's court would be relieved to see him removed, and support the empire's edict. However, despite sending a message beforehand requesting an audience as a matter of urgency, citing major affairs of state, he was kept waiting. The Ambassador chided himself for thinking Melyobar would have responded rationally. He should have insisted on an immediate audience, or even had his men force their way in. Instead he clung to his diplomatic instincts. He had the foolish idea that his mission could be realised civilly, with the Prince giving way to the higher authority Talgorian represented.

Now Talgorian was ensconced in an anteroom bordering the royal quarters while, at his hosts' insistence, his troopers loitered in the humbler surroundings of a nearby guardroom. He paced the opulent chamber, on the verge of acting. Then something caught his eye and he stopped.

A previously hidden door in a far corner was edging open. Fearing some kind of treachery, Talgorian tensed.

A young man furtively entered. He wore the distinctive robes of a sorcerer, specifically a version that identified him as being in the service of the sovereign. He looked young for a ranking sorcerer, and unlike most of his brethren, he was clean-shaven.

'It's all right,' he whispered, holding up his hands placatingly, 'I'm not here to harm you.'

'Who are you? What do you want?'

'My name is Okrael. I'm a one of the palace's sorcerers. In fact, we've met before. I think we even exchanged a few words.'

'You do look familiar. But why the cloak-and-dagger tactics?'

'I need to speak with you, Ambassador.'

'There are official channels. If you'd care to get in touch with –'

'I have to speak to you now.'

'This isn't an ideal time. I'm expecting to be called in to the Prince at any moment.'

'That's exactly why I need to talk to you now, before you see His Royal Highness. I have something to tell you.'

'What?'

The young wizard looked hesitant. 'I'm taking a hell of a risk here . . . Can I trust you? Can you be relied on to do something?'

'About what?'

Okrael nervously scanned the room. 'The Prince.'

Talgorian wondered if he should explain that that was why he was here. But he thought it best to be cautious. 'What of him?' he said; adding, 'Anything you say will be treated as privileged. You can trust me.'

'I've no choice, I suppose. But then, what's there to lose? If he goes ahead with his scheme we'll all be dead anyway.' Okrael looked pale and sick.

'I know that his Majesty's methods can sometimes seem a little draconian, but –'

'No, no, no. I'm not talking about the small, everyday cruelties; I'm referring to something far more profound.'

Talgorian glanced up at the ceiling and the several objects silently hovering there. 'Is this the most appropriate time and place for such a discussion?'

'Don't worry, I've temporarily immobilised the spy glamours. We can talk freely. But not for long.'

It occurred to Talgorian that this was all an elaborate plot to trick him into saying something incriminating.

As though he'd read his mind, Okrael said, 'If you're worried that this is some kind of ploy, since when did Melyobar bother with trifles like evidence?'

'Are you implying that His Majesty would employ summary justice in the case of someone like me? I am Gath Tampoor's

Imperial Ambassador, after all.' He found it hard saying this without a slight swelling of the chest.

'Do you really think that would sway him in any way if he wanted your throat cut?'

The self-evident truth of that deflated the Envoy somewhat. 'All right, I'll listen to what you have to say. But I hope you're not wasting my time.'

'Then I'll keep it brief. The Prince has had us working on a special project for months now. A project with only one objective: mass murder.'

'But he has no legions under his command, no army to wreak destruction. There's no more than his palace guard, essentially. How are they to undertake a slaughter?'

'You're thinking conventionally. Melyobar has no intention of killing by force of arms.'

'Then how? Magic?'

'Magic's played its part. But you might say that what he's really employing is nature.'

'Explain yourself.'

'A great deal of effort's been put into making this place even more independent of the outside world than it already is. We've not only taken on enough supplies to feed a city, we also have things the Prince wants preserved.'

'Preserved?'

'Animals, for example. Beasts of all kinds in mating pairs. The lower levels are crammed with pens and cages. It's a zoo down there.'

'They're just diversions, surely? For His Highness's entertainment.'

'No. They're not there for his edification; he has them because he wants them to survive. To populate a new world.'

'How could he possibly –'

'It's all about his obsession with death, of course. Putting one over on his old adversary. The way Melyobar reasons is, what better way to find a man hiding in a forest than to burn down the trees?'

'You're saying he plans destruction, but by what means?'

'He's had us collecting corpses, putrefying flesh, all manner of vile, corrupt things. The aim was to identify those humours that breed in filth and bring sickness, and having isolated them, to produce a distillation of pestilences. The plan is a cleansing of the world through the spread of plague. He claims his dead father gave him the idea.'

'Could it work?'

'Oh, yes. We've arrived at a particularly virulent strain of the malady. We know it works; it's been tested on live subjects.'

'It's Melyobar's objective to introduce this . . . essence into the world?'

'He favours scattering it with the catapults you'd have seen arrayed on the battlements. Though in truth it could just as easily be introduced into wells or rivers, or in any number of other ways. Simply forcing people to drink the distillate and sending them out contaminated would spread the disease.'

'And the result would be . . . ?'

'With no known protection against the strain, and no cure, numerous fatalities. Perhaps even the world denuded of human life, as Melyobar dreams. Purged of all, that is, except him, his servants and obsequious courtiers.'

'All the better to see Death.'

'Yes. At last, there'd be no hiding place for the Prince's enemy.'

'Why are you telling me all this?'

'I didn't become a sorcerer to have a hand in massacring my own people. It has to be stopped. Few outsiders come here, and you're the only one of late with any power, Ambassador, and not in his thrall. At least I hope so.'

Talgorian was reeling. Okrael's story had an awful ring of plausibility. 'As it happens,' the Envoy said, 'our aims regarding the Prince aren't dissimilar. I'm here to bring about changes.'

'Then I'm more relieved than I can say. But you have to hurry. The quintessence is almost ready.'

'You said magic had a part in this. I don't see where.'

'The essence is unstable. Extremes of heat or cold can neutralise its virulence. Magic binds it, keeps it sure.'

'You're a sorcerer. Can't you interfere with that binding?'

'I'm far from being the only one working on this, and certainly not the most senior. One or two of my brotherhood are sympathetic, but most are too frightened to express an opinion. I don't know who's against me or with me. I can't do more than I'm doing, Ambassador. Now it's down to you.'

'Very well. Before the day's out, things are going to be very different, Okrael, I can assure you of that.'

They made their farewells, promising to talk again later, under a new regime. Then the wizard slipped away, leaving Talgorian to mull things over.

A long time seemed to pass before they came to fetch him, though in reality the minutes elapsed were barely into double figures. He was guided by a pair of liveried servants, who true to form remained aloof.

He was surprised to find that he wasn't taken to the throne room, where audiences usually took place. Instead, he was escorted up flights of stairs to a much higher level. He asked his guides what was going on, but they remained non-committal. His anxiety built, and he found himself nervously fingering the document he had in his pocket.

Finally they reached what Talgorian thought of as the wheelhouse; the area from which the palace's movement was controlled. The spacious room was dominated by a large panoramic window that occupied almost all of three sides. Its view was one of nearly complete murk, patterned with swirling snowflakes. The glamour orbs that lit the space had been dimmed to improve visibility.

There were a number of people present, mostly the wizard crew, along with guards and various servants. It was very much the way it had looked the only other time Talgorian had been there.

Melyobar sat on a throne-like chair set higher than any other, not far from the wheel that directed the massive palace's movements. He was addressing an individual Talgorian recognised as the Captain. The Ambassador caught only the end of their exchange, but apparently the Captain had objected to the route the travelling court was about to take.

'Enough!' the Prince exclaimed. 'I've no interest in your snivelling misgivings! We're following a course through the great lakes area, and that's an end to it. Unless you want to have your loyalty put to the question.'

The man grovelled, apologised and withdrew crushed. No one else seemed in the least interested in his humiliation, an indication of how common such occurrences were.

Only then did the Prince notice Talgorian. 'Ah, the Ambassador has arrived,' he announced loudly. 'Come, step forward. Let's not delay the progress of affairs of state.'

The Envoy did as he was bidden, thinking that perhaps the monarch was a little sharper than usual. 'Greetings, Your Highness. I trust I find you well.'

The Prince ignored the banality. 'And what brings you to court with such urgency?'

'These are difficult times, Your Highness. As you'll be aware, your nation and mine are engaged in a military mission of great importance.'

'Are we?' A look of befuddlement fleetingly occupied the Prince's face.

It was something Talgorian often found when talking to
Melyobar about the wider world, and it gave him brief
comfort. 'Indeed. A Gath Tampoor fleet, including represen-
tatives of our Bhealfan allies, is dealing with an enclave of
rebels as we speak.'

'And what do you expect me to do about it?'

'As such, Highness, nothing at all. I merely draw your attention to events in order to give my succeeding statements a
relevant context.'

'We're at war again. What's so different about it this time?'

Was his attitude a mite more aggressive than usual?
Incisive, even?

'It's not so much a matter of difference, sire. I mention it
only in order to illustrate the great burden our dear Empress
shoulders at such times, and to underline the difficulty of
the decision she has had to make.'

'Decision?'

Talgorian slipped out the document he'd been harbouring,
and unfurled it. 'I think it would be best, Highness, if I were
to read you the edict drafted by Her Imperial Majesty's
advisers.' He looked about and saw that furtive eyes were
on them. 'Bearing in mind that this refers to matters of a
delicate constitutional nature, perhaps Your Highness would
prefer to be informed of its contents in private?'

'No,' Melyobar responded bluntly.

'Very well.' He cleared his throat. 'In accordance with the
powers invested in me by the relevant authorities, I, Andar
Talgorian, Imperial Ambassador to the Royal Bhealfan Court,
do hereby submit an official proclamation relieving Prince
Melyobar of his position as –'

'As I suspected!' the Prince roared. 'Treachery!'

'This is a situation I'm sure we can reasonably discuss
and –'

'Guards!' Melyobar yelled. 'Guards!'

Men rushed forward with swords drawn and seized the Envoy.

'Unhand me!' he demanded. 'Don't you know who I am?'

'Their loyalty lies with me,' Melyobar told him. 'Though I wish I could say the same for all my subjects.' He raised an arm and clicked his fingers.

The signal brought in a group of guardsmen shoving a bound prisoner, and Talgorian's heart sank.

Okrael could barely walk. His face was bruised and bloody.

'Your co-conspirator,' Melyobar announced.

'No,' Talgorian replied. 'There's no plot, only the writ of higher authority. I act under orders, Your Highness. I'm just the deliverer of my superior's wishes.'

'You must think I'm very stupid,' the Prince snorted.

'I'm not here alone. I have an escort of –'

'Your cohorts are in no position to help you. Did you really think I'd allow a band of assassins to wander loose in my palace?'

'Assassins? Your Highness, if those troopers have come to any harm, Her Imperial Majesty will be extremely displeased. Likewise this man.' He nodded towards Okrael, who blinked back through unfocused eyes. 'He may have evidence germane to my mission, and as such should be afforded the empire's protection.'

'So you do admit you're in this together.'

With an icy fist clutching at his innards, Talgorian could see that he was getting nowhere. 'Please be aware, Highness,' he said, playing his last card, 'that I have the backing of the Empress herself.'

'The backing of my enemy, more likely! Death's agent!'

'This is absurd, sire! You're making a terrible mistake!'

The Prince glared at him malignly. 'We'll see how much of a mistake I'm making when torture extracts the truth. Take them to the cells!'

*   *   *

It was still snowing on the Diamond Isle, too, albeit less fiercely.

Vivid eruptions and the flicker of magical beams lit up the night. On the redoubt's parapet, Serrah and Caldason gazed towards the sea. They could just make out a multitude of masts, shrouded in white canvas.

'I don't care what your parentage is, Reeth,' Serrah said. 'It's you I love. Everything else is background chatter.'

'Look at it from my point of view.' He gestured in frustration. 'I'm proud of being a Qalochian, but ashamed of my Founder blood. That Founder heritage has effected me in all sorts of disturbing ways. My rages are obviously due to it; the two opposing sides of my nature are at war, I see that now. And maybe there are other little gifts I don't even know about yet.'

'But if it hadn't been for the life extension the blood gave you, you'd be an old man now. Or quite possibly dead. We would never have met.'

'I've thought about the irony of that a lot, Serrah, believe me. I've also worried about the great age difference between us.'

'Oh, don't start that again, Reeth. It's not a problem for me; it shouldn't be for you either. Let's just be grateful that fate brought us together, shall we?'

'You're right. But that's kind of ironic too, isn't it? Finding each other at a time when future prospects hardly look bright. Assuming we have any future prospects.'

Serrah looked at him meaningfully. 'We have each other and we have the moment. That's more than a lot of people get. Look, forget us for a minute and think about the bigger picture. What did you make of what Praltor said about the Founders surviving?'

'It occurred to me to wonder if it was some kind of mistake, or if he was imagining it all.'

'Reeth. I know it's hard to take, but don't go into denial over this. It wasn't Praltor's opinion, it was from the Source. He couldn't fake that.'

'I know. As you said, it's not easy discovering certain things about yourself.'

'Look on the bright side. It's not every day you find out you've got such influential relatives.'

Caldason had to smile.

They kissed.

A chorus of shouts went up. The lookouts stationed on the battlements were sounding an alarm.

'What is it?' Serrah said.

'Look.' He pointed.

A wagon was heading for the redoubt, accompanied by a handful of riders. The group rode hell for leather.

Serrah had a spy tube. 'Reeth! It's Dulian and Quinn.'

They were being pursued. Several dozen mounted soldiers were after them, their horses huffing white clouds in the chill air.

One or two of the redoubt's sentries began unleashing arrows. Serrah and Caldason ran for the stairs, and went down them in a breakneck clatter.

When they reached ground level they found the gates had already been opened. Defenders were roaring encouragement at the approaching wagon, and adding to the rain of arrows zeroing in on its pursuers. The latter had already slowed, cautious enough not to get too close to the fortress.

As the wagon and its smattering of outriders neared safety, there was another development. A body of soldiers emerged from the treeline, their uniforms grey against the night's blackness.

'How many, do you think?' Caldason asked.

'Forty or fifty, maybe more. Shit, Reeth, they've got to us already. The island must be overrun.'

'Not necessarily. It's a basic tactic to send in advance groups of shock troopers. These are probably pathfinders. Small in number but veterans.'

The wagon and riders thundered into the redoubt, to cheers. A mass of defenders put their shoulders to the gates and got them rapidly closed.

Karr and Disgleirio looked shaken but were unharmed. Several of the men with them had minor wounds.

'We were lucky,' Karr explained as they helped him down. 'Which is more than can be said for some of our comrades, I'm afraid.'

'What happened?' Caldason asked.

'We were simply overwhelmed,' Disgleirio replied. 'It was all we could do to get out.'

'What about the fortress?'

'Holding, and quite well, I'm pleased to say. But they only have to wait it out, of course.'

'It's a chaotic situation out there,' Karr added. 'Defenders are holding some parts of the island and invaders others. We've got pockets of our people cut off all over the place. It's anarchy.'

'Any idea where Darrok is?'

'No.'

'Is there any good news at all?' Serrah wondered.

Before anyone could speak, the lookouts were in full voice again, bellowing warning.

'And that's unlikely to be any,' Caldason reckoned, making for the wall.

Serrah and Disgleirio followed, along with scores of others. They crowded the grilles and arrow slits. What they saw was a lone rider heading their way, with a mob of invaders on its heels.

'Looks like a straggler,' Disgleirio said.

Serrah had her glamour tube. 'Gods. It's Pallidea.'

'Are you sure?'

'There's no mistaking that red mane. Here, look for yourself.' She handed him the tube.

The rider's pure white horse swerved to avoid a line of invaders blocking the way, then took off in the direction of the half ruined fairground.

Serrah clutched Caldason's arm. 'We've got to help her, Reeth.'

'Come on.'

They hurried back across the courtyard, to find that Phoenix and Goyter had joined Karr. Swiftly, they told him what they'd seen.

'We can't spare a sizeable number to go after her,' Karr told them. 'In fact, I can't see that we're in a position to send anybody, whoever needs rescuing.' He looked genuinely pained. 'I'm sorry, but defending this place has to come first.'

'Of course,' Serrah replied. 'But you've no objection to us going?'

'I have, actually. I don't want to risk losing you both. But I know that what I say won't make the slightest difference. Just promise me that if things look too hopeless you'll abandon the idea and get back here.'

'We will.'

Goyter waved in a groom leading a pair of horses. Across the saddle of each was a breastplate and helm.

'I'm not wearing those,' Caldason stated.

'You need all the help you can get,' Goyter insisted. 'Both of you. And the armour's surprisingly lightweight. Now hurry up and get into it.'

Caldason surrendered and hefted the breastplate. Serrah was already in hers. Several people clustered around to help tie their stays.

'I've something else that might be useful,' Phoenix said, showing them a small black cube on his palm.

'What is it?' Caldason asked.

'A personal deflection shield. It's got enough of a range to cover both of you, providing you stay together, and it'll protect against most edged weapons or projectiles. Have either of you used one before?'

'Never,' Caldason said.

'A few times,' Serrah acknowledged. She was fastening the strap on her helmet.

'Then it can be in your care,' the magician decided, handing it to her. 'But don't forget that it's short-lived.'

'How short?'

'About ten minutes.'

'Can we get a move on?' Caldason pleaded.

They mounted their horses and the gates were opened.

'Gods speed!' Karr shouted.

Caldason and Serrah galloped out. The gates closed behind them with a mellow thud.

The enemy foot soldiers kept their distance, contenting themselves with jeers and threatening gestures.

'Looks like there isn't too much in the way of cavalry about yet,' Serrah said.

'The few we saw seemed more interested in catching Pallidea. Come on, she went this way.' He spurred his horse.

They rode further inland, towards a cluster of abandoned amusement houses and pleasure domes, remnants from the days when the Diamond Isle was at its height as a resort for the rich. At first, they saw nothing but semi-ruined buildings overgrown with weeds and creepers. Then there was movement in the clutter.

Serrah and Reeth spotted riders milling amongst the ruins, swords drawn, slashing at the undergrowth. As yet, they hadn't been seen themselves.

'What shall we do?' Serrah mouthed.

Before he could answer, the decision was taken for them.

There was a commotion ahead. A figure broke cover and dashed their way, her flowing red hair unmistakable.

'Hang on, Reeth!' Serrah yelled. She slapped the tiny black cube against her thigh, cracking it like a raw egg and casting the spell. As the near invisible glamour spread to cloak them, a tingle ran through their flesh. 'Remember, stay close!'

They took off towards Pallidea, and found themselves riding into a barrage of arrows. The bolts ricocheted off the protective shield, some snapping in two with the force of impact, as Caldason and Serrah raced on.

Pallidea's horse had been downed and she was limping from the fall, yet she moved like an athlete. A pack of riders were behind her, and gaining fast.

Serrah and Caldason pounded in. He leaned from his saddle, arm outstretched. Pallidea grasped it, and with a mighty effort, Caldason heaved her up and onto his mount. All the while, both horses were describing an arc, so that as Pallidea was anchoring down, the two beasts had already turned and were heading back in the direction they'd come.

The manoeuvre gave the enemy a chance to narrow the gap. Now it was a chase, pure and simple, with arrows continuing to glance off the protective cloak. Serrah and Reeth spurred on their mounts, and started to gain a lead.

Then the glamour shield ran out.

They only knew because an arrow plunged into the back leg of Serrah's horse. The animal whinnied, stumbled and went down. Serrah was pitched headlong and bounced across the frozen ground.

Caldason pulled up and slid from his horse, signalling Pallidea to stay put. Taking in Serrah, the injured horse and the charging pursuers, he made an instant decision.

'Go!' he yelled.

Pallidea was shocked. 'No, Reeth! I couldn't poss –'

'Get to the redoubt! We'll be fine! Go, go, go!' He slapped her horse and it bolted away.

Serrah was on hands and knees, shaking her head to clear it.

'You all right, love?'

'I . . . yes.'

He hauled her to her feet. 'Then get ready to move.'

The first of the empire riders were bearing down on them. Caldason plucked a snub-bladed knife from his belt and flung it. The blade struck the foremost cavalryman square in the chest. His fall caused a moment of chaos for those following. A rider was unhorsed. Several others had to swerve sharply.

Caldason's gaze flicked towards the redoubt. Pallidea was well on her way to reaching its gates, and horsemen were charging out to defend her.

But Pallidea had been lucky. A number of enemy troopers were moving across the plain, cutting off Reeth and Serrah's way to the redoubt.

'This way!' he bellowed, snatching her arm.

They headed for another cluster of ruins, dominated by a tower, weaving as they ran. At their rear, hooves thundered, and arrows, spears and even a hatchet were lobbed. A shaft clipped the side of Serrah's breastplate and she felt the blow like a punch. Reeth tugged at her, keeping her moving.

The tower seemed to be the only halfway substantial building in their path. They made for it, praying its door would prove unfastened. Long moments later, gasping from the effort, they arrived at the tower's base, and were relieved beyond measure to find the door ajar. They slammed it behind them practically in their pursuers' faces, quickly securing it with an iron bar.

The place was a watchtower, part stone, part timber, but it hadn't been built as a defence, or even for any overtly practical purpose. Like so much on the island, it was ornamental; a prop to enhance someone's fantasy vacation. As such, it wouldn't withstand a determined assault for long. Even now the door shook under a battering, and was unlikely to hold.

They looked around. There was nothing but rickety wooden stairs leading to the tower's summit, and Serrah and Caldason began running up them. The stairs creaked and swayed, while below, the pounding at the door grew more violent.

As they reached the second flight, the door's restraining bar buckled and splinters flew. They kept climbing, and by the time they clambered up the last flight, they were breathing heavily.

At the top of the tower was a belfry, where a frame supported an iron bell large enough for a buffalo to wallow in. It hung above an open trap. Waist-high stone walls enclosed the belfry's four sides, and there was a wooden crown above, but otherwise it was open to the elements. A bitter wind cut through, bringing a smattering of snowflakes.

'They're going to have that door down any second,' Serrah said.

'I've been in worse defensive positions.'

'Really?'

'Well, not by much.'

The door was holed. Looking down, they could see the tips of spears, and probing hands searching for the bar.

'What do we do?'

'Stand well back,' he told her.

One hand against the bell frame, he scaled the wobbly banister. Then he drew his broadsword. At a stretch, he swiped at the stout rope holding up the bell. The blow bit into the rope, but didn't sever it, and he struck again, gouging deeper. Strands popped as the fibres grew taut.

There was a rise in the level of noise from downstairs. The last remnants of the door were kicked in.

Caldason was about to deliver a third stroke, but there was no need. The rope snapped and gravity took the bell, sucking it neatly through the open trap. From that point it fell less tidily. It hit a balustrade, shattering it, and crashed into the wall, dislodging masonry and emitting a sour note. Then it dropped true.

The bell struck with a tremendous, almost melodic crash, sending clouds of dust billowing. It came down at an angle, one edge of its lip driven into the ground, its dome wedged against the entrance.

The staircase shook violently. Barely keeping his balance, Caldason hopped lightly to the belfry floor and froze. He and Serrah stood motionless, listening to the bell's echoing death knell and waiting for the stairs to collapse. After what seemed a very long time, Serrah whispered, 'I think they're staying up for now.'

Caldason crept to the edge and looked down. He wasn't sure, but he thought he saw limbs sticking out from underneath the bell.

Serrah edged over to join him. 'Seems awfully quiet down there.'

'This was just a hitch. Don't run away with the idea that we stopped them or anything.'

'Let's see.' Moving low, she led him to the belfry wall.

For the first time, she noticed that an elaborately carved gargoyle stood at each corner, looking out across the island. She and Reeth huddled beneath one, then they took a peek. Almost immediately a roar went up from below, and arrows quickly followed. One hit the gargoyle's head, chipping an unsightly ear. Reeth and Serrah ducked back down.

'I made it twenty or more,' she reported.

'Me too. Add the ones we couldn't see and –'

'And we have a lot of murderous bastards who want to get in here.'

'Of course, we're just two people. They must have better things to do. Perhaps they'll give up.'

'Do you think so?'

'Not really.'

He removed his helmet, then began unlacing the breast-plate. 'I hate wearing this stuff.'

'I'm grateful for it.' Nevertheless, she was taking hers off, too, revealing a spreading bruise from the arrow strike. At the bruise's core, the skin was broken.

'You're getting a good black eye as well,' he told her. 'But don't worry, I like dark-eyed women.'

'Ha, ha.' She dabbed at the bruise with a cloth, and winced.

'Give it here,' he said. He produced a hip flask and damp-ened the cloth.

'What is it?' she asked.

'Brandy. Good stuff, too. Darrok gave it to me.'

'Trust him to have the best. Ouch.'

'That should stop any infection,' he said, pressing the cloth to her wound.

'Which might not be our greatest worry at the moment. I mean, infections need time to take hold, don't they? And that could be something we haven't got a lot of.'

Neither spoke for a moment. Then she added, 'Do you think Pallidea got through?'

'It looked like it. About that. I meant to say . . .'

'What?'

'Did I do the right thing? I kind of took the decision for you, didn't I? Maybe you're the one who should have had my horse.'

'There was hardly time for a debate, Reeth. And yes, what you did was right. You usually do. It's one of the things I like about you.'

'Here's some more irony for you. For decades I wanted

nothing but to die. Now I've found you and I want to live, just when –'

She placed her fingers on his lips, quietening him. 'Who said the gods haven't got a sense of humour?'

'The joke's on us this time.'

'No, Reeth. As long as we're drawing breath, and as long as we're together, there's hope.'

'And the longer we stay here, the larger their numbers are going to get.'

It was nearing dawn, and the snow had all but stopped, though it was colder than ever. They heard noises from below, and dared another peep over the wall's edge. This time there were no jeers or streams of arrows; the invaders were too busy lugging wooden props, buckets, shovels and bundles of faggots towards the tower.

'What's the betting those buckets are full of oil and pig fat?' Caldason said. 'They're going to undermine the walls with fire.'

'I don't much fancy the idea of being on top of a funeral pyre.'

'You won't be. The tower's going to collapse long before that.'

'Great. What are we going to do, Reeth?'

He hesitated, looking hard into her face. Then he dug into his pocket and pulled out a small grey pouch.

'What's that?' Serrah asked. 'A glamour? Some charm that's going to blast us out of here or –?'

'No.' His expression was deadly serious. 'It's something else Darrok gave me.'

He spread the pouch's neck and showed her the contents.

'What the hell?' she whispered, actually taking a step back. The colour was bleeding from her face.

'Listen to me.'

'Is this some kind of sick joke?'

'It's the only way we stand a chance of getting out of here.'

'You want me to take that shit? When you know what it did to Eithne?'

'I'm not suggesting this lightly, Serrah.'

'Why the fuck are you suggesting it at all?' she hissed.

'Because I can't think of anything else that might get us out of here alive,' he replied calmly.

'Oh, yes, taking a dangerous drug's really going to help in this situation, isn't it?'

'Think. When you were in the CIS you faced gangs who used this stuff. Remember how greatly their stamina was increased? How aggressive they were?'

'They were bandits. Scum.'

'That's not the point. Ramp can give you an edge that just might make the difference.'

'The damn stuff took so much from me.'

'Then let it give you something back.'

'I notice you're talking about me taking it. What about you?'

'Which one of us has a form of near immortality? Which of us gets berserk rages? Who needs ramp most to get us out of here?'

'I'm scared,' she confessed, eyes misting.

He embraced her. 'Of course you are. But did you think I'd ask you to do this if there was any other way?'

'It's dangerous.'

'No more so than facing what's outside without it.'

She pulled away. 'All right, I'll do it. But right now, and don't say anything more, Reeth. I don't want any reason to change my mind.'

'Give me your hand.' She was shaking slightly. 'I'm with you,' he assured her. He poured a quantity of the crystalline substance into her open hand.

She stared at it.

'Here, wash it down with this.' He passed her the canteen. 'You know how it goes, don't you? You'll roar for a couple of hours before it wears off. After that you'll feel pretty washed out, but otherwise you should be all right.'

'I may never forgive you for this, Caldason.' She lifted her hand to her mouth and lapped the crystals, then she pulled a face. A swig from the flask gave her a brief coughing fit. 'What now?' she said huskily.

'We wait. It should take effect soon.'

'How will I know?'

'You'll know.'

31

'Oh.'

'What is it?'

'My heart,' Serrah said, laying a hand on her chest. 'It jumped.'

'Take a couple of deep breaths,' Caldason advised.

She did.

'All right?'

'I'm fine.' Her eyes looked strange.

'We should put the armour back on.'

'Nah, fuck it.'

'I think the ramp's working, Serrah.'

She massaged her forehead for a few seconds. 'You could be right.'

'How do you feel?'

'I feel . . . I feel light-headed. I feel like I want to be sick, and dance. Or fight, run, cry, laugh . . . I don't know.'

'Yes, it's working.'

'What happens now?'

'Soon you'll start to feel a surge of energy, and well-being. Your reflexes are going to get faster. A lot faster. And you'll probably feel reckless. That's something you have to be careful about, Serrah. This isn't a situation where either of us can afford to be careless.'

'Uh? Sorry, my attention drifted. What were you saying?'

He spoke deliberately. 'Ramp changes the way you think. It can affect your judgement. Do you understand?'

'Gods, but I'm spoiling for a fight.'

'I think you just answered my question.' He took her firmly by the shoulders. 'The ramp gives you stamina, and it'll make you fight savagely if it comes to a brawl. But given the odds, it's better using that extra energy trying to run for it.'

'You're no fun.'

'We've got to act soon, Serrah. We need a plan.'

'To run? How much of a plan do we need for that? We should – Oow!' Her face clenched.

'What's wrong?'

'I think it just kicked in harder.'

'It's going to get more intense before you reach a peak.' He looked to the breaking dawn. 'We need to move soon, before it gets much lighter. How are you with that?'

'All right. What do we do?'

'We keep it simple. What we want is a diversion to give us the chance to get clear, and ideally grab a couple of their horses.'

'What kind of diversion?'

'I thought we could use this.' He was rummaging in a pocket again.

'You're a cornucopia. Is it something else Darrok gave you?'

Reeth brought out a small cloth-wrapped bundle. 'No. This is thanks to you, actually.' He opened the package and showed her.

'Dragon's blood? It needs salt water to set off. Got any?'

'No. But does it have to be sea water?'

'I don't know, we've never tried it with anything else.'

'Maybe it'd work with any liquid, and we've got the brandy.'

'What about salt? Do you happen to have a ration of that on you?'

'No, but you have.'

'I don't.'

'You do in a way. The ramp raises your body temperature quite a bit. Unless you're different to everybody else who's ever taken it, you're going to start perspiring soon.'

She smiled, just a little manically. 'Sweat and brandy. Cute. It might just work.'

'You still all right?' He was studying her closely.

'Gods help me, Reeth, but this stuff is nice. So hurry up. I'm finding it hard keeping a grip.'

'The drug's making you restless. Do some more deep breathing while I sort out the dragon's blood.'

He tapped a little heap of the powder onto two thin strips of cloth, then added a couple of masonry chips for weight. Finally he wrapped and tied them.

'So we lob those out to keep them busy below, then . . . what?' Serrah asked. 'I mean, we've got a bloody great bell blocking the only entrance. How do we get out of this place?'

'Down the outside.' He nodded at the bell frame. 'There's plenty of rope.' He began unwinding it. 'You might use up some of that energy by giving me a hand.'

When they had two sufficiently long lengths secured, she said, 'So what are we waiting for?'

'Hold still.' He touched one of the packages to her forehead. It came away stained with damp. He did the same with the other, and handed it to her. 'Ready?'

She nodded.

He took the flask of brandy and doused the packages. 'You throw from this side, I'll throw from the other. We go over the wall there.' He pointed. 'All right?'

Her expression had grown severe, her eyes hard. 'Let's just do this, shall we?'

Their bundles started to smoulder.

'Damn,' he said. 'We forgot to put the breastplates back on. Too late now.'

'They'd only slow us down,' she stated matter-of-factly.

He kissed her. 'Right? Go!'

They tossed their combustible packages over the low wall, then immediately grabbed the ropes. A loud report rang out, accompanied by a dazzling flash. Instantly, it happened again.

'Now!' he yelled.

They rushed to the wall and looked over. As they'd hoped, most of the invaders had dashed to the other side of the tower to investigate the explosions. There were only a handful of men below, and not too far beyond them, a string of horses. Time was in short supply. Reeth and Serrah vaulted over the wall and began to abseil down.

Caldason thought they were going to get down unspotted, almost to the point where their feet touched ground, but then things got messy.

Somebody shouted. Another voice joined in, and another. As they were releasing the knots on their ropes, a dozen men or more swept in to face them, and any idea of slipping away under cover of chaos was shattered. Rapidly drawing their blades, they moved forward to meet the enemy.

It was no time for finesse. Caldason met his first opponent with direct brutality, felling the man with a single, massive blow to his head. Without pause he ploughed into the next two, dealing them wounds that were grievous if not fatal. He worked like some kind of automaton, designed for no other function than butchery. Foes were cut down ruthlessly, pumping blood, shedding severed limbs.

Serrah fought just as mercilessly. To those trying to stop her, it seemed she moved at almost eye-blurring speed. She countered blows with ease, apparently anticipating attacks before they were made, and simply engaging her blade was too thorny a task for most of the men trying to block her way.

From her ramp-stoked point of view, it was like strolling through a waxworks. The manikins she weaved around and slashed at were sluggish, dull-witted creatures, too inept in their responses and too slow to fall. It seemed to her that hacking at scarecrows would have provided more of a challenge.

Curiously, one part of her mind remained disengaged from the task at hand. A morsel of her consciousness was like a bird in a gilded cage, looking out at events with the detachment of a spectator, and whatever unpleasantness might be occurring all around, much of it prompted by her crimson blade, the world had a certain fetching quality. She was particularly taken by the lovely green and purple shimmer around the edges of her vision.

A face appeared in the centre of her dream. She would have swatted at it with her steel scourge, and made it go away like all the rest, except there was something familiar about the image.

'Serrah! Serrah!' Reeth was shaking her roughly. 'Come on, Serrah!'

She focused and looked around. They were surrounded by corpses and groaning wounded.

'The others are coming,' he told her. 'We have to move!'

He grabbed her arm and all but dragged her away from the tower's base. There was an outcry behind them, and the sounds of pursuit. Caldason pulled her towards the line of tethered horses they'd seen from above. Somebody loomed in their path, an axe raised. A bout of hacking cleared the obstruction and added another wash of red to the trampled snow.

A mob was at their heels. Caldason's intention had been for them to take a horse each, but he wasn't sure if Serrah could handle one in her state, so he untied a single mount, bundled her on and swung into the saddle himself. Arrows were flying again. Ducking to avoid a hit, he spurred the horse meanly.

They galloped out into a grey, cold new day.

A group of riders, around a score, chased them towards the redoubt. But at the halfway point they fell away, reasoning perhaps that expending such resources on two people was hardly cost effective. And doubtless taking comfort from the fact that their quarry would soon share an inescapable fate.

On their sprint back to the redoubt they saw great black columns of smoke rising from various points along the coast. The islanders, it seemed, were putting up a spirited defence. On the plain facing the redoubt itself, enemy forces were massing. Not the full strength of the empires' armies, which must surely be on their way, but advance troops, though still numbering many hundreds.

The demilitarised zone surrounding the redoubt was ample enough to allow Reeth and Serrah to get in. They were lucky; from now on it would be impossible.

Inside, all was abuzz. People were dashing in every direction, and men and women bolstered weak points in the defences with sandbags. Teams of sorcerers sealed entrances with charms and prepared their magical munitions.

There were no non-combatants anymore. Weapons were being distributed to the old and lame, and children took up positions on the battlements, clutching spears twice their height.

Pallidea rushed from the crowd. She embraced Serrah and Reeth, and delivered the thanks there had been no time for earlier.

'Any sign of Darrok?' Caldason wondered.

'Yes, he got back too, thank the gods. Actually, I was just trying to find him.'

'There's Karr,' Serrah said.

They excused themselves and pushed their way to him. The ageing patrician was with Goyter. They were accompanied by Disgleirio and a quartet of Righteous Blade swordsmen. When he saw Caldason and Serrah, Karr's relief was palpable, even given all the other concerns weighing on him. He looked drawn and unwell. 'To think that we were once talking about currency and roads,' he mused sadly. 'Now we can only think of how to achieve a quick, dignified death.'

'That's enough of that,' Goyter informed him sternly. 'It's not like you to give in to pessimism, Dulian, so don't start now.'

He smiled, grateful for her strength. And despite her austere manner, Goyter was clutching his hand.

'You look a little wild, my dear,' she told Serrah, not unkindly. 'I hope everything's well with you.'

'Couldn't be better.' Serrah noticed that the older woman was wearing a sword. 'Looks good on you, Goyter. What's the news on Tanalvah?'

Goyter's expression darkened. 'The girl's still troubling us all. Something's not right there. I wish we could afford to spare more people to be with her and take the pressure off Kinsel. Not that he'd agree to such a thing.'

'I'll go and check on them.'

'Try to get them to move deeper into the redoubt. With what's going to be happening here they could be safer.'

Reeth took Serrah aside. 'Don't be long,' he said.

'No. I'll just see how things are. Somebody's got to make sure they're all right.'

'How are you feeling?'

'I could still kill a lion with my bare teeth.'

'That'll pass soon. You won't feel like it, but try to eat something. It'll help mop up the ramp.'

Serrah nodded. 'I'll be back,' she promised.

No sooner had she left than Kutch and Wendah appeared.

'You two shouldn't be here,' Caldason told them. 'Get yourselves to a bolthole.'

'We have magic,' Wendah said.

'We can help,' Kutch added. 'Phoenix has assigned us to one of the defence covens.'

'It's dangerous,' Caldason stressed.

Wendah pointed. 'There are kids much younger than us on the walls over there.'

He couldn't argue with that. 'All right, but be careful you don't –'

A roar went up from the ramparts, then alarm bells were pounded.

'To your positions!' Karr ordered, his voice magnified by a booster glamour.

Disgleirio and his men were making their way past Caldason. 'Where are you stationed?' the Qalochian asked.

'We're roving. Filling holes where needed.'

'I'll be doing the same. Good luck.'

The redoubt had catapults, admittedly few in number, and they began a bombardment of the advancing forces. Uncertainty spells and terror hexes were unleashed from the battlements, and archers fired off streams of bolts in deadly arcs. When the first besiegers reached the walls, scalding oil and blisteringly hot sand was poured through the fortress's murder holes.

Caldason was never still. He attended every breach, helped beat back many incursions. Like all the defenders, he fought tirelessly, and watched as comrades fell with arrow wounds or from searing sorcery.

None of it made any difference. The enemy were at the gates in shockingly little time. Their numbers and force of arms, and superior magic, paid off, and now they were breaking through.

Disgleirio had Karr and Goyter pulled back to safer reaches, the pair of them protesting bitterly. As the gates and walls succumbed to a human wave, the rebels began a pre-planned retreat. Some made for reinforced outbuildings, while others fell back to the main house, with its labyrinth of corridors, hideouts, keeps and subterranean tunnels. They could at least make it a costly prize.

When he saw that no more could be done to defend the walls, Caldason joined the withdrawal. Even as he made his way down, the gates were yielding. There was organised chaos in the courtyard below. The first of the enemy were trickling in, fortifications were being scaled.

Kutch and Wendah hadn't got very far.

'Come with me,' Caldason said.

'We're supposed to be with the defence coven,' Wendah protested.

'Forget that. We have to fall back. Come on.' He led them to one of the redoubt's stables as the invaders began to flood in. His thought was that a horse might give him an advantage fighting off the invaders, or that he could direct a stampede their way. He also hoped to find somewhere for the two young people to hide, but all he could really think about was Serrah, and the possibility of them dying apart.

There were no horses that he could see. They must have been used in the battles being fought on various parts of the island, or more likely there was a shortage, just as there was of everything else.

Caldason was about to tell Kutch and Wendah to find another hiding place when the sound of a door slamming came from their rear. He turned, hand on sword.

Devlor Bastorran swaggered into the stable. The freakish looking meld accompanied him, and another, younger man, in uniform.

'How very gratifying to see you again, Caldason,' Bastorran announced. 'I do hope you'll be able to find the time for a little chat.'

Kutch was transfixed, but not by the paladin. His astonished gaze was set on the young officer with him; and the officer stared back in apparent amazement.

Caldason hid his own shock. 'Always happy to accommodate someone who's travelled so far to see me,' he replied casually. 'Let's hope your visit's not going to be too much of a disappointment.'

Bastorran grinned as he reached for his blade. 'I doubt that.'

Hurrying along one of the redoubt's many corridors, Serrah passed an open door and noticed that someone had left a tray of food on a table inside. She had no appetite, but remembering what Reeth had said, went in. The tray must have been there for a couple of days, and the meat and fruit looked suspicious. She contented herself with a hunk of stale bread, washed down with water. The effects of the ramp were starting to wear off, and she was feeling weaker, but this was no time to give in to energy loss. She forced down a couple more mouthfuls.

There were noises outside. Dimmed by distance and thick walls, but unmistakable all the same: the onslaught had started in earnest. Serrah discarded the powder-dry crust and continued her journey at a faster pace.

Everybody she passed seemed to be going about their own urgent business, understandably, and largely they ignored her. When she got to her destination, she found Kinsel outside the door.

'Serrah, I'm so glad you've come.' He was obviously relieved to see her.

'What's up?'

'We were promised a healer, but nobody's come.'

'I wouldn't hold your breath, Kinsel, given the state of things out there.'

'I know, and I feel selfish when everyone's so stretched. But I'm worried about Tan.'

'Is she in desperate need?'

'I don't know,' he sighed. 'That's what I was hoping a doctor would tell us.' He moved closer and his voice dropped. 'Though I'm starting to think she might need a priest; not a healer.'

'Is she that bad?' Serrah replied, alarmed.

'No, no, you misunderstand me. It's just that what ails her seems more . . . spiritual than physical.' He added in a whisper, 'I suppose I mean her mental state.'

'I've not seen that much of her since she got here, but she does seem . . . well, almost a different person. What happened, Kinsel, do you have any idea?'

'She had a hard time in Bhealfa before getting away, of course. I've never been able to find out exactly what she went through, though we can be sure it was difficult. But I'm no less in the dark than you, really.'

'Perhaps it's the baby. It's her first, remember, and sometimes that can be a trial. Maybe once it's born –'

'Yes, of course.' He looked at her, as though he'd pulled away from his own concerns and was seeing her properly for the first time. 'I'm sorry, Serrah; you must think me terribly self-obsessed. I haven't even asked how you are.'

'I'm fine.'

'Are you sure? You do look a little wasted, if you don't mind me saying. What have you been up to?'

'It's an involved story, and it'll keep. Look, things outside are turning critical. That's what I came about.'

'We know we're hardly in a good position here, but –'

'It's going to get a lot worse. I want you to think about letting me arrange a move for you all, seriously this time.'

His worried look deepened. 'I thought you said we were safe here.'

'I did. You are. But you'd be safer nearer the redoubt's core. You're too close to the outside of the building.'

'What's the point? The situation's hopeless, isn't it?'

'That attitude's not very helpful to Tan, is it? Or the kids. And what's your alternative, giving up and cutting your throats? There's always hope. Hang on to it.'

'You sound like the way I was once.'

'Good. Be that way again, it suits you.' She squeezed his

arm affectionately, noting how much bonier it was. 'Something will turn up.'

'The Source?'

'Our secret weapon?' She had to bite back her cynicism, lest she negate her last little speech. 'It's not proving fantastically helpful at the moment. But it has come up with some interesting facts.' There was no need to burden him with horror stories about the Founders. 'Again, I'll tell you later.' Assuming there would be a later.

'Something else worries me.'

'Haven't you got enough to be going on with?'

'Seriously. I wonder what I'd do if it came to me being all that stood between Tan and the kids and those invaders. What price my pacifism then? How would I be able to protect them? Then I think about how I'm leaving the fighting to others, and feel perhaps I'm just a coward after all.' He bowed his head.

She stretched a hand to his chin and gently lifted his head again. 'That's between you and your conscience, Kinsel. I know what I'd do in that situation, but you and I have a slightly different way of looking at the world. And you're no coward. I couldn't do what you do. That turning the other cheek stuff takes a lot more self-discipline than I've got. Does that make either of us a coward?'

He gave a mild smile in gratitude. 'We'll have to hope that the enemy behave honourably and are merciful towards women and children.'

'I'm sure they will be, if it comes to that.' She thought it would be nice to believe that herself. 'Kinsel, time's pressing. Can I see Tan?'

'Yes, of course you can.' He stood aside to let her in.

As before, Tanalvah was in her bed. Her appearance wasn't greatly improved from the last time Serrah had seen her. She still had a pasty, unhealthy pallor, and her breathing was shallow to the point of improbability. Her eyes were closed. In the room's meagre light, she could have passed for a corpse.

There was no sign of the children. Serrah assumed they were behind the closed door of the adjoining room, hopefully sleeping.

Sensing Kinsel and Serrah's presence before they made a sound, Tanalvah opened her eyes. There were unmistakable embers of pain in them, but she smiled at Kinsel.

'I seem to spend my life asking this,' Serrah said, 'but how are you, Tan?'

'I'm going to be better,' she replied. It came out with a decisiveness she hadn't shown for a long time.

'That's the spirit, my love,' Kinsel approved.

'I'm going to be better once I've made a clean breast and begged forgiveness.'

'Iparrater doesn't need you to beg,' Serrah replied, taking it as a reference to Tanalvah's faith. 'You've often said yourself she's a benign god.'

'I've made my peace with her. I'm content with whatever punishment she sees fit to inflict on me. No, I'm thinking of more worldly forgiveness.'

'You've done nothing to be forgiven for. If you're referring to your old profession, well, you hardly had a choice about that, did you? Come on, Tan. A child's birth should be a joyous time, whatever else is going on in this crazy world.'

'It will be joyful to me if my child isn't born in my sin. Which is why I must make my confession and –'

'Tan? Tan.'

Tanalvah's face twisted, her body writhing in agony.

Kinsel peered at her, anxious. 'My love?'

'It's . . . time.' Tanalvah said it through clenched teeth. Another shudder wracked her.

'She's right,' Serrah reckoned. 'Those are contractions.'

'We need a healer.' He looked distraught.

'They're all busy.'

'Then we have to do it. Serrah, you –'

'Because I'm a woman I have to be an expert midwife, is that it?'

'Who else does she have but us?'

'Oh, shit.' Serrah felt a little ashamed, as well as fearful. She really wanted to get back to Reeth. And if she was being totally honest, given the ramp still coursing through her veins, the action. 'Bring hot water and towels,' she said. As he moved off, she called, 'And keep the kids out of here!'

'Good odds,' Caldason said, his gaze flicking from the paladin to the meld and the young officer.

'They're under orders to leave this to me,' Bastorran told him.

'Ah. I meant only the three of you. Good odds.'

'I'm going to enjoy shutting that mouth of yours so much.'

'Then perhaps it's time you stopped flapping yours and got on with it.'

Kutch was still gawping at the uniformed stranger, and Wendah was staring perplexedly at him.

Bastorran took the lure and came at Reeth, sword swinging. Their blades collided, giving off a peal that echoed through the empty stable.

The opening rash of strokes and counterstrokes should have determined top dog. Instead it showed there was little between them in terms of prowess. But that initial few seconds reminded Reeth of something he had observed the last time they met. Their skills might be more or less equally matched, but their fighting styles differed. Like all paladins, Bastorran had been trained in the classical tradition. Caldason was more of a street fighter. He put a greater emphasis on instinct, and less on standard combinations and textbook passes.

Not that classical meant fair. Fencing as the paladin

employed it was no less ruthless in intent than the actions of the lowliest back alley vagabond. Bastorran may have wielded his blade with grace, even a certain elegance, but still the object was to drive steel into his opponent's gut.

'Not so easy this time, is it, Caldason?' he mocked. 'No speeding wagons to hurl your victim from. No gangs of traitors to spirit you away.'

'Whereas you've only brought a pair of back-ups. Or should that be three, counting the grotesque?' Caldason nodded at Kordenza. The meld, acting as a lookout at the door, glared back.

Bastorran went on the attack again. They slashed at each other, probing defences, seeking a breach. But the intensity of their blows was rising in direct inverse ratio to the speed at which they moved. Most duels were short, intense affairs, settled quickly in passion. When two swordsmen of like stature met, stamina was often the deciding factor.

Wanting to avoid the descent into a messy slog, Caldason put on a spurt in hope of finishing things. Bastorran tried to match him, and for the first time looked to be faltering.

As they battled, Caldason shot a glance at the unnamed officer, who remained to one side, motionless, as though a mere bystander. His function was presumably to prevent Kutch or Wendah joining the fight, though he had no blade drawn. In fact, Caldason thought he saw him wink at Kutch, but realised that was absurd.

Now a fresh burst of energy infused their clash and it turned frantic again. Thrusts and parries, blows delivered and offset. The pace was feverish. Neither man would relent, but there was no disguising Bastorran's growing uncertainty. He seemed to struggle just that little bit more to drive home his strikes. Blocking Caldason's passes seemed just as much of an effort.

Despite his boast that he would take Caldason alone, the reality was proving too taxing for the Clan High Chief. His eyes conveyed as much, and the signals were directed at his aide and Kordenza.

The gestures were subtle, but Kutch picked them up. The young officer remained immobile, giving no hint that he'd comprehended his master's tacit summons. In any event, Kutch no longer seemed interested in him. His covert attention was on Aphri Kordenza. The meld had understood Bastorran's command, and was readying herself for a move.

Kutch was nearest to her. When she transferred her weight from foot to foot, presumably limbering before action, he noticed something strange. As one foot lifted slightly from the floor, there was a glow from under her heel. It was a distinct purplish light, and it appeared, bizarrely, to have the characteristics of a gummy substance. Strands of incandescence linked foot and ground for a second, like miniscule lightning bolts.

Kutch knew magic when he saw it. And now, with his spotter talent kicking in, he saw into the heart of it. Wendah surreptitiously followed his gaze, and she saw, too.

Slipping a hand into his coat, Kutch fingered the handle of the knife Serrah had given him just before they escaped Bhealfa. She seemed to have forgotten about it, but he'd kept it close ever since. It frightened him, as most weapons did, but what he saw in the meld frightened him more.

Caldason and Bastorran continued to fight. The paladin battled with an air almost of desperation, his swipes becoming wilder and his aim less sure. But there were still flashes of brilliance. He put together a mix of passes and feints that wrong-footed Caldason. For a second, everything was in flux.

Kordenza took her chance and moved. Too fast for Kutch to react, but not Wendah. The girl scooped a handful of tiny green pellets from her pocket and tossed them into the meld's path. Hex cracklers were at the milder end of the barrage glamour spectrum, more or less toys, but they detonated with an impressive report.

Caldason and Bastorran were probably as startled as everybody else, but too seasoned to be put off their stroke. Their battling didn't waiver. On the other hand, Kordenza recoiled and hastily drew back, a stunned expression on her face.

Wendah had acted instinctively. Her deed had prevented Kordenza from aiding Bastorran, but it also triggered the meld's anger. Enraged, Kordenza went for the girl and swiped her savagely across the face, hard enough to knock Wendah to the ground. The meld reached for her sword.

Kutch was there, pointing his dagger at her, hand trembling. 'Leave her alone,' he said.

The meld sneered. 'Think you can stand up to me, little boy? Let's see, shall we?' She swept up her blade.

Another barred its arc. It belonged to the silent young officer.

'How dare you stay my hand?' Kordenza flared. 'Whose side are you on anyway?'

'Certainly not yours,' he said, speaking for the first time. 'You want Kutch, you go through me.'

'I'll enjoy it.'

Their swords came together and another fight broke out.

'What the hell are you doing, Meakin?' Bastorran yelled.

'Looks like you don't inspire quite as much loyalty as you thought,' Caldason chided.

They fenced on.

Still clutching the knife, Kutch backed away from the violence and helped Wendah up. Her lip was bleeding and she looked shaken, but not seriously hurt. He embraced her protectively.

In Kordenza, Meakin had chosen an opponent far more skilled than himself. But he acquitted himself well, bravely even, knowing that he faced a professional killer. The meld chose to increase her advantage yet further. She retreated a few steps and began the repugnant process of disgorging her twin.

'Don't let her do that!' Kutch cried, for he'd seen what she was, and what she could become.

Meakin dashed forward, evaded the meld's sword and encircled her in a bear hug. Their struggle took them to the ground, limbs thrashing.

That particular distraction was poorly timed for Caldason. He deflected a blow imprecisely, then took a second hit at an awkward angle. The upshot was that his sword, the only one he wore this day, was knocked clean out of his hand. It landed tip down, quivering, in the impacted earth of the stable floor. He dived for it, sprawling full-length, a finger's length short.

Bastorran was nearer. He contemptuously kicked the blade away. It bounced beyond reach.

Caldason was at his mercy. The paladin loomed over him, lifting his sword for the killing blow. 'You don't know how much I've longed for this,' he announced sardonically, relishing the moment.

The blood pounded in Reeth's ears. Kutch yelled something that sounded like, 'The sword, Reeth!' He looked to the weapon. It was tantalisingly near but past hope of recovering.

Bastorran's blade was raised high.

Wendah gave a shrill little scream of horror.

Caldason's gaze returned to his sword. An indescribably powerful surge of wanting rose in him.

The sword moved. It shifted jerkily at first, as though tugged by an invisible hand. Then it flew, smooth and dart-like, hilt first to fill his waiting hand.

Bastorran watched all this in frozen astonishment, his own sword poised.

Reeth took his chance. He delivered an upward thrust. The steel sliced into Bastorran's abdomen, and Caldason felt it go in deep. He wrenched it free, ready to strike again. The wound erupted crimson.

The paladin wore an expression of bewildered disbelief. A look that spoke ill of a Fate that could have him snatch defeat from the jaws of sweet victory. The sword slipped from his grasp. His blood flowed more freely still. He fell.

Caldason was numb. The blade in his hand could have been a viper from the way he stared at it.

There was a commotion. Kordenza ran for the door, cloak aflutter. Meakin was getting to his feet and looking to chase her.

'Let it go!' Caldason shouted. He thought the young man lucky to have survived one encounter with her. A second could well prove fatal.

The young officer obeyed. In fact, his attention was now on Kutch, and the two of them came together. They hugged.

It seemed to Caldason that the world had just got crazier. Standing, he said, 'Kutch, who is this?'

The boy turned his head Caldason's way. His eyes were glistening. 'This is Varee, Reeth. My brother.'

'Your what?'

'It's true,' Varee told him. 'Kutch and I are siblings, and we haven't seen each other in a long time. In fact, until recently I felt sure he was dead.'

'And I thought you must be,' Kutch said, his voice near breaking.

'Varee Pirathon?' Reeth queried. 'Bastorran called you something else.'

'Meakin. Lahon Meakin. Under that name I've been his aide for the last six months.'

'You better be able to explain this.' There were sounds of fighting from outside the stables, a reminder of the greater conflict. 'Only not right now. Later, if we're still alive.'

'He's all right, Reeth,' Kutch insisted. 'He's my brother. Look how he took on the meld.'

'You do deserve thanks for that, Varee,' Caldason conceded. He turned his attention to Wendah and Kutch. 'And so do you two.'

'Forget that,' Kutch replied excitedly. 'What about that magic you pulled off? That was awesome, Reeth!'

'No. No, I didn't do that. It was a fluke . . . a . . . It was really you, wasn't it, Kutch? Or you, Wendah?'

They shook their heads in unison.

'Neither of us could do that,' Wendah informed him.

'It was you, Reeth,' Kutch added. 'You're a natural. That Founder blood.'

Caldason was horrified. He resumed studying his sword.

Varee looked thoroughly confused.

In brotherly empathy, Kutch said, 'Don't worry, I'll explain. Though there's a lot to tell.'

'I know some of it. I've been trying to help your cause, in a small way. And I want to help now.'

'Then get rid of that uniform,' Caldason advised, pulling himself together. 'There are several hundred rebels out there waiting to riddle it with arrows.'

'Gladly.' The elder Pirathon started peeling off his tunic, revealing a plain shirt.

Kutch looked on in something approaching adoration. And Wendah looked happy for him.

'The fighting's nowhere near over,' Caldason reminded them soberly. 'Not to mention that meld's still on the loose. Let's get out of here in good order, and keep your weapons handy. Kutch, Wendah, you stick close.'

They trooped past Bastorran's body and to the door. On the way, Varee picked up a discarded horse blanket and draped it around his shoulders against the cold.

Things were a lot quieter outside. The invaders had been repelled, just, and at a dreadful cost in lives. Islanders were mopping up the last pockets of fighters. Most were being forced into a retreat through the gates, or back over the walls. Kordenza was nowhere to be seen, and was presumably among them.

Caldason couldn't stop thinking about what had just

happened with the sword he carried, and what Kutch had said about it. He walked on, leaving the brothers and Wendah behind in their slow-moving, engrossed huddle.

Darrok swooped in on his flying dish. 'Good to see you, Reeth.'

Caldason returned the greeting distractedly.

'Thanks for saving my woman,' Darrok added gratefully. 'Look at that,' he went on before Reeth could respond. He pointed at a corpse half immersed in a horse trough. The man wore pirate clothing. 'More of Vance's men siding with the empires.' It was obviously a running sore for him.

'Something should be done,' Caldason replied mordantly.

Darrok was in a mood to take that literally. 'You bet something should be done. And I'm the one to do it, given the debt I owe the swine.'

Caldason kept walking, leaving Darrok to stare at his back before gliding away. He went to one of the walls, clear of invaders now, and found a little stretch of his own. The soldiers they'd driven out were jogging towards an army massing on the plain. A force bigger than the entire rebel population of the Diamond Isle, and with more arriving. He knew that everything up to now had been a skirmish.

Wendah came and stood beside him. 'They want to be together,' she explained. 'They don't need me there.' It was said without rancour. She took in the scene. 'It's bad, isn't it?'

He nodded. 'Yes.' He was thinking of Serrah. All he wanted was to be with her, and that was the next thing he was going to do.

'You have the power,' Wendah reminded him. 'Use it to help us.'

He was going to deny it, but heard himself say, 'I don't know how.'

32

It had been profound, frightening and awe-inspiring, and it wasn't over yet.

The ramp was slow leaving Serrah's system, and it was beginning to outstay its welcome. She certainly could have done without it while trying to assist a birth.

But now Tanalvah's baby was born. It was a boy, and apparently healthy.

The same couldn't be said for his mother.

The birth had been long and difficult, with Tanalvah lacking stamina, and seemingly the will to get through it. Only when they reminded her that the child's well-being was at stake did things improve. But birthing took a terrible toll on her. She endured great discomfort, with no painkiller except a few sips of brandy, and there had been copious blood loss. Serrah and Kinsel did their best without the help of a midwife or healer, and finally they got her settled down, but Tanalvah was far from well.

Fortunately, Teg and Lirrin didn't have to witness her ordeal. Kinsel had managed to persuade one of the older women to look after them in her quarters nearby.

The whole experience had been made even more fraught

by the realisation that the invaders could break through at any time. Sounds of fighting and destruction had been a constant backdrop to Tan's labour. But now, thank goodness, things had quietened considerably, though everyone knew it was just the calm before the storm.

As soon as the baby was born, Serrah had taken him into a little washroom that comprised part of their quarters, to check that he was hale. She didn't want any unpleasantness in front of Tanalvah, who was distressed enough. Now she was gently bathing the newborn. It brought back sweet memories of Eithne as a baby, and other recollections, less happy.

Kinsel came through from the room where Tanalvah had given birth. His face showed a mixture of emotions, but the moment he saw the child he was nothing but misty-eyed. 'Is he well?'

'He seems to be fine.'

'I don't know how we can ever thank you, Serrah. If it hadn't been for you –'

'Forget it.' She nodded at the bundle she cradled. 'It was worth it.'

'She wants to see him.'

'Good. I'd be worried if she didn't. We're just about done here. Aren't we, darling?' she cooed at the babe. 'Here, go to daddy.'

'Oh.' Kinsel accepted the child gingerly, then beamed at it.

'Typical man. Don't worry, it won't break.'

His smile faded. 'I'm not sure we can say the same about Tan.'

'No improvement?'

'I think she's a little worse. As far as her state of mind's concerned, that is.'

'She's still in pretty bad physical shape, too. Once I got a proper look at her I was shocked at how much she's been neglecting herself. But I'm hoping we'll be able to find a healer this morning and –'

'No. I mean yes, her physical state worries me, of course it does. But right now I'm more concerned about some of the things she's been saying.' He was clearly very troubled.

'She has been coming out with some nonsensical stuff lately, it's true. But it's likely she's feverish after what she's been through.'

'I don't think it's just that. This is more specific.'

'You mean this fixation she has about confessing?'

'Yes. I'm starting to think she might really have something she needs to get off her chest.'

'We know that Tan killed a violent client over in Rintarah. But she has no reason to feel guilty about that. It was self-defence.'

'It's not that she's been referring to.'

'What, then?'

The baby began to cry.

'He's got his dad's lungs,' Serrah said. 'It's all right, he just needs feeding. I'm not sure Tan's up to it though. I've got some milk here. We can warm it for him.'

'I'll do that and bring it through.'

'Sure?'

'I'm a father now, I've got to learn these things. Here.' He gave back the baby. 'I think you'd better go in.'

In Serrah's arms, the child calmed down almost immediately. She found Tanalvah looking as white as the fresh sheets Kinsel had put on her bed, but her bleak expression brightened when she saw the baby.

'Here he is,' Serrah announced cheerfully, trying to lift the tone.

'Is he all right?'

'He's a fit, beautiful little boy, Tan. Can you manage?' She gently lowered the baby into her arms.

Tanalvah gazed at her son with the adoration of a new mother, but there was an evident sadness in her expression, too. She kissed the child and whispered soft endearments.

Kinsel arrived with the milk. He'd poured it into a small pottery flask with a teat made from a twist of spongy wool.

'Let's see that,' Serrah said. She shook a few drops of the milk onto the back of her hand. The improvised teat worked pretty well. 'Fine, and it's not too hot. I can see you're going to be good at this.'

Giving them some privacy for their baby's first feed, she went back to the washroom. Filling a bowl from a jug of tepid water, she washed her face. She was exhausted. A lack of sleep, taking narcotics, and a big expenditure of emotional energy really took it out of you, she had discovered. But she dared to hope that things might improve with Tanalvah now she had the baby to hold.

Serrah was towelling herself dry when Kinsel came back in.

'Can you come, please? I need you.' His tone and looks invited no argument. Serrah tossed the towel aside and followed him.

Tanalvah still had the baby, but she was trying to hold it away from herself. She appeared physically worse than she had ten minutes before.

'What's this?' Serrah asked. 'Are you tiring?' It was an absurd question. Tanalvah was patently shattered. But it wasn't that.

'I don't deserve him,' she said. 'I'm not worthy.'

'You what?'

'You'll think so too, when you know.'

Serrah could see that Tan's arms must be aching from the effort of pushing away her son, not to mention the stress she was subjecting herself to. So she took the child and handed him to Kinsel, who tiptoed to the other side of the room and laid him in a cot someone had found for them.

Meanwhile, Serrah perched on the side of the bed. 'Now

what's this nonsense about you not being worthy of your son, for the gods' sake?'

'It's the way it is, Serrah. He'd be tainted by me.'

'Look, Tan, I know some mothers feel down in the dumps after they give birth, but it passes. There's no way your boy's going to be tainted by you or anything else except loved.'

Tanalvah laughed. There was absolutely nothing joyful or amused about it. It was weak and cynical and despairing. 'You wouldn't make excuses if you knew what I –'

'And what is it we should know?' Serrah was fatigued enough to be feeling irritable, and starting to show it, despite her sympathy. 'You keep hinting, Tan, but you're not telling us. What is it that's so terrible? Please, tell us, and let us be the judge of how awful you think you are.'

'It's about the great betrayal.' She spoke low, almost in a whisper.

'Did something happen to you at that time, darling?' Kinsel asked kindly. 'Something bad?'

'You could say that.' Her eyes moved to Serrah. 'You vowed to kill the traitor, didn't you?'

'Damn right I did.'

'Well . . . go ahead.'

'You're not making sense, Tan.'

'You can honour your vow, Serrah.'

'Karr told me somebody called Mijar Kayne was suspected,' Kinsel offered.

'A Righteous Blade man. He's supposed to be dead.'

'But if you know better, Tan,' Serrah put in, 'if you've seen him alive somewhere or –'

'Listen to me,' Tanalvah demanded, 'both of you. I'm the traitor.'

There was a moment of silence, then Kinsel responded, 'That's in poor taste for a joke, my dear.'

'It was me,' she repeated.

Serrah and Kinsel exchanged concerned glances.

'Why would you do such a thing?' he said.

'For you, my love, and for the children. For all of us as a family. I thought I'd be saving life, not taking it.' She broke into a coughing fit. Kinsel held a mug of water for her to drink from, his hand at her nape. The drink seemed to help.

'How did you do it?' Serrah wanted to know.

'I went to the clans. Eventually I got to see Devlor Bastorran. I gave him a little information, to let him know I had the connections. He didn't take much convincing.'

'What did you expect to get in return?'

'Kinsel. I wanted him back from that terrible galley. Bastorran said he could do it. And he told me nobody would come to harm if I told him things about the Resistance, so I did. But he lied.'

'How could you expect him to do anything else?'

'Just a minute, Serrah,' Kinsel interrupted. 'You're not taking this seriously, are you?'

She didn't reply. Her instinct was to say, No, it's insane. Tan would never dream of doing such a thing. However, she was starting to think the unthinkable.

'Come on,' Kinsel pleaded, 'this is hysteria or something.'

'It was a terrible, terrible mistake,' Tanalvah said, 'and I'll burn in hell for it.' There was the shadow of enormous weariness on her face.

'You're asking us to believe something incredible about you,' Serrah remarked.

'Wouldn't it be even more incredible if I made up something like this?'

For Serrah, that was close to being the clincher, but there was another possibility. 'You've been sick, and under a lot of pressure. How do we know it isn't your illness talking?'

'Because this is a deathbed confession, Serrah.'

'Nonsense,' Kinsel mocked, not entirely convincingly. 'Isn't it, Serrah? It's rubbish. You're just run down.'

On a hunch, Serrah reached out to the sheet covering the bed. Tanalvah didn't try to stop her. Their eyes locked, and Serrah saw something of the old Tan there. Serrah pulled back the sheet.

'My gods, no,' Kinsel gasped. He involuntarily looked away.

The bed was soaked through with blood, as was Tanalvah's nightgown. Serrah looked on in horror. She didn't know where to start, what to do.

'Now do you believe me?' Tanalvah said, her voice barely above a whisper.

'You didn't say. If you'd told us you were losing blood again we might have been able to help you. Gods, Tan, we were standing here talking to you, and all the while . . .'

'I'm beyond help in this world.' The strength was going out of her.

'We have to get a healer,' Kinsel said.

'Kinsel . . .'

'Don't look at me like that, Serrah. What do you know about it? You're not a doctor.'

'No, but I'm a fighter. I've seen blood loss before.'

'We can't just –'

'Kinsel,' Tanalvah whispered.

Kneeling, he grasped her hand and pressed it to his lips. 'My love.'

'I'm so sorry, dear.'

'As far as we're concerned, you've nothing to be sorry for.'

'You are the most wonderful man a woman could have. I treasure every moment we spent together. Take my love to Lirrin and little Teg. Don't let them all grow up hating me.'

'That I can promise you.'

'Forgive me, Kin.'

'I forgive you. I forgive you and I love you. I love you . . . so much.' The tears flowed freely now.

Tanalvah's eyes seemed to be unfocused, as though she gazed at a scene they couldn't see. But in an undertone she distinctly said, 'Forgive me, Serrah. Forgive me, if only for being a fool.'

Serrah didn't move or speak. Kinsel looked up at her.

'Her time's short,' he said, as though imploring.

'I know,' she whispered.

'Do this one last thing for her, Serrah. Please.'

'You're telling me that my friend, your woman, was responsible for untold deaths of people we knew, but that I should forgive her?'

'Try to imagine how I feel. She did it for me.' He almost couldn't go on. 'The suffering can't be undone. But how does making her death even more miserable put right any of the wrongs?' Big teardrops were running down his cheeks. 'We have little enough power in this world. The one thing we have in our command is forgiveness.'

'It's so hard. I've lived in hatred of the traitor. I swore they'd die if it was up to me. But to find out it was . . .' She gave way to sobbing herself, hands to her face.

'I know. But I'll say it again: we've only one gift to give her that means anything.'

Serrah nodded, sniffing. She moved to kneel by the bed, alongside him. 'Tan? Tan?'

Her eyes had been closed. Now they fluttered open. She recognised Serrah, and smiled. 'Don't cry. There have been enough tears shed on my account.' With some trepidation, she asked, 'Do I have your forgiveness?'

'I can't give you absolution. That's for a higher authority. But, yes, I . . . I forgive you.'

Tanalvah looked to Kinsel, her smile broader. Neither of them spoke.

The light started to leave her eyes. He leaned forward and kissed her. And when he lifted his lips from hers, she was dead.

Kinsel and Serrah stayed where they were for what seemed like a long time. Until the new baby cried and roused them.

Grief had subsided to some kind of numbness, and Serrah did her best to get things organised for Kinsel. He was crushed, and for a moment she had the irrational fear that he might decide to join his lover in death. But it took no more than a reminder of the children to stiffen his resolve.

Serrah thought how tough it had been on Teg and Lirrin. To lose their natural mother was bad enough. To go on and lose their adoptive one was indescribably awful. For the second time in their young lives they were going to be told something that would break their hearts. She didn't envy Kinsel's task.

She comforted him a little by telling him that at least they had a kind, decent, loving father. But they both chose to ignore the fact that even this could be in doubt once the empires' armies took the island.

Serrah found him and the children new quarters deeper in the redoubt. The rooms weren't as big as the ones they were leaving, but the set-up was more communal, and there would be people about to help and distract. It was considerably safer, too. She made sure Lirrin and Teg would be waiting, and she accompanied Kinsel there. He carried a couple of bags of possessions, she held the baby. She left him with the children clustering around the good news of the newborn, preparatory to the bad.

Her promise to Kinsel was that she would go back and lay out Tan decently. She'd also try to rustle up a priest and a burial detail, though that wasn't going to be easy in the middle of a war. Apart from that, there were a few things he wanted from the apartment, but couldn't face going for himself.

This was all in her mind as she trudged the endless corridors.

And Reeth, of course. It felt like an age since they had last seen
each other. She had no real fears about him being able to look
after himself, but she longed to set eyes on him.

That was the last coherent thought she had for a while.

Reaching the section where the apartment was located,
near one of the fortress's external walls, but still a brisk walk
away, she turned a fateful corner.

No sooner had she entered the corridor than it was bathed
end to end in a flash of blinding light, followed soon after
by an ear-splitting explosion.

The floor bucked like a living creature. Doors imploded,
windows shattered, chandeliers fell. Bricks and timber flew
in all directions. There were clouds of smothering dust. Then
the roof came down.

Something, a number of somethings, pelted and pummelled
her. And at the last she was on her back, unable to move,
covered by a barely tolerable weight. Instantly, all of her fears
about being trapped in a confined space became horrible
reality. But the mind is a strange and wondrous thing, and
no more so than in extreme situations. Instead of panic occupying her consciousness, she could only dwell on the question, who did she think the Resistance had stolen the dragon's
blood idea from in the first place?

Serrah's assumption was substantially correct. Out on the plain,
and on the tops of a few low, flat hills not far off, the invaders
had set up giant catapults and massive glamour launch tubes.
They were using a mixture of rocks the size of houses and
magical munitions in their bombardment. It was one of the
latter that had struck the part of the redoubt Serrah was in.

Caldason ran for the fortress as fast as he could, heedless
of any in his path. Well behind, Kutch and Wendah, hand
in hand, dashed after him. All the while, the barrage
continued. Massive jagged projectiles ploughed into fleeing

islanders and crashed through roofs. Hex shells fell like hail, spreading the pestilences of fire, vitriol and noxious gas.

Inside the redoubt, people were already working frantically to clear debris and free the wounded. Several dead bodies were evident. In the chaos, Reeth spotted Kinsel. He had no way of knowing about his loss, and took his dazed appearance to be a result of the carnage.

'Have you seen Serrah?' he demanded, catching his sleeve.

'Reeth! Yes. That is, I came to look for her when I heard the –'

'Do you know where she might be?'

Kutch and Wendah arrived, panting.

'She was heading back to our apartment,' Kinsel explained. 'But they say that's where the main strike was.'

'Stay with your kids,' Caldason told him. He ran in the direction of the collapse, bowling people aside and cutting a path for a breathless Wendah and Kutch.

There were few people in the area of the worst roof fall. Rescuers had yet to arrive, and anybody there at the time of the strike likely had problems of their own.

Caldason surveyed the downed walls and mounds of debris. The dust was still settling. Shouting Serrah's name might have been an option if there wasn't so much echoing noise already. 'Where do we look?'

'We can help,' Kutch said. 'Or Wendah can, rather.'

'Can you, Wendah?'

'My skill's similar to Kutch's but not the same,' she said. 'I could see things for Praltor, find things.'

'Could you find Serrah?'

'I can try.' She started to wander into the wrecked corridor.

'Be careful,' Reeth warned.

A couple of minutes later she stopped at a pile of twisted junk no different to any other. 'There,' she said, pointing at it.

'Are you sure?'

She nodded.

Caldason cupped his mouth. 'Serrah!' he called. 'Serrah!'

There was a muffled response three or four paces away. Caldason began sifting through the wreckage, and Kutch came to help him. They kept calling, and narrowed their search by the responses. At last they came to a door, lying embedded in rubble. They heaved, Wendah adding her modest strength, and at last managed to shift it just enough to reveal a hollow beneath. The pasty white shape they made out in the darkness there was Serrah's face.

'Thank the gods,' she said.

Caldason went down on all fours and stretched his hand into the hole. He touched her face, and she kissed his hand.

'Afraid I can't return in kind,' she explained. 'I can't move a limb. Can you get me out?'

'Of course we can, my love. Are you all right? Anything broken?'

'It's hard to say when you can't move. I don't think so.'

A shudder ran through the whole of their side of the building. Plaster and small bits of masonry bounced around.

'This stuff on top of me isn't very stable,' she told him. 'I can feel it shifting. And if it shifts the wrong way . . .'

'We'll get you out,' he promised. 'Just stay calm. We're right here and we're working on it.' Then he looked about and saw the enormity of the task. There were pieces of stonework in the way that a dozen men would struggle to move. The sheer quantity of wreckage was daunting.

There was another shift in floor and walls. Serrah cried out. He scrambled back to the hole.

'It's getting tighter down here,' she complained. 'If you're going to come up with something, soon would be good.'

Caldason reassured her again. His frustration was starting to find an outlet; as in combat, he felt the creeping onset of a berserk. He couldn't see that being helpful in the present situation and tried to calm himself. He turned to Kutch and Wendah. 'How? How are we going to get her out of there? At the best of times it'd take a small army to clear all this. And at any minute the lot could slip and crush her.'

'You're going into one of your tempers,' Kutch said. 'I know the signs.'

'I'm trying not to.' He added crankily, 'What the hell has that got to do with it anyway?'

'No, no, no,' Kutch replied, 'it's good. I mean . . . not *good* good but maybe it's good for this situation.'

'I'm not following this, Kutch. Does it have a bearing?'

'We've discussed it, Wendah and me. Your rages are due to the Founder bit of your parentage, so it could be the best way to connect with that part of you.'

'Why would I want to?'

'Because of what happened in the stables today,' Wendah told him. 'Tapping whatever Founder magic you've got in you could help get Serrah out of there.'

'How?'

'We don't know,' Kutch admitted. 'But we do know the Founders had really powerful magic. Who can say what it might be capable of? Surely it's worth a try?'

'I can't believe I'm saying this but . . . yes, it's worth trying. What do I do?'

'Ah. That we're not entirely sure about.'

'Oh, great, Kutch.'

'No, wait a minute. You're already halfway to a berserk, so that kind of puts you in the right frame of mind. Now we need some kind of catalyst.'

'What?'

Kutch shrugged.

'Damn it! I'm out of my depth here, boy. If this was a swordfight I'd know what to do.'

'That's it.'

'What is? You want me to attack this mess with a blade?'

'Do you remember the times you talked to me about the no-mind technique you use in fighting? That's a particular frame of mind, like the berserks. If you could combine them –'

'I see where you're going, but I'm not sure how easy it'd be trying to reach a meditative state while a berserk's building. That's a boat tossed on a very choppy sea.'

'Try it,' Wendah urged.

'Maybe if you treated this as a martial exercise and drew your sword . . .' Kutch suggested.

'What's happening up there?' Serrah wanted to know.

'We have to do a bit of . . . figuring out,' Caldason replied. 'Hang on!'

He crept away from the aperture, unsheathing his sword. 'Wendah, Kutch; try to keep her occupied. I need to be able to concentrate.'

He moved a little way off, adopted a stance he knew to be conducive, then opened himself to no-mind. In his hand he held the same sword that had earlier saved his life. He had no real idea of what he was supposed to be doing, which in no-mind terms was an asset.

Wendah and Kutch were at the hole, comforting Serrah and letting her know what was happening.

Another rumble came, along with the sounds of splitting timbers and cracking glass. Serrah screamed. Kutch and Wendah didn't look to her. As one, they turned and peered in Reeth's direction. What they saw was awesome.

He came to them. Nothing about his appearance had changed, with the exception of his eyes, and they would have been hard put to say what was different about them. It was through the filter of their talents that they perceived the really important transformation. They saw something terrifying and inspiring in equal measure, and as he approached they realised that they had no privilege in their view. Anyone would be aware of the power Caldason now embodied.

There were no words. He simply gestured for them to move. Once they had, he took hold of the door and ripped it away like paper. He discarded it as easily as a plucked flower, sending it crashing halfway along the corridor. Then with no apparent effort he tore into the mass of debris imprisoning Serrah, tossing it clear.

Nothing impeded him, stone, wood, tile or glass. He snapped iron supports in two and swatted aside masonry chunks twice his size. In no time he was hoisting Serrah free and they were in each other's arms.

She knew, too. No wild talent was needed to show her what was so obvious. 'You've done it, Reeth,' she said, mesmerised.

'I feel . . . omnipotent,' he told her.

She gazed into his now so atypical eyes and saw a story there. The war of good and bad, his divided legacy, each side struggling for dominance.

'You're full of contradiction,' she told him.

'Yes. I have to keep the balance. If I slip into the dark . . .'

They hadn't noticed that the level of noise outside the redoubt had been rising. Now the sounds of battle were unmistakable, and they could hear the crash of more projectiles. Somehow, none of them doubted that Caldason could hear a lot more.

'Don't you see?' Kutch said. 'It's what they were trying to hide! It's what's inside you! The Founders didn't want you having what you're feeling now. Your mixed heritage, it makes for something different to them. Perhaps more powerful, because you have their remarkable magical strength tempered with humanity.'

'You can do something, Reeth,' Serrah told him. 'You can go against that horde out there before they kill us all, along with the dream.'

'How?'

'You'll know.'

He looked up to the shattered roof and the dark clouds above. Then he looked to himself, and he understood.

Reeth Caldason was a lightning bolt. He streaked into the sky. It was like his visions. Exhilarating, hyper-real, filled with potential. He knew that the Dreamtime must have been something like this.

He floated far above the land and the petty affairs of men. Majestic, ethereal, he felt only contempt for them. Then his human reason countered and he saw distinctions, a golden divide between nobility and evil. He started to pay attention to what was happening on the ground, and swiftly picked his targets.

It only remained for him to become an avenging wraith, an exterminating angel, a force of nature.

He dropped like a stone, dived like a bird, moved from air particle to air particle like something other than a man.

The enemy's great siege engines, catapults and glamour tubes were so much kindling for Caldason. He swept them from the plains and hills, and down onto the heads of the advancing armies. He caused fire to rain on the invaders. He turned their black clouds of arrows into silk scarves. He sent them needle-sharp ice slivers in their hundreds of thousands. He harassed their supply lines and spread contagious paranoia.

Then he moved to the ocean and set about their ships, burning and sinking them at random, strafing the crowded beaches with shards of quartz and raw diamonds. He sowed the sailors' ranks with venomous serpents and downpours of blood.

The further reaches of the sea caught his eye. He soared high and saw another mighty, ill-assorted fleet there, unrelated to the empires', which was heading for the island. And no sooner had he seen it than a surge of attraction swept over him. He wanted to go there.

But something changed. He began to experience a falling away of his power. The possibility of his corporeal existence became an issue again. He felt less indomitable.

He headed back to the ground, his energies bleeding. The island rushed in all directions to meet the horizon, became a rough map, then showed its detail. He saw the redoubt, a box surrounded by armies he'd only begun to decimate. The fortress's inner square was visible, and shortly, the people in it.

Caldason, almost fully himself now, drifted down to land in a clearing the islanders had pulled back to create.

There was some cheering and applause. But just as much silent amazement or trepidation.

A little delegation pushed through the crowd. Karr led it, Disgleirio and Phoenix at his side. Kutch and Wendah were there, and best of all, Serrah. She embraced him.

'That was . . . fantastic, Reeth,' Karr said, plainly amazed. 'You did brilliantly. You've dealt a grievous blow and thrown them into disorder.'

'You were awesome,' Kutch volunteered.

'But what went wrong?' Phoenix asked. 'Why did you stop?'

'I had no choice in the matter. One minute I had the power, the next it was being taken away. Just after I saw the new fleet.'

'New fleet?' Disgleirio echoed.

'Another one's on the way. Not from either empire. I don't know whose it is.'

'Another force coming against us and your power's failed. What's going to protect us now?'

'Perhaps it was my lack of expertise,' Caldason offered. 'Maybe if I try again –'

'No,' said Phoenix, 'I don't think so. Something else is happening here. The scrap of Founder magic in me makes me feel it. You should too, Reeth.'

Caldason remembered the feeling he got looking at the

unknown fleet, and the attraction it held for him. 'Perhaps you're right.'

'We can sense something,' Wendah piped up. 'Well, more me than Kutch actually, because I'm more sensitive.'

'I'm getting it a bit,' Kutch assured them.

'Can you describe it?' Karr asked.

'I don't like it,' Wendah replied. 'I've not had this feeling before and it's all wrong.'

'Precisely,' Phoenix agreed.

They all fell silent after that, as though there was a mass perception of something imminent and strange.

Then somebody said, 'Hear that?'

Everyone strained to listen. It wasn't so much something that could be heard, as felt.

The first they knew about it in Rintarah was a deep rumbling, similar to an earthquake.

In many ways, an earthquake would have been preferable. It would probably have been more benign.

For most, it started with the energy grid. The lines began to glow, pulsate, crack, and in some locations erupt in geysers of raw magic. Instances were so numerous that the licensed sorcerers and emergency glamour-dousing crews were overwhelmed. The pure magic, lacking restraint or expert direction, manifested as hordes of random glamours. Town streets and hamlets' cobbled lanes swarmed with exotic, grotesque, surreal, frequently dangerous nightmares. The sky was filled with their flying brethren.

Everything that depended on magic began to malfunction or fail. Lights went out, impossibly beautiful courtesans vanished in puffs of lavender-scented smoke. Public statuary froze, or ran amok. Fountains spewed molten lava. Lavish, shimmering gowns faded to drab rags. And all the while the populace was under siege from running, crawling, flying, swarming, exploding, melting, scalding, freezing onslaughts.

As the magic escaped in ever greater quantities, its absence from the very structure of the environment began to be felt, very much like an earthquake. Tall towers were the first to go, their great weight no longer stable. Buildings collapsed, bridges swayed. Fissures opened up in country lanes and city boulevards, big enough to swallow horse-drawn carriages.

What became apparent, to those able to observe it, was that in fact the magic was being negated; not leaking but ceasing to be. And with it went everything it supported, in all senses, so that public anarchy and civil disobedience added to the chaos in normally well ordered Rintarah.

In the capital, behind the rulers' forbidding walls, things were no better. Jacinth Felderth, the empire's most powerful individual, was in his beloved rose garden when catastrophe struck. The spectacle of witnessing his elegant blooms wither and turn to dust was made all the more unedifying for knowing the same was about to happen to him.

All over Rintarah, but most especially in the capital, the families of the ruling elite, which is to say surviving Founders, were suddenly seen as they really were. The rapid onset of the ageing process, making up for the countless centuries cheated, informed an outraged populace. Tyranny they could tolerate. Being ruled by something not quite human was a different matter. The scales fell from their eyes and there was something akin to a general uprising, fanned by remnants of the Resistance. Their task was made the easier with the disappearance of the authorities' magical defences.

Gath Tampoorians first had an inkling of what was to come when many observed a deep rumbling, of the kind an earthquake makes.

Overall, their experience was very much the same as

Rintarah's. City and countryside saw the wholesale escape of magic. They had their cracks and geysers, too, and a plague of glamours. Their proud buildings and shunned hovels fell, just the same. Dams broke, forests burned and streets were ripped up with the force of it.

Like the citizens of their rival empire, they saw their rulers in their true light. Indeed, some of them met their ends at the hands of their own subjects, notwithstanding the ageing acceleration process would have got them anyway. There was much bewailing of the loss of magic, in common with Rintarah. And here too, the people fell to insurrection, aided by what was left of the Resistance. A prolonged period of uncertainty and confusion was predicted, and the fate of the empire was by no means assured at the end of it. In this respect, Gath Tampoor also mirrored Rintarah.

Empress Bethmilno was at the matrix pit in her palace throne room trying to reach her Rintarahian counterpart, Felderth, when the pit erupted. The subsequent discovery of what was left of her corpse threw no light on the case. Her family suffered similar fates, or speedily aged to dirt.

Commissioner Laffon, head of the infamous CIS, was in Merakasa for an audience with the Empress. He was said to have been identified by a vengeful mob and chased through the streets. His demise came about when the chase took him into the path of a collapsing forty-ton ornamental column.

The column belonged to the headquarters of the Gath Tampoorian Justice Department.

33

In Prince Melyobar's floating palace they knew nothing about possible earthquakes.

The court was moving above a landscape of almost pure white, and snow was still falling hard. There were steep mountains on either side of the airborne procession, and a network of sizeable lakes, frozen over and snow-covered, not far below. The route had been insisted on by Melyobar himself, for whatever reason that seemed pressing to him at the time. But the weather conditions meant that the sorcerers tasked with steering the behemoth had kept it flying low. Thousands of the camp followers who relied on non-magical transport were finding their way across the ice-bound lakes. But as many chose to take a long detour.

Talgorian had been held in a dungeon, roughed up a little and not fed, although they did give him a small amount of water. He had no idea what had happened to the detail of troopers he'd brought with him, and knew nothing of the fate of Okrael, the young sorcerer who tried to warn him about the Prince's lunatic scheme. As yet, Talgorian had not suffered the torture that had been threatened when he was seized.

They came for him without warning or explanation. He was given a heavy fur coat to put on, and thick gloves, which surprised him. But it became clear why when he was taken, not to an audience chamber or to the throne room, but outside, onto one of the palace's upper battlements. It was here that the Prince had ordered the installation of powerful catapults, and it was Okrael who had revealed what they were to be used for. In addition to the catapults, and set well away from them, there was a structure that looked worryingly like a gallows.

It was bitterly cold. He wondered why anyone would want to conduct business of any kind in such a place. Then he remembered that the 'anyone' was Prince Melyobar.

The Prince himself sat, incongruously, on a throne mounted on a dais, over which a canopy had been erected. There were various nobles, officials and military types about, as usual, and the higher-ups had their own parasols. Nobody else got an awning, naturally. Or a seat.

Talgorian was frog-marched into Melyobar's presence like a common criminal. It had been his intention to dispense with formalities like bowing in order to show his displeasure at how they were treating him. Unfortunately, one of the thuggish guards enforced the protocol with a clout to the back of Talgorian's head.

The Envoy was also frustrated in his next planned snub. He meant to offer the Prince no ceremonial greeting. This was thwarted by the simple fact that Melyobar spoke first and ignored etiquette himself.

'I trust a night in the cells has helped bring you to your senses,' the Prince said.

'My senses about what precisely, Your Royal Highness?' Talgorian didn't quite have the nerve to dispense with the man's correct titles as part of his protest.

'Your sedition. Your conspiring with enemies of my rule.'

'Those charges, if that's officially what they are, Your Majesty, are patently absurd. I've not been seditious and I don't associate with the enemies of authority.'

'Well, of course you'd be inclined to lie about it, wouldn't you?'

'I take great exception to that slight, Your Majesty. And if I may say so, I think this whole episode is an appalling way to treat an Imperial Ambassador. I intend complaining to the Empress about it in the strongest possible terms.'

'Complaining to my arch-enemy, more like. Complaining to . . .' He almost always lowered his voice when referring to death. '. . . Him. Do you deny it?'

'Yes! That is, what exactly am I denying, sire?'

'Your attempts to confuse this hearing are typical of the methods employed by your sort.'

'Hearing? In what way does this represent a properly consti-tuted legal tribunal, my lord?'

'It's officially constituted as far as the rules of my court are concerned.'

In other words the Prince was making it up as he went along, Talgorian thought. 'If this is a form of trial, then I respectfully request the benefit of legal representation.'

'There's no need. I afford you something much better than that.'

'Sire?'

'You're allowed to talk for yourself. Who's more qualified to put your case?'

'What case? How can I defend myself when I'm unaware of the exact nature of the offences I'm supposed to have committed?'

'So you admit you have no case. That won't go well for you.'

Talgorian wanted to scream. Instead he chose to speak as though to a child, which had worked in the past. 'I don't know what I'm supposed to have done, Your Highness. If it were possible for you to graciously inform me, perhaps I could then assist Your Highness.'

The Prince lifted a sheet of vellum from his lap and spent an inordinate amount of time studying it. At length he said, 'It amounts to treason.'

'But I'm not even a Bhealfan subject!'

'Ah, and neither is he. So you're making the further admission that like my enemy you're not a Bhealfan subject. This is all starting to sound rather damning, isn't it?'

The Ambassador took a steadying breath. 'You mentioned conspiracy, Majesty. Would you be kind enough to outline the nature of that charge?'

'You're accused of conspiring against me, and by extension, the people of Bhealfa.'

'If that's the basis of the accusation against me, sire, then I'm forced to draw to your attention the plot which you yourself are said to have instigated. A plot whose aim is to exterminate a large number of Your Majesty's own subjects. Is that not a conspiracy against the people of Bhealfa?'

'You say plot, I say project. I'm afraid your own terminology betrays you. For who would describe a project as a plot unless they saw themselves as a victim of it? And to see yourself as a victim must mean that you stand as an enemy of this administration. Indeed, the very fact that you have knowledge of the project indicates an element of espionage, and should constitute another charge against you. So consider yourself lucky on that count.' He slumped back in his throne, evidently pleased with his display of superior logic. 'Do you have anything to say before judgement's passed?' he added.

'I –'

'Suit yourself. Having considered the evidence in some detail, there can be only one verdict on these grave charges:

guilty. And offences of such gravity can attract only one sentence: that you be hanged by the neck until dead. And further, that your remains be contributed towards manufacture of the essence I'll be employing to cleanse the land.'

Shocked as he was, what really lodged in Talgorian's mind was that he had been given a coat and gloves so he wouldn't feel discomfort at his execution.

'Is there a plea for mercy?' the Prince asked. 'Would the condemned man care to confess his guilt, supply details of the conspiracy and throw himself upon our mercy?'

'This is an outrage!' the Envoy yelled, resorting to the diplomat's trump card, indignation. 'The Empress herself shall hear of it!'

'I see no reason to delay the sentence,' Melyobar decided. 'But it's a pity really, because you'll miss seeing the launch of the project, which starts just as soon as this weather clears. Guards!'

Talgorian, voicing objections, was prodded towards the scaffold.

The Prince gestured to an official standing by a door leading into the palace. 'I'm very pleased to say,' he announced to those present, 'that on the occasion of this execution we are honoured to have with us our inspiration, our leading exemplar of moral rectitude, the Grandfather of the Nation and originator of the project we're soon to see underway. Please welcome my father, King Narbetton.'

To smatterings of polite applause, muffled by gloves, a small procession made its way out of the open door. At first sight it appeared to be a funeral, an observation that sent a chill up Talgorian's spine. In fact, technically the six uniformed bearers were carrying a glass-fronted cabinet, not a coffin. It contained the comatose body of the not-so-late monarch, dressed in finery and clutching a grand broadsword. His cabinet was manhandled to an upright position and made secure with props, so that he appeared to be standing, albeit on a lower level than his son.

Talgorian was being hustled to his own stage, for a performance he'd rather not give. His wrists were bound, which meant removing the gloves, and his hands immediately began turning blue. They positioned him beneath the gibbet, just next to the trapdoor that would open and cause his neck to snap. The trap was as big as a small barn door, indicating that the scaffold was used for mass hangings.

Somebody slipped the noose over his head, leaving it lightly about his neck. At least it wasn't snowing so heavily.

All they needed now was for the Lord High Executioner to put in an appearance. His absence caused amusement among Talgorian's guards, prompting whispered jokes about how Melyobar had probably had the hangman executed. Jests Talgorian considered in poor taste, under the circumstances, though he had no argument with the executioner being late.

From his raised position on the gallows he could look over the ramparts to the wintry landscape beyond. Turning his head slightly, he saw the other levitated palaces that formed Melyobar's court. They followed the royal residence in a well established pecking order, travelling single file and snow-caked, looking like an enormous string of pearls.

The Prince and his courtiers were growing restless waiting for the hangman. Talgorian's worry was that Melyobar would lose patience and order a lowly soldier to do the job. If he was to be hanged, the Ambassador's position required the attentions of no less than the Lord High Executioner himself. He didn't want to lose face over this.

Standing on his windy perch, surveying a view the others couldn't see as easily, the Envoy noticed something strange. Ahead, at the mouth of the next valley, a small town clustered, just visible in the greyness because of its lights. As he

watched, those lights flickered in unison. Not individually or
in segments, which might be explicable, but all of them at
the same time. He couldn't imagine why the town's entire
glamoured lighting should gutter simultaneously. Then it
happened again, twice in quick succession. The fourth time,
all the lights stayed out.

His guards hadn't noticed. They were stamping their feet and
huffing into their hands. Going by their resentful glances, they
were more anxious to see the executioner than he was.

The officials around Melyobar's throne conferred in groups.
Messengers were dispatched.

He looked to the town. There were lights again, but they
were different. They flashed, pulsed and shimmered, and they
were multicoloured. Some took the form of brief, intense
bursts. Perhaps a celebration was taking place. A melancholy
thought for a man waiting to be hanged.

Then he thought he saw movement on the mountain
slopes near the town. It was hard to be sure, but it looked
like a large body of snow sliding earthward. An avalanche?

Another door opened on the battlements. A man hurried
to the Prince at speed. He wore the robes that marked him
as one of the sorcerer elite responsible for controlling the
palace's movements. He bowed low to Melyobar, then began
an animated discourse.

All the palace lights flickered. The lights on the other
palaces did the same, and in unison, like the distant town.

An odd noise greeted this unprecedented event. It sounded
like the buzz of an enormous swarm of insects. In fact, it was
a mass murmur; the startled outpourings of the many people
on and about the palace, and the ones following. As the floating
buildings made no noise, and the snow-blanketed day was
equally silent, it was quite possible to hear such things. People
hailing each other from one passing palace to another, using
just their lungs, was not uncommon, though there were those

who considered it vulgar. The misbehaviour of the lights caused a definite stir among Melyobar's entourage. Much coming and going ensued, and the sorcerer who had briefed Melyobar left even faster than he had arrived. Watching all this, Talgorian was afraid they'd forgotten him. He spiked that thought. On balance, he was more afraid they hadn't.

When the lights flickered, Melyobar's personal bodyguards naturally moved closer to him. The Prince's instinct was to move closer to his father.

Glamour-heated, Narbetton's cabinet was pleasant to the touch on a winter's day. Melyobar embraced it, and began an edgy, whispered dialogue with the old King.

Some of the courtiers went to the battlements and looked down on the army of camp followers. Things seemed to be out of the ordinary there, too. There were more lights than there should have been, many of them overly busy, and some kind of turmoil was evident. Sounds accompanied all this. They drifted up as pure clamour, but there were higher-pitched, faintly distressing chords woven in. The courtiers took to exchanging anxious looks.

'Father says it's all right!' the Prince reported. 'It's just a little glitch in the magic, due to . . . the bad weather,' he ended weakly.

The entire palace lurched. It took a drop of perhaps a second's duration, though it felt much longer. Stomachs turned. Breaking glass could be heard, and loud curses. People screamed.

'Father thinks it might be best if we were to bring the palace down to as near the ground as possible,' the Prince announced. 'Not that there's any danger, of course. I'm issuing an order to that effect.' A lithe messenger sped off with it as he spoke.

A full half minute passed before the next scare. Another tremor ran through the palace. This time the effect was more violent, with the structure not just descending sharply, as it had before, but drifting alarmingly off-course as well. The sheer wall of the mountain on their right loomed uncomfortably close.

The other palaces had similar problems. Several dropped in height appreciably. One was spinning, apparently uncontrollably. Small explosions blossomed on their surfaces, dislodging debris, and in one case, a balcony.

On the royal palace, the mood was one of barely suppressed panic. One of the military brass in the crowd milling about the Prince remarked, 'This is a fine time for the executioner to turn up.'

Melyobar caught the remark, and followed the officer's gaze. Tiers of stone walkways lined the side of the palace above the battlements. On the lowest there was a figure. It somehow gave the impression of masculinity, although there were no obvious signs. He was tall and slender, and dressed entirely in black. The mantle he wore covered him completely. His hood was up, and it was impossible to see his face. His hands were the only visible part of him. They were strikingly pale and long-fingered. Some might say skeletal.

The figure didn't move. He just stood there, looking down at the Prince.

In many respects his demeanour conformed to the image of an executioner, dressed for anonymity and come to earn his coin.

For Melyobar, there was another, more dreadful possibility.

He pressed himself to his father's cabinet, their faces inches apart. 'A fine time for the executioner, father, is that it? Or the perfect time to foil our plan?' His breath misted the glass.

The palace swung alarmingly. It began unsteadily revolving on its axis, looking for all the world like a demented children's fairground ride. Columns, statues and strips of filigree dislodged and dropped away. One of the catapults broke its restraints and rolled across the battlements, scattering everyone in its path and crashing into the restraining wall, before beginning the return journey as the palace started to tilt in the opposite direction.

Hysteria broke out. People ran in all directions, aimless, screaming and shouting. The few trying to maintain order were overrun by the panicked majority. Cracks rippled through floors and walls.

The other floating palaces were in just as much trouble. Towers crumbled and causeways collapsed. Fires erupted. Several of the manors bumped each other, the jolting impacts breaking a thousand windows and fracturing their marble facades. Two collided head on with a sound like thunder.

Terror held sway. Giving in to irrationality, or simple desperation, many on the royal palace had deserted the battlements and fled indoors. None, not even his personal guard, had elected to stay with or protect their prince.

'Father?' he whispered, hugging the cabinet. 'Father? What do I do?' He listened attentively, and at last said only, 'Oh, yes.'

The Prince again lifted his gaze to the parapet where the figure had stood. He saw what he expected.

Melyobar returned his attention to the cabinet and his father's severe countenance. 'Look, daddy, look. Watch me. Watch me, father.' He smiled. 'Are you ready? Watch me now. We . . . all . . . fall . . . down!'

Magic deserted them.

The distance to the ground was not that great, being equivalent to a moderate cliff face, or even some of the remarkably tall trees found in tropical regions. But height is irrelevant when plummeting objects weigh untold thousands of tons, and the locality over which the court travelled was not without bearing.

The royal palace and its attendant chateaux, mansions and citadels dropped like a handful of pebbles released by a bored god. They came down in a region dominated by lakes. Lakes much deeper than wide, and very wide indeed.

Not all of the buildings fell on iced-over lakes. Several came to grief on marshes and farmland, and in one case, a road. But that wasn't the fate of the majority, including Melyobar's palace. They smashed through ice, breaking up on impact or plunging into the freezing water whole. As they sank, the increasing pressure stove in windows and doors, and a deluge invaded their warrens of corridors, their state-rooms, grand apartments and auditoria.

The lake was greedy. It swallowed everything. Or almost. Melyobar came to himself in the murderously cold water. An object nudged him. It was King Narbetton's glass sepulchre, floating serenely by. The look of inscrutability on his father's face was the last thing the Prince saw before the water took him.

A head broke the surface.

Andar Talgorian took great gulps of air, his lungs burning. He was so numb from the cold that he couldn't feel his body except as pain. Somehow, the bonds tying his wrists had broken.

He didn't imagine surviving for more than a couple of minutes in this cold. The irony of escaping death twice in succession, only to fall at the last hurdle, was not lost on him. Perhaps the gods were set on him dying.

It was getting harder to keep afloat, or even to think straight. His stamina was draining away, and his limbs were growing weaker. The cold was beyond cold, and seeping into his very bones. What he found amazing was that the equivalent of a sizeable town had just dropped into the lake and you wouldn't know it. He couldn't see anyone or anything else.

Then he heard a sound. Or thought he did; his ears might have been cut off for all the feeling he had in them. There it was again. A voice. Correction, voices. Shouting. He saw nothing the way he was facing. So laboriously, painfully, he turned himself about.

Something was coming towards him. He couldn't make out what it was. As it got nearer it began to look like two figures walking on the water. Crouching, more like, the closer they got. They were calling and waving. They hauled him out. He lay gasping on their makeshift raft, the hangman's rope still about his neck. One of his rescuers put a pocket flask to his lips. The fiery alcohol brought back some feeling as it burned its way through his system. As his senses returned, he realised that the sodden clothes the two men wore were uniforms.

'Nechen and Welst, Palace Guard Auxiliary,' one of them said. 'How are you, sir?'

'Thank . . . you,' Talgorian managed.

'Glad to share our good fortune, sir,' the other told him. 'Why, if it hadn't been for this piece of wreckage, we wouldn't be here ourselves.'

Talgorian focused on the slab of wood supporting them. It was the trapdoor from the gallows.

Many stories were told about the day destruction swept the empires and their many protectorates. Some would become legends.

One concerned a notorious pirate chief who threw in his lot with the empires against the fledgling rebel state.

It was said that on that fateful day a man came seeking an accounting with the pirate, a man terribly wronged and ill-treated by him. He came not by sea, but through the air, riding a wondrous flying disc. Alone he overcame the pirate's band, raining down magic from above that blasted and seared, until at last only the pirate captain himself stood against him.

The release of the magic caused great convulsions, in many ways. One was uproar in the balance of nature. Many disasters were triggered, and there were earthquakes as the world accommodated itself to the loss. Where these happened at sea, their offspring was tidal waves.

As the pirate and his foe battled to the death, a cluster of breakers as tall as mountains swept their way. They crushed the buccaneer's armada, sinking every ship bar his. It was taken by the biggest wave and flung into a portside hamlet on the Diamond Isle, giving the pirate the island he coveted, though not in a way he had intended.

Many believed the avenger perished too, paying the ultimate price for bringing his enemy's predations to an end.

And then there was the way things ended on the Diamond Isle itself.

The island suffered its own upheavals, but the redoubt was comparatively untouched. Being too impoverished to have much in the way of magic was an asset for once.

Initially, the islanders were unclear as to what was happening in a wider sense. Being in the middle of an invasion, that was understandable; and they had enough remarkable things happening to keep them stretched as it was.

As the disturbances began to subside, there was a tense lull in which to prepare for the final onslaught.

Serrah and Reeth volunteered for lookout duty, and found themselves stationed on one of the redoubt's battlements. It was the first time in many hours that they were able to be alone. Across the plain, the empires' combined armies had gathered in even greater numbers.

'They could just walk in here any time they like,' Caldason reckoned, 'and we couldn't do a thing about it, other than making them pay a price in blood. So why are they holding back?'

'It was you, Reeth. You did them some real damage.'

'Only enough to slow them down. Whatever stopped me did it before I could finish the job.'

'Finish? You're not seriously saying you could have defeated a horde like that single-handed, are you?'

'I don't know what I was capable of in that condition. But I do know that it felt . . . It's difficult to explain, Serrah. It felt as though I could do anything. The potential, the power . . . it's why the Founders have fought over me for so long, and why some of them wanted me dead.'

'But you've not been able to do it again.'

'I've only tried once. But it was like there was nothing there.'

'Maybe you need to recuperate, build up your strength or . . . I don't know. There's too much going on, Reeth. It overwhelms you after a while.'

'Doesn't it just? And this thing about Tanalvah, it . . . beggars belief.'

'That's what I thought, at first.'

'There's no doubt?'

'I don't think so. It was a deathbed confession. And I believed her. You would have too, if you'd been there.'

'What would make her do something like that?'

'She thought she was saving Kinsel. She did it out of love.'

'I sometimes think as much evil's done in the name of love as hate.'

'That sounds cynical.'

'It's not supposed to; it's just an observation.'

'Well, let's be sure our love never generates evil, shall we?'

'It couldn't.' He put an arm around her, and they kissed.

'Anyway,' she said, 'I can't think of Tanalvah as evil. Sounds crazy, I know, after what she did, but I still don't see her as bad.'

'It's about potential again, isn't it?'

'I don't know what you mean.'

'We're all capable of being righteous or wicked. Sometimes both. The seeds of good and evil are in us, just waiting for something to set them off.'

'You think we're all capable of murder?'

'That's a strange question for you and me, isn't it? It was your profession, and I've done more than my share.'

'That wasn't murder, any more than taking an enemy life in this siege would be murder. The people we killed were bad.'

'A pacifist, like Kinsel, would say that was trying to justify it.'

'Sometimes you have to defend those who are weaker, or protect your own life, or –'

'You don't have to convince me. I'm a Qalochian. Well, half of one, anyway, and you don't get much more martial in outlook than that. But we'd be offended to be called murderers. I'm just saying that given the right conditions, enough of a shove, anybody could be a murderer. A killer in that bad sense. According to Praltor, even the paladins were noble once.'

'Does it bother you that Tan was a Qalochian?'

'Bother me? You mean like letting the side down or something?'

'I suppose I do.'

'Being of the Qaloch didn't make her any better than anybody else. We're not saints.'

'You never really got on with her.'

'And you think what she did confirmed my opinion? Actually, it wasn't my opinion; it was more a case of her not favouring me too much. Though I admit I think I made her uneasy, reminding her of our heritage.'

'She had that heritage taken away from her. You of all people should understand that. She grew up in Rintarah; it was natural she'd take on their customs.'

'I wonder how the funeral's going to be.'

'What kind of service, you mean? It'll be presided over by a priest of the Iparrater sect. Kinsel's quite keen on that actually.'

'It's the Qaloch gods who should be invoked.'

'That's a bit rich coming from you, Reeth. I thought you had your doubts about gods of any kind.'

'I do, but it's funny how the prospect of almost certain death can make what you were taught as a child seem meaningful again. Anyway, how is Kinsel?'

'I think you can guess. Having the new baby and the children to care for is the only thing keeping him going, I reckon. He feels ashamed, you know. For what Tan did. He sees it as reflecting on him.'

'He shouldn't. He wasn't responsible for her actions.'

'You're right. Oh, just a minute. Stand still.' She reached up and plucked something from his head.

'What was that?'

'A grey hair. I'm damned if I know what to do to help Kinsel, Reeth. How do you get somebody through a thing like that?'

'By being there for them. Which of course might not be possible.' He nodded towards the brooding enemy forces. 'And don't forget the other complication. There's a fleet in these parts that's not either empire's. We don't know what difference that's going to make to the balance.'

'Whose might it be?'

'I think we can guess.'

Disgleirio appeared, bounding up the battlement stairs with his usual athleticism. He made for them.

'What's up, Quinn?' Serrah asked.

'Phoenix asked me to relieve you.'

'Why?'

'I don't know. He'll be here directly to explain.' He looked out at the enemy ranks. 'Sobering, isn't it?'

'You could say that,' Caldason replied.

'What I don't understand is what they're waiting for.'

'That's what we wondered.'

Somebody was moving along the line of defenders on the battlements, dispensing water from a pail. He proved to be Kutch's newly returned brother.

'Good to see you don't think water carrying's beneath you,' Serrah said.

'I'm happy to do anything to help,' he replied, putting down his load. 'But when the fighting starts I expect a much more active role.' He patted his sheathed sword.

'We need everybody we can get. Oh, I don't think you two have met properly yet. This is –'

'I know,' Varee said. 'Quinn Disgleirio. I'm honoured to meet you.' He held out a hand.

Disgleirio took it. 'And you're Kutch's brother. Well met. But how do you know me?'

'I've seen you, more than once, back in Bhealfa. In fact, I once got very close to you indeed.'

'Really? I don't recall.'

'You weren't supposed to notice. It was during a riot. I managed to get a note into your pocket.'

'It was you, was it? I've been wondering ever since who had the inside knowledge to warn us. Given your connection with Bastorran, it makes sense now. Well, I'm grateful.'

'I'm still not clear on you, Varee,' Caldason admitted. 'What's your story?'

'That's something everybody seems to want to know.'

'Just tell us,' Serrah advised him, 'we're notorious gossips.'

Varee smiled. 'I'll make it quick, I've got thirsty people waiting for me.'

'How did you come to turn from the paladins?' Caldason wanted to know.

'I didn't. I've always hated them. I got into their ranks

because I hated them. I'm not clan blood, of course, but they take a certain percentage of outsiders to fill administrative posts. That was how I worked my way up to Bastorran.'

'Why?'

'You and I have something in common, Reeth. We both wanted revenge on the paladins. The only way I could see to do it was to climb as high in the organisation as I could, leaking bits of information to the Resistance as I went, anonymously.'

'To what purpose?'

'To get close to the highest-ranking officer I could and kill him. But you kindly undertook that part earlier.'

'Sorry if I deprived you.'

'Don't apologise. I could never have taken Bastorran in a straight fight. You know he killed his uncle, to get the leadership?'

'It didn't take much guessing.'

'The meld did the actual deed. It killed two birds with one stone for Devlor: he got the leadership and you conveniently took the blame.'

'But why did you want revenge so badly?' Serrah said.

'With respect to Reeth, the Qalochians weren't the only ones to suffer at the paladins' hands. The Pirathons were farming folk for generations. Then a local lord decided he wanted our lands, and all our neighbours', too. The paladins were contracted to do the job, and used utmost brutality, needless to say. We were just an unregarded backwater and nobody outside our community cared.'

'This was before you and Kutch were born?'

'Before Kutch. I was about two at the time. But that wasn't all. Our father could never accept the unfairness of what happened to us, and he spent years trying to get justice. Petitioning officials, begging audiences with governors, trying to find somebody in authority who'd listen to him. I'm as sure as I can be that it's what got him killed. He just became too much of an irritant, and eventually he simply disappeared. From what I've seen of clan records since, it's pretty obvious they got rid of him.'

'Kutch never mentioned any of this.'

'He doesn't know. Our mother kept it from him, and evidently didn't tell him after I left to join the clans. In fact, she thought I'd enlisted in the army.'

'You never saw her again?'

'I didn't want to run the risk of them finding out about her and Kutch. So I sent money when I could and bided my time. I'm going to tell Kutch everything, but not just yet. I think he needs time to get used to me being back first.'

'So getting here to the island was part of your plan?'

'No, not really. Bastorran ordered me to accompany him. But by then I knew Kutch was with the Resistance, so it suited me well. It goes without saying that it was Bastorran's intention to kill you. The meld was along as back-up. Or possibly some kind of scapegoat, knowing Devlor.'

'Where is your brother?' Caldason said.

'I don't know. But here's a man who probably does.'

Phoenix arrived, stern-faced. He got straight to the point. 'Serrah, Reeth, come with me.'

'Now?'

'You'll want to see this.'

He led them to a cluster of wooden buildings on the far side of the square. One was an unprepossessing storage silo with no windows and a single door. Inside, at the very back, behind stacks of crates, a small group of rebels were gathered around something. They moved aside for Phoenix and the others.

'Well, now we know what happened to Kordenza,' Serrah said.

'Do we?' Caldason wondered.

The meld was stretched on the floor, unmistakably dead, her face hideously contorted. There was an extensive, gaping wound down her left side, from which innards had seeped. A trail of blood and a glistening, mucus-like material ran to a large burnt stain in a corner.

Phoenix pointed to it. 'And that must have been her glamour twin . . .'

'Aphrim,' Caldason supplied. 'What happened here?'

'Self-evidently the twin killed his host by trying to escape from her body. That or something went wrong when she was bringing him out in her usual way. Look at this.'

They went back to Aphri's body. For the first time, they noticed that one of her feet was bare.

'She removed the boot herself,' Phoenix explained. 'If you were to examine her heel, you'd find that an object's been inserted just under the skin.'

'I'll take your word for it,' Serrah assured him.

'It's a device Covenant's familiar with, though it's rare. Its function is to draw energy from the grid, almost certainly with the object of keeping her symbiote status permanent. It clearly failed her.'

'Not a pleasant death,' Caldason remarked.

'Not at all,' Phoenix agreed. 'Come on, there's more.' He marched for the exit.

As they trailed him, Serrah spoke to Reeth in an under-tone. 'You look a bit ashen, my love.'

'My energy level's down a bit. I'm all right.'

'Maybe it's what I said earlier: you need to recharge.'

'Maybe.'

This time, the sorcerer took them into the redoubt itself. The damage from the attack was still very much in evidence, though the worst had been cleared. Phoenix made his way to the chamber where Praltor Mahaganis was lodged.

Kutch and Wendah were there, by the old man's bed. He

didn't look good. It was as though he'd appreciably aged in a matter of hours, and his skin was like ancient parchment. Yet his countenance had an ease, a look of contentment, they hadn't seen before. His eyes were closed, but he breathed steadily.

'He says it's gone,' Kutch related.

'What has?' Caldason said.

'The Source. Praltor says it's not there anymore, inside him.'

'It isn't,' Wendah confirmed. She appeared shaken.

The old man opened his eyes. The obvious signs of blindness remained, but again there was a different, calmer look. 'It's true,' he said. 'The weight's left me. I can't describe the relief.'

Serrah leaned in to him. 'How did it happen, Praltor?'

'Not through any doing of mine, or these wizards. It was wrenched away. There was pain in that, but nothing compared to what's gone.'

'Your life's going too,' Wendah murmured resentfully.

'My dear,' the old man soothed, reaching for her hand, 'I've had more than my allotted span. More than I deserved.'

'No, that's not true.'

'Shh. I've lived long and well, Wendah, and after all these years of carrying that terrible burden, I welcome rest.'

'But what will I do without you?'

'You'll be fine. And you're not alone. You have Kutch now, and you couldn't wish for a finer young man.'

She took Kutch's hand, and a tear rolled down her cheek.

Phoenix gestured for Reeth and Serrah to follow him out, and they left quietly. In the corridor, Phoenix drew them aside and said, 'I'm sorry, Reeth. I realise he's close to you and it must be distressing. The gods know we've seen enough loss in recent days.'

'These are distressing times, Phoenix. And yes, he's important. I wouldn't be here if it wasn't for him.'

'He's going to die soon,' the sorcerer announced bluntly.

'That was obvious.'

'Come on, Reeth, you must see the implications for you in all this.'

'What are you getting at?' Serrah demanded.

'The magic. There's been some unprecedented malfunction, or worse. I can feel it ebbing away. Kutch and Wendah feel it, and Praltor certainly did, as you just heard. And it's what killed the meld.'

'Go on,' the Qalochian prompted.

'You and I and Praltor are all in the same boat, Reeth. Or similar. Founder magic's kept us going longer than we should. Now the debt's being repaid. Does any of this strike a chord with you?'

'I . . . don't know.'

'You said you felt drained, Reeth,' Serrah reminded him.

'My stamina's low, it's true.'

'Look at the back of your hands,' Phoenix suggested.

Caldason did. There were brown splotches there he hadn't noticed before. Liver spots.

'Like Praltor, I'm reconciled to my end,' Phoenix continued. 'I see my life as fulfilled, and I have my certainties about what's to come. How about you, my friend?'

Reeth stared at him.

Then sounds of uproar drifted in from outside. Scores of alarm bells began ringing.

'Here they come,' Serrah whispered.

They broke away from Phoenix and ran.

They joined the hundreds making for the walls. On the battlements, they found Karr with Goyter, watching the advance. The plain was black with advancing troops.

'So the last chapter is finally written,' Karr said.

But the great army slowed, and stopped. Just two men continued walking towards the fortress, one of them waving a white flag.

'Must we parley with them?' Goyter asked.

'That's a flag of truce,' Karr reminded her. 'We must honour it. I'm going out.'

'Are you sure, Dulian?'

'It's my place to. Reeth, would you come with me and carry our flag?'

'I'd be honoured.'

Somebody donated a shirt and a makeshift flag was quickly constructed. The gates were opened a crack and Karr and Reeth left the redoubt.

As they walked towards the little delegation, and the countless, silent thousands beyond them, Karr said, 'What if their terms are too harsh? Do we refuse them and fight on?'

'You have to be the judge of that. For my part, I'd want nothing to do with any surrender that involved retribution against our people.'

'Neither would I.'

They reached the two men. Both wore uniforms, one of Rintarah, the other Gath Tampoor. The latter asked of Karr, 'You're in charge here?'

'Insomuch as we have a single leader, yes.'

'We're the two highest ranking surviving officers of our respective forces,' the Rintarahian explained. 'We've come to discuss terms of surrender.'

'I must make it clear that we won't be party to any capitulation that involves reprisal killings or draconian punishments.'

'We're glad to hear it,' the Rintarahian replied. 'We had our fears that you might exact an even higher price than you already have.'

'How could we when we'll be your prisoners?'

'*Our* prisoners? I think we're talking at cross purposes. We're here to agree the surrender.'

'So you said.'

'Our surrender,' the Gath Tampoorian informed him.

Karr was too astonished to speak.

Caldason said, 'Let's get this straight. You are surrendering to us?'

'Of course. You must know things are in chaos on our side. And we had some rulers with us. When we saw what happened to them . . . well, frankly most of us haven't the heart to carry on.'

'Tell me,' the other man added, 'how did you do it? How did you kill the magic?'

'We didn't,' Caldason admitted. 'But I think I know who did.'

It was probably unprecedented in war that a surrendering army, many times larger than their captors, had volunteered to regulate their own captivity. However, as the islanders had neither manpower nor resources to police their prisoners, that's exactly what happened.

That evening, the fleet Caldason had seen arrived, and the Diamond Isle hosted the biggest collection of ships in history. And by now, no one was in any doubt as to who was about to pay a visit.

The warlord didn't demand that anyone come to pay homage to him. He travelled to meet the rebels. Not in a victory procession with marching soldiers and drummers, but modestly, in a simple open carriage, accompanied only by two aides, one of whom drove.

Everyone was struck by his extraordinary ordinariness of appearance, underlined by a lack of any finery or ostentation in his dress. They were at least as impressed by the indefinable quality of his presence.

When he entered the redoubt's inner square he was met by a delegation led by Karr. But it was Disgleirio who spoke first.

'Do we bow?' he asked, an edge of defiance in his voice.

'No,' Zerreiss told him. 'No more bowing, or any retribution. I'm not conquering you.' The warlord looked about as he said this. His eyes rested on Caldason. 'I thought you were like me,' he said.

'I am,' said Caldason, eyeing him coolly.

'I meant in respect of my talent.'

'I meant in our antipathy for magic.'

'Yet magic linked us in our dreams.'

'I believe that's because our relationships to it, though different, are equally strong.'

'There's some sense in that.'

'So you made all this happen?' Caldason indicated the scene with a sweep of his hand.

'Yes, and more.'

'Are you a god?' Wendah piped up.

Zerreiss laughed, and at his back his aides smiled. 'So many people make that assumption. No, young lady, I'm not a god.'

'What are you?'

'I'm a man.'

'How do you do what you do?' Serrah said.

'How is a question I can't answer categorically, I can only speculate. I was born with a very simple talent, but I tend not to think of myself as an aberration, but rather as a little ahead of my time.'

Phoenix pushed forward. 'Will you explain that?'

The warlord noted Phoenix's robes. 'Ah, a sorcerer. I've had occasion to be at odds with your calling in the past. Today I can only offer my regrets at the termination of your profession.'

'I was just getting the hang of it,' Kutch complained.

'It was getting the hang of you, young man. Hopefully you'll come to see that. To answer the questions; I believe I'm an example of what's to come. Look about the world. Nature selects the lifeforms best equipped to survive and thrive. It favours the most adaptable, and what the race of man needs now is the adaptability to shake off the stifling hand of magic. We need to breathe free air, think free thoughts and guide our lives with rationality.'

'You say you've always had this power?' Karr said.

'From birth, and despite there being nothing out of the ordinary in my parents. I found out early that I could affect magic, but the talent was a feeble thing when I was a child. It grew as I did. I learned to control the ability to some extent, and to extend its influence more and more. So that now it takes just my approach, if I will it, to negate the magic. I never chose this path. A religious man might say I was supposed to be a catalyst and had no choice. I tend to a more rational view, as you might expect, but at root I don't really know. What I do know is that if I'm the first, it's the first of many. The majority. All, in time.'

'It's sad,' Kutch said, 'the magic going.'

'It must seem that way to you. And yes, there's much that's wondrous and beautiful, and even good in it. But it's an illusion. It kept us transfixed, like moths around a flame. What's to come, without it, will be an adventure so much greater. But certain things have to happen before that.' He turned to the Patrician. 'You're the one called Karr?'

'I am.'

'You have authority here?'

'I believe so.'

'Then you have some organising to do, and on quite a scale. Don't be alarmed, you'll get the help you need. The fact is the empires are finished. If they don't know it yet, they will once I've cleansed any remaining pockets. A new order's needed, but it won't be run by me. I've never wanted power, only to do my job. It seems to me that the only organised, untainted force is the Resistance. I know it's taken some terrible knocks, and you've lost a lot of people, but it's still out there, along with a lot of sympathisers. It's going to fall to you to step in, organise, rebuild. From here on the Diamond Isle will be the hub of a new civilisation.'

'You don't believe in setting modest tasks, my lord.'

'Plain Zerreiss, if you please. I don't believe in one man being regarded as any better than his fellows, and I would hope you'll build a world enshrining that, but it's up to you. I can only create the conditions.'

'Conditions of chaos.'

'All creation came from chaos, the priests tell us. You should be able to construct a paltry civilisation. It won't be easy, granted, and it'll take time. But do you have a choice?' Zerreiss looked at each of them in turn.

'Will you play any part?' Caldason asked.

'Where I can. But mainly as a taker of satisfaction for what I've been able to do. And what of you? You find yourself in a difficult position.'

'Do I?'

'You already differ from the man in my dreams. Your bloom is withering. The going of the magic brings back the years. Stay where I've been and you'll die.'

'Can't you make it not apply to Reeth in some way?' Serrah almost pleaded.

'I'm sorry. I wish I could, but I can only take away, not give. However, I need to consolidate, and guide my people to aid yours. There are places in the world I haven't got to yet, and might not for a long while. Think on that.' He turned to leave. 'I'm glad I met you, Reeth Caldason.'

*   *   *

Early next morning, Zerreiss moved on with the bulk of his entourage. Others were left to help deal with the empire prisoners, and to begin the work.

Around midday, a wagon rode into the redoubt. It carried Zahgadiah Darrok, minus his dish.

'Did I miss anything?' he asked when Pallidea had finished covering him in kisses.

He was able to tell them of Vance's fate, and explained how he himself barely escaped on the vanishing residue of magic in his flying disc. Landing scarcely in time, and awkwardly, he was found by islanders, shaken but not seriously injured.

'Your disc,' Pallidea bemoaned, 'how are you going to get on without it?'

'I did once, before I could afford it. I'll think of something. Providing you're about to help me. I'm assuming you haven't gone cool on the idea of squiring a cripple?'

'I never will.'

Darrok had arrived in time for a hastily arranged ceremony. There were several reasons for it. The first was the christening of Kinsel and Tanalvah's baby.

'I've decided the boy will be called Dulian,' Kinsel announced, Teg and Lirrin looking on wide-eyed.

It was a popular choice, and there was applause.

'I'm taken aback,' Karr replied, 'and honoured, of course. Dulian Rukanis. Has quite a ring, doesn't it?'

'Rukanis-Lahn,' Kinsel corrected. 'Unless you or any other has an objection?'

No one spoke. It was the first small step on the path to Kinsel's healing.

'Dulian Rukanis-Lahn, first citizen of the new order,' Karr declared.

The second point of the get-together was for Karr to announce that his age and health meant he had to step down from heading the United Revolutionary Council.

Although not unexpected, the news was greeted with cries of displeasure and displays of genuine affection.

Goyter would be his companion during retirement, and their relationship was to be cemented by the public exchange of vows. Karr nominated Quinn Disgleirio as his successor, a commendation the Council was expected to approve. Neither development came as a great surprise to most people.

The final purpose of the gathering was to bid farewell to Reeth and Serrah.

A ship had been provided. It was small but fast, and its volunteer crew were the best that could be found. As Zerreiss had made least headway in the far south, that was the direction chosen, to islands hardly known, and perhaps a rumoured land beyond them, if it wasn't a myth.

Phoenix and Praltor Mahaganis were offered places. Neither seriously considered it. Both were in decline, especially Praltor, and pronounced themselves content.

The hardest decision was not to suggest Kutch went with them. Serrah argued it would be unfair to ask the boy. It could ruin his budding relationship with Wendah, should she choose not to go. And what of Varee? Was he to come too, or risk losing his brother again? Above all, what if no haven was found, and Kutch had to watch Caldason die, and comfort his grieving lover? The Diamond Isle offered him some kind of stability, and the prospect of a future. Reeth had to agree.

Neither favoured speeches. They said their goodbyes privately and without fuss. Now they stood on the deck of their ship, about to catch the tide and waiting for the last farewell.

'Are you sure about this?' Caldason said.

'Of course I am. What purpose would my life have without you?'

He was a little more drawn. Faint lines had appeared on his face and neck. Serrah had plucked more of his grey hairs.

'Looking at it now, I can see that the first time I knew I loved you was when you tried to take your life, back in Bhealfa. It was then that I realised I couldn't lose you.'

'And you haven't. We're in this together, to whatever outcome.'

'Ironic, isn't it? That I should spend my life shunning magic, and now I'm hunting it.'

'I said the gods liked a joke.'

'Bastards.' He grinned at her, showing love in every line of his face.

'Ah, here they come, Reeth.'

Kutch, Wendah and Varee appeared on the dockside. Serrah waved them up the gangplank.

Wendah and Varee didn't delay their goodbyes. Sensing the need for privacy, they quickly left. Then Serrah found herself suddenly fascinated by the view further along the deck. She embraced Kutch and kissed him, then left him alone with Reeth.

'What do you think your chances are?' Kutch asked.

'I might have thought you could answer that better than me, you being the only expert on magic present.'

'There's no point in knowing anything about it now. It's gone.' He was doleful. 'But the thing about Zerreiss is that he kind of pushes the magic out of the land as he advances, like squeezing wine out of a sac. So it's possible you'll find somewhere where magic still occurs. I hope you do,' he added quietly. 'I'll never see it again.'

'You'll see another kind of magic. With the life you've got ahead, with Wendah and your brother, and with whatever it is you decide to do with yourself. Things will be better without magic, believe me.'

'They won't be better without you.'

'Thanks, Kutch. I'm so glad I've known you.'

The boy flew into his arms and hugged him tight. 'Don't go,' he pleaded, tears rolling.

'I have to go. You know that.' Caldason gently moved him back, hands on his shoulders. 'You've been the best friend and companion a man could have. Now get on with your life.'

Kutch looked as though he was going to speak. Instead he simply stared, then turned away. He took three steps, looked back and said, 'I'll never forget you.' He ran to the gangplank and down onto the harbour.

When they started to move off shortly after, he was still standing on the quay. He shouted something, but they couldn't hear what it was.

The Diamond Isle was soon swallowed by mist.

Together, Reeth and Serrah set off into a new world.